I0695313

ENTWINED LIVES

A NOVEL

Shuvashree Chowdhury

First published in India in 2018 by CinnamonTeal Publishing

ISBN 978-93-86301-97-0

BISAC Code: FIC000000/FICTION/General

Typesetting and Cover design: CinnamonTeal Design and Publishing

CinnamonTeal Publishing
an imprint of CinnamonTeal Design and Publishing
Plot No 16, Housing Board Colony
Gogol, Margao
Goa 403601 India
www.cinnamonteal.in

For the city of Chennai

Contents

1. The Impeccable Groom   9

2. A Perfect Marriage   29

3. The Two Women and the Man   43

4. Her New Life   57

5. The Self-reliant Woman   76

6. The Emotional Entrapment   90

7. Reconstructing her Life   102

8. The Fisherman's Cove   110

9. Love and Alcohol are Potent Analgesics   124

10. Making Love versus Sex   138

11. The Marriage at a Crossroads   149

12. The Handsome Englishman   166

13. An Unwarranted Guilt   183

14. You Cannot Run Away from Love   193

15. A Lonely Marriage   210

16. An Internet Love Affair   221

17. Power is the Ultimate Aphrodisiac235

18. Expensive Gifts247

19. A Pillar of Strength267

20. The Price of Love277

21. The Compulsive Womaniser297

22. Upholding Faith in Humanity305

23. The Wife Versus the Girlfriend321

24. Freedom at Last332

25. At the Cliff's Edge344

26. The Hairpin Turn358

Chapter 1

The Impeccable Groom

"Nikhil only has a little time left, Aparna," the harried male voice said over the phone. "The doctors have given him twenty-four hours at most. Until yesterday, we had no idea he was this sick."

Aparna's initial shock at the news she had received early this morning had turned to irritation and then an assumed indifference. Nikhil had been admitted to the Lilavati Hospital in Mumbai with jaundice last night after a severe bout of vomiting. He was in a critical condition. Why should she care now what became of her ex-husband? Even during the few years of their marriage, Aparna had been wearied of his recurrent trips in and out of the hospital. But this was not surprising when in a marriage to an alcoholic, who spent days together binge-drinking.

The aircraft gradually ascended from the tarmac of Chennai airport. Over the armrest between their seats, Kartik's hand clutched Aparna's, as she leaned over him to look out of the window. She felt that familiar unease in the pit of her stomach, but she was not sure it was due only to the flight taking off. It was just after sunset, and the sky was a blend of purple, orange, and yellow. She watched the silhouettes of houses, trees, and roads briskly recede, till they become a web of green and brown landscapes. Once the aircraft was on a steady cruise, only darkness visible through the window now, Kartik's hand relaxed. Aparna leaned back in her seat and shut her eyes. But the events of the day flashed in her mind, making her restless.

It was the sharp recollection of how devastated their son Kartik would be at losing his father that had jolted Aparna into sweeping aside her bitterness for Nikhil. It was her love for Kartik that had urged her into taking this flight to Mumbai. She had to admit that Nikhil had been a good father, even without taking any real responsibility. After all, that was as good as any alcoholic could possibly be. In fact, Kartik's vacations had been compulsorily spent with Nikhil lately, as he had been granted this right by the court at the time of their divorce. Over the years, with the time they had spent together, Kartik had grown to genuinely love and adore his father. After the call this morning from Nikhil's father, Aparna had remembered that it was barely a month since Kartik had returned from Mumbai, after his summer vacations with them. The memory of Kartik's excited chatter on the drive home from the airport, filling her in on the good time he had had, came to her, wrenching her heart at his loss.

It was with that memory that Aparna called her office's travel desk and requested them to arrange for two plane tickets to Mumbai. After attending the daily late-morning meeting with her team that she thought wise not to cancel, Aparna had picked up Kartik from school and driven him home to get ready. On the drive to the airport, explaining their sudden trip to Kartik had made Aparna fight to control her tears. He had been through so much in his twelve years already and losing his father now could crush him. But much to her surprise, he maintained a cool, aloof silence, staring outside the taxi window. Kartik took the news very sensitively for a boy so young.

After his last vacation, Kartik had reported to Aparna, "Daddy has been rather weak lately and nauseous a lot, particularly in the mornings after waking. I begged him to visit a doctor, but he just wouldn't listen to me." Then, after some thought, Kartik had sadly added, "He continued to drink, go out with me—eating at restaurants, playing tennis, jogging at the Marina, and swimming at the club. Then, when Grandmother called the doctor home, Daddy went out just as he arrived."

On the flight now, Kartik continued to remain quiet, and then dozed off from exhaustion. Aparna, her head leaning against the seat, her eyes closed, could not stop her thoughts from racing into what lay ahead in their lives. After struggling to build a career and secure a future for Kartik, just when her life had fallen into a comfortable pattern, with a promotion and a salary hike, this jolt in their lives was unwarranted. The sounds of the cabin crew

  Shuvashree Chowdhury

serving meals broke into her thoughts and she opened her eyes abruptly. Aparna woke Kartik up, so he could eat. His next meal was uncertain, given the circumstances now, but he declined. In coaxing him, she decided to eat, though she had no appetite. After consuming their respective spinach and corn sandwiches, along with tetrapacks of orange juice, mother and son withdrew into their private cocoons.

Aparna thought about how lucky she was to have the support of her parents now. It had been an imposing task initially, to convince them to let her live with them after the separation from her husband. They had worried about how their middle-class neighbours, their friends, extended family, and the society would react. Then Aparna's thoughts skipped to how, after a few months of living with her parents, concurrent to Nikhil's regular telephonic arguments with her, she had goaded him to join a rehabilitation centre. She had promised Nikhil she would return to him if he did. But after resorting to ultimatums, threats, cajoling, and coaxing, she had come to terms with his incapability to even admit to his drinking problem, let alone give up drinking.

It was then that she had decided to leave him for good and set about to convince both sets of parents. This was no easy task. They insisted that Nikhil was intrinsically a good person, but unfortunately a slave to his addiction. Aparna conceded this view. However, she contended with the optimism of the elders that he would stop drinking, if given her support. Aparna, by now, was convinced that Nikhil was not even interested in trying; it was impossible that he would reform. Aparna had tried everything before accepting her failure to keep Nikhil from the allure of alcohol and his addiction. She reminded his family as well as hers how violently volatile Nikhil became after a few drinks. There was no way it was safe for her, that too with an infant, to live with him alone.

"Living with an alcoholic father is surely no environment to bring up our son," Aparna had said firmly and passionately every time the parents tried to make a case for the need for the presence of both parents in a child's life. Then when the pressure on her to accept and reform Nikhil would mount, she would defiantly add, "That too a father who has no respect for his mother, is rough and violent with her, and does not even go to work. The child will only become insecure and confused and I cannot allow that."

Aparna vividly recalled the infant Kartik's fear and bewilderment at his father's sudden outbursts. Nikhil would throw fits of abusive temper, his rage directed at Aparna and the maid. One night, he even locked Aparna and Kartik out of their apartment in Mumbai in a fit of rage. Aparna's offense, enormous in Nikhil's eyes at that point in his addiction, had been that she had cleared the house of all his alcohol bottles. It had been too late at night for him to procure more, driving him crazy. Nikhil had roughly dragged her out and left her to sit on the staircase all night, in a nightgown and carrying their two-year-old son. In the morning, as if awaking from a nightmare, Aparna had telephoned her in-laws from a neighbour's house. They had then come over promptly and taken her, along with their grandson, who was their real cause for worry, to their house, in a scruffy and mentally distraught state.

Nikhil's parents were rather disappointed that marriage and a child had not sobered him as they had expected. But they would have to convince Aparna to stay, as there was no way they wanted his drunkenness back on their hands. Nikhil had awoken almost at noon that day, with a severe hangover. It took a while for the events of the night to come back to him, through a pounding headache, the queasiness, and lethargy. Then, unable to find his wife and son, expecting for them to be sitting outside where he left them, he was livid. After enquiring with the neighbours on their whereabouts, Nikhil drove to his parents' house in a frenzy. He didn't want to call in case Aparna had not gone there.

As he barged into his parent's house, on seeing Aparna sitting calmly on the sofa, a fresh bout of rage surged through him. Nikhil slammed the glass living room door. It came crashing down. Aparna rushed to protest, but Nikhil pushed her aside violently and then struck his father who had dashed to save her. Nikhil then demanded to know how Aparna dared to leave without telling him. Moreover, how dare she call his parents and tell them what happened? He insisted that his drinking and losing his temper was all really Aparna's fault. She always criticised him on his inability to earn as much as she had expected of him, so as to sustain her dream lifestyle.

To Aparna, this incident had been the actual point of culmination of their marriage. She refused to return home with Nikhil that day, in spite of all his tantrums. His parents also did not insist on it, having seen first-hand the risks it entailed to send her and the child to live with him. Nikhil was getting more and more violent, and they could not offer to keep him and Aparna at their house either. Thus, the next day, escorted by her in-laws, Aparna had collected her personal belongings from her marital home, never to return to it again. Though at the time, neither Nikhil nor his parents took Aparna's firm resolve not to return seriously.

The next afternoon, with Kartik in her arms, Aparna had waved goodbye to her in-laws at the Mumbai airport. They expected her to get over her distress and return, after a short visit to her parents. There was no going away for her now from this marriage, they concluded, what with the child. In addition to that, Nikhil would be calm soon, regretting his impulsive and violent outbursts, and then would miss his wife and son. He was a soft-hearted child in their view. But Nikhil's parents did not realise that they were to forever regret allowing Aparna to leave that day. They knew their son well, but did not gauge his wife's nerve. It was over a decade now since Aparna took that flight to Chennai—where she lived to this day, with her parents and son.

* * *

Aparna Srinivasan's had been an arranged marriage, through the classified column of the only newspaper her family subscribed to and trusted, the *Hindu*. She lived with her family in Chennai then. Nikhil Shekar, from Mumbai, had all the prerequisites of the perfect groom any girl could desire. He was handsome—tall with an athletic build and sharp facial features. He was also academically well-qualified with an engineering degree followed by an MBA degree from the UK. To boot, he came from an affluent, reputed Tamil Brahmin business family, settled in Mumbai now. Aparna's family did not match Nikhil's financially or in terms of social standing. They were respectable service-class people, Tamil Brahmin as well. Nikhil had visited Aparna's home in Chennai along with his family, after preliminary communications along with exchange of profiles and photographs. Aparna and her family felt blessed and were elated with their good luck that they should find such a worthy groom and family in every way. Aparna did not meet the conventions of traditional beauty as she was dusky, though she was quite attractive with good features. So, getting a handsome groom was lucky indeed.

When she first met him, Aparna had been deeply impressed by Nikhil's good looks, personality, charming manners, and, above all, his values. Nikhil's passionate statement in response to her quizzing him—"My work is my first love and love is my life."—had convinced her that he was a determined and conscientious worker. She had found no reason to delay her acceptance of the alliance, even though it came at a time when she was not yet mentally prepared for marriage. She had been working at a reputed luxury hotel chain, rather enjoying her work and the newly acquired financial and personal independence it brought after a conservative upbringing. Still, after the mutual customary background checks of prospective bride and groom, Aparna had married Nikhil. Their wedding was a traditional ceremony, one December morning, at a reputed *kalyana mandapam* in Kilpauk, Chennai. It was presided over by a Tamil priest, and attended by their close friends and relatives. This was followed by a lavish, traditional, multi-course banquet in the evening.

It was only on their honeymoon in Goa that Aparna first got an inkling of her husband's passion for drinking. They had room reservations at the Park Hyatt Resort, a gift from his parents, a perfect setting for the newlywed couple to get to know each other. But in the week that they stayed there, they spent more time frequenting the pubs and beaches of Goa than at the resort. While pub-hopping and beach-lazing with the excuse of celebrating their new life, Nikhil guzzled one drink after another, then yet another and many more. Aparna, herself a teetotaller, though shocked, consciously decided not to put up a resistance. She would rather not be labelled as a prude so early in her marriage by her westernised husband. Her friends at work, at the upscale Taj Coromandel,

     Shuvashree Chowdhury

thought she was too traditional and had spared no opportunity to rub it in. She was not going to prove them right.

It was after her wedding was all set that Aparna had applied for a transfer to the Taj Mahal Palace Hotel in Mumbai. She was due to start work there on return from her honeymoon in Goa. As yet, other than Nikhil's affinity for alcohol, she had no misgivings about her choice of groom. Nikhil was witty, spontaneous, and sensitive. Aparna was confident, once they got back to Mumbai and to work and this celebratory phase was over, Nikhil would prove to be the responsible husband she had chosen for herself. Moreover, Aparna had to admit that Goa, with its scenic beauty, warm, fun-loving inhabitants, and vacationers from all over the world, encouraged one to forget inhibitions and have a good time. Aparna too had found herself absorbing the bonhomie of Goa, letting down her reserve, to truly enjoy herself for the first time in her life.

Once back in Mumbai, settled into Nikhil's room at his parent's house, Aparna resumed work as reservations executive at the Taj Mahal Palace Hotel. It was a ten-minute drive from where they lived in Colaba and she got dropped and picked up by Nikhil or in the family car. Aparna adjusted spontaneously to married life, and it soon fell into an easy rhythm. In the evenings, once back home from work, she would spend time with Nikhil's family—his parents, elder brother and his wife whom she referred to as her co-sister, till Nikhil joined them on his return from work. He usually came late, just in time for dinner. This didn't seem unusual, as Nikhil worked at their family's electronic gadgets chain store's head office, as head of marketing.

The entire family usually had dinner together, before retiring to the privacy of their rooms. Aparna and Nikhil would then discuss their respective days like any average couple, watch television in bed for a while, make love, and retire for the day. Aparna was content and could not have asked for more out of life. After all, this is what she had expected out of married life. She was even more grateful now than before marriage, for having found the perfect life partner and family.

It was only after three to four months that Aparna started feeling the strain of balancing work with making time for her extended family. Her mother-in-law often expected her to accompany her on lengthy and elaborate shopping sprees or to social engagements in the evening, and thus they returned home very late. Then Aparna would become tired and fall asleep, unable to spend time with Nikhil. He was also returning home increasingly late with the passing days. She noticed that when she returned late, and when he did as well, he would be drunk. This made him snappy and irritable. Aparna now attributed his drinking to his boredom due to her being away and inability to spend time with him as before.

So, when Nikhil announced they would be shifting to a rented apartment, Aparna felt God had solved her dilemma. With more space and privacy, Aparna was sure their life would be better, thus improving their flagging relationship. She could then maintain a cordial relationship with Nikhil's family from afar, saved from their day-to-day interference in her life. Aparna did not realise that Nikhil had taken the initiative to move out from his own need for privacy and space, not for theirs as a couple. In fact, he had been in a hurry to move out of his parents' house, as he was unable to drink freely in their presence or even return too late without them raising objections and questions about his whereabouts. More so, he could not stay away from work at their home without justification and drink all day. Nikhil's parents, tired of altercations with him, were also eager to have him move out of their house. They were sure that Aparna would take over their son's responsibility.

It was their moving out of his family house that had been the real beginning to the end of Aparna's marriage. She was now rudely awakened to the extent of her husband's alcoholism. He began to get violent when she restricted his drinking at home, or questioned his returning late, on knowing he had been drinking at a pub or a friend's place. It was not long before he began staying home to drink all day instead of going to work. Aparna would not have realised this if she had not returned home early one day to find him completely inebriated. After that, she resorted to calling Nikhil's office during the day, to check whether he was there. When Nikhil learned of her probes, realising people in the office would talk, he became furious with Aparna. In the course of time, in order to hide his alcoholism, which was severe by now, he restricted everyone including her friends, even family, from coming to their

     Shuvashree Chowdhury

apartment, let alone staying over. He became a total recluse and a violent one at that.

On days that he went to work, Nikhil either turned up drunk or reached very late, with a hangover or at best in a foul mood. It was not long before his father's elder brother, the managing director of their company, prevented his coming to office. He convinced the rest of the directors, including Nikhil's parents, that Nikhil made a bad impression on employees, spoiling the company's image at large and the family's reputation. This made matters worse for Aparna. His ego having taken a beating in front of his family, he became perpetually angry and overbearing with her, blaming Aparna for all his problems.

One evening after work, Aparna was surprised and a little apprehensive to see Nikhil waiting for her outside the hotel's staff gate. She had been taking a taxi to and from home, since they left his parent's place, not wanting Nikhil to come and pick her up in his car. Nikhil noticed her walking out with her colleagues, a number of whom were male. This enraged him, drunk as he was, and he walked towards her with a violent look. Aparna, recognising his angry expression, to save herself the embarrassment of the tirade she knew was coming, pretended not to notice him. She quickly walked away from him and towards their car parked across the road. For Nikhil, this refusal to acknowledge him in front of her colleagues was a severe blow to his flagging self-esteem.

Nikhil strode after her, and promptly opened the car doors with the remote key. Once both were seated inside, he almost spat on Aparna in his drunken drawl.

"You whore, how dare you insult me in front of your friends?" he yelled, hitting the steering wheel, setting off the horn. "Who the hell do you think I am, your chauffeur? You are going to pay for this."

Then Nikhil revved the car's engine and stared at her menacingly. Satisfied with her meek and embarrassed look as her colleagues waved at her, he sped the car away, driving like a maniac. At a high speed, swerving crazily on the road to scare her, Nikhil threatened Aparna.

"I will kill you, you bitch," he screamed, racing the car recklessly. "In fact, I will kill both of us this very instant, you will see … if you don't promise me that you'll quit this job. You must be going up to the rooms, whenever possible, with those guys you were out with … don't you? Then why, of course, the rich guests, right, the foreign ones especially, they probably pay rather handsomely for an hour with you in their room, isn't it? That's why you are always late in returning home?"

This abusive display of drunkenness frightened Aparna terribly. It was not so much his words, which she was used to, but by the way he drove on the somewhat empty Colaba roads by the sea on the road better known as the Queen's Necklace.

Left with no alternative, to save their lives at this juncture, Aparna screamed aloud, "I will quit my job … I promise you, I will leave immediately. Now just please slow down, Nikhil."

"Repeat what you just said. I have to ensure you mean it," Nikhil mocked, laughing outrageously and wrenching the steering wheel.

She repeated, gritting her teeth, "I will quit my job. I am giving you my word. Now you keep yours, and drive properly."

Nikhil now reduced the car's speed, swerved to the road's side and continued to drive, as he grinned at her menacingly. "Now you've learned a lesson, haven't you?"

Aparna knew that she needed the job more now than ever before, not only for her own empowerment under the circumstances, but also because Nikhil was now without a job. His family had cut off all remuneration from the business that was due to him as one of the directors. They transferred his earnings to his mother's account, as his wife was still too new and he might coerce it out of her. They hoped this lack of funds would serve to reduce his drinking.

In fact, he had come to pick Aparna up from work for money, to get her to withdraw from her account through an ATM on their way back home. Aparna had no option but to give Nikhil the money he demanded, after he pulled up in front of an ATM and signalled to her. Then she waited desolately in the car outside the wine shop while he staggered out. He came back grinning, with two bottles. Sitting behind the car wheel, Nikhil promptly took a swig out of one of the bottles. Then he smiled lovingly at her, patted her cold and stiff hand, and then drove away.

    Shuvashree Chowdhury

Back home safely, Aparna quietly heated Nikhil's dinner for him. She herself went to bed without any, having lost her appetite He tried to initiate sex that night, trying to hug her from behind as she slept on her side, but she pushed him away with all her might. After getting his way with her on quitting the job and the money for the drinks, he chose to spare her the physical overpowering that night and dropped off to sleep beside her.

The next morning, Aparna tried to reason with Nikhil.

"We need my job now, Nikhil, don't we? Even to pay for your drinking, we need my job, don't you understand that?" Aparna cajoled, as softly as one would in taking a candy out of the tight grip of a child.

But Nikhil was resolute as he firmly replied, "I am the man of the house and it is my business to provide for our home."

Aparna knew well that his dramatic speeches were mere glib talk and Nikhil liked to feel good that way, though it infuriated her. His theatrics were a reminder to her, a slap on her face every time, of how she had been fooled by his initial dialogues into marrying him. Aparna, however, realised how embarrassing it would be for Nikhil to land up at her work place and create further scenes, which she knew he was quite capable of doing. An alcoholic, with no control of his senses when drunk, obviously has no self-respect, so why would he care for her respect?

In exasperation, Aparna just did not go in to work that morning, chucking her job like setting sail into a stormy and evil sea. Every moment ahead seemed bleak. Since she had only recently joined, Aparna thought no one would really miss her at work. So she sent her resignation by email, to the front office manager, citing an unexplainable and urgent family exigency.

* * *

Incapable of bearing Nikhil's atrocities any further, Aparna was steeling herself to leave him for good, when to her horror, she learned that she was pregnant. Her initial thought was of terminating the pregnancy. How could she carry the child of a man whom she could not bear to live with any longer, let alone rear a child with? But her parents, whom she first broke the news to, as well as her in-laws who then learned from them, pressured her into carrying the child to term.

"A child is a blessing from God," her mother declared over the phone, even as her mother-in-law added, "The baby is coming as a messiah of harmony in your life. Things will get better after the child's birth. Nikhil will change, you'll see. He'll become responsible once he becomes a father."

Aparna was thus swayed, in spite of all her misgivings, to carry the child to term and thereby give her marriage another chance.

Nikhil's uncle, though still adamant about restricting Nikhil at the office, offered Aparna a job in the family business. Aparna graciously accepted and started working promptly, even though she felt weaker as her pregnancy progressed. The job kept her sane and financially independent. She now felt fortified with the family's support, and also in knowing that if Nikhil landed up at her office to create any nuisance, he would be dealt with severely.

In the meantime, Nikhil, now cut off from all sources of income other than what little he could wheedle out of his mother or Aparna on occasion, was forced to reduce his drinking. With Aparna's persuasion, he was able to start a business in partnership with a friend. He coaxed his mother into giving him a reference in order to sanction a bank loan. Armed with the money, along with his partner, Nikhil set up a medical transcription call centre. It was a good business module back in 1999. The initial setting up and running of the business caught Nikhil's interest and he drank lesser and was reasonably sober. Aparna was thus convinced she had taken the right decision to carry their child to term and give their marriage another chance.

In time for the child's birth, Aparna went to Nikhil's parent's house. They had not allowed her to go back to Chennai while she could still travel by air as much as she and her parents had wanted to. They had feared she would divulge the details of her marriage to their alcoholic son, and then perhaps her parents might convince her to stay back along with the child. So the child was born in Mumbai and Nikhil's grandmother was to later name him Kartik. He was born a healthy baby at the reputed Lilavati Hospital, in West Bandra. Nikhil and his family, as well as Aparna's parents,

Shuvashree Chowdhury

who had come to Mumbai to usher the child into the world, were overjoyed.

It was after three months that Aparna felt strong enough to return to work in the family business. She hired an ayah to take care of Kartik in her absence. Nikhil, who was ecstatic at the birth of his child, spent as much time as he could with Kartik, which was as much as he could spare from his now successful business. It all worked out well. Nikhil would spend a good part of the day at home, keeping an eye on the baby and the ayah, then go to work in the evening once Aparna returned. She was grateful to God for finally taking the baton of her life, in bringing it back on track, and now guiding her steady run. But this harmonious state and sense of well-being sadly did not last long. But by the time problems erupted again, luckily, she had recouped her physical strength. She had also recovered emotional and mental agility from working fruitfully and earning well.

After a year and a half of running the call centre amicably, differences crept up between Nikhil and his business partner. It was not long before their problems got so out of hand that they had to end their partnership. This left Nikhil in the lurch once again. He was lucky to be able to recover the money he had invested, in parting ways with his partner, and to be able to return the bank loan shortly. But his good luck was limited only to that as he was once again without a job. The stress of his failed venture and the renewed frustration of being jobless again, with no focus in life, threw Nikhil back into the doldrums. It propelled him into the open arms of his old love—alcohol that cradled his low esteem in its lap. This time, it took Aparna and his parents a while to figure out his return to his old habits, as it was gradual.

By now, their son Kartik, nearing his second birthday, was increasingly restless and naughty. He would crawl all over the house, throw things about, and, often breaking them, would gurgle in mirth. Then when scolded and handled firmly, the child would howl and grow hysterical. Nikhil, now always either in a drunken stupor or a hangover, found it difficult to handle Kartik—who was too unruly for the ayah to manage herself. Aparna being away at work, Nikhil would get angry and then violent when Kartik cried, yelling at him to shut up. By the time Aparna returned home,

Nikhil would have reached the limit of his endurance. Though she had seen much worse, this behaviour towards their son shocked her. Her shock then turned to fear for the child's safety, especially when she was away from home.

Nikhil's conduct towards Aparna was also becoming frightfully menacing and this would alarm the child. Nikhil would push Aparna violently, even twist her arms, then hit her if he was not yet satisfied that he had hurt her enough. The purpose was to alleviate his frustrations by deliberately causing her immense physical and emotional humiliation and hurt.

Nikhil would yell and create a ruckus if the food was not piping hot, whenever he returned home drunk, be it at any odd time of the night. He forbade Aparna from keeping his food in hot cases to eat from when he desired, or even in microwaveable dishes to heat at his own convenience. So he would brusquely force Aparna to wake up at odd hours to serve him, waking Kartik who was asleep beside her and causing him to bawl. Then Nikhil would coerce Aparna into heating his food, while she attempted to pacify Kartik. With a smug grin at Aparna, Nikhil would then not eat the food—which was often sautéed vegetables, *sambar*, and rice—she had just heated. Then when she had gone back to sleep again, the food having grown cold, he would once again wake her forcefully to reheat every item. Thus, in teasing and taunting Aparna, crushing her self-esteem, Nikhil's bruised ego found a sadistic outlet.

Kartik's ayah too complained to Aparna incessantly about Nikhil's behaviour. Of how he pushed her and the child violently if she was unable to get Kartik to stop crying and disturbing Nikhil's drunken stupor. Aparna did not say anything to Nikhil about it, as she knew it was useless trying to reason with a man who, overpowered by alcohol, had lost all ability to reason. Also, she knew how violent Nikhil could get, having been on the receiving end of his verbal and physical lashings on numerous occasions. But when Aparna resorted to silence in order to deal with his abuse, Nikhil turned more aggressive and violent. He construed her silence to be a mockery of his pathetic demeanour and felt he had to punish her for humiliating him. Then even as Nikhil hit or pushed her, twisted her arm or pinched her, Aparna would rush

		Shuvashree Chowdhury

to pick up a crying Kartik. She tried to save his witnessing this spectacle, duty-bound to protect his tender mind, by holding him close to her.

Aparna fervently prayed for God to uplift her from this gutter of a life she had fallen into or at the least give her a sign on what she should do. The only way out of this mess, Aparna concluded, was to leave Nikhil and return to her parents in Chennai. But she was undecided about the final move, as there was the issue of a child to be raised away from the father now, in another city. But Aparna soon found the signal she desperately sought from God, which spurred her to leave Nikhil. It was in his pushing her out of the house along with Kartik, the night they spent sitting on the staircase. Once safely home with her parents, Aparna called her mentor and boss Balaji, Nikhil's uncle in Mumbai, and updated him on what had compelled her to leave. In empathising with her, much to her relief, Balaji assured Aparna she had taken the right decision in leaving Mumbai.

"Don't think of the future now," Balaji had advised.

He had begun to care for Aparna, in working closely with her, and felt sorry for all she had undergone. She was a sincere girl, full of love and warmth, and surely deserved much better in life.

"Yes, I'm just so tired to think of anything now," Aparna replied. "But I am relieved to be back in Chennai and away from that constant stress and struggle."

"You must first rest, distance, and recuperate from the trauma you've undergone,' Balaji said tenderly, "And then you will find the strength to take the next course of action wisely. But then, explain to Kartik why you left. You must tell him about his father's illness. That is what Nikhil's alcoholism is, in reality, Aparna. I hope you understand that he is not a bad person. Kartik should not grow up confused and rebellious because of these memories."

Thus, in the first months of her return to Chennai, Aparna focussed on regaining her emotional strength, spending as much time as possible with her son Kartik. Her parents, were at first shocked, then horrified and empathetic, when she narrated the details of her marriage. But they were worried about what their extended family, friends, and neighbours would think about Aparna living with them again.

"Our son-in-law Nikhil is travelling abroad on work for an extensive period," Her parents told everyone they met. "Aparna will be staying with us a while."

Aparna was also asked to tell people that she was visiting while her husband was travelling. It was a sound justification for people not to probe further.

* * *

After six months of being at home in Chennai, her parent's worries and nagging peaked. Aparna's troubled existence started taking a toll on her. She started to get irritable with her parent's behaviour in controlling every aspect of her life, leading to heated arguments with them. Aparna concluded that her financial dependence on them was what made her answerable to them for her every move, even though she was thirty. She raised the issue of taking up a job, but her parents strongly dissuaded her. Their reasoning was that with Kartik away from one parent, Aparna owed him her undivided attention. Moreover, if she took up a job here in Chennai, the neighbours would gauge something was amiss in her marriage and raise eyebrows. Their views seemed justified to Aparna.

So, in spite of her restlessness to get on with her life, heightened by financial stress and her inability to buy anything she liked for herself or her son, Aparna did not broach the subject of working after that. She decided to wait a couple of years for Kartik to start school before taking up a job. During this time, Aparna also had to deal with constant pressure from Nikhil and his family to return to Mumbai. They visited Chennai in turns, at first staying with her family, then checking into a hotel near her home, trying to convince and then threaten her to return to Mumbai.

"Nikhil, you will have to go through a session of detoxification," Aparna insisted conclusively, every time on meeting him, or when he called, "If you expect Kartik and me to ever return to live with you."

"Now, enough is enough, Aparna," Nikhil replied menacingly, "don't use my drinking as an excuse to live with your parents, after taking my son away from me. I am not an alcoholic, as you make me out to be. A few drinks do not construe to being an

     Shuvashree Chowdhury

alcoholic. In fact, it is your egotistic, argumentative, self-centred behaviour that induces violence in me, not alcohol. It is your fault."

"Nikhil, not admitting to your drinking problem is the first and surest sign of an incurable alcoholic," Aparna would say in exasperation, "Then worse still, if you want to blame me for all your problems, so be it. But I insist you go into rehabilitation, if you dream of ever living together with us as a family again."

"It is up to you to return or stay with your parents, Aparna, but you have no right to keep my son with you. I will take you to court, you just wait and see," Nikhil had roared, then slammed down the receiver after concluding "I will ensure you return my son to me, Aparna."

This would be the usual thread of conversation between Aparna and Nikhil in every interaction. Then weeks would go by, when neither Nikhil nor his parents would call. Aparna always assured herself that Nikhil would not take on bringing up Kartik by himself and neither would his family. They were threatening to take Kartik away in an attempt to get her back to Mumbai for their convenience. Nikhil's life was difficult without her to keep house through his drinking binges. There was no way his parents would take him back into their home. Neither would he return. He and his family wanted Aparna to return and take charge, but for how long would they wait for her, she wondered. A nagging fear of losing Kartik soon crept in and was filling Aparna's mind with every passing day. She knew that if Nikhil filed for divorce, she might lose custody of Kartik, since she had no personal income and Kartik was almost five now.

Aparna's family was not as affluent as Nikhil's—who would easily be proven more appropriate to bring up a child, in giving him the best in life, in the event of a divorce. In spite of this fear, Aparna firmly decided not to return to Mumbai till Nikhil admitted to his drinking problem and agreed to seek professional help. But so far, there was no initiation on his part in that direction. What was really strange was that there was no move even from his family. They had made this serious issue of his alcoholism into one that would uphold their fragile ego to Aparna, what with Nikhil's elder brother being alcoholic as well, though not as violent as Nikhil. Since his wife was accepting and adjusting to marital life as women tend to, along with their ten-year-old daughter, the family was complacent Aparna would do the same in time. That was why, though she was under a lot of stress and anxious about Kartik's future, Aparna was firmly resolved never to return to Mumbai or remain in her defunct marriage.

Aparna's father, a State Bank employee, had just retired from service the year before, and her mother, a school teacher, was due to retire shortly. Aparna decided it was high time now for her to take up a job, whatever her parents' opinion, if she wanted to keep Kartik and provide for a good life for him and the family. The child's well-being should not be compromised by his own father and paternal family, due to her financial incapacity to achieve his judicial custody and bring him up well. She was going to fight them all, Aparna decided, in spite of comprehending the difficulties in being a single mother.

Kartik, by now, had started his schooling at Padma Sheshadri Bala Bhavan, one of the most reputed group of schools in Chennai, with very high academic standards, after a much apprehensive wait in the admission process. Aparna's father, now that he had retired, could look out for Kartik outside of his school hours and her mother could watch out for his studies. Aparna convinced her parents of her need to take up a job and they consented. It was not possible for her to return to Mumbai, they conceded after witnessing Nikhil's temper themselves. They agreed that Aparna's working would ensure Kartik would live with them for good, now no longer able to envision a life without him.

Aparna got in touch with a few of her old friends and associates in Chennai. It took her a few months of doing the rounds of firms and recruiting companies to finally find employment through a friend's reference. It was at a reputed media house. Even though the job profile and remuneration did not impress her, Aparna judiciously took up the appointment. After some experience there, she could find a better opportunity in a hotel as before, or an airline perhaps, she thought. With a long break in service, it might be a while before she found a job of her choice, so it was not prudent to let go of this. And so, it was in January 2004 that she joined the *National Daily* as a features reporter. A recipient of honours in English from the top-ranking Stella Maris College, that had one of the best English departments in Chennai, adding to her inherently charming personality, also her work experience at the reputed Taj Hotels, Aparna's employers were happy to take her on as a stringer to start with. But this too was after a written test and an interview, both of which she excelled at.

Nikhil, on learning of Aparna's job, started calling her repeatedly again, harassing her even more. His insecurity was the driving force behind his attempt to hurt Aparna's pride, to reduce her sense of security. He found her new self-assured attitude intimidating. It was in reality his own self-doubt that spurred him to drink immeasurably and then become jealous, moody, irritable, and angry. Then this conduct came in the way of his retaining any job or doing well in business, in spite of his superior academic qualifications and skills. All of this was a vicious cycle which soured his relationships with people, even family, especially in marriage. An insecure man tries to prove himself to others, as much as to himself, leading to arrogance, boasting, backbiting, and undercutting. He cannot stand for another to be more successful, physically fit, in love, richer, happier, and more intelligent, so will do whatever he can to bring the secure ones down to his insecure size.

People like Nikhil are destructive to themselves as well as to those they love. They abuse their wives, parents, girlfriends, children, and harass people who service them, or work for and with them. Insecurity may be termed as the primary reason for most of the troubles we as humans have in relationships. A secure man is successful in a relationship, does well in his career, for he does all it takes to be successful. He enjoys challenges, takes responsibility, manages adversity, and thus leads, provides, and gives support to his loved ones. While a secure man is able to admit when he feels insecure, shy, or doesn't know how to do something, an insecure man usually can't admit to any shortcomings and blames destiny and everyone who it brings into his life. It is such a man or woman who will use alcohol, even religion perhaps, as a prop.

Nikhil's anger over his wife's perceived superiority, combined with his fear of losing her forever now that she had taken up a job, impelled him to come to Chennai. He violently exhorted her to return to Mumbai, threatening to take Kartik away. But by this time, Aparna was a determined woman and there was no stopping her now.

          Shuvashree Chowdhury

Chapter 2

A Perfect Marriage

Sujata Srinivasan was married before she turned twenty. She had barely completed her graduation when her parents had begun shortlisting prospective suitors from newspaper matrimonial columns. It was on responding to an advertisement in the *Hindu* by Anand Krishnan's family that her profile and picture had been shortlisted. After the usual preliminaries, Anand and his family had come to meet the prospective bride at her residence in Nungambakkam. The two families were seated in the drawing room exchanging pleasantries when Sujata, led by her mother, walked in with her head bowed, looking demure. She was dressed in a blue and red pure silk *sari* which emphasised her slender frame. Her long silken hair was in a braid wrapped in strings of jasmine flowers. She had a luminous complexion, slanting, somewhat oriental eyes, a small but shapely nose, wide conspicuous mouth, and overall a pleasant endearing appearance. Sujata was attractive, though not beautiful in the conventional way.

Anand's gaze followed her closely, from the time she entered till she shyly took a seat across him. It took him just about that time to decide she was the girl he wanted for his wife. However, one look at Anand and Sujata was sure she would never have him as her husband. Anand was of average height, plump, with small facial features, brown piercing eyes, and dressed unfashionably in white shirt and black trousers. He was not as smart and handsome as her sister Ramya's husband, who Sujata idolised and thought of as the best-looking man she knew. With the shallowness of youth, Sujata firmly decided that there was no way she would take on someone as plain as Anand for her husband. She thus relaxed, knowing she had to only bear this visit cordially, answer a few questions, and then go back to her regular life. Maybe she could join a post-graduation course.

Hopefully, it would be a while before another marriage alliance came knocking on her door, ensuring Sujata was well into her new academic course by then. Her parents would surely then wait for her to complete her Master's degree, before pressurising her to get married. Anand, on the other hand, in his resolve to convey his assent on this alliance at the end of this visit, engaged Sujata in a conversation. He asked about her interests and hobbies, the subjects she had just studied at college, also her views on movies, books, and current affairs. Sujata responded affably, conveying her lack of interest in books, English movies, and current affairs. Anand was disappointed in her disinterest in all of his passionate interests, but that did not deter him in his resolve to marry her.

Having gauged Sujata's warm and congenial nature, Anand was pleased. But her perfect mix of intelligence, innocence, and simplicity, rare in modern young women attracted him even more. She was refined, visibly respectful of elders, and conversant with household chores. He inferred this from the deft way in which she made and handed around the tea, along with an assortment of sweets and snacks. Whatever qualities Sujata lacked from his ideal of a dream wife, Anand decided, could be inculcated with ease in one as young as Sujata. In fact, he would influence her interests too, he decided, so they could grow in steady companionship. Anand knew from the warmth and ease with which his parents and younger brother had taken to Sujata that they would all wholeheartedly support his choice of bride.

On their way out, Anand's father, shaking hands with Sujata's father, said, "Thank you so much for your warm hospitality. We will convey our decision in a day or two, after discussing with our son. After all, it is his life and it should be his decision." Then, smiling warmly at Sujata and her mother, he added, "You will also need to discuss this with your daughter. Her consent should be considered."

After the guests departed, Sujata made her disapproval clear to her parents: "I will not marry this man," she stated. "He's made no impression on me whatsoever. He is not good-looking, neither does he have an impressive personality, nor any conversational

     Shuvashree Chowdhury

skills either. How can you ever expect me to marry a man like him?"

Sujata's father, firmly reminding her of the affluence of this alliance's family, said "Sujata, but you want to marry a rich guy, and you've stated that clearly. Now you cannot find everything in one man, can you? This family is one of the most reputed and also wealthy families in Chennai. You know that well yourself."

Her mother did not say anything to Sujata. Sujata's aloofness to Anand had told her of her daughter's disinterest. She conveyed her opinion to Sujata's father that night, and they decided not to pressurise Sujata. Her parents thus set themselves up mentally to finding more suitable candidates from the newspaper, also to communicate afresh with others already shortlisted. Internet matrimonial sites like Shaadi.com and Bharatmatrimony.com, which would become so popular in the coming years, were not yet on the horizon. Few used the Internet at home yet, in 1997, even though Sujata's father used it for his business. Sujata did not even have an email account then.

The only dependable way for finding an alliance, other than through matchmaking firms and through family and friends, was the newspaper classified columns. Since Anand's family owned a reputed media house that also published newspapers, they had not mentioned the details of the groom and family in any identifiable way in the *Hindu*, which was actually a rival of their newspaper. It was only when they came to visit Sujata's family and found them to their liking that they divulged their real identity. Sujata's parents were rather impressed. But Anand's family's background had no impact on Sujata, except that it amused her and would add spice to the stories she would tell her sister and her close friends about this meeting.

The next morning, Sujata's father had just started to read the newspaper while sipping his filter coffee when the phone rang. He was just about to give the news a quick look and then turn to the matrimonial column, it being Sunday. It was Anand's mother on the landline.

"Good morning, Mr. Srinivasan," she said cheerily, identifying his voice correctly from their conversation the day before. "I'm calling to say that we rather liked your daughter Sujata, also your family and home. My husband and I discussed it with our son and we are all interested to take this marriage alliance ahead, if you have no objections."

How could Sujata's father turn down this proposal from such a respectable, affluent family? He was honoured that they had shown interest to begin with, and were now confirming their acceptance of an alliance he had not even imagined of for his daughter.

So though knowing of his daughter's outright rejection of Anand, he politely replied, smiling into the phone, "Thank you so much, Mrs. Krishnan. We liked your son and family too. Sujata would like a little time to deliberate though. She is still very young and keen on studying further. Moreover, marriage is a lifetime's decision. We would rather give her some time to think things over, and perhaps even interact with your son before deciding. I hope that is alright with you."

"Yes, of course, please allow her to take her time. There's no hurry at all." Anand's mother said confidently, "Just that I wanted to convey our decision, so you may not be keen to look at other alliances before considering ours well."

After Sujata awoke, a little late now that college was over and there was no pressing demand on her sleep, she was summoned to the privacy of her parents' bedroom. They could not allow their daughter's shallow views on the boy's plain appearance and personality and his poor sense of dressing come in the way of her assuredly happy life. It was a chance to climb the social ladder for them as well. Moreover, their elder daughter was married to a man who fit right into the bill of the ideal partner in Sujata's mind. But her sister lived a life of constant financial struggle. Her parents were determined not to allow Sujata, with her unrealistic view of life, to follow in her sister's impractical footsteps. Sujata's father convinced her mother of the need to ensure that Sujata did not lead a similar life of struggle. They did not want to be anxious on Sujata's account as well as that of her sister's.

In the meantime, Anand learned of Sujata's father's response from his mother. He judiciously read into it his impending rejection by the woman whom he was now determined to marry. He made up his mind to woo her with his charms. Anand wrote a

Shuvashree Chowdhury

beautiful, handwritten letter, using all the expressions and poetic skills he naturally had a flair for. He would later laud this timely intervention, in clinching the deal of his alliance with Sujata that her parents had failed to. For their attempt to convince Sujata, far from achieving the outcome of its well-executed agenda, only proved to Sujata's parents the stubbornness of their daughter's character. She knew her mind too well, whether or not for her own good. Their well-meaning attempts were thwarted by her persistent reasoning and conclusive decision that she would not marry Anand. Sujata's parents were liberal and open-minded. They did not wish to compel their daughters into any choices, whatever the consequences.

"This man Anand does not measure up to Ramya's husband Prashant's suave personality," she had asserted firmly, however silly it might sound to anyone, including her parents. "An impressive personality is my criteria for a prospective groom, just as was Ramya's. It's only that I haven't met anyone myself, as she was lucky to. I'm not attracted to Anand in any way, either physically or intellectually, so how can I marry him? Then also, this will be a bone of contention between us sisters and with my husband, if I were to wed someone as unattractive as Anand."

"But we want you to think hard about this, before your final decision," Sujata's mother had concluded, sounding exasperated. "We cannot allow you to throw away your bright future on a whim, just like your sister did, with a similar immature arrogance. We would not have been so sure about our views had we not been witness to Ramya's emotional struggles. What with the women her husband constantly attracts with his looks and the financial problems which won't allow her to ignore it."

It was thus much to the shock and satisfaction of Sujata's parents that Anand's poetic, elegantly written first letter impressed Sujata. The letter overrode his lack of physical appeal and style. She now saw him in a new light. His written words achieved what his personal disposition could not. Sujata replied to his letter, though only to turn down his interest in a polite way in two sentences. The writer of such elegant lines, Sujata thought, deserved a decent rejection at least. This was not what her first impression of the man had been. Anand, instead of seeing her two-line reply as a rebuff, read into it a cause worthy of a proper pursuit. He was shrewd enough to know that he had managed to grab her attention. For Sujata had opened the lines of communication which had seemed padlocked, except in sheer politeness, on his visit to her house.

Anand decided that he would charm his future wife with his intellect, and the gift of the written word that God had endowed him with. It didn't matter that he was not very good-looking or didn't have a charming personality. Much of his unease on the occasion of their visit to Sujata's house had been due to the presence of his parents, especially his father, which did not inspire confidence in him. That did not hamper him while writing letters. In the ensuing two months, in firm determination, with his deluge of poetic letters that he followed with telephone calls, Anand was able to wheedle his way into Sujata's heart. He seduced her mind with his words, thus gradually attracting Sujata physically too.

Once she had replied to his letters after much delay and hesitation, through them and also their ensuing conversations, Anand caught glimpses of her soul. Then Sujata had not been difficult to win over. Luckily for Anand, boosting his confidence, he had her parents as aides, in making inroads into the nooks and corners of Sujata's mind and heart, hitherto never traversed by any man in her twenty years.

Sujata's parents had proposed to her, as she saw it, a life based on security and luxury without love, a path that she dreaded to tread. They had their elder daughter Ramya's case to fuel their apprehensions of a marriage without financial prosperity. But now, with the joint forces of love and their logic acting upon her in tandem, it was not long before Sujata consented to the marriage with Anand with all her mind and heart. It was a traditional Tamil Brahmin wedding, with all the incumbent rituals, at a large and reputed *kalyana mandapam* (marriage hall) on Cathedral Road in central Chennai. Later, they had a lavish reception on the sprawling lawns of the recently opened Dakshin Chitra, a famous living-history museum and cultural centre on the East Coast Road. Their guest list read like the who's who of Chennai's glitterati. The functions, attended by a number of celebrities, were given elaborate coverage in Anand's family's English and Tamil newspapers, even though the fact that the

     Shuvashree Chowdhury

couple had found each other through a rival newspaper was a family joke.

* * *

It was the end of their honeymoon in Bangkok and Pattaya that turned out, literally, to be the end of the honeymoon period of Sujata's marital life. She moved into her marital home in T Nagar, a mere ten-minute drive from her parent's house in Nungambakkam to commence her conjugal life. But it was after the celebratory phase that she was startled into the reality of the immense difference between the two households in terms of culture. The contrast in open-mindedness and liberality of the two homes hit her hard. Sujata was soon brought face to face with the idea that, as a woman, she was an underprivileged member of her husband's household and society. She was inducted to the customs and practices of the women of the household. Her life was now on to be governed by the dictates of her husband and, above him, her father-in-law as the head of the family.

Sujata's mother-in-law, who had perhaps once been in the same position as Sujata was now, had only lately with age and the passing of her elders, risen to being the one in command in all household matters. Her husband was rather busy with his business and, though her mother-in-law dictated terms, she did not have a loving bond with her husband. Her parents-in-law, to Sujata's immense surprise as it was so unlike her parents and those married couples she had known, slept and practically lived in separate rooms. It was only much later, over the years, that Sujata found out from extended family that the bone of contention between the aging couple was the man's alleged affair with his wife's sister. It was rumoured that Anand's cousin—his aunt's son—who managed the Tamil newspaper might be his father's son and his half-brother.

All this gossip would reach Sujata's ears only much later. For now, as a new bride, she was presented with the achievements and reputation of the family. This was to impress upon her the need to conduct herself as befitting her new position. It was made clear to Sujata that she could only wear a *sari* at all times, whether day or night. Only after a few years of marriage had she been able to break this rigidity by wearing a nightdress, once she was in her bedroom with the door shut. She rose early every morning. After a mandatory bath, she had to dress her hair in strings of jasmine flowers, kept ready by the elderly house maids. She had done this first, on the day Anand's family first visited her home, for their benefit. This ritual was followed by the daily puja along with her mother-in-law. After supervising the drawing of the *kolam* in front of their four-storey house, Sujata was to serve filter coffee prepared by the maids to her parents-in-law, husband, and his younger brother. While the men finished their coffee over reading the newspapers and then got ready to leave for work, Sujata helped with the breakfast and supervised the packing of their lunch boxes.

Almost every evening, Sujata visited one temple or the other, along with her mother-in-law. It could be a walk to the small Ganesh temple behind their home, or a drive to the grander Venkat Narayana temple on the road named after its presiding deity nearby. Then they might visit the Partha Sarathy temple at Triplicane, sometimes the magnificent Kapaleeshwar temple at Mylapore. These visits often ended with attending dance recitals or classical music concerts at the temple premises, or at Vani Mahal on G.N Chetty Road or other *arangams*. Sujata had never visited temples as many times in all her twenty years as she had in the twenty days since her return from the honeymoon with her husband. Her own parents were believers, no doubt, but not staunchly devout. They had not brought up their daughters in such traditional piety and subservience. After a couple of months of this culture, Sujata felt that she could take it no more.

However, the only time Sujata got respite from all of this ritualism was in the few days of her menstruation. She was not permitted to do anything during the time. She couldn't cook or perform the daily puja; she couldn't even enter the kitchen and puja room. She could not touch anything in the house other than her personal stuff in her room and also had to eat there. She was not to step out of the house for any reason whatsoever. Though in the first few months, she enjoyed the break from all the routines during her periods, the fact that this asceticism was imposed soon began to frustrate Sujata. Then, in addition to all this, there was the vast difference in food preference here as compared to her

     Shuvashree Chowdhury

parent's house. Her mother-in-law discouraged the cooks from anything but traditional Tamilian food; she was not particular about how it was served either. Sujata's parents had encouraged the preparation of pan Indian and any international cuisine, so long as it was vegetarian. Also, they were particular about the presentation of the food.

As she was so young, Sujata settled into the ways of her new home without much protest or fuss. But it was the gradual change in the attitude of her husband that now stuck in her throat. She perceived it as a fishbone that refused to dislodge in spite of the incessant tears she attempted to flush it out with. He had recently been given independent charge of the reputed English paper owned by his family, the *National Daily*. Anand was kept away from her often and long, touring the country, at times travelling globally. She might have overlooked this if he gave her quality time when he was home, but he was always glued to his newspapers or a book even in her presence. Where had the poetic verses and their romantic writer vanished, Sujata wondered dejectedly? It was like Anand had married and brought her home, as one would a trophy, to display and keep as his family chose—who, in turn, were proud of this feat.

In all the time Anand was wooing Sujata, she had believed he had actually fallen head over heels in love with her. She had assumed he was so charmed by her that he would give in to all her likes and dislikes. So Sujata now expected Anand to stand up to his parents for her, to tell her that she need not follow all the traditions imposed by his mother and the restrictions by his father. But she was surprised when he seemed to enjoy the immense joy his parents took in playing with the doll he had brought home for them. It was later that Sujata realised that Anand had wooed her with honeyed words for his family's sake. He loved her only obligatorily, Sujata soon concluded, out of convenience perhaps. Someone as self-absorbed as him was obviously incapable of true love.

Anand was kind to her when he felt like it. He took Sujata on luxurious vacations abroad, and to lavish lunches and dinners at expensive restaurants— only five-star when in Chennai. They went to movies of his choice, usually English, when he was in the mood.

Anand also gave her money for expensive *saris* and jewellery, and also to buy gifts for her family. In return for all this, he expected Sujata to dedicate her time and life to his family, which he was unable to do himself. His work was his life and life for him was all business. For many women, this would have been a fair barter, but not for Sujata. She had married Anand because she had believed that he was in love with her. But now she knew that he had secured her hand in marriage much as he might clinch a business deal. Thus he did just enough, as he would to retain a valuable client.

Anand's absences bothered her most when Sujata became pregnant within a year of their wedding. Already in an emotionally and physically fragile state from the pregnancy, she felt marooned at home, in an island prison where she was the only inmate. Her parents-in-law seemed like the jail warden and superintendent. At times, Sujata's parents, sister, and her sister's husband visited. But their visits were always in the presence of the in-laws. Due to this awkwardness, the visits slowly became rarer and then stopped. During this time, Sujata found some comfort in the conversations she had with Anand's brother. Their common ground was their mutual distaste for Anand's condescending, increasingly arrogant, and negligent attitude. They both agreed his attitude was due to his parents. He had been made director without ever having to prove his mettle.

Things reached the breaking point, when Anand was absent at the time of Sujata's childbirth. As he was away on work, his parents did not find it necessary to summon their son to the birth of his child, or even to inform him of it. Only when he returned home in due time, in a couple of days, Anand was introduced to his child as though he were a visiting uncle. The explanation the new parents were offered for this was that his business prospects could not be disturbed over something as mundane as the birth of their child. Sujata's parents and sister, also not informed in time, made it to her suite at the Apollo hospital only much after the child's birth. The fear and isolation she had undergone strengthened Sujata's resolve to emotionally distance herself from those with power to hurt her, most of all Anand.

To add to Sujata's misery, she was shocked to see that Anand took an instant dislike to their son, whom Anand's father had named

     Shuvashree Chowdhury

Varun. To Anand, the child represented an end to his quiet routine at home and his jaunts with Sujata. Anand could not endure such interference, even from his own child. He insisted that Sujata leave Varun out of their bedroom at night, in the ayah's care. Anand also wanted her to go out with him as she did before. But Sujata would not comply; in fact, she increasingly clung to the baby as if he were her lifeline. Anand interpreted this as Sujata losing interest in him. He did not understand that she was shutting herself off from him emotionally. The more he demanded of Sujata's time, and thus avoided their child, the more it angered her.

In time, Sujata's simmering anger at Anand and her own family for coaxing her into marriage, along with her alienated motherhood, turned into a festering wound. It erupted at Anand, who usually came in its way. At the slightest provocation, she would slip into caustic remarks and ill-tempered jibes. The financial help she had provided her family after marriage served as fodder for her rage against them. Though in her sister's husband, who was jealous of Anand for his financial affluence and success, she found a growing empathiser. Then Anand's brother Murali got married. The budding rivalries of his wife, the new woman in the household, and Sujata brought an abrupt halt to their one-time camaraderie. Also, Anand and his brother found themselves on opposite sides of the fence. Their mother favoured her younger son and wife and showed this preference by gifting the new bride jewellery and *saris*. Whether unwittingly or not, this clear preference drove a wedge between the brothers and alienated Sujata further.

* * *

It was not long before Sujata came to the conclusion that the only way to find mental and emotional stability was to engage in a productive enterprise. This would give her the personal identity she badly needed and the financial independence she could well do with. Her current equation with Anand meant that she could not ask him for money for her expenses any longer. He, in turn, stopped giving her the money of his own accord and waited for her to ask, turning it into a powerplay of sorts. When she did ask, he tried to lighten the mood by some jokes about her overspending.

This had the opposite effect of hurting her deeply and freezing him out even further.

Sujata's son was to soon start school and she didn't need to be with him all day now. She was thus determined to find an occupation. It was in the process of looking for a job that the recruitment firm she approached offered Sujata a role as a research analyst for their executive search division. At first, there was tremendous resistance to her working from her in-laws. No woman in their family had ever worked and they perceived this new development as a huge disgrace. Her parents felt she would be neglecting her son by working, starved as he was for the attention and time of his father. Surprisingly, Anand was supportive. He hoped that the job and exposure to the outside world would improve her mood and, in turn, their relationship. Moreover, he felt that their son would gain from a mother who was confident, independent, and happy. Though she was sceptical about Anand's support, Sujata went ahead and took up the job.

Her work entailed research for headhunting mandates which Sujata was allocated by her boss, the head of the consumer, retail, and services vertical, a lady based in Mumbai. She was assigned to a team for every mandate, comprising a consultant and two or three other research analysts. First, the researchers made a long list of companies from which the prospective candidates for the position might be searched. Once this list was approved by the consultant, who worked closely with the researchers, and the client, Sujata and other researchers called the prospective candidates from out of these companies through their board lines. On acquiring the cell phone numbers of the prospective candidates, the researchers then called them up. They introduced themselves, their own firm—a reputed multinational one—and the client company, and detailed the job profile on offer. A list of interested candidates, along with a brief on each, was then submitted to the consultant and meetings were fixed between them and each candidate for further assessment.

This was a challenging job, one Sujata found herself sucked into like quicksand, though wholeheartedly. She began to enjoy her work and being with her colleagues during coffee and lunch breaks. The interaction with people at senior levels had seemed daunting to

        Shuvashree Chowdhury

Sujata in the beginning, but soon she found discussing a position with candidates and the ensuing conversations stimulating. It built her confidence tremendously and often Sujata joined the consultants at candidate assessment meetings, whether in office or outside, and each of these sessions was truly a learning experience. Even without ever personally having worked her way up the corporate ladder, Sujata steadily climbed the ladder of experience, knowledge, and wisdom. In two years, she was promoted to the position of an executive search consultant. This gave her self-esteem a boost as it did her personal finances.

The changes in her personality and the confidence she exuded now were a stark change from the shy, introverted, and unsure girl Anand had married. In a year of working, Sujata stopped wearing only *saris* and now wore *salwar* suits as well. This was made possible also because after considerable acrimony between Anand, his brother, and their parents over business issues, she and Anand, along with their son, now lived separately on a different floor of the same house. By this time, with his own business exposure as managing director, Anand had developed a distinct sense of style and sophistication of his own. He had taken membership at the Park Hotel's gymnasium and swam in the pool regularly, as it was close to his office on Mount Road. He also visited the salon and spa there and altogether was a new man. Anand now played tennis on occasion at the Cosmopolitan Club as a member.

All these lifestyle changes and his successes at work augmented Anand's personality. He was a much better conversationalist now. Sujata had taken over the job of shopping for Anand's clothes and accessories since their marriage. She did a good job of buying stylish clothes from renowned branded stores for him even now. All these changes had a positive impact on their relationship. With their son now quite grown up and busy with school and extracurricular activities, Sujata and Anand had more time for themselves. They could now go on holidays and outings together, without Sujata always feeling guilty over leaving Varun home alone with the maids.

This was the start of Sujata and Anand's second and better phase of marriage. Age and experience allowed them to meet on a more equal platform. Now they even discussed their respective work and found companionship in their matured selves. Anand found Sujata's interest in current affairs refreshing. They watched and discussed the news, both on television and newspaper reports. Sujata took an interest in the working of Anand's newspaper, and matters related to the media and the publishing industry. It helped her as she still worked in the consumer, retail, and services vertical that included media. Anand too learned about the corporate world that Sujata was always abreast of.

Sujata had once been conscious of Anand's mediocre looks and personality, when they went out with her extended family and relatives, along with her sister and her husband. But now she was confident of Anand's new, suave personality, and not reluctant to go out with him. His mother's blind support for her younger son and his wife, despite his incompetence, had alienated Anand from his parents and brought him closer to his wife. He no longer took his parents' side over her, and showed her respect even in their presence, unlike earlier. Sujata too was content with this state of affairs.

It had taken Sujata and Anand over seven years to reach this level of mutual respect and understanding. It was only when they had separately worked on themselves, enhancing their respective self-esteem and confidence, that they were able to achieve conjugal harmony.

	Shuvashree Chowdhury

Chapter 3

The Two Women and the Man

Anand was sometimes the last one to leave office, once the next day's paper had been put to bed. He left the office premises on Mount Road much after midnight. On most days, when he left his cabin, there was no one at their work stations outside, the hall empty, dimly lit by a light or two. Many of the employees would still be outside the main gate though, around a tea vendor on a bicycle. The security guard and a peon would be chatting in the reception area of the floor his cabin was on, waiting for Anand to leave, to lock up his cabin. One evening, when he stepped out of his cabin after an overseas conference call, his secretary long gone by now, he was surprised to see an employee pounding away rapidly on her computer keypad. He walked up and stood behind her. The computer screen displayed what seemed like a list of questions, the last in midsentence.

The lady turned around instinctively and Anand recognised her as the new employee Aparna Nikhil. He had been introduced to her a few weeks back, during the final interview for selection. It surprised Anand that she was still around so late, as she was with the magazine supplement, not the main paper. Why had her department head and colleagues left the new employee behind by herself, he wondered?

"How come you are still at office, so late?" Anand asked.

"Sir, I was preparing a questionnaire for an interview I have tomorrow morning, so I came back to the office. I have to email it tonight," Aparna said, promptly standing up and then hesitantly added, "My computer at home is not working."

"Please sit, sit down, Aparna," Anand said, pulling up a chair next to her and sitting down. "You don't have to justify what you're doing. Also, please don't call me sir. Everyone here calls me Anand."

"It's alright, Sir, err … Anand, Sir," Aparna stammered as she sat facing him, her mind still on her work.

"Aparna, it's been a few weeks now that you've been working with us, isn't it? So how do you find working here? In fact, I was intending to have a chat with you soon, to get your feedback. I do that with all staff a month or so after their joining. This newspaper can well do with fresh ideas and who better than someone who has newly viewed our practices."

"Sure, it will be a pleasure to chat with you at any time of your convenience," Aparna replied politely, then in an apologetic tone, added, "But now, I have to send out this questionnaire urgently, before the interviewee retires for the night. He's the chairman of the Royal Hotels chain."

"Yes, yes, please continue now," Anand replied, standing up, "Have you got a vehicle? Or I hope you have informed someone from the main paper to wait for you. Otherwise, the staff drop cars will all leave."

"Thank you. I've informed the security people, and they will inform me before the last car leaves," Aparna replied. With that, Anand walked briskly to the exit, carrying his laptop bag with him.

Aparna anxiously returned to finishing her work. She would have no way to go home, if the last car left, and she didn't want to take an auto. She avoided autos late at night in Chennai, though she had not hesitated to take one or even a taxi, however late, when working in Mumbai. Moreover, her parents would be awake worrying till she got home. At least, her mother would. She often sat up waiting in the balcony when Aparna came late, now that she had recently retired as a maths teacher from PSBB School where Kartik now studied. Feeling guilty, Aparna would insist that she not stay up and wait.

But her mother would reply, "You know, I cannot sleep when you are out at night. It makes me so anxious. Why can't you finish your work early?" Then bitingly, she would add "After living in Mumbai, you take coming and going late very lightly."

Aparna could not help thinking, on the drive back home, how

     Shuvashree Chowdhury

she would have managed bringing up Kartik as a single working parent. Without her parents, it would have been rather difficult and she might have had to send Kartik to boarding school. Aparna had put him to sleep on completion of his homework and dinner, and only then left home. Her father had insisted on driving Aparna to the office as it was late. Only after talking to the security staff and ensuring an office car would drop Aparna home, did he agree to leave. Aparna recalled fretfully that her mother would still be awake, waiting for her to return. Living with her parents came with its fair share of disadvantages too. Though she was a grown woman with a job, Aparna was answerable to them in every way and felt restricted. She had assumed, once she started working, they would ease out on her, but just the reverse happened. They were always worrying now, and tried to make her feel guilty for her absence.

Aparna rang the doorbell of their apartment with trepidation. Opening the door, her mother looked at her angrily.

"Your father and I are old now, Aparna, and all this stress is killing us," she said in a firm voice. Then as Aparna stepped inside, shutting the door noisily, she added, "You hardly spend time with Kartik. Poor boy! As it is, he is without his father, and then his mother too has no time for him."

"Amma, how can you say that?" Aparna replied sharply, dreadfully weary, "I was here till he finished his homework and dinner. Now that he is grown, he does not need to be put to sleep like a toddler." Then after a pause, as her mother looked at her exasperatedly, Aparna added, "But then you know, I wouldn't be out late unless it was necessary. I'm doing the best I can, and I must be serious at my job, to establish myself professionally to improve my pay. It's all for him, isn't it, that I'm working?"

Then dropping her hand bag on the sofa in the living room, Aparna washed her hand in the washbasin in the dining room. It irked her that most old houses in Chennai still did not have wash basins in the bathrooms, though there would invariably have to be one in or near the dining space. In the bathrooms, there always was a tap at a low level to wash the feet. After her Mumbai stint, Aparna found the way one felt compelled to hold on to age-old traditions in Chennai, however irrelevant they were to modern life, irritating. Aparna's father appeared. She was surprised to find him awake. He pulled out two chairs at the dining table and, after she was seated, sat down alongside her. Her mother presently joined them, as the food was already on the table in hot cases. It had been too early for Aparna to have dinner when she left at eight o'clock, but she had insisted her parents not wait for her.

"I had to complete and then email an urgent questionnaire to the chairman of Royal Hotels, for an interview tomorrow," Aparna said, chewing on *appam* dipped in vegetable stew—a Malayali dish.

Her mother made *appams* couple of times a month as it was Aparna's favourite dish. As she hungrily tore another large piece of *appam* and dipped it into the stew, Aparna could not help feeling emotional about her mother doing so even though she did not particularly care for it herself and neither did her father. She was touched by her parents' gesture in sitting up with her.

Looking at the clock on the mantelpiece, Aparna said passionately, "Oh my God, it's almost 2 a.m. and you both are still up. I'm so sorry. Now both of you, please go to sleep. I'll wake Kartik in time for school and get him ready, so you both sleep late."

But Aparna's parents rose only after she finished eating. She took her plate to the kitchen, while her mother carried the serving dishes. They scolded her often, no doubt, but Aparna knew it was from worry, and out of their love and concern for her. She appreciated all her parents did. But their jibes about neglecting Kartik stung her, as it added to her own guilt. She went to office only a couple of days a week, emailing stories from home, and yet they complained. Aparna had been lucky to get a job as a stringer with such a reputed newspaper. This job gave her flexibility and yet decent earnings to start with. She had got this job only through a friend's recommendation. The man knew of her flair for writing through her blogs when in college, and had introduced Aparna to Radhika Nair, the editor of the city supplement *Urban Plus*. Aparna's experience at Taj Hotels, her understanding of the hospitality industry and the lifestyles of the rich and celebrities, in addition to her writing skills along with her self-confidence and charm, had clinched the job as a features writer for the magazine.

After meeting Radhika Nair, an attractive, stylish, and articulate

 Shuvashree Chowdhury

lady, Aparna had been called into Anand's cabin for a final round of interview. As chief editor and managing director, Anand met all correspondents before their final recruitment, to ensure they would add value to the paper his grandfather had founded. It was a highly competitive market and the paper's survival depended on the quality of new recruits and the training given to experienced employees. Anand noticed Aparna's charming personality, awareness of the hotel industry, and knowledge of city celebrities. He agreed with Radhika and the HR manager that Aparna had the much-needed fresh perspective, even without journalistic experience. Radhika had asked Aparna to write five hundred words on the hotel industry in Chennai, as a test. Then she had shown Anand the write-up and he agreed that Radhika would develop Aparna's skills well over time.

In spite of only a couple of hours of sleep, Aparna sprung up to the alarm at 6 a.m. She woke up Kartik and ensured he was wide awake and brushing his teeth. Sometimes, he would climb back into bed. He had to be ready for his school bus at 7.30 a.m. Aparna took out the *idli* batter along with the *chutneys* from the refrigerator, which she knew would be there as usual. Her mother ensured that two *chutneys*—an onion and a coconut— and *idli* batter was prepared and stored for the next day before she went to bed every night. After that, Aparna collected the three milk packets left by the milkman in the plastic basket outside their main door. After emptying the milk packets into a large, stainless steel vessel with a brass-coated bottom, she put the vessel to boil on low heat so it would not spill over, as she went about her other chores.

Quickly, Aparna washed and placed a cup of *toor dal* along with water, salt, and turmeric in a pressure cooker on the stove, beside the boiling milk. After this, she poured the *idli* batter into the moulds and left them to cook in the *idli* maker. By the time the milk boiled and the *dal* cooked, Aparna chopped carrots, onions and drumsticks, extracting the tamarind paste, and got together all other ingredients along with curry leaves, for the seasoning of the *sambar*. Then she briskly stirred in two tablespoons of Bournvita into a glass of milk for Kartik and placed it on the dining table to cool. After the *sambar* and *idlis* were ready, she quickly bathed and dressed Kartik. She got him to drink the milk first, to ensure he finished it without the excuse of being too full from the food. She then made two *dosas* and fed him, dipping it alternately into *sambar* and the *chutneys*.

Then four *idlis* wrapped in silver foil and the *chutneys* in two small plastic containers went into Kartik's tiffin box, placed in a side pocket of his school bag. She also packed some buttermilk, which she had taken the time to make, in a glass-shaped Tupperware container. Satisfied that her son was in no way neglected in comparison to children living with both parents, Aparna and Kartik went down to wait for his school bus. After handing Kartik's school bag to the bus helper, Aparna watched him settle into a vacant window seat. She waved to him, as the bus rolled out, struck by his increasing resemblance to Nikhil. She could not help making a quick, desperate plea to God that the similarity between father and son remained limited to Nikhil's good looks and intelligence, and not his inherent weaknesses and bad habits.

As she walked away from the bus stop, suddenly depressed, and took the lift up to their apartment, Aparna could not help but feel the nagging fear creep up her spine again. The thought that she could lose Kartik to alcohol one day was more than she could bear. He was only five years old now and it would be a while before any tendencies in that direction would make themselves known. If Kartik grew up and wanted to drink, there was little she could do to stop him. She could only hope that it wouldn't affect him the same way as his father. In Chennai, most men Aparna knew drank liberally, however inhibited they might seem outside their home. It was an accepted thing. Her father did not drink now, but he had had his fair share when he was young.

By the time Aparna returned home, her parents were up and her mother served them all a cup of filter coffee. Aparna was more grateful for its strong aroma this morning, to chase away the old clouds of worry. It was probably the lack of sleep and the thought of a challenging day ahead that had caused them to rear their head again. With the last sip of her coffee, Aparna vowed to coach her son to be strong-willed and build up high self-esteem, so no temptation of vice or addiction would ever crush him. After their coffee cups—the small steel tumblers traditionally placed

        Shuvashree Chowdhury

over steel bowls that her mother still preferred to use—were put away into the kitchen sink, her parents left for their usual morning walk.

Aparna pulled on her stretch pants and rolled out a yoga mat in the privacy of her bedroom. The next half hour was her mental haven. It was a respite from all the trying roles she had to play as a woman—as mother, daughter, and journalist. This was above and beyond the benefits of yoga to body and mind that Aparna now relied upon, to keep her sane and equipped her to meet the world head on. By the time her parents returned from their morning walk, Aparna was bathed, dressed, and ready. She was draped in a rose-pink georgette *sari*, with a string of matching pearls around her neck and pearl drop earrings. Aparna preferred to dress up Mumbai-style, rather than follow the conventions in Chennai. The *sari* was her usual choice of attire when she went to interview or to meet someone for the first time. On the second meeting, she might wear a *salwar kameez* or even a pantsuit, whichever she deemed suitable.

That morning, Aparna was meeting a very senior luxury hotel chain owner and wanted to appear mature and professional. A *sari* had that effect. It lent an air of composure, confidence, and elegance. A western pantsuit, while making her look professional and dynamic, also made her look much younger and inexperienced. Aparna's meeting with the elderly hotel owner at his flagship property in MRC Nagar went off rather well. It took place in his luxurious office cum residential suite, on the top floor of the hotel. Aparna was able to draw her interviewee out with her gregarious, witty charm and her knowledge of the hotel business. She was surprised at how well-prepared he was, based on her questionnaire. His secretary had received the email with the questions attached this morning and had had a printed copy sent up early to his room along with coffee.

Aparna's insightful questions, tempered with curiosity and a passion for the industry, pleased him. It was not just an interest in his personal matters. He wondered why more journalists couldn't be like her. The silly, often irrelevant questions many of them asked demonstrated that they did not even have the respect to do their homework before a meeting and that tended to annoy him. He mentally made a note to call her employer Anand, who incidentally was a family friend, to commend him on his employee's approach and affability.

After her meeting, Aparna took an auto and went straight to the office. It was her first major story and she felt she had better discuss it with Radhika. Also, Aparna preferred to write her story immediately, so she could reproduce the discussion with all its subtleties. She made minimum notes and didn't use a Dictaphone either. She preferred not to distract the interviewee, so as to allow it to be a congenial chat, but more so as not to miss subtle cues herself. By the time she walked into her office building and went to her workstation, most people had gone to the canteen for lunch. Aparna was not hungry after her heavy breakfast. Also, at the hotel, she had been offered an assortment of delectable pastries from their patisserie, two of which she had enjoyed along with coffee. But she still went to the canteen as it was there that she could bond with her boss and the rest of the department. Over a glass of buttermilk and a banana, two of the staples on the lunch menu at the canteen, Aparna told her team about her meeting with Mr. Thyagarajan, the hotel's chairman.

"You know what, his elder son has gotten a divorce, and the younger son's wife just returned from the US after a nose job," she told the group seated at their usual table.

Aparna had learned that such gossip was enjoyed here and helped team members bond.

"The old man told you all this himself?" Sunil, Aparna's friend from college who had initially introduced her to Radhika, quipped. "He must have really warmed up to you, to give you this kind of information. He's usually reticent about his personal life, especially after his wife passed away. She was an active partner in his businesses as much as in his life. She practically ran everything. In fact, the hotel business was her pet project. The couple had met when his first hotel was being built and he had interviewed her for the position of front office manager."

Aparna was glad she had opened the discussion with her team. It helped her gather more information from journalists who had been around much before her. They would already have a repertoire of stories for her to use as a framework for her work.

    Shuvashree Chowdhury

She had researched Royal Hotels and its owner Mr. Thyagarajan in detail, by way of the Internet. But this kind of personal information would hardly be available on the net.

Aparna went back to her workstation and retrieved the questionnaire she had prepared the previous night, and which was pasted on her desktop now. She added the answers from the notes she had taken this morning. This was over the café latte with Mr. Thyagarajan, in his luxurious office-cum-residential-suite on the tenth floor of the hotel. To this, she would add flourishes, by way of her observations, then weave the personal conversation with Mr. Thyagarajan subtly into her story, leaving out the private specifics. She was not going to break the man's trust in her.

After Aparna had left Mr. Thyagarajan's office, he had asked his secretary to get Anand on the line for him.

"I liked this girl Aparna from your paper, whom I met this morning," he said, after the two had exchanged pleasantries. "She's intelligent and affable. What I particularly liked is her earnestness. It's great that you're taking some fresh talent from the service industry, with customer-handling experience, in addition to the journalism graduates I meet everywhere."

"Thank you, Sir. I'm glad you liked Aparna," Anand replied, pleased with Radhika for her choice and his own judgement, "She just joined us a couple of weeks back and I'm happy she is living up to the promise we saw in her."

When Aparna walked into the office building that afternoon, before she headed to the canteen, Anand was stepping outside for a lunch appointment. They had crossed each other in the lobby and she had politely nodded at him. He was tempted to ask her to meet him in his cabin later in the day for a discussion but caught himself, just nodding back at her instead. Anand decided to wait to see Aparna's story in print on Sunday, before talking to her, so he could gauge for himself if Mr. Thyagarajan's appreciation was justified. He firmly believed that a person's intellect could be evaluated in their ability to convert thoughts and observations appropriately into the written word. What use would Aparna's exuberant nature and affable manner be, if she could not convert her interactions and sensitive observations into logical, stylish sentences for enthusiastic readers?

After his return from lunch, Anand first called Radhika into his cabin, to get her feedback on Aparna. He did not mention Mr. Thyagarajan's call or his own views of her. He did not want to set any rivalries in motion or make it look like he favoured the much younger woman who had recently joined. Radhika, having personally referred Aparna to him after her own evaluation, now justified her decision to him. She praised Aparna and narrated her interactions with Mr. Thyagarajan which she had heard over lunch at the canteen.

"Since her arrival, I have asked Aparna to read international magazine articles and interviews, recommending them to her personally, to get her to learn the nuances of writing such articles." Radhika said, and then added passionately, "Luckily, the girl already has a flair for writing, which just needs to be polished."

Anand was pleased with Radhika's report and her obvious protective streak towards her subordinate—but then he knew how she cared about the development of her team. He was concerned about Aparna in particular, as she seemed promising, with the potential to take on larger responsibilities soon. Yet Anand was sure that there had been some tragedy in her life. He could see the sadness lurking behind the careful façade and forced cheerfulness. Anand was intrigued by her overtly expressive face, the large eyes that failed to hide the emotions that flitted through them as she spoke.

* * *

Anand's thoughts were interrupted by the ringing of his direct phone line. He glanced at the caller ID and, recognising the number as being his wife's, promptly picked up the receiver. She preferred to call the office number lately and Anand could not help wondering if she did so to check on his whereabouts. It was her usual post-lunch call enquiring if he had eaten. She quizzed him on what he had for lunch, to ascertain if he ate the home-packed lunch she insisted on his taking along, knowing his preference for fast food. In spite of his high blood pressure and blood sugar levels now that he was just over forty years old, Anand abhorred restricting his diet and his lifestyle.

 Shuvashree Chowdhury

Sujata was now seven months pregnant with their second child. She had quit her job as executive search consultant, as she had been advised strict rest by their doctor. A combination of pregnancy hormones, a lot of time at her disposal, and distress over quitting the job had made her very sensitive.

"Have you had lunch?" She said, on hearing Anand say "Hello". Had she imagined the amused tone? She added, "What did you eat?"

"You know, as usual, I had the lunch you packed for me," Anand laughed now, adding deliberately, "It was the sautéed carrot and beans with *sambar* and rice, along with the buttermilk and the banana you never forget."

He had taken a look into his box before asking his secretary to share it or give it away to the peons, before he left for the lunch meeting. Anand thought it wiser to lie about eating the packed lunch, rather than risk her anger on learning he had eaten mutton *biryani* and fried chicken, followed by *firni*.

That night, on reaching home, late as usual, Anand found Sujata sleeping with their son Varun on his single bed. She slept curled up, like a child herself, her face radiant in the blue night light. He had the dinner the maid laid out for him on the dining table. Its preparation, he knew, had been personally supervised by Sujata. By now, living on a separate floor of his parent's house after Anand's severe altercations with his mother, Sujata supervised everything herself. When Anand was ready to go to bed, he woke Sujata up to take her along to their bedroom. It always took consistent nudging to wake her up late at night. But Anand never relented to the resistance she put up reflexively, being pulled out of deep sleep. Whenever at home, Anand made it a point to sleep on the same bed with his wife. Often, he had to literally drag Sujata to their bed, after the bad fights and her silences wherein she would consciously refuse to go with him.

It was not that Anand was looking to make love to Sujata tonight in her late pregnancy. It's that he believed the marital bed is the rope binding a couple. Whatever the issues threatening to snap it, they can be kept at bay if they hung on to that rope together. Over the years, there had been a number of instances when the strain on their marriage had been considerable, but it had somehow survived complete breakdown. A couple of years after their marriage, after the birth of their first child, Sujata had been shocked and deeply hurt to find that her husband's interest in her sexually had waned. But even then, Anand had insisted on sleeping on the same bed as her, though he snubbed her shy sexual advances with vague excuses of tiredness and work stress. At first, Sujata had believed his pretexts, but soon the continuous disinterest and rejections had hurt her pride and left her frustrated.

To Sujata's deep dismay then, she was to learn that it was really her that Anand had lost interest in, not that he had developed a general disinterest and apathy to sex. She had at times woken up late at night to what she initially thought was him working on his laptop. But her curiosity had got the better of her and she had found a way to peer into his laptop without his noticing her. He was watching pornographic movies, she learned. Then, a few times, she found him chatting—there were a couple of chat windows open. It did not take Sujata long to deduce he was carrying on one or more Internet affairs and thereby attributed this to his romantic disinterest in her. Sujata concluded that Anand now preferred visual titillation to real sex. He was perhaps too lazy or selfish to satisfy his partner in bed, and thus found greater satisfaction in self-indulgence wherein one's own pleasure is paramount. Sujata concocted varied theories to mentally justify Anand's behaviour, but none helped allay her immense hurt, the bruising of her pride and ego.

Sujata began to avoid Anand completely, in bed and out of it. She would not allow him to even touch her, not even hold her hand, or embrace her in sleep. He would attribute this to the fights or disagreements they were simultaneously having, insensitive to her anguish from his physical rejections. This was also the time when Sujata was deeply hurt by Anand's negligent attitude towards their growing son Varun. Anand's not showing overt love or concern for their child, insistence on leaving him out of their holidays and outings, never bringing him chocolates or gifts from trips as fathers do, all of this enraged her. Varun craved the tenderness, the demonstrations of love that he saw bestowed upon his two cousins, Ramya's children, by their father Prashant. Sujata found the stark difference between her husband and her sister's

          Shuvashree Chowdhury

husband galling. As it is, since meeting Anand, she had found him not conforming to the standards of an eligible husband set by Prashant.

Now to her horror, Anand did not also conform to her views of a decent, let alone good, father. Sujata had never complained of Anand's neglect of her, out of sheer pride. But that did not stop her from throwing her views on his neglect of their son on his face. Anand's attitude towards their son sharpened the dagger of her feeling of being conned into marriage by his poetic declarations of false love. The rope Anand thought he bound her in by merely sleeping on the same bed thus enraged Sujata by the hypocrisy it projected. But Anand always defended his stance, though futilely to Sujata, that he did not have time to devote to her and their son because he was too busy building an empire to leave Varun someday.

It was after Sujata had started working that she had gradually found her self-worth returning. Then she was able to forgive Anand, to allow her anger at him to dissipate somewhat. It caused her volcanic personality to become dormant, with only cursory eruptions on and off, as if from the fissures of her mind. Anand, however, attributed Sujata's erratic behaviour, not to his own lapses, but to a personality disorder. Then with time, Anand and Sujata had reached a stage of harmonic coexistence, as housemates, their association now friendship of a kind. Their sexual relationship that had come to a complete halt resumed sporadically. Sujata no longer found his lovemaking to her taste, though she relented sometimes as she felt she owed it to their newfound amity.

It was during this new friendship phase that Sujata and Anand, after the initial years, once again took a few international vacations together. They visited Europe, Australia, the US, and Middle Eastern countries. Sujata insisted on taking their son Varun along. He was a shy, disciplined child—absolutely docile, perhaps more out of fear of his father. By now, Anand was reconciled to being pleasant to Varun, to include him in their outings, as that was the only way Sujata would be pacified and even agree to go out with him. Luckily for him, Varun was, in his father's presence, unusually quiet, more often whispering into his mother's ears if he wanted anything. Early in life, Varun had learned to act like a grown-up or he knew his father would be displeased. Sujata, even though she tried to get used to Anand's cold behaviour towards their son, could not understand it even remotely. She definitely could not absolve the hurt it caused her, from her heart, but decided to tolerate it.

Sujata conceived their second child on Anand's return from one of his official trips. It was one of their sporadic nights as real man and wife, now that they had a bond of amicable friendship between them.

"It was by accident," she liked to say, laughing, to her family and friends. "We didn't plan for a second child and least of all expected it."

Both Sujata and Anand had, in fact, been quite opposed to the idea of a second child, for very different reasons. Anand was having trouble adjusting to the immense changes to his lifestyle, just due to the presence of one child. A second baby, he knew, would further take away his freedom. Sujata was emotionally and physically tired of being a single parent. And with another child on the way and the job she desperately wanted to return to, she felt she might lose her sanity. With Anand's lack of involvement in Varun's life, Sujata had given her life to teaching Varun, coordinating extracurricular activities, attending her son's school functions and parent-teacher meetings, all this alone as a single parent.

Sujata had proceeded with the second pregnancy only after her parents convinced her that Varun needed a companion, a sibling, as he was a rather lonely child. Anand was also induced by his parents that a second child would give their business another heir. So even though seriously contemplating an abortion, Sujata agreed for her son's sake. Anand also eased his opposition. It felt to Sujata, when she was compelled to give up her job, like she would have to find fulfilment in her life as a woman only as a mother.

		Shuvashree Chowdhury

Chapter 4

Her New Life

Aparna had made a few friends at work, especially two girls in her department. Now that she felt more secure about her work and life, she found it worthwhile to get to know Chennai a little better, the city she was born and grew up in. Before moving to Mumbai, like other women from conservative Tamilian families, she had led a restricted life, unexposed to the city's vagaries. And her early marriage and move had prevented her from ever exploring the place. But since she had started work, no longer a prospective bride now, she was free to go out a lot. Also, she was now able to justify it to her parents that it was in order to become a good features journalist. It was late on a Sunday that Aparna along with her two new friends—Priya and Meera—decided to go to 10 Downing Street, the pub chain that had just opened in the ground floor of a small hotel. She had heard much about it from her colleagues who visited often, and it was only recently that she learned much to her surprise, that for any place in Chennai to get a commercial bar license it must be part of a hotel or guest house with a minimum of twenty rooms.

This sudden idea to go to the pub was after a day spent relaxing at home, listening to her son Kartik's chatter in between being taken for his tuitions and painting classes by her father. Her mother had taken care of the cooking that day, giving Aparna a much-needed, rare break. But the realisation that the weekend would be over in just another few hours made her morose. Aparna felt she could well do with an outing with her friends before the grind of an entire week set in. Even though going to a pub was not exactly her cup of tea, alcohol being at the root of all the ordeals she had gone through, her friends insisted. The previous evening, she had taken her parents and Kartik for a movie and then to dinner at the City

Centre mall. Aparna had lately noticed that if she spent a weekend entirely at home relaxing, though feeling rested on Monday, she did not feel mentally recharged.

Aparna decided to go along with the suggestion of her friends to go to the pub, as she could not offer any better alternative herself. Moreover, she had better go along to the latest hotspots to keep abreast of the city's night life, she decided. It was better to go as a regular partygoer to get the real essence of a place, than scrutinise such places as a journalist on a story. Aparna was ready, enthusiastically so, by the time her two friends picked her up from home. Though she could have taken the family's car, her parents felt a lot better about her being out late only if convinced she was to be safely dropped back home. They worried a lot when she drove herself. The fact that she was being picked up by two women would also put to rest any speculation by the neighbours, now that it was common knowledge that she was separated from her husband.

At the portico entrance to the pub 10 Downing Street, when they were waiting for valet parking, Aparna took in the crowd with surprise. She might as well have been transplanted to a city in any western country, with people dressed trendily in chic, contemporary attire. She was used to this modernity in Mumbai and in Goa where she had gone with Nikhil for their honeymoon, but not in Chennai, not even in her time working at the Taj. Aparna had long concluded women here only wore the *sari*, or at most a *salwar-kameez*, with strings of jasmine flowers wrapped around their hair. Even her own relatives, friends too, were conservative dressers, and until she had moved to Mumbai, she had never waxed, worn makeup or western outfits outside of work.

People were trooping in and out of 10 Downing Street, even as Aparna looked around, now eager to go inside. The air was electric with so many young people and music, drinks, and food. The crowd was dressed in the latest fashion, many sporting expensive brands of clothes, shoes, and bags. The latest hair styles and colours were on display. Aparna recognised her own hairstyle in a number of women in the crowd, one that she had recently acquired at Bounce, an upscale stylist's salon in Nungambakkam. The only other popular stylist in the city she had been referred to by her

		Shuvashree Chowdhury

friends was Habib's. The Tony and Guy, Studio Profile, and such other beauty salon chains were to set up shop in Chennai a few years later and Aparna, as a lifestyle correspondent, would then find herself writing about them.

Aparna walked in with her friends through the dimly lit foyer, getting their hands stamped, but without paying an entry fee, as it was barely an hour to closing time at 11 o'clock. They were surprised by the crowded place and the packed dance floor. It took Aparna a while to distractedly identify the Hindi film songs, mixed by the DJ with as much gusto as those dancing to it. This being the biggest surprise since their car pulled up at the entrance, Aparna realised she had been rather judgemental from her lack of exposure, to assume Chennai only clung to its traditional and ethnic spirit, and abhorred modernity. It was liberating to note that the city of temples, classical music, and dance could also party hard to Bollywood music. What Aparna loved about the Chennai she was getting to know now as a journalist was that it allowed you to be the way you wished to be, to live and to let live. It opposed drastic change for itself, but the city did not restrict modernity and change for those who preferred it. In Mumbai, for example, you were conspicuous if you were not dressed trendily, but in Chennai, if you were fashionable, you might stand out on the streets and most public places. A majority of women still preferred their hair oiled and adorned with fresh flowers that their men loved. It is only in Chennai that you might spot women in trousers and western tops, often sporting a *bindi* on the forehead and flowers in their hair, retaining the essence of tradition in modernity. Here, tradition and modernity co-exist as nowhere else. A woman could be impeccably dressed with well-coordinated accessories and such women, or even men for that matter, are usually very brand conscious or she could just be casual, even at a formal function attended by glitterati, without raising an eyebrow. She might wear bright silks, heavy gold and diamond jewellery, even her wedding attire if she pleased, to a cocktail party, and yet not come across as loud and ostentatious. Now a woman is entitled to all her varied moods, isn't she?

Aparna's favourite haunt in Chennai lately till she visited the 10 Downing Street had been Zara on Cathedral Road. It was a speciality Spanish resto-bar. She loved the lively set-up, not to mention the pitchers of Sangria her friends ordered, that she merely tasted, along with their Tapas. This is a place you were better off going to in a large group. They had few two-seater tables and it might be ages before you found yourself a seat at a larger one. The Leather Bar at the Park Hotel, a lounge bar, also was a place she had grown to love, for the kind of music they played, especially the fusion variety, of which Prem Joshua was her favourite artist. Then the Pasha at the Park Hotel, Havana at the Raintree Hotel, and Dublin at the Park Sheraton, she had been to a few times, and it's where upper middle-class Chennai partied, if not at house parties. Distil was another pub at the Taj Connemara that Aparna liked to visit, and had been to on a few Fridays—it was the Ladies Night. They served two cocktails on the house for ladies to get you started for the evening or to have your fill of—for the night.

Among the restaurants Aparna liked, there was Tangerine in Alwarpet, Little Italy in Nungambakkam, and Casa Picola on Kader Nawaz Khan Road, for their continental food. Other than at luxury hotels, these restaurants served the best continental food. However, a list of her favourite haunts in Chennai would be incomplete without the mention of the Woodlands drive-in restaurant where sitting in her friend's cars, they were served excellent *chole bhature* and a host of North and South Indian savouries along with filter coffee. Aparna liked the Woodlands restaurant in T-Nagar beside Nalli, the reputed *sari* shop, too. In spite of her mother being an excellent cook, Aparna loved their *idli-sambar, dosas,* and the *sapar* (traditional full meals) they served. She preferred it and the one on Cathedral Road to the renowned chain of Murugan Idli, Sangeetha Veg Restaurant and Saravana Bhavan eateries that seemed forever crowded, with the weekend queues outside the outlets of Murugan Idli spiralling long on to the road in front.

Chennai's craving for Murugan's fare was in spite of its residents having their fair share of the similar *idli-dosa* and *sapar* at home. Aparna knew her own people well and they were in general not an experimental lot, but especially when it came to food. They were reserved and resistant to new tastes, preferring to hold on to traditions and customs. To what else could you attribute the need for curd-rice after every meal—be it continental or pan-Asian?

     Shuvashree Chowdhury

Aparna's entrepreneur cousin had told her in amusement of how, when she had taken her colleagues out to lunch at Little Italy, they requested for curd-rice after a pasta meal. Thus, the variety in taste the common man in Chennai might care to opt for in their lives was just variations of what they usually consumed at home. One would not see so many eateries serving Marathi food in Mumbai or Bengali food in Kolkata for that matter, she rued, as there is of local cuisines in Chennai. But with the increase in industry and inflow of expatriates, along with the inclination of people from the north and east of India to move to Chennai, it was fast becoming multicultural. There was a time when a North Indian or one from the west or east when transferred to Chennai, tended to perceive it as a punishment posting, feeling culturally alienated, but not so much now.

The changes that the city was undergoing at breakneck speed meant that this was the perfect time for Aparna's entry into the world of journalism. Already, there were plans on for a number of luxury hotel chains to open up their Chennai gates. A host of international retailers were setting up shop, adding to the multitude of traditional *sari* and jewellery stores abundant in Alwarpet and T Nagar—the retail hub of the city. The city was conducive to industry and trade and the authorities proactive to easing bottlenecks in the set-up process. In time, there would be a variety of international cuisine restaurants like Japanese, Korean, Russian, amongst a number of pan-Indian. Chennai was thus truly a city of intriguing contrasts. Aparna, by now enjoying herself at her new job, considered she was lucky to be hired even at an entry-level writer's position, able to record this change through her writing. As a features writer, she would never be short of stories to tell, she was sure.

What Aparna had missed most when away in Mumbai was the temples of Chennai. They are an embodiment of the culture, customs, and spirituality of the Hindu faith and are known for their rich mythology and traditions. Thousands of devotees come here to catch a glimpse of these deities. While the temple architecture and overall upkeep is awe-inspiring. Aparna was always infused with immense mental strength from visiting the Kapaleeshwar temple at Mylapore and the Balaji temple on Venkatnarayana

Road, T-Nagar, more than from visiting any temple elsewhere in the country. It was her visits to these two temples that saw her through her worst times since her return to Chennai and inspired so much devotion and faith. She had visited both these temples consecutively on the eve of her final interview at the newspaper. The confidence she imbibed sitting meditatively in front of the deities got her the job, she believed.

"To be a writer, you have to love to write—it's that simple" Anand, managing director and chief editor of the *National Daily*, had said to her at the interview, "You can take all of the journalism classes you want, but if it's not in your soul, you won't love what you do or even tolerate it."

"Working at a newspaper can be stressful, you know, Aparna, depending on the day." Radhika, editor of the *Urban Plus* magazine, had said, "It's not all glamour to be a features writer, as you might assume. Since we work on deadlines, everything comes down to the last minute, whether it's editing a story to make it fit in the little space we've been allotted or finding filler wire stories for the extra space we've suddenly acquired due to a last-minute cancelled advertisement."

"I am serious about wanting to be a writer," Aparna had replied self-assuredly, realising she was being told all this for the interviewers to gauge the seriousness of her intent to take on this job.

"I'm sure you are serious," Anand had smiled, noting the positivity in her voice, "But you're not aware of what you're getting into, so it all seems easy."

"You see, Aparna, I'm still a writer first," Radhika had said on cue, looking at Aparna earnestly, "As that's my passion, I'm not just an editor. In addition to overseeing the features department, I write human interest stories and write one to two columns per week on topics of my choice. I generate research and write feature stories, edit the work of other writers, and also lay out the section for production. You must be mentally prepared for all of it, if not in the months, then in the years ahead. Since this is a new career path for you, please think judiciously before you consider joining. We would not like you to look upon this as a mere job. That would waste our time and yours and you won't learn anything. You must

     Shuvashree Chowdhury

be prepared to grow along with the paper and make this a long-term career path."

It was at this stage that Aparna, in spite of her confusion, decided to make journalism her vocation, and replied "I'm going to do all it takes to excel at my work."

Anand was impressed with her attitude and he smiled warmly, looking from Radhika to Aparna. Radhika nodded at Aparna, but continued.

"Speaking for myself personally, I don't feel I maintain a healthy work-life balance, because I can never go home and not think about work." Radhika said passionately, "Whether it's someone calling me about a rewrite or worrying about a story I can't quite capture, I take my work home all the time. But I truly love what I do. I've fallen in love with several of the subjects I've interviewed for feature stories over the years. I feel like I've found my stride telling someone else's story that may not have been heard otherwise. The people I meet and interact with make my job seem like a bonus. The newspaper business is a very stressful job, as it is extremely deadline-oriented. But I get out of bed every morning and come to work because I really am excited by what I do. I get to meet a whole lot of interesting people, listen to their stories, and then translate them for others—it's a wonderful thrill. I feel really warm when I get a call or a thank you note from someone saying they liked what I wrote about them. It's not life-changing, what I do, but it changes me a little every day."

Aparna had listened intently, and then nodded firmly. The HR manager, dressed in white shirt and trousers, with wavy oiled hair, and thick black framed glasses that he kept pushing up the bridge of his nose with one finger, asked her, "I hope you are getting the drift of what you're walking into, Aparna?"

"The challenges I face at work are usually pretty manageable when you look at the big picture," Radhika had promptly adjoined, then looking earnestly into Aparna's eyes, she continued, "Although, when they're happening, it doesn't seem that way. An example of my daily challenge is when the advertising department at the newspaper gets to hold the paper layout so they can sell more advertising space for the next day. What this means is that, we at the editorial departments can't lay out the paper for the next day. So even if it's midnight and we've been here since noon, I sometimes wait. Then it's very hard for me to secure any vacation time, and when I do, I usually get phone calls demanding that I take my substitute through one process or another. So, no, I'm never able to fully relax or be at ease during the little vacation time I manage to take. What I'm trying to tell you is that in considering working at a newspaper, you have to have a lot of resilience, but firstly and above all else, love what you do."

"I am prepared to do the same, all of it," Aparna had replied passionately, convincingly, deeply inspired by Radhika's speech, also in awe of Anand, thus clinching this job that she now knew would become her life.

* * *

It was the Monday after Aparna's article on the Royal Hotel chairman had appeared in *Urban Plus's* Sunday issue. After evening tea, Anand asked his secretary Rose, a short girl with sharp, beady eyes, shoulder-length hair, and a warm smile, to call Aparna into his cabin. He would get her feedback now, as he had suggested to her that evening on his way home. Anand had just read her article and recalled the Royal Hotel owner's praise of her.

"May I come in, Sir?" Aparna said softly, standing at the door, her eyes unobtrusively taking in Anand's plush cabin.

There was his large, oval teakwood desk, with the high-back leather chair. The paintings on the beige walls were softly lit by the beams from the brass holders above them. And there was a white sofa along with a coffee table at the far end away from his desk, with a white bone-china tea set on it.

"Yes, please come in" Anand replied, looking up from typing on the keypad of his computer. Signalling to the chair across his desk, he said, "Please be seated, Aparna, and don't call me sir, will you?"

Aparna looked him at him shyly and then nodded, as she settled down on the chair, her hands clasped in front of her on the desk.

"Please, just give me a minute to wrap this up," Anand said, indicating what he was typing and then, in a casual tone, added

"So how did your meeting with the owner of Royal Hotels go? I read your piece, but I'd like to know your personal views on the hotel chain, of the man himself."

"It went very well, I should think," Aparna replied enthusiastically, with a broad smile, "He was a rather warm and affable person, compared to what I had expected of a business tycoon like him. I had heard a lot about his volatile temperament, but didn't see it in all the time that I spent with him."

"Well, he seemed to have liked you too!" Anand smiled, having set aside the work at hand. He turned his attention squarely on Aparna, noticing her large eyes that twinkled in merriment like a child's and her face flushed with amusement, reflecting the bright pink of her cotton kurta. He added, "And I can see you're quite taken with him. Now tell me, how has it been working here since you joined. Does it meet your expectations?"

"I love it," Aparna said passionately. "Radhika has been very supportive and so have the others. They've been guiding me and referring me to a lot of good writing that I can learn from. This is in addition to taking me along for their assignments, in fact, all over town, to gain practical exposure on how to go to meetings, interviews, and press meets."

"How long has it been since you joined us? Should be over three to four months now, right? Now would you consider being a journalist permanently, of making this a career?"

"Yes, I would definitely think so," Aparna gushed excitedly, her eyes twinkling. "I am rather enjoying myself. But now what needs to be seen is how good I can become at my work, in order to grow here."

Her face, Anand deduced, was the most expressive he had ever seen and he was charmed by her inability to conceal what she was thinking, quite unlike the usually reserved demeanour of people in Chennai he was used to. "With this passion towards your work, I'm sure you will do well and grow with us," Anand said, and then absorbing her congeniality, letting his usual reserve drop, he grinned and added jovially, "That is, if you don't go overboard with excitement on assignments with people who prefer a sombre expression."

"Oh, I can pull off one of those expressions too," Aparna

laughed aloud, completely at ease now. She drew her breath in and pulled a mock serious face.

Anand laughed too, and then looking intently into her jet-black eyes, after he took in the wavy crop of dishevelled, shoulder-length, thick hair, he said, "You are quite a caricaturist, Aparna, aren't you … and I hope this congeniality helps you forge ahead, just as it did with the last interview wherein you charmed the usually grouchy old man of Royal Hotels."

"I'll ensure that I make people laugh out and perhaps cry even as they tell me their stories straight from the heart. Yet I'll do my best to protect their space and privacy."

"Now that sounds like a good beginner's resolution to me," Anand replied, even as he caught the flicker of sadness in her eyes. "If you genuinely respect people, build relationships, and yet ensure not to break their faith over cheap shots at personal fame, I am certain you will be a name to contend with in this industry very soon."

"I really hope so," Aparna replied softly, looking down, "I need to build myself a secure career, one I can grow old with respectfully and is financially sustainable."

"Aparna, by the way, what does your husband do?" Anand asked, seizing the opportunity now, to delve into what lay behind this mask of merriment she tried desperately to keep on, that both intrigued and drew Anand.

"We are separated," Aparna stated emphatically. She looked at Anand and caught the flicker of concern on his face at her pained expression. She blurted, "We've filed for divorce."

Anand was silent for a while, looking at the top of Aparna's bent head. He waited for her to regain her composure and look at him again. He gauged that there was a lot bottled up inside her and the façade, this show of elation, was a desperate bid to hide her pain from the world. But he was not about to probe, even though he was curious and instinctively wanted to reach out to her. His intent, he knew, should be to ensure she was settled in here and making herself useful, the paper providing the right circumstances for it and no more. When Aparna looked up, feeling composed, she found Anand looking at her with concern. The quiet steely strength of his persona, reflected in his piercing look, abruptly tore into the thin

 Shuvashree Chowdhury

veil of her control and her eyes abruptly welled up. Aparna became acutely embarrassed now. In silence, she tried to distract herself, as her facial muscles twitched from trying to will the welled-up tears away and prevent herself from cracking up completely. She was making a fool of herself, she thought desperately, when she had really intended to show him how strong and emotionally resilient she was.

"It's all right, Aparna," Anand said softly, smiling comfortingly, "Don't worry about the impression you're making on me. I'd rather you tell me your story, but only if you feel comfortable."

Aparna looked intently into Anand's eyes. The concern and compassion she saw, the self-assurance he exuded in the face of her ungainly behaviour, stirred the bottled-up emotions inside her, and like a dam breaking, the tears gushed from her eyes.

"I'm so sorry," Aparna muttered, almost in a whisper, choking on the few words. She grabbed a handful of tissues from the box Anand thrust in her direction. "It's been really stressful lately ... I'm really sorry, Sir ... er ... Anand Sir, no, Anand ... I didn't mean to create such a spectacle ... really."

"Now you don't worry about this at all, Aparna," Anand said. "We all, each of us, have our predicaments that we struggle to cope with. When it gets unbearable, it's bound to erupt at times when you least expect or wish it to."

"It's my son. I'm under tremendous stress over my son," Aparna blurted feebly, feeling compelled to confess, to let out her grief, if for nothing else but his advice perhaps.

"You have a son? How old is he?"

"He is just over four years old now," Aparna replied, then in a steadier voice continued, "Since we filed for divorce, my husband and his family are threatening to take him away from me. They are rich and powerful. I fear the court might grant them custodianship after he crosses five years of age. The family claim they can give him a much better life. But how do I give my son—my life—away and allow an alcoholic to ruin his life like he has his own?"

"Alcoholic ... who ... your husband?" Anand asked, looking quizzically at Aparna.

"Yes, that's why I left him in Mumbai and came here with our son, to live with my parents," Aparna replied, feeling calmer even as she did. "He was physically abusive and very violent when drunk, which actually was almost always. I tried to adjust, to help him out of his problem, but how could I allow our son to grow up in such an unhealthy environment, in trauma, watching his mother subjected to constant abuse?"

Anand looked at Aparna sympathetically. He read a lot more of her pain and anguish in her eyes and voice and on her face, than from the words itself.

"But how can he take your son away under the circumstance?" Anand said vehemently, angry now at the unfairness of Aparna's plight. "How would the court make him custodian, if you prove his drinking? They would never allow him to raise a child."

"Yes, if he was seeking custody by himself and not along with his parents." Aparna sighed, fidgeting with her hands on her lap. "You see, they are rich and well-connected. They will project that they are more capable of raising the child than I can ever hope, giving him a better education and lifestyle, that I cannot do myself. At best, as his mother, I may get to keep him till he is five years old."

"But now you're working and you also have the support of your parents."

"That is why my job is so crucial for me now. So that I might build a career for myself and my son's future," Aparna said emphatically, her inner strength taking over the helpless aggrieved soul of minutes ago, leaving her calmer and much composed. "I am indeed lucky that my parents have ultimately come around and accepted that my marriage is over for good. It took me a long time to get their support, worried as they were of what people might say."

Anand nodded slowly, then said, "You've taken the right decision so far. Now don't worry and concentrate on your work. Life has a way of sorting itself out."

"I try to do that, to forget about my past and look ahead, since I've decided what I must do going ahead. But the constant calls from my husband and his father or grandmother, their insistence on my return to Mumbai with the child, the threats, and emotional blackmail to take my son away really get to me."

"I can understand, but you have to learn to let it bounce off," Anand said forcefully, "with the awareness that your job and

     Shuvashree Chowdhury

ensuing financial stability is what you're building your life on now. If you exude confidence in yourself, in your decisions and purpose, your husband and his family will relent. Also, now on, if you are in any trouble or face any problem, or if you just need to talk, all you have to do is call me."

Aparna nodded, drawing strength from Anand's supportive words, his concern, and the thought that she now had a strong support system in him. Radhika walked in at this juncture and both Aparna and Anand looked up at her simultaneously. Aparna was relieved she was composed by now. She did not want Radhika to think she was trying to ingratiate herself with Anand. That would spoil her equation with Radhika who so far had been very protective and helpful. The three had a short discussion together and Aparna excused herself and went to her desk. Surprised to see that it was late and some work stations around hers were empty, some people having left after 6 p.m., Aparna realised that she had been with Anand for more than two hours. Sitting at her desk now, she took stock of her emotions that had let her down in this abject way in front of the person she had intended to create a positive impression on. But what was done was done. She felt free.

Opening up her heart to Anand, whatever be the circumstances, Aparna had to admit that she felt better. It was the first time she had ever talked openly about her circumstances to anyone, other than her parents. But talking to them stressed her out, as she sensed them absorbing her worries, then getting more aggrieved, which in turn only stressed her further. But talking to Anand, she realised, gave her a newfound strength and support. It had put certain things in perspective. She made up her mind to hold on to her son at all costs, believing in her ability to bring him up well on her own. She had been worrying about whether she was being selfish in wanting to keep her son with herself. After all, it was true that his father's family could give him a much better education and lifestyle, which she could never afford. But talking to Anand had made her realise that none of that would matter over the nurturing, attention, and sound upbringing that only she as a mother could provide.

It was on the auto ride home that Aparna conceded that if she took her work seriously, she could work her way up the career ladder and, in time, steadily enhance her income to give her son a balanced and meaningful life. That was more important than mere affluence in bringing up a child. It is by far better to bring up a child with good values than to just shower him with expensive things and experiences, to overcompensate for time spent on personal care. Aparna was glad she had been open with Anand and that he had been empathetic. It made her feel positive and in control. She still regretted breaking down in his presence as he was after all her employer. Over his discussion with Radhika on Aparna's progress at the job, Anand went over part of the conversation he had just concluded with Aparna in his head. Even so, he did not disclose Aparna's circumstances.

It was not relevant, he decided. Radhika did not need to know yet. All this information and the fact that Aparna had confided in Anand, not her, might prejudice Radhika. Also, any mistake in her work, any lapse even in punctuality and attendance, would be attributed to her personal circumstances. Aparna's revelations had obviously rattled Anand, but he was not going to do her the disservice of blurting it out to anyone. Her distraught face as she fought to control the tears was perhaps indelibly etched in Anand's mind.

This image of Aparna, along with their exchanges, kept lingering in Anand's thoughts. She was on his mind, as his driver deftly manoeuvred the car through the rush hour traffic to the Savoy Hotel on Cathedral road. He used their gym every other day, other than the one at the Park Hotel, and then returned to office for the evening. Anand could not forget Aparna even when he climbed the stairs to his second-floor home later that evening. He thought of her right through dinner and the attempt to concentrate on a book he habitually read till he fell asleep. He knew she had not intended to reveal so much, and must be pretty shaken and embarrassed at the turn of events, in spite of all his efforts to pacify her.

As for Aparna, she had sought to protect her private life even from friends. The burden she was carrying in her heart had snapped at the most inappropriate time, spilling its contents embarrassingly. But was it the weight of her problems that had made her talk to Anand, or was it his warmth and compassion, the understanding and emotional strength he exuded? Had she read his interest in her intuitively and that actually touched her heart, allowing her to

     Shuvashree Chowdhury

open its doors, with a ray of hope? Aparna was to ponder over this and her conversation with Anand, repeatedly, for days after. That Anand was now privy to Aparna's personal life connected them inexplicably, created a bond, even though they would perceive its impact only gradually.

The next day at work, after lunch, again Anand asked his secretary to call Aparna to his office. Shortly, she was at the door. Today, she was dressed in a green *kurta* and jeans, her wavy shoulder-length hair as usual in a state of disarray. Anand noticed her embarrassed look. With a warm smile, he gestured for her to sit. Aparna, averting her gaze, briskly walked in, and took a seat across him without looking directly at him.

"Aparna, hope you're feeling alright, perhaps better now that you've let out some of the weight you've been carrying around?" Anand said, trying to meet her gaze that steadily avoided his.

"I'm so ashamed about yesterday," Aparna blurted out, looking downward, "I really am. I don't know how I could be so unprofessional, the way I behaved."

"Please don't worry about that. I'm not judging you for it, nor will I discuss it with anyone, not even Radhika," Anand said reassuringly. "When the heart is heavy for long, it tends to expunge that weight in the most unlikely circumstances. I'm glad you've blurted out some of what's troubling you, even if you didn't intend to confide in me, and hope it's made you feel better."

"Yes. Though I'm embarrassed, I must admit I feel much better than I have in a long time. Also, I am relieved that there is no need to hide my circumstances any longer." Then after a pause, waiting for Anand to say something, Aparna added, "In any case, there was the possibility of you learning of this from other sources, perhaps with a lot of distortion. That's why I'm glad I told you myself. But I would not like you to think I'm expecting sympathy and leniency at work in any way due to my circumstances."

"Of course not." Anand smiled. "Don't worry. I called you in now so you don't worry yourself over yesterday's meeting and my opinion of it. Concentrate on your work now, as that's going to stand you in good stead in the long run. And remain positive about the custody of your son. You should also get out a bit and explore the city. That will help your work too."

"Thank you so much!" Aparna replied, "Yes, I have been going out a lot with friends, to reacquaint myself with the city I was born and grew up in, and also to get story ideas. They've taken me to quite a few places already. I'm really lucky to have bosses like Radhika and you. I don't know what to say … You're both so kind."

"Please call me anytime you need help, personal or otherwise. Don't hesitate at all. Now I'm not going to keep you any longer. You can carry on."

Aparna nodded silently, looked straight into Anand's eyes with all the gratitude she could summon from the bottom of her heart, then got up and walked out.

Anand looked at Aparna's retreating form thoughtfully, though it was her beguiling large eyes that he was thinking about. He could not help go over all she had told him yesterday, word for word. Perhaps this would help him get her out from under his skin.

"You see, sir, I was madly in love with my husband by the time we got married, even though ours was technically an arranged marriage." Aparna had said through a flood of tears, in a barrage of breathless words. "Nikhil wanted me to marry him so much, and I was flattered by his interest. He had plenty of money then, or so my family had found out, but I'd have married him even if he had none. I was so taken by him. He was so charming in those days, so handsome, so gay and light-hearted. What fun we used to have together in the initial months! He had immense vitality then. He was so kind and gentle and sweet—when he was sober. Then when he was drunk, he was noisy and boastful and vulgar and quarrelsome. It was terribly upsetting when he was like that and I used to feel so humiliated. But I couldn't be angry with him for long though, as he was so repentant afterwards, and he'd promise he wouldn't drink. All this was in the first year.

When he was alone with me, he was as sober as anyone. It was only when there were other people that he got excited. Then, after two or three drinks, there was no holding him. I would wait till he would be so drunk as to allow me to lead him away, drive him home, and put him to bed. I did everything I knew to make him stop drinking, to cure him. I read everything I could find on

    Shuvashree Chowdhury

alcoholism on the Internet, but it was useless. I don't believe any longer that a drunk can ever be cured. But I was so optimistic then and didn't believe my marriage and life could be going so horribly wrong. I kept hoping this was just God's way of testing me."

Aparna drew a long breath and continued, "It angered Nikhil when I tried to restrain him, but I had to try. I could not give up on him as his family had. Then when he stopped working and forced me to give up my job, we had no money, none at all. His family cut him off from the family business in an attempt to control his drinking, but luckily, they later gave me a job. All my jewellery was with his family, so we could not sell them, as his parents knew their son well. Often in frustration, I would lose my patience and fly into a rage with Nikhil and then we'd have an awful fight. He would even physically strike me, as he fumbled with words as that irritated him.

Sometimes he would not come back all night. At first, I thought he might have gone off to some woman's place, maybe one he'd just met at a bar. After all, he was a good-looking man. I used to be jealous, unhappy, and bitter. But then I began to wish he wouldn't come home, for if he came home he'd insist on making love to me with his breath stinking of stale alcohol, all hunched and slouched over, and his face distorted. And I knew it was not love but the drinks that made him want to sleep with me. I hated every moment, as he forced himself on me and I was physically powerless to resist his strength. It was like being raped every other day. And I knew it made no difference to him, whether it was me or any other woman. And his kisses, even his breath and proximity, made me sick to my gut, and his desire horrified and humiliated me. He would force himself on me, and when it was over, he'd drop into the snoring sleep of drunkenness. I hated him most then, I hated him from all the humiliation of it."

"But why didn't you leave him right away then, when you found out"? Anand asked, looking at her in a state of shock, enraged at the images her words had painted.

"How could I leave? What would I say to my parents, that all their aspirations were shattered after the huge amount they spent on my wedding, and I was not even willing to try my best at my marriage? That I was a quitter so soon? But no, that's not all, let me be honest. Nikhil was so dependent on me. When anything went wrong, if he got into trouble, if he was ill, it was me he came to for help. He clung to me like a child." Aparna's voice broke, and after a few seconds, her whole body shuddered as if from the immensity of her emotions. Then, her eyes brimming with tears, she had continued softly, "He was so broken then that my heart bled for him. Though he was unfaithful to me, though he hid himself from me so that he could drink without restraint, though I exasperated him so much that he hated me, deep down I knew he always loved me. He knew I'd never let him down and he knew that, except for me, he'd go all to pieces. He was so beastly when he was drunk that he had no friends, and would not allow me to have any, only some wasters like him, that he went drinking out with. He knew I was the only person, other than his parents, who cared if he lived or died. I knew, just as he did, I was the only person who stood between him and absolute ruin."

The tears were flowing down Aparna's face and she made no effort to restrain them. Anand, thinking it would relieve her to cry, had sat still and said nothing. Presently, he lit a cigarette. He took out another cigarette out of his case and handed it to her.

"No, thank you, I don't smoke." She said, "I'm sorry to have got so emotional."

"When did you return to Chennai?" Anand probed. Now he had to hear it all.

"About two years back, after over three years of that hell that I lived in. It was all for our son that I opted to give my marriage up finally, or I could have never left Nikhil. I knew my life was wretched with him and we had nothing to look forward to but hopeless misery. But I somehow felt responsible to save him from total destruction. When I was leaving, I had gone to our apartment to collect my stuff and Nikhil said to me, 'I've always loved you, Aparna.' She sighed, then continued. "And I replied, 'I know that, Nikhil, but not enough to give up drinking for me and our son.' And he stupidly said, the child at heart that he was, 'But if you loved me, Aparna, you would not leave and I would surely go to rehabilitation as you insist. But now that you're leaving, why should I listen to you?' I knew he would not go for rehabilitation,

          Shuvashree Chowdhury

and I know he can never give up drinking. It isn't in his control, or curable for that matter, any longer. So I left."

Chapter 5

The Self-reliant Woman

When Sujata got married, she had just completed her graduation—a Bachelor of Science degree is what she had brought with her to her marital home along with her bridal trousseau. But this did not help her more than giving her the dignity of being labelled educated—as a graduation is considered its basic level in Indian society. At the start, she was relieved to have been done with studies. How she had detested the regular classes, notes, the tutorials, the exams being the worst part of it all. Was it not only to be married then that she had been raised into thinking a graduation was compulsory? The process leading up to finding a groom, all the searches through newspapers and matchmakers, and the uncertainty of life beyond that had seemed daunting at the time. It was like the preparation for board exams, filled with nervous tension and stress, but culminating in a sense of relief once the exams are over.

But then, the post-exam relief is fleeting, as worry over results and college admissions set in. Similarly, once the wedding celebrations are over, the stress of adjusting to a new life grips the newly-wed couple. Sujata had thought that marriage was the end of all her efforts, little realising that it was only the beginning. The first year of her marriage had gone by reasonably smoothly for Sujata, in a heady mix of love and passion, in spite of cultural and lifestyle adjustments with the new family and the ways of their household. But at the time, Anand was on her side, morally supportive of her difficulties, even though he did not vocally stand up to his parents in support of her. With the birth of their first child came the steady flow of disappointments, from her youthful expectations of a husband, her child's father, and marriage crashing on the hard ground of the reality she now faced.

     Shuvashree Chowdhury

Then Sujata began to work, soon earning a promotion as executive search consultant. It earned her the respect she sought from Anand and elevated her position in the world. Their relationship had improved considerably for a while. But the troubled second pregnancy, her health having borne the brunt of her long-endured emotional upheavals, had compelled her to quit the job she loved. After the birth of the second child, it had taken her a long time to regain her strength to even be able to go out of the house, and much longer till she could contemplate working. There was then not only the gap of over two years since her last job to justify in finding a good job, there was the reality of having a toddler on her hands again. Added to this was the need to spend more time at home, that there were two children, with the first vying for her attention more now than ever before.

But it was not long before Sujata determined that the only one she could, and thus must depend on, was herself. She decided to become financially independent again, irrespective of what anyone thought of a woman from a wealthy family of repute stepping out to work. She could not go back to a full-time job, now that she had so much on her hands at home. The remuneration from a part-time job would not make the time and effort away from her children worth it. The best thing would then be to start an enterprise herself, Sujata decided after much thought, on a small scale initially. At first, she had no idea what it was she could do. There was also the reputation of her husband and his family to consider, which was crucial. She could not afford to tarnish any of it in her forays into financial acquisition and independence.

Her first job with the multinational headhunting firm had given her sound experience and enough exposure to start a business on her own. Also, Sujata, in the early years of marriage, had started purchasing jewellery that would add to her personal assets, even though she hardly cared to wear any. Whenever Anand had asked her what she wanted, she opted for money with which she bought jewellery, especially diamonds. She knew their value would appreciate fast, compared to gold. Also, diamonds, especially solitaires, were easier to store as compared to gold of similar worth. The driving force of her life, now that her marriage was just a farce, other than bringing up her children, was gaining her financial independence and winning back her compromised self-esteem. Sujata knew that only then could she lead her life free from Anand's and his parent's constant control. She could then take decisions not only about her life, but on behalf of the children independently. Anand was not overtly controlling, like most chauvinistic men she knew in Chennai were of the women in their lives. Rather, he was a quiet and assertive man who had to have his way in everything. What option did Sujata have now but to comply, as he was the one paying for everything and she depended on his money for herself and the children? It was more for the children. As for her, there was not much that Sujata needed personally. The further deterioration of their relationship after the birth of the second baby meant that she loathed to ask him for money.

Sujata had to live and provide the children a lifestyle suited to the family's social status. Earlier, Anand gave her money even before her asking, but lately he had stopped giving it readily. Rather, he was using it in their power struggles, as a way to melt her icy behaviour towards him. Though she wouldn't talk to Anand for days after a fight, she would be forced to break her silence in asking him for money. But to Sujata, it was much more than his mere breaking of her silence; it was the forsaking of her pride. Yet when she needed the money for the children, Sujata asked Anand, even though it hurt her self-esteem, realising he was purposely withholding it to assert his control over her. It was at this point that Sujata became determined to start earning again. The jewellery she had would serve as an asset to set up a business.

After some thought, her parent's house, which was very centrally located in Nungambakkam, struck Sujata as the ideal location to set up shop in. The ground floor was in the form of a large hall that her parents, in spite of a lot of discussion, had never put to any commercial use. It had been used to host the pre-wedding and after parties of both their daughters. It was there that they hosted parties often—be it for Diwali, Golu, and there were the grandchildren's birthday parties too. At Golu, the Tamilian festival which is celebrated during Navratri leading up to Dasshera, Sujata and her sister, along with their children,

    Shuvashree Chowdhury

decorated a large tiered stand with colourful dolls—mainly
of gods and goddesses, which was displayed here in this hall.
Many people from the neighbourhood were invited to attend the
celebrations and view this exhibition, and were served a lavish
traditional Tamil dinner on the lawn behind the hall. The caterer,
along with his cooks and aides, was allotted the corner of the
lawn, under a makeshift shed.

At the yearly Diwali parties, this lawn, which was an extension
of the hall, was used for the grand fireworks display, while the
dinner buffet was set up to its side. Sujata and her sister, ever
since they were children, had helped her parents organise these
events. In fact, Sujata was rather good at managing such parties.
When in college, at these house parties, because of her detailed
planning, followed by her personal coordination and supervision
of decorations, lighting, florist, and the caterer, her friends had
often joked that she might as well set up an event management
company of her own. When contemplating what enterprise Sujata
could set up, this suggestion of her friends came to mind. Even
now, she was the backbone of all parties at her parent's house.
Then why not make something she loved and was good at the basis
of her business plan? Her passion would stand her in good stead in
making a success of her enterprise.

Sujata spoke to her mother, who initially had reservations on
the security of the house being compromised as they lived upstairs.
But Sujata hired round-the-clock services of a professional security
agency. She had not told Anand the real reason for her new business
venture, except that she would have a good time at it. Thus, she
was confident she could get money from him, if she really needed
it. Her parents trusted her enterprise, and for a monthly rent of
Rs. 15000, they allowed Sujata the use of the ground floor hall
and lawn. Sujata insisted that her mother, in spite of her initial
reluctance, take the rent money from her. Her father's business was
suffering as he could not devote much time to it. But the rent also
meant that she would have independent charge of the place.

Sujata got the place restructured, repainted, and renovated,
spending a good amount of money on all of it. For money, she sold
a pair of diamond eternity bangles that she had bought in the early
years of her marriage, from Tanishq on Cathedral Road, by saving

from the money Anand gave her for expenses over time. She had never worn them and Anand did not know of them as she always kept the bangles in her personal mini-vault in their bedroom. Their value had appreciated and she got a good price for them. All the work on the hall started after the Diwali party that year. It was completed well in advance of the upcoming wedding season. At the Golu and Diwali party, Sujata had floated the word around of her forthcoming enterprise and her friends, trusting her venture, enthusiastically spread the word around.

Sujata was clear she was not just going to rent out the hall. The services of the decorator, florist, caterer, and other allied facilities required would all have to be taken through her. It was going to be an event coordination service and she would put in all the elements of her personal taste and style into making each event unique and special. It was Sujata's creativity that was to be the chief draw for her clients. Sujata registered the company in her mother's name, calling it "Sundari Enterprises". At one corner of the large hall was a small room with an attached bathroom, which Sujata converted into her office. In it, other than office furniture and filing cabinets, she installed a tea and coffee vending machine that was to be used during the functions as well, for serving guests. In this office, she met with prospective clients as well as vendors.

Sujata's rates were as per the market, every break-up in cost accounted for by the varied vendors, over which she added the rent of the place and her service charges. Her first client luckily was a family friend whose son was getting married. She had known the couple since childhood and as guests of her family over the years, they had encouraged her managerial skills. So she was at an advantage in executing their event self-assuredly. When someone has faith in your capability and trusts that you would do the best you could for them, you're already ahead in the race. Her first event was a success and this gave Sujata the confidence to go ahead full steam on this venture. Her parents too were reassured that they had made no mistake in letting out the place to Sujata. She also contacted the companies she had worked with in her earlier job as executive search researcher and consultant, knowing as she did their HR and the administrative departments well.

Due to her persuasive sales pitch, these companies showed

    Shuvashree Chowdhury

interest in holding daylong training sessions and workshops at her hall. She made sure that these events went off without a hitch, arranging for everything from morning tea to evening tea. The vending machine she had installed for the wedding parties was thus put to good use. Though she herself detested the machine-made tea and coffee and always went upstairs for a freshly brewed cup of Darjeeling tea or filter coffee prepared by her parents' cook. For these corporate event lunches, she got her regular wedding caterer, all too happy with the additional off-season business, to prepare well-planned, wholesome packed meals which would have everything in it. They would come with cutlery and included a salad, the main course of rice and paratha along with a paneer or chicken dish and sautéed vegetable. It had to include a portion of curd rice as well, along with a sweetmeat from the neighbourhood Krishna Sweets as dessert. These boxes reduced the lunch time and also saved the hassle of a number of waiters. The staff and the corporate administrative teams preferred this option over a buffet. Sujata personally supervised the nutritional quality and taste of the lunch boxes.

She soon learned that when you execute your job with passion, clients perceive your sincerity and keep coming back to you. Weddings are one of the most important occasions in people's lives and if you value them as such, to give your clients and their guests an experience no less than you would expect at your own, they are grateful. The execution of these wedding and other family events gave Sujata scope to showcase her work to a large number of guests, and her business grew by word of mouth. It was not long before hers became a flourishing business as there is never a dearth of occasions in people's lives. Sujata's relationship with Anand was satisfactory at this stage. When one's own self-esteem suffers, relationships suffer the most as hers had. But now Sujata was not so sensitive to Anand's every word or action, and didn't have the mental space to dwell on his insensitivity, perceived or otherwise, that had once seemed so crushing in its assault on her emotions. As Sujata now had an air of self-possession, and from this state it is not easy to be offended and hurt, she had an elevated sense of place in the world. Now that her children were doing well in the top-ranking Shishya School where she had made up her mind from the start to admit them, Sujata had an enhanced sense of emotional security. During this time, she again started taking care of her appearance and clothes. Though she preferred to wear *salwar-kameez* or *sari*, as she was as yet shy and uncomfortable in western wear, her clothes were tastefully selected from fashionable boutiques. She wore them with élan along with well-matched shoes, bags, and light jewellery. Needless to say, she received plenty of male attention. There were young men she met, who tried to get close. She was, no doubt flattered, even flirted in a friendly way. Her husband, though friendlier, warm even, now hardly noticed her as a woman.

But Sujata never went out with any man, not even for coffee or lunch, lest anyone should see her and thus gossip. She could not jeopardise her reputation now that she had her own business identity, or of her husband and his family, but mostly she worried about the effect any gossip could have on her children. All Sujata could do then was chat telephonically, with the few male friends she had. They were usually business associates from the corporate world whose events she conducted, and whom she respected and trusted from their senior positions in reputed organisations. One such close male friendship with Shekhar Ravindran, whom she had first met on a business trip to Mumbai during her stint as an executive search consultant, had stood the test of time to become her strongest support through all these changes in her life. This, in addition to the love of her sons, became her source of emotional sustenance. Anand noticed the changes in his otherwise shy wife—the frequent phone calls, the long chats, and the attention to her dressing. Even though he taunted her, he was relieved she was in much better spirits. He welcomed the renewed self-assured woman. Another peaceful phase of their relationship began thus.

* * *

One of Sujata's clients, Manas Das, the HR head of a renowned tea and coffee company of South India with plantations in Coonoor and Munnar, was one of the men Sujata had become close to. He was a tall, handsome man, with somewhat oriental features and a sharp nose, who had charmingly pursued her. He was originally from Guwahati, but had been in Chennai for over five years now.

    Shuvashree Chowdhury

He had a wife and daughter back home in Assam, who lived with his parents. Manas went home every few months when he could. Sujata had initially interacted with him only telephonically as an executive search researcher and then later as a consultant. After she had contacted him and introduced her event management enterprise, he had asked her to come and meet him. From the moment she had walked into his Pantheon Road bungalow office wearing a floral printed royal-blue georgette *sari* pleated to perfection, Manas was drawn to her. Over tea in his plush cabin on the ground floor, brought in by a smart uniformed waiter, they had first acquainted themselves with each other's lives and circumstances.

When you meet someone for the first time, it's the physical chemistry that comes into play instantly, often completely changing the dynamics of the connection you might have made over prolonged telephonic, email, or social media interactions, even with photographs or through video chats. And Sujata and Manas had not even seen each other's photographs, let alone had video chats over strictly professional exchanges. Sujata however found that Manas was as authoritative, persuasive, and charming in person as his voice had sounded. While Sujata had a soft, girlish voice that had sounded unassertive, Manas had instinctively assumed her physical bearing would be as such. But in person, Sujata carried herself with dignity and grace. He found himself overwhelmed by her pleasant face and feminine personality. Sujata, raising her head from her perfectly brewed cup of tea that she had expected from a tea company of such repute as his, noticed Manas looking at her intently and admiringly. This set her heart aflutter, as she found him irresistibly handsome, similar in looks to her sister Ramya's husband.

From the way he kept hanging on to her every word, Sujata realised that Manas was very much attracted to her. This excited and, in turn, attracted her further to him. Sujata had been neglected for so long by her husband, physically and emotionally, that Manas's obvious interest was very gratifying. She had randomly given Anand the silent treatment, but it did not have the effects she had desired, leading both to become irrevocably disconnected. The silent treatment, though commonly used by women, creates feelings of heartache that may eventually lead to the end of the relationship. What seems to work for the moment in getting attention may lead exactly to what you don't want in the long run—a deepening sense of detachment. It was due to Anand's inherent aloofness, perhaps not an intentional coldness on his part, that Sujata was so hurt. As she had tended to think, she must be doing something wrong to bring it on. When he had thwarted her efforts to get close, it had left her alone, abandoned, anxious, and scared.

But all that was well behind Sujata. She now had her heart sealed akin to a vault, to Anand's emotional encroachment, the door lined and thickened with casual flirtations that fortified it to his attempts to penetrate it. Manas's attention and attraction came to Sujata at a time when she much needed the reassurance she sought in her reinvented persona. This was even as the much older Shekhar Ravindran, whom she communicated with constantly since their meeting in Mumbai, continued to remain her primary mentor and anchor. In spite of her immediate attraction to Manas, Sujata was very cautious and shy in her interactions with him. She had not even had a boyfriend before marrying Anand, and her exposure to men even after marriage was limited and she was thus reticent in her interactions with men. Manas flustered her, making her feel self-conscious at his open and bold flirtations. He had begun to call her rather frequently, at first on the pretext of business, then casual chatty calls. The charming speaker that he was, he caught and ensnared lonely Sujata's fancy.

Sujata now looked forward to Manas's calls, and was often in a flushed state and full of smiles and blushes while talking to him. He would always ask her out to coffee or lunch, but Sujata firmly turned down such invitations. There was no way she was going to be seen in public with him. After all, she lived in a conservative society and her husband and his family were well known here. Also by now, she was well known too. Thus, she did not meet Manas, not even go over to his office anymore as it might grab attention. Manas couldn't come to her office as her parents would be at home upstairs, and might get suspicious if a young handsome man came around often. Though he used her hall and services for all conferences and vendor meets, the coordination could be

        Shuvashree Chowdhury

handled by junior members of his team and he was not required to visit personally.

It was really through telephonic conversations, text messages, and Gmail chats that Sujata and Manas become close. Manas kept insisting that Sujata meet him, but she always declined, however tempted she was to meet him. Then one day, after much persuasion, Manas drove down to her office. He called her from his car.

"Come out and see me," he said firmly. "Or I'm sitting here till evening when you leave office and then I can see you."

"But I'm not appropriately dressed to meet you now," Sujata giggled. "So please go away, Manas. I promise we'll meet soon, I will come to your office."

"You will look beautiful however you're dressed and it doesn't matter," he insisted, "I must meet you now or you pay the consequences of my sitting out here parked at your gate till someone notices me."

Sujata's heart raced, even as she rushed out, with the anticipation of meeting Manas as much as with the anxiety of someone noticing them together. As she stepped into his car and sat beside him, clutching her bag that she had remembered to grab, Sujata's heart constricted. She was drawn into the overwhelming power of his physical magnetism as she climbed into the high seat of his black sports car that added to his suave personality. His masculine musk cologne enveloped her. She looked ahead, afraid to look at his handsome face, as Manas revved the engine of his car left on for the air conditioning and the music system, and drove out of their lane in Nungambakkam. She noticed the twinkle in his eyes—their sides crinkling. Then she took in the satisfied smile on his thin lips that the shapely moustache on his chiselled face could not hide. Manas manoeuvred the car deftly into the rush of traffic on Mount Road. Then taking a U-turn, he drove towards the Gemini flyover.

Sujata turned to him sharply and, in a tense voice, said, "Where do you think you are going? I'm telling you, I don't want to be seen with you ... you don't understand, do you, that I cannot risk my marriage and the lives of my children?"

"Wait and see where we are headed..." Manas said softly, in a placating tone. "And just relax. No one can see us, Sujata. Notice the dark shades? We won't be getting out of the car anywhere."

He took a smooth left turn under the Gemini flyover, quietly crossing the American Consulate gates, and drove down Cathedral Road crossing the cathedral gates and then accelerated and drove up on the flyover.

"Are you taking us to Marina Beach?" Sujata asked, her anxiety giving her tone a sharp edge, overwhelming her shyness at his proximity.

"Yes, I am, and we can park the car there and sit and talk. Now don't ask me why there—as where else can we park without being noticed? At this time, the beach will be deserted."

At the Marina beach, Manas drove down the length of the parking area looking for a secluded spot—not so isolated as to seem suspicious to the cop squads driving around constantly. He parked on a height overlooking the sea, the road running between them and the thick-walled parapet, after which the sand stretch ran for quite a distance into the sea. It was not warm outside, but it was really in fear of being noticed that they did not roll down the window panes for fresh air. For Sujata's sake, he had to be absolutely cautious that they were not seen together. After turning off the ignition, pushing back his seat and reclining it back really low, then stretching out comfortably, Manas turned to look at Sujata. She was still viewing him with a curiosity mixed with much apprehension. As he met her gaze, then held it for a while, Sujata noticed the glow in his eyes and the indication of his attraction for her.

A chill ran down Sujata's spine. It was a queer mix of elation and excitement, with anxiety at the realisation of how drawn she felt towards him as well. As he looked at Sujata, trying to hold her gaze, Manas stretched out and gently took her right hand in his. Sujata tried to retrieve her hand, but Manas held on to it with one hand, lightly patting it with the other—as if to pacify her—as he leaned backwards with his back to the window and kept looking at her. His calmness by now seeped into her somewhat, as Sujata slowly relaxed enough to begin to enjoy the close proximity to him. Her hand still in his, they sat staring out into the distance at the sea merging with the sand in a shimmering white stretch in the afternoon sun. Music played softly in the car. Suddenly, Manas

                    Shuvashree Chowdhury

bent towards Sujata who was looking ahead, as if he was going to whisper into her ear. When she turned to look at him coolly, Manas took her by surprise, kissing her gently and lightly on her lips.

Even as she was recovering from the shock of the exhilarating sensation his touch had aroused in her, Manas kissed Sujata passionately. She did not respond for a while, but did not resist him either, trying to feel the sensation that was seeping through her lips into her being. She was not used to kissing, as her husband, the only man she had had the opportunity of kissing as yet, did not favour it. He preferred to have sex without its hassle, rather did not quite see the significance of kissing for arousing emotional and physical intimacy, for a satisfying and pleasurable sexual act, especially for a woman. Sujata slowly reciprocated. She was afraid Manas would figure out her ineptness and she was anxious about cops coming over to their car. But once she had overcome the initial hesitation, she allowed her instincts to guide her. As Sujata gradually gave in to her passion, she found to her surprise that she actually liked kissing.

Manas pulled back slowly. He was pleased to have overcome her reserve and awakened her dormant passion. He smiled at Sujata, patted the top of her hand, and looked around to see if all was well. After this, they did not talk much and they quietly sat hand in hand, staring out into the sea. Then Manas slowly pulled out of the parking area and drove them back to her office. He wanted Sujata's desire for him to grow, so that it would propel her towards him of its own accord. He was not to be disappointed in throwing his bait into a deep turbulent sea. That evening by the Marina beach kick-started an exhilarating phase of Sujata's life. She was ready to set sail on a high tide, as she looked forward to meeting Manas often, now that she felt secure of her place in the world with the stability of the boat of her business in new waters. Manas's calls became her lifeline.

Anand and Sujata's parents noticed the twinkle in her eye, the constant and long vivacious phone conversations, her never leaving her mobile phone unattended, and the lightness in her steps. They were happy to meet the new woman who had emerged out of a fulfilling career—in their view. Sujata's mother did know that there were men who gave Sujata attention and that surely had something to do with the lightness in her voice and step. She also knew of Sujata's disenchantment with her husband, and so approved of her need to have a little fun. But she was anxious of Sujata's thereby neglecting her children who already lacked their father's attention, but she was most afraid of it leading to her abandoning the security of her marriage altogether. At it is, at this time, Sujata did not have much inclination to her other good friend in Mumbai, Shekhar, who had filled her mind and heart for so long. But she made it a point nevertheless, to keep in touch with him and to faithfully tell him of the new romantic interest in her life. He tried to dissuade Sujata from her friendship with Manas, as he knew him professionally. But Sujata paid no heed, as she attributed it to his jealousy and possessiveness.

It was Manas who was to shortly veer Sujata out of her current event management business into starting a headhunting firm. He had first known her as a research analyst and then worked with Sujata as a search consultant. She had worked in the consumer, retail and services (CRS) vertical as a researcher, then in the manufacturing and real estate vertical, that had the highest revenue earning potential in the current Chennai landscape, as the city was racing towards development.

Manas, on one of their outings, as they sat in his car gazing at the Marina, had casually suggested, "Headhunting would be a more stable, lucrative, and long-term business, that you can sustain with advancing years. You will be at an advantage now, from the urgent market needs. So much is happening in this city now. But more than that, it will lead to good and meaningful associations for you, rather than chasing vendors all day in this event management business. After all the effort you put in, isn't it difficult to maintain quality and totally satisfy your clients—dealing with unreliable manual labour and their less educated supervisors?

"Yes, that's true," Sujata had replied thoughtfully, "It does get difficult and exasperating too, chasing the caterers, decorators, florists, so many of them."

"In headhunting, your personal skills and effort would set the stage and spearhead your firm's reputation in the market. And Sujata, I know you are good at your work. Trust me on it." Manas had stated firmly, "You are good at sales too."

     Shuvashree Chowdhury

Sujata was enthused by the idea, but decided to call Shekhar and tell him what Manas had suggested. She would not think of this seriously until Shekhar gave her the vote of confidence. She still trusted him over anyone else, and then he was a senior HR professional and would know best.

"You know, Sujata, I dislike Manas. I don't trust his motives," Shekhar had said in response to her call. "But in this case, I'll admit he is right. It would be better for you in the long run."

Initially, Sujata was to continue with the events business, while working independently on headhunting mandates that both Manas and Shekhar in Mumbai helped her clinch. Her mother and sister filled in for her on the event management, when she was away on the new business. She registered a new firm at the same address. Also, she had taken on two researchers, a young man and a woman, and trained them well, to help get the new business set to her high standards. Then later, she was to hire a couple of experienced consultants. By this time, she had set and regularised standard operating processes for her firm. As she grew confident with the success of her new enterprise, Sujata stopped taking on more events and closed that business.

Once her finances were stable, the new firm making profits, she moved to a new location. This was also near her parent's house, so she could leave her boys with them when required. Her parents loved the boys and were happy to take them on as and when required. This gave Sujata immense support and ability to surge ahead at work, even as she travelled. She did not feel guilty in burdening her parents, as she gave them a good sum of her earnings every month, along with a steady flow of gifts and a lifestyle they would not afford on their own. She felt happy and fulfilled. But Sujata did not depend on her parents or sister solely, just as she had stopped relying on Anand. She ensured to take on more domestic help now that she had her own money, only for the sake of the boys. She was now a self-reliant woman.

Chapter 6

The Emotional Entrapment

"**S**ir, *samosas*," the office attendant announced, as he placed a small plate of it on Anand's desk at work one evening, along with a cup of coffee on a tray.

"Who ordered them today?" Anand asked, still looking into his computer screen, with his hands flying over the keyboard in response to an email.

"Sir, Aparna madam."

"Ah! Take them away," Anand said abruptly, "I'm not in the mood for them today, and get me the usual biscuits."

The attendant brought out the round glass container of biscuits from a side cabinet and left it on Anand's desk. He walked out with the plate.

"What happened, Sir's not having *samosas* today?" Aparna asked the attendant, as soon as he stepped out of Anand's office past his secretary.

"No, he asked for the regular biscuits," he replied, "Sir even asked me who ordered them today and I told him it was you."

Aparna returned to her work station, irrationally very dejected, not in the mood anymore for the *samosas* she had ordered from the canteen. Every other evening, someone or other ordered snacks from the canteen for everyone on the office floor, at the time that the attendants came around serving tea and coffee. Aparna had merely followed the prevalent culture, so why would Anand not have *samosas* today as he always did? There were days when Anand ordered sandwiches or *medu vadai* or other snacks for all the staff, just as he ate what others ordered. On staff birthdays, the HR department customarily ordered a cake for everyone, and the one whose birthday it was usually ordered the snacks to go with it over tea and coffee. The cake was cut in the conference room usually at

5 p.m. as most employees would be present then. Anand made it a point to attend these birthday celebrations and to interact with staff as if he were one of them.

Anand's refusal convinced Aparna that he was avoiding her. In the initial weeks after that feedback meeting with him, when she had revealed her personal life, he had been compassionate. When he came around to their work area to talk to Radhika or anyone else, or after a meeting, Anand had made it a point to enquire about Aparna's work, of how she was doing. He would ask about her assignments or which story she was working on. Sometimes he would call her to his office over some story she had done or he wanted her to write. It was during these chats Aparna told Anand more about her life. Anand, in turn, told her about his family, his marriage, and his children.

Then one day, even as Aparna passed by him on her way home and enthusiastically tried to talk to him, to her surprise, he ignored her outright and walked away. At the time, Aparna had thought Anand might be preoccupied or worried about something and had assuaged her disappointment with the presumption. Then the next day, she went and met him in his office and all was well again. However, since then, much to her confusion, now that they had graduated to being friends, Anand had been blowing hot and cold. When she expected him to be friendly, he would snub her and, when she disregarded him in turn, he would be warm and enquire about her work, her son, and about her parents. Aparna was often left wondering what she had done to deserve Anand's ire, his snubs, or his ridiculous behaviour—in her view. Only when Anand was warm again to her as initially, Aparna relaxed. She was always on edge, not knowing what to expect from him.

But, Anand had begun to go out of his way to nit-pick on Aparna's work—commenting on her stories, even reprimanding her for some inane issue or other at the meetings. Then he would call her into his office and talk as if all was normal and the rudeness was merely part of work. All this really upset Aparna, more because she was still in an emotional turmoil from dealing with Nikhil's random calls to threaten or cajole her in turns to return to him. She could not even turn to her parents for support, what with their constant worry, and the pressure they created on her with regard to her son. Whatever may be her current personal disposition, Anand's mood and conduct was irrational. It began to affect her. His words bore deep into Aparna's psyche. She became hypersensitive to his public insults. Anand was a quietly reserved, polite person, but could easily become caustic and abrupt when he chose to. At such times, seeing Aparna's pained face, the tears abruptly filling her eyes, though she would check them from spilling over, Radhika would attempt to comfort her.

"Don't take it personally, Aparna...." she would say after meetings, "We've all gone through our early years of this mental coaching to be where we are today. Anand is merely being tough to groom you for your progress on the job. You're doing well and he's pleased with your progress. And I am too."

In spite of Radhika's assurances, as she returned to her desk that evening, after Anand had declined to have the *samosas* on learning she had ordered them, Aparna felt nausea sweep over her. This was also appended by his snubbing her story idea and views at the meeting before that, in the presence of her entire team. Aparna had ordered the *samosas* today of all days, in the hope of clearing the air with him. She had been planning on going into his office thereafter and, over coffee, asking him what was wrong with her story idea and why he had completely rejected it. But now that he did not have the *samosa*, she felt too let down to go and meet him. Aparna could not help the sinking feeling whenever Anand snubbed her. Somehow, she felt connected to him and couldn't shake off his influence. In the squall that was her current life, Anand had appeared as a raft which she had felt secure holding. But whenever it threatened to throw her off balance, as had happened a lot lately, she became petrified. Slowly and surely, without consciously planning to, as a creeper plant grows on a wall, she had become emotionally dependent on him.

* * *

On his part, since Anand encountered Aparna, first at her final interview, then on his way out of office the evening when she was still around, he had been curiously attracted to her. The mysterious look in her large, compelling eyes on her swarthy, luminous oval face had stayed with him for days. After that, the

 Shuvashree Chowdhury

meeting at his office, where she had become emotional, divulged all about her personal life, and then burst into tears, had shaken him. With each interaction thereafter, Anand found himself drawn to Aparna. He had thought that, with the passage of time and the regular interactions, the attraction would wear off. It was not like he had not been attracted to other women who joined his paper before. But it was true that he had never made any advances, however slight, in their direction. But he welcomed and basked in the attention that quite a few of the women gave him, especially the younger ones, overawed as they were with his power and personality.

When Aparna had called him late after working hours, a few times, to discuss the latest circumstances of her divorce and to seek his advice, Anand had been very warm and supportive. He had listened to her intently, and given her his opinion, mindful that she was in a vulnerable point in her life. Then one night, she had called him rather late when he was already in bed. She was sobbing inconsolably after a telephone conversation with her husband. He had insisted he was going to get the custody of their child at any cost and his lawyer was going to go all out to prove Aparna was incapable of bringing up the child well. Anand had quietly listened to her till she calmed down. Then he told her he would speak to her the next day after work. After he had disconnected the call, he noticed his wife Sujata sitting up beside him, looking at him with immense irritation.

"Why the hell is this woman calling you so late at night?" Sujata had thundered "And the way she was wailing, as if someone has died. I could hear her right through your mobile. Isn't she the new employee who called you a few times before?"

"Yes, her name is Aparna and she's very troubled," Anand replied casually.

"How come she's calling you, of all people, with her personal woes?"

Anand had no valid response, so he remained silent. He knew Sujata was justified in her opinion. Why would he be involved in the personal affairs of one of the staff, a young lady at that? Aparna had called a few times earlier in Sujata's presence and she had given him suspicious, disgruntled looks each time. Her anger and mistrust had more than good cause, Anand knew. It had been provoked when Sujata had chanced upon overtly flirty text messages between him and a girl from office, on their vacation at the family's bungalow in Munnar. This was right after the birth of their second son. The girl who was from the main paper's city desk—Sujata had verified later—had texted Anand, much to Sujata's indignation. This proved her suspicions that Anand, far from discouraging such entanglements, actually fanned the flames.

"I love you so much I cannot live without you, Anand sir," the message read.

"Missing you too … It's beautiful here," he had replied, "See you on Monday."

It was true that Anand welcomed female attention, even craved and basked in it, now that it was finally coming his way. He was not all to blame for it, he justified to himself. His wife's lack of confidence in him and embarrassment that he was not as handsome as she would have liked was partly to blame. Sujata was never proud of him as he was not suave and charming like the other men of her family, especially her father and her sister's husband, thus hurting his pride.

Sujata had not kept her opinions to herself. She would often tell Anand, "People find your company so boring, as you try to show how intellectual you are … thus have little to contribute to casual or party conversations. I am embarrassed at family get-togethers when you just ignore everyone and remain silent. It's as if you are superior to everyone else."

Anand never tried to explain that his reserve was really due to an inherent shyness and inability to make small talk. He never showed that he was hurt by her biting remarks, laughing it all off in projecting that he was much amused. But there was a feeling of emotional coldness he nursed, that his wife was never in love with him. Then when female colleagues started giving him attention that he was not used to in his youth due to his quiet and reticent personality, Anand felt his ego swell. And so, he had gone all out when the opportunities presented themselves, to allay his insecurities, by garnering all the female attention he could come by.

At his office, Anand did not need to impress women with his looks and physique, though they had but improved since he started working out at the gym and going to the salon at the Park Hotel and the Savoy Hotel regularly. Sujata shopped for his clothes which were now sophisticated too. But the women at work were impressed by his intelligence, wit, quiet humour, decisiveness, and the power he exuded as the boss. This had led to Anand's casual flings, the last one with the girl whose texts Sujata had read, snatching his mobile up as it had beeped incessantly. They had been sitting cosily on the plush white and green floral-printed sofa by the fireplace. What had hurt and humiliated Sujata most were Anand's responses to the string of messages, especially the last one that read 'Missing you too.' It was particularly galling when they were on what Sujata had assumed was a romantic interlude to try and fix their marital problems.

It had hurt Anand to see Sujata's distraught expressions on seeing the text messages, then watch her expression harden. She had become suspicious of his flirtations, but thought they were casual and harmless. But that he could be missing some other woman on a supposedly romantic vacation with her had hit her hard. She had become silent, and would not give him a chance to explain that it was merely a casual flirtation that did not mean anything to him. In trying to assuage Sujata's feelings, Anand did promptly severe all personal connections with this woman from his office for good, but the damage to his marriage was done. Sujata never got over that incident. Though she did show her temper over household issues and the children at times, she had all but frozen him out of her life.

With Anand's relentless efforts, Sujata did warm up to him somewhat, in spite of learning of his other flirtations from time to time. It was then after a few years now that Aparna's calls had made Sujata become agitated over again. Perhaps Anand's recent distractedness and the way he spoke to Aparna with his tone all soft and concerned, and her calls on personal issues even late at night, had caught Sujata's suspicion. Then Sujata also had her contacts in Anand's office, from whom she learned that Aparna walked into his cabin randomly, and was rather bold with him at meetings, speaking her mind always, not in the least hesitant like the others.

But this time around, Anand did not pacify Sujata, as there really was nothing between him and Aparna. It was true that, since that first meeting with Aparna, she had haunted his thoughts. But that was nothing to justify to Sujata, he had done nothing wrong. He thus ignored her angry outbursts, hoping in time she would realise there really was nothing to worry about.

Anand knew that he was inexplicably drawn to Aparna, unlike other women in the past, though he was not sure yet what he really wanted from her. Did he want to be in a relationship, to act upon his attraction, or merely capture her attention? The more he toyed with this idea of the two of them together, especially each time he met and interacted with Aparna over work, he became more certain of his attraction. Then one evening after gym at the Savoy Hotel on Cathedral Road, over drinks at their popular pub—Sparks—with two of his close male friends, he blurted out to them, that there was a woman in his office whom he found very attractive. In the course of describing her to them, he became aware that his attraction had grown beyond his desire to withhold it any longer.

These friends of Anand's, who were incidentally tall, good-looking, with well-toned bodies and a flair for charming women, even though not high achievers like Anand, encouraged him to act on it. One was none other than Sujata's sister Ramya's husband Prashant—the one she was so much in awe of. The other, Rajeev, had a steady girlfriend who was Sujata's cousin and one of her close friends. Yet they did not find their committed relationship statuses a hindrance to a continued need and desire to have their egos stroked, over their ability to make women drool over them. The friendship between these men had obviously blossomed over time, through the considerable time they spent together as they were extended family. Both of Anand's friends conceded that a man must have diversions outside of the wife and children, in order to perk up his life and make living worthwhile. They shared with Anand their individual master strokes, in the game mastered lifelong, of courting women.

"You need to give a woman a lot of attention at first, then ignore her while you shower attention on other women in her presence. But don't ignore her so much or for long as to allow her to lose interest in you," Prashant said, while Rajeev elaborated, "This will

     Shuvashree Chowdhury

result in the woman first being pleased. Then when you ruffle her feathers and confuse her, you grab her attention. Slowly but surely, you get under her skin, then control her mind and emotions thereafter."

By the time the three men left the hotel, Anand was convinced on improving his life, by bringing the zing back into his married life.

"But Anand, you must ensure not to get emotionally attached, or to ever consider leaving your wife and children for another woman." Sujata's brother-in-law Prashant cautioned him, conjuring a family loyalty however feigned, just as they were about to get into their respective cars. Rajeev added, "Otherwise it will no longer be fun. You get it, man!"

Anand, his mind now made up even as he stepped into his Mercedes Benz driven up by his chauffeur, was as a man on a new and thrilling space mission.

* * *

Aparna, with the assurance and moral support she had received from Anand since confiding in him of her circumstances, had found in him great strength. She didn't really have anyone to talk to since coming back to Chennai with her son. Aparna's parents, in the midst of their worry and fear about her situation, of what would become of her after they passed, but most, of what people were inferring and talking about her return, could not provide her the emotional support she much needed. They felt anxious and mentally burdened too financially with her return and the end of her marriage, after having spent much above their means on the wedding that they had considered an investment on her secure future. Added to which, they were genuinely worried and felt responsible for her son's upbringing now. Aparna had an old friend, a young woman who had worked at the Taj Coromandel with her before marriage, with whom she discussed her situation now, but it was not the same as the strong male support she found in Anand.

Aparna had thus been pleased with the attention Anand gave her over other staff and had begun to seek it in various ways. She came up with novel story ideas he might like, diligently filed more stories than others, and never forgot as she wrote any piece for the newspaper that Anand would be reading it. His commending her work, soon seeking her opinion on official matters along with Radhika's, gave Aparna the confidence to approach his cabin at any time, and to call him after working hours, either with official or personal issues. And Anand had always been forthcoming initially. Radhika, a mature woman, had by now learned of the circumstances of Aparna's personal life and was also kind and supportive. This was perpetuated by the fact that Aparna was soon more productive than many in Radhika's department—the daily *Urban Plus* supplement. The need to please Anand and to seek his approval had given Aparna a surging passion for her work, a conscientiousness otherwise not possible perhaps with her current circumstances.

An inner joyfulness awakened in Aparna, along with a sense of security, from her love for her work and Anand's presence in her life. Her husband Nikhil's threats, the impending divorce, along with the fear of losing her son were all seemingly more in her control now. Since she was not so distressed herself, Aparna was able to see her parent's perspectives and provide them with the moral support they needed in dealing with all that had befallen them due to her circumstances. This was especially after Aparna had been able to get her son Kartik admitted into one of the best schools in Chennai, the PSBB. He was a smart boy and Aparna was able to clear the parent's interview as well, explaining that her husband was in Mumbai on work and they travelled between the cities.

Aparna was confident that as expenses rose with Kartik's school years, so would her salary increase. This was also another pertinent driving force for Aparna to excel at work, so as to benefit from the performance-based increment culture in the newspaper. Aparna's faith in God had been reinstated by now, convincing her that he tests one surely, but not indefinitely. When Anand's attitude towards her took a severe U-turn, with his ignoring her, being rude in public, it shook her to the core. This erratic behaviour of his, based on advice from his friends that evening at the gym, started at a work meeting. It was Aparna's story idea for

Shuvashree Chowdhury

the *Urban Plus* to showcase the latest eateries in Chennai.

"It's high time you come up with something more original and new, Aparna!" Anand had said sharply, "You keep doing the same thing over and over again on hotels and eateries. Can't you find something new, better than the string of stories you've been churning out lately?"

Aparna looked at him in surprise, her eyes narrowing. Then as the biting cruelty of his tone and words registered in her mind, her face contorted and her eyes welled up. She quickly made a mental note of her last stories, the one on the airline industry—low-cost carriers and a SWOT analysis on them, on the multiplex theatres in Chennai, and a variety of other write-ups. Anand continued speaking to the others with absolute disregard for the sharp, wasp-like sting she had imagined on her face, and the thumping of her heart in embarrassment even as she distracted herself in recalling her earlier stories. She looked downwards, as the rest of the group looked at her slyly—few with sympathy and the rest with satisfaction. In their view, it was high time she was put in her place. She had been high-handed with people, encouraged by the attention she received from Anand.

After the meeting, Aparna had followed Anand out of the conference room. He was on his way to his cabin. But he stopped and smiled at her as though everything was normal.

"I'm in a rush today, Aparna," he said "If there's anything you need to discuss, we'll have to do it tomorrow or you talk to Radhika if it's urgent."

"It's okay!" Aparna replied in a small voice. "I'll talk to you tomorrow. Just wanted to discuss what you said inside, whether you really meant it."

"I know you're upset," Anand said, smiling wryly. "And you must hate me this moment. But I don't care. I know you have the potential, so I'm not going to stop going after you, whether you like it or not. You have the right attitude for this job, Aparna, and it can take you places, if you only stay focussed."

Aparna nodded, her spirit lifting as abruptly as a bird soaring as she walked towards her work station. Perhaps he had snapped at her in the presence of everyone to shake up the team, and push them into being more cognitive and creative. She felt enthused to come up with fresh ideas in readiness for the next meeting, so as to win his appreciation. As she passed, Radhika asked her what Anand had said. But Aparna chose not to share the cause of her change in mood and the elation, after the putdown at the meeting. She feigned a sad look for Radhika's sake, as well as those who could see her through Radhika's glass cabin, and basked in everyone's sympathy in the bargain.

After a while, at about 8 p.m., Aparna left for the day. An auto-rickshaw she hailed outside the office in Royapettah, would take her home to Kilpauk. On the way, Aparna mentally went over the evening's meeting and her conversation with Anand later. His apparently quiet and reticent attitude hid a waspish tongue, Aparna recognised. When unleashed, it could slash through one's soul like a whip. She felt ashamed at the sudden tears it had brought in the presence of everyone today. Radhika's effort to assuage and motivate her later had only embarrassed her further. But she had developed a newfound respect for Anand. He had first crushed her pride as one would a paper cup, but instead of chucking it out, had straightened it and placed it on his desk again with his motivating words later. This had driven him further under Aparna's skin, perhaps never to dislodge.

"You have the right attitude for this job and it can take you places," he had said.

She now joyously carried home his concluding words in her heart, as a pigeon does a prized portion of food to its nest, in its beak.

Aparna could not wait to share her happiness at home. Anand's words would cheer her parents too, and reassure them of her security and well-being at work.

The next day, when Anand crossed Aparna's desk on his way to Radhika's cabin, he did not even look her way, while smiling at the others around her. At first surprised, then distracted and impatient while he was inside, Aparna tried to keep her calm, as he would surely come out and talk to her. But when Anand came out, he walked past Aparna without looking her way. It took a few seconds for Aparna to realise he had ignored her purposely. She got up involuntarily and followed him.

"Anand, I would like to have a few words with you," Aparna

                    Shuvashree Chowdhury

said, a step behind him, in the corridor just outside his office. "Please, may I come in?"

"Aparna, I'm busy now," he replied snappishly. "Please speak to Radhika."

Astounded by Anand's curt behaviour, the way he brushed her off without even talking to her, asking her to talk to Radhika instead, hurt Aparna deeply. She felt a lump in her throat, and a desperate need to cry. But her eyes remained dry—though they widened with shock and emotion. She briskly walked back to her desk and looked into the computer screen where she had left a write-up midway, glad to have the comfort of staring into it, to hide her pain from those around. Aparna now firmly decided to distance herself from Anand and retain a formal relation, as expected of any employee.

Chapter 7

Reconstructing her Life

Sujata heard the tone of an incoming message on her cell phone when she was collecting her handbag after security check at Chennai airport. After reinserting her laptop into its bag, while walking towards the departure gate, she retrieved her phone to view the message. It was from Shekhar, she noted, smiling to herself. His steady flow of messages never ceased to cheer Sujata up and insulate her from the real problems of her world. Her friend Manas was still in her life, but after the initial year, the charm of her romance with him had worn thin for Sujata. He did not give her the sense of mature security that Shekhar did. And he had become rather demanding of her time and emotions which she could ill spare now from a demanding new business. Shekhar, on the other hand, with his HR expertise and experience, had become her sturdy guide and mentor in the strategic building of her business. Sujata made all decisions only with his advice.

On her way now to Mumbai for a business meeting, Sujata knew Shekhar would have some witty comments to distract her from the unease of leaving the children in the care of the maids at home. Her parents and in-laws would check in on them, but this awareness could not dispel the guilt and heaviness in her heart from leaving them alone, considering their father was also out of town travelling on work. Her elder son Varun, eight now, had held her hand with a forlorn look at the door, though knowing his mother would not leave them alone overnight unless it was urgent. The younger boy Vishal, at three years, was too young to comprehend the situation and had been playing with their large, friendly Alsatian, Pamela. It was on settling into a cushioned seat at her designated departure gate that Sujata opened Shekhar's message. Its mere presence in her inbox having

Shuvashree Chowdhury

comforted her disquiet, she was startled now by the formal tone of the message.

"Dear friends," she read, sitting upright with a stab of jealousy at not being sent a personal message, "I deeply regret to inform you that my dear wife is no more. She left for her heavenly abode early last morning. We cremated her a few hours back."

It took Sujata a few minutes to swallow the news, shocked and more than a little hurt that Shekhar had not sent her a personal message.

Sujata felt closer to Shekhar than to anyone else and she believed he felt the same. In the five years of their friendship, she had shared everything about herself and her life with him. So now she felt betrayed he had not apprised her of his wife's illness, not even over their prolonged conversation late into last night. In fact, his wife must surely have been ill for a while, Sujata construed, as Shekhar's message did not seem like he was shocked by her death. The impact of Shekhar's wife's death to her own future striking her, trepidation set in. Sujata could not help but think now that, perhaps, Shekhar had allowed their companionship to reach this level of closeness knowing his wife would not live long. Her relationship with Shekhar had been without expectations or promises so far, but with him widowed now, the equations would surely change. She wanted to call him right away, clarify again her stance on being committed to her family for the sake of the children, as she had in the past. But this was not the time for that. Added to his emotional state, his family and friends would be with him. She chose to send him a text message instead.

"I am very sorry to learn of your wife's demise," she typed before switching off her mobile in readiness for her flight. "May her soul rest in peace and may God give you and your sons the fortitude to bear your loss."

The aircraft had barely come to a halt at Mumbai airport when Sujata switched on her cell phone. She expected to see a message or a missed call from Shekhar. But to her dismay, there was neither. By now, having harnessed her troubled thoughts, she felt composed. On the flight, she had recalled how Shekhar had never pressurised her into anything against her wishes, not even to meet or talk to him, let alone to consider leaving her family for him. She realised how unfair it was to him, after how truly considerate he had been, to construe that he would have planned for their relationship to happen ingenuously. They always spoke on the phone when convenient for her, chatted over Skype when she could and the children were asleep, and hardly met, even when in the same town, because she was afraid of being detected by anyone. It was Sujata who had the reins of their friendship in her hand, for her to tighten or loosen according to her convenience. He had always indulged her, afraid that if she felt threatened she might snap all ties with him.

Sujata's husband and their family were well known in the social circles of Chennai, and their reputation widespread in the country due to their paper's image. She did not wish to jeopardise her husband's reputation or that of his paper, and risk her marriage and the emotional well-being of her children by her careless behaviour. Shekhar had always been there for her when she needed him and she needed him a lot emotionally. Over the years, with a busy and emotionally absent husband, Shekhar had become her best friend, guide, mentor, sounding board, and life line. At fifty-two, he was considerably older than her, and she depended on him to guide her through life, mentally holding her hand. He put her needs before his and listened to all her troubles rather than tell her his own. She had undergone much in her thirty-five years. At times, he had hinted at his own turbulent marriage, resulting from his wife's arrogance and dominating nature, but had left it at that. Perhaps he had not mentioned his wife's illness so far, Sujata concluded, to prevent her feeling coerced towards any expectation of a commitment.

Sujata realised the tension she felt now only confirmed that Shekhar had been right in not telling her of his wife's illness. If the news of her death now could cause Sujata paranoia after a five-year friendship, doubt of her absence earlier might have prevented her opening up to Shekhar the way she had. Sujata had been firm on her stance from the start, that she could never leave her husband whatever the provocation. Her children had to have a secure upbringing and future. With her current personal success since setting up her own executive search firm almost four years back, she could provide for them financially, no doubt. But her earnings

   Shuvashree Chowdhury

would never match her husband's in a long time and the family reputation he provided. Moreover, she valued the presence of their father in the lives of her children, however distant and formal, especially since they were boys. It was the fear of her excessive attachment to Shekhar that had kept her from meeting him often, in spite of her constant urge to. She knew their regular meetings, with his pampering her the way he did, and the emotional bonding would push her into throwing away her already dysfunctional marriage for a life with him.

After landing in Mumbai, on the drive to her hotel, Sujata warmly reminisced about her first meeting with Shekhar five years back, in this city. She had been an executive search consultant with the firm she worked for then, and he the human resource director of a multinational company. They had interacted through email and telephone, but the mandate for a chief executive for a new division had required Sujata to meet him in person. Shekhar had been referred to her by his team, who had used her firm's personalised services under their previous boss, much to their satisfaction.

"Sujata Anand understands our needs well," one of the HR managers had told him, "She is familiar with our current organisation structure, style of operation, culture, and role linkages. Therefore, she is the best for our senior-level placements."

Shekhar had emailed Sujata, requesting her to come and meet him in person, in order to discuss the headhunting search plan for this role.

The chief executive for the new division was no doubt a very crucial position for the company but his selection was more important for Shekhar personally. He had to make the best impression on the board of directors, as it had only been a few months since he had joined them. He had called Sujata to discuss and share with her the coordinates of the search position, in collaboration with his board of directors. Then an elaborate search brief would have to be drawn up by her, to be approved by all the directors. The search brief, which might be amended at any time during the search process if the need arose, would detail the job responsibility and reporting relationships of the position, the critical attributes and personal profile required of the candidate, as well as chart the prospective career growth and possible lateral movement for the selected candidate. Sujata understood the outlook and growth pattern in the FMCG industry well and was aware of their selection process and the tight time frame. She had taken with her a long list of companies, both local and international, along with a list of suitable candidates from these companies for this position.

On her arrival at Shekhar's office building, after a brief wait at the reception, followed by cursory exchanges with one of the three HR managers whom Sujata knew well, she was escorted to his cabin. "Mr. Ravindran, Ms. Sujata Anand is here to meet you," Shekhar's secretary announced.

Sujata, over her interactions with Shekhar, had imagined a much older man as the HR director of such a large company. She was surprised to see an unprepossessing forty-five-year-old man with an air of authority and magnetism about him. Shekhar looked up in time from his laptop to catch Sujata's quizzical expression. He smiled at her with a warm glow of familiarity in his eyes, trying to hide his surprise at how attractive she was, with her small yet charming facial features, slender, upright frame draped in a blue and black silk *sari* pinned neatly as a service industry professional, with her hair held in a chignon.

Shekhar said, "Very nice to meet you finally, Ms. Anand. Please sit down."

"Thank you! Nice to meet you too, Mr. Gupta," she had replied, a little conscious about the admiring look in his eyes, as she sat down. "Please call me Sujata."

"I hope you had a comfortable flight, Sujata." Shekhar smiled, noting how vulnerable she looked in person, as compared to the tough, older image he had envisioned. "And I'm Shekhar. Would you like some breakfast?"

"No, thank you, Shekhar," she smiled back, "I ate well on the flight."

An attendant had walked in then, with cups of tea and coffee. Sujata and Shekhar accepted a cup of coffee each. Then they briefly chatted about their professional and family lives, breaking the ice. Sujata found she became comfortable with Shekhar faster than with other clients or candidates she tended to chat amiably with, as if she had known him for a while.

     Shuvashree Chowdhury

Now, even after all this time, Sujata could feel the warmth of Shekhar's gaze on her face as on that first meeting. So much had happened in the last five years, and now his wife's death. But the recollection of how his light brown eyes had borne into her the first time made her feel flushed even now. His gaze had been different, more intimate than any touch she had ever known. It had just been a look, but in the space of the few seconds that it lasted, she had known the warm feeling it generated would never leave her. It was different from any other she had felt, and to this day, she carried its essence wherever she went, as an emotional shield from the cold harsh realities of her life. How she wished things were normal and like before. She would have finished the meeting for which she was carrying with her the assessment reports of the shortlisted candidates for a head of finance position and then spent the evening with him over the usual seafood dinner they both loved.

On checking in at the Kohinoor Continental, a four-star business hotel in Bandra that Sujata's staff had made reservations in, she decided to remain in the privacy of her room till the next morning. Luckily, there was nowhere to go and no one to meet, till the meeting with her client—a retail giant—the next morning at 9.30 a.m. After a shower, relaxed in her night gown, with a cup of hot chocolate, Sujata switched on the television. But none of the news channels she kept flipping through impatiently could quell the uneasiness within her. It was almost like a physical pain. The death of Shekhar's wife, to her surprise, was impacting her deeply. It was as if she had suffered a personal loss. Sujata felt her apprehension at the probable turn their relationship might take now turning into a deep sense of empathy for him.

Sujata wanted to reach out to Shekhar, talk to him, to connect with him, but could not decide between calling and texting him. Also, she was at a loss for the right words in a situation like this. A sadness creeping out of the depth of her heart seemed to be dissipating to every part of her being. Sujata felt overwhelmed by the enormity of her feelings and soon a fear different from the one she had felt earlier gripped her. This fear arose from her recognition of her deep emotional connection with Shekhar. He had become such an integral part of her psyche that, even without communicating with him, she was feeling his pain. Somehow

Sujata was not jealous now at the thought of his heart ache at the death of his wife. After all, Shekhar had been married for thirty years and he had loved his wife dearly, in spite of his growing closeness to Sujata over the last few years.

The next morning, Sujata arose to the alarm on her cell phone at 6 a.m. She checked for a message or perhaps a missed call from Shekhar. But to her dismay, there was none. Perhaps, with his wife's death, guilt over his relationship with her had overtaken Shekhar. Why else would he suddenly be ignoring her, she thought. Quickly showering and dressing, while waiting for her breakfast through room service, she texted Shekhar: "How are you coping? Hope you've slept well."

"I am fine," was the prompt response, "I slept well, thanks so much!"

"I'm glad. Please take care of yourself," she typed back, and then in order to keep the communication casual, in allowing him the space and time to tell her everything at will, she added, "I'm in Mumbai as you know, on my way to the meeting we discussed. I will connect with you after my meeting … later in the day."

The interaction with Shekhar cheered Sujata somewhat and gave her strength for the day ahead. She had reached out to him in the morning, knowing that without the assurance of his presence in her life, she could not face the meeting confidently. Sujata checked out of the hotel, carrying her Hidesign overnight strolley suitcase, along with the laptop bag of the same brand, to the meeting with her. She would be taking the evening flight back to Chennai. The meeting went off well, and her clients were pleased at the thoroughness of her preparation—her long list of companies, and the list of candidates for the position. They handed her a check of rupees five lakhs, as retainer, for exclusivity of their search mandate. After lunch at the client's office canteen, along with two of their directors, Sujata took a taxi to the airport. It was after check-in, when she was seated in the departure lounge awaiting her flight to be announced, that Sujata's mind returned to Shekhar and his wife's death.

"How are you feeling now?" she texted him, "I'm on my way back home. Thanks to your inputs, the meeting went off rather well. They liked the proposed search plan. I even got the retainer check.

                     Shuvashree Chowdhury

"That's great news, Sujata. And I'm fine," he replied. "My elder son is here from Dubai with his wife and the younger one who lives in Delhi is also here with his wife. Then my mother is here too. We have a number of relatives and friends dropping in all the time, so it is a little overwhelming. I will call you soon."

Sujata was relieved to learn that Shekhar's family was with him. She wished she could be there in person to comfort him, and be of some use, but decided on giving him time to deal with his loss. She felt he needed space now so she would wait patiently till he was ready. Sujata boarded her flight with a lingering sadness, her spirits low. On landing at Chennai's Kamraj airport, on telephoning her driver, she was relieved he was outside, waiting to take her home.

As she walked into the second-floor apartment of their four-storey family house, both her sons rushed to meet her. Their innocent faces were bright, and eyes aglow. They tugged at her hands, each trying to get her attention. Bouncing right behind them as usual was Pamela the Alsatian. She grabbed Sujata's attention, overpowering them all with her immense size, her front paws promptly raised and resting on Sujata's shoulder. The two maids came to greet her, one carrying a tray with a glass of water. Sujata playfully pushed Pamela away after a loving pat on her head, and then bent down to hug the boys simultaneously.

As Sujata walked into the living room and sat down with the glass of water, she realised her spirits had soared. All of a sudden, the remorse and sadness, even the longstanding one pertaining to her relationship with her husband who was more often missing from all their lives, had vanished. The children and Pamela gave her so much joy, and were always emotionally available. This warm homecoming to their innocent, earnest love, and this feeling of being needed and missed was what Sujata knew she could not ever trade for a full-time romantic relationship.

Chapter 8

The Fisherman's Cove

It was almost dusk on a late July day. Anand waited in the back seat of his car, in front of Aparna's apartment building at Kilpauk.

His chauffeur had pulled up his black Mercedes by the sidewalk, behind a white Maruti Swift car, whose driver now curiously looked at Anand through the rear-view mirror. Anand dialled Aparna's mobile number.

"I'm here in front of your building," he said urgently.

"My God! You're here already … I thought you'd call before you left home, so that I could get ready," Aparna replied anxiously. "Well, just give me a few minutes."

"It's alright, take your time," Anand said, as he hung up, leaned back on the plush seat, and then turned up the volume of the car stereo with the remote control.

The chauffeur got out, leaving Anand to wait in the car. Sitting alone, his thoughts went out to when he had been either ignoring Aparna at office, or was critical or rude with her. Then suddenly, he would be warm and friendly without preamble. These vagaries in behaviour had been in keeping with the suggestions of his gym friends. All that was not so long ago, six months back perhaps, when he had first set out to get her attention. The recollection of her agonised look, eyes welling with tears, as Aparna barged into his office that afternoon, seeking an explanation for his undue outburst at her at the meeting just concluded, made him wince now. He had distressed her so much over his wanting to get her attention, he thought ashamedly. The full realisation of his desire for her had sneaked up on him only gradually. The intensity of his feelings, as it grew with every small interaction, had shocked him, even as it made him powerless to behave naturally with her.

 Shuvashree Chowdhury

At times, the large shocked eyes brimming with tears when he made a snide remark, her face visibly crumpling, propelled his longing for Aparna. Then the glint of happiness in the same eyes if he praised her, or when she threw her head back and laughed raucously at his words, all, heightened his persistence to win her over. There was no better way Anand had identified, other than his friends' suggestion, to handle his feelings and to make Aparna want him in turn, than to blow hot and cold with her. But it had certainly achieved his goal, he thought, smiling smugly to the strums of the lively Bollywood music that he loved since his college days, on the car stereo. So it had all been worth it, after all. It was one afternoon, a month back, when Aparna came into his office and slapped her resignation on his desk, then burst into tears, which in a bid to hide she was almost running away, that Anand had grabbed her hand. He had held it firmly, till she turned around and looked him in the eye.

"I'm so sorry," he whispered, looking meaningfully into her eyes.

"Sorry?" she repeated, then said, "Do you have any idea to what lengths I've gone to please you with my work? I put in the most time and effort and yet I'm always the target of your temper."

Anand had stood there rooted to the floor, in shock at this sudden turn of events. But he did deserve it, didn't he, he thought desperately. The thought of losing Aparna forever looming large over him, as he looked at the resignation letter on his desk, all he could do was squeeze her hand in an instinctive gesture of pleading. He continued to hold on to her hand tightly, so she would not run away, looking pleadingly into her eyes. Aparna was still emotionally fragile, what with the upheavals in her life since returning to Chennai. There was still the drunken harassment by her ex-husband to deal with, even now after the agonising divorce a few months back. This was from Nikhil's threats to get their son to return to Mumbai, since she had been accorded custody of Kartik, and which in his drunkenness, he would not accept graciously. Thus Anand's guilty look, his pleading, compassionate attitude, after his prolonged coldness, emotionally crumbled Aparna, and brought her as if to her knees.

Aparna squeezed his hand back unthinkingly, and controlling

the sudden urge she felt to hug him, she withdrew her hand and hastily retreated from his cabin, shaken to the core. Anand was desperately worried, but called Aparna only late at night on his way home, rather than talk at work. He wanted to profusely apologise, to convince her to withdraw her resignation. He was afraid if he didn't act promptly, she would leave her job and he would lose her irretrievably. And he could not afford to lose her. Anand became sure of that only now when faced with the harshness of her leaving. His fear prompted him to admit his feelings to her, in justifying his recent erratic behaviour. Aparna's heart already bursting with love for him, she expressed her feelings for him as well. But right after that, they were at a loss as to what to do next. Then it was over two months of emails, text messages, and stolen interactions at the office that had finally brought Anand to Aparna's door this evening, to take her out to dinner.

Suddenly, looking out through the windshield of his car, Anand noticed Aparna standing near the white Swift car parked in front. She was looking about her for his car, her mobile phone to her ear, having dialled his number. She wore a navy blue, long-sleeved knitted top with a black border that clung to her, emphasising her curves, over fitted jeans. He opened the door of the car and waved to her. Aparna walked over quickly, and slid into the car as Anand shifted to the right side, behind the driver's seat. The driver, as if on cue, got behind the wheel and turned on the ignition. As he revved up the engine, Anand looked at Aparna and grinned broadly, and she smiled back, as he put his left arm over her shoulder.

Then instinctively peering into the rear-view mirror, he signalled to the driver to go with a tilt of his head. Anand whispered to Aparna, "He can see us."

Aparna nodded, yet caught and held his hand over her left shoulder in a way that neither of their hands would be visible even if the driver could really see them. Aparna felt the warmth of his palm and was acutely conscious of it, even as she moved closer to him on the seat and fit snugly into the crook of his arms. He playfully ruffled her hair, and they looked at each other simultaneously and grinned broadly, recalling all the events and interactions that had brought them finally to this point in time. Both looked radiant—their skin fresh and hair damp from the

Shuvashree Chowdhury

showers they had just taken, smiles lighting up their world, even as darkness descended upon them as they drove out onto the East Coast Road.

"So where are we going?" Aparna asked casually, not actually caring as long as she was with him and as close to him as they were now.

"I thought we could try a quaint place, where it would be quiet and cosy, with not too many people, what do you think?" Anand asked softly, looking into Aparna's eyes questioningly to which she nodded. He then said to the driver, "Sunil, take us to the place you mentioned, two lanes to the left after the toll tax point, beyond the VGP resort—what's it called—Kipling Café? I looked it up on my iPad as we waited, their website seemed good."

As the driver nodded quietly and stepped on the accelerator, Anand slowly brought his hand down from Aparna's shoulder and onto his lap. Aparna, midsentence, narrating an incident about someone she had recently interviewed, instinctively clutched his hand and held it on his lap, as they continued to talk about her work. It was after a long drive past the VGP resort that Anand, looking outside, asked Sunil where they were. Aparna and he had been so physically aware of each other, engrossed in their conversation, that the driver had driven way beyond where they proposed to go. It was only after asking for directions, taking a U-turn, and driving back down the way they had come for a while, that they found the sign for Kipling Café at the entrance to the lane that housed it. The lane, even though broad, had a rather uneven and bumpy mud road, and the café was flanked by cars parked on either side of the road, marking it easily.

At the entrance, Anand and Aparna were greeted by a petite, North-east Indian hostess, clad in a silk *sari*, who ushered them through a long, covered area, amidst a garden, into the main café. They followed her into another garden edged with thatched hut-like pavilions housing round or square tables, each with seating capacity of six or more people. Amidst all the huts, there was a rather huge one for larger families or groups. The garden café was dimly lit, creating a warm and cosy ambience. In one of the huts, there was a group of westerners and in an adjacent one a large South Asian group—perhaps Japanese or Korean. With Anand leading the way, they walked ahead to check out one of the huts ahead, with a hope of getting a view of the sea beyond it. But there was no visible sign of the sea, not even a breeze or the sound of it. As they walked over to another such hut, they discovered there was no sign of the sea here either. Anand was rather disappointed. Going through their website, he had envisaged a sea view in a quiet and isolated place, with the breeze caressing them softly. That was why he had opted for a quaint place for their first outing.

There was an adjacent rooftop place the café had, they were told, which alone had a view of the sea. But it was now closed. A waiter was trailing them around, having taken over from the lady hostess, answering their queries about the place.

Anand suggested, "Let's have a drink here, now that we're here. Then we can go to another place."

Even as Aparna nodded her consent, they walked back to the centre of the garden. The waiter led them to a table there. They sat down facing each other, their faces aglow from the lamps hanging overhead. But perhaps, the months of longing and the heady rush of emotions now fanned by their physical proximity was also responsible for it. They liked each other immensely, were fiercely drawn both mentally and physically, so it could be judiciously concluded they were already very much in love. The waiter brought them the menu, and handed a copy to each of them. But Aparna set hers down on the table, looking to Anand to order for her. After an absent-minded glance at the drinks menu, Anand ordered a Martini for himself, looking at her questioningly, waiting for her to nod. She did, rather hesitatingly, and he ordered one for her too. Their drinks were brought in quickly. Anand called his driver.

"Sunil, don't go for your dinner yet, as I asked you to. We will be leaving for another place shortly, so you can have dinner somewhere near there."

After a few sips of their well-mixed Martinis, they both slowly relaxed, the tension from their necessarily clandestine meeting and the anticipation which had built over the months easing.

"Instead of looking out for a quiet, secluded place to meet, wouldn't it have been simpler if we had checked into a room somewhere here?" Anand joked, looking at Aparna with an amused expression, even as she replied laughing, "So what, we simply go

   Shuvashree Chowdhury

over to some resort and say we want a room for a few hours?"

"Yeah, why not?" Anand grinned, looking at her unfinished glass, unaware that she did not usually drink—more so now with the memory of her ex-husband's drinking problem still haunting her. She had gone along with his order just to please him. He turned her glass around, and said "Have it from this side, the salt's all here," then he casually added "We'll just say we're horny and we'd like a room. Do you think they'd have a problem with that?"

"Why would they?" Aparna replied smiling, though shocked at his frankness. They had discussed their mutual physical attraction over a long telephone conversation one memorable Sunday afternoon. And Aparna had admitted, after much cajoling, that she wanted him to make love to her more than anything. Suddenly, in reflection of his candid and playful mood, now she added, "Yeah, we could, but what would we say, turning up without even an overnight bag? In any case, I'm going to wait in the car, when you go and conclude the registration formalities."

Anand smiled indulgently at her reciprocation of his outspoken mood, understanding that she was doing it for him, in spite of her inherent shyness. He looked at her glass and noted that she had finished her drink. Perhaps it is what gave her the nerve now, he thought amusedly, as he waved to the waiter hovering nearby, to get their bill. Then they walked out, back through the garden, with Anand's hand comfortably resting on her shoulders. He was a couple of inches taller than Aparna and they were a good match physically. By the time they settled back into the car, Anand had decided where they were going. On the drive to the Fisherman's Cove resort further along the East Coast Road, they sat together in comfortable closeness, holding each other's hands. Aparna drew immense strength and comfort from Anand's touch, and she held Anand's hand as if she would never let it go, even as she chattered nervously. In spite of the air conditioning being on high, Anand felt Aparna's hands sweating profusely. He thought it might be the alcohol or maybe his nearness. He drew her attention to it, and teased her. She became more conscious and shy, trying to justify that it was indeed a very hot day.

Shortly after that, the driver pulled in through the gateway of the Fisherman's Cove resort, drove up the gravel path amidst the garden, and came to a halt at the porch. Anand and Aparna got out, and asked the driver to go and have his dinner. Anand leading the way, the couple, now cosy in each other's company, crossed the open front lounge—a breezy, lively place with a spattering of indistinct noises of people of varied nationalities conversing. They passed the adjacent Seagull Restaurant to the left that overlooked the swimming pool to their right, walking over the narrow pathway through the grassy stretch, and then went down the flights of steep stony stairs. Stopping by the washrooms to freshen up, they proceeded to the open-air restaurant—Bay View Point. It was a picturesque sight on the dimly lit beach, lit by the faint lights coming from some of the open cottages to their left. They descended hand in hand towards it, with the sea breeze caressing them. Aparna and Anand turned to look at each other. They smiled and, clutching each other's hand with renewed passion, strolled into the open-air restaurant.

After a brief wait, they were able to get a table for two, but not at the edge of the beach as they requested. Though they were assured once a table overlooking the beach was available, they would be shifted. Anand pulled out a chair with its back to the beach, drew it up beside the one facing the sea, and signalled to Aparna to sit. They now sat in warm cosy comfort, softly lit by an overhead lamp hung from a tall pole, looking at the dimly lit beach at an angle from each other, so they could also look at each other. The white foam over the soft waves seemed to approach to caress them, along with the breeze. The waiter took their order of a seafood platter and chilled draught beer. They opted for it rather than anything more alcoholic due to the sultry heat even in the pleasant breeze.

After a brief silence to take in their beautiful surroundings, basking in their newfound companionship, Anand and Aparna resumed their conversation over slow sips of beer. He responded to her queries about his personal life. Aparna also filled him in on the latest developments in her life, without his initiation. She mentioned the unwarranted control Nikhil still wielded on her life, due to his rights over their son, that did not allow her the mental riddance of his annoyances. Anand had been evasive with

     Shuvashree Chowdhury

her about his life till now. It was too early for him to trust her implicitly. Also, he had not been emotionally ready to talk of his sour equation with his wife Sujata and the banal one with his elder son, though he was attempting to create a bridge with the younger one recently. But after the Martini they had had earlier and the beer now, Anand had become more open to talk.

"What can I say? My wife Sujata is aloof with me, cold even, after volatile bursts of temper," he said softly, when probed. "The only thing of interest to her is the children and her work. It is my financial contribution to all their lives that keeps us bound, otherwise Sujata makes all efforts to distance me from their lives."

The breeze was gentle and soothing, as it stroked their glowing damp faces, impelled by the few bottles of beer they had consumed between them. It was a sultry evening in late July, with a cloudy, overcast sky. Once the food arrived at their table, with portions of the day's catch, Anand served large helpings of the fish, lobster, crab, and shrimp on to Aparna's plate. Then he placed a small *naan* that was a bread accompaniment to the seafood platter, to the side of her plate. Aparna was deeply touched by Anand's doting gestures that made her heart melt and trickle down to the pit of her stomach. Aparna continued to talk about her life, her marriage, and her family. By now Anand had finished eating, she noticed, while her plate was still full. He signalled to her plate urging her to eat, and then scooped out the remnants of the flesh from the lobster shell for her.

"All we've spoken of since we met is our families, our spouses, things that distress us," Anand snapped, as the waiter cleared their plates and set down another bottle of beer. "I don't really want to hear about that ex-husband of yours anymore. It just makes me so angry. But more than him, I hate to talk about my life. In all this time, we have spoken nothing of ourselves. What a waste of good time."

Aparna suddenly felt distressed and very conscious of how boring she must be. She wondered why she had been talking of such things. Was it because she was seeking to become comfortable and to emotionally connect with the man she loved – usually an inherent need in a woman before she allows physical bonding?

"I was only trying to get to know you better, and to share my thoughts," she said quickly "I'm so sorry to have bored you, and to have spoilt the evening. I feel terrible."

"It's just that people's personal lives are boring to relate and listen to," Anand replied impatiently, his sensitivity obviously disturbed. "We've spent all this time, hours literally, discussing your ex-husband, nothing about us." Then he repeated angrily, "I just don't want to hear of him anymore, you know. It makes me so angry."

Aparna's gaze meeting Anand's was as guilty as she felt. She realised that her stories of her suffering had distressed Anand and spoilt his mood. But she didn't know how to fix it. Suddenly, looking around, Aparna noticed all the other tables were vacant, and it was silent except for the soft lashing of the waves. Only a couple of waiters hovered around, clearing and cleaning the tables. A few people walked on the sand stretch in front of them in the dark. The lights of the restaurant were all turned out by now. Anand asked the waiter to shift their glasses, along with the two bottles of beer he had ordered when told the bar was closing, to a table right by the beach. Aparna and he walked over and sat down, overlooking the sea. In front of them, across the iron grille, a young couple strolled hand in hand. They were visible till quite a distance, as Aparna and Anand looked on, and then dissolved into the sand and the darkness.

"I am a great fan of your work and professional ability," Aparna said softly, looking ahead. "But I'd also like to know you better as a person. That's why I asked you the personal questions, not to judge you in any way. Do you like people to love you for your work alone, not the person you really are?"

"I don't know...." Anand replied uncertainly, staring ahead. Then as Aparna turned to look at him, he said, "I agree it's really nice to know more of each other." Then smiling, he added, "I'm more of a hill person, you know. The sea is alright though."

"Well, I'm a hill person too," Aparna smiled now, "but since the sea is at hand, I've learned to love it too. Keep looking at the waves for a while. Isn't it calming? That's the effect the sea has on you, it soothes your mind. For that matter, staring at any flowing waterbody, like a stream or river, has that effect too."

     Shuvashree Chowdhury

As they turned towards each other, they smiled. Aparna now tilted her head sensuously towards Anand, her hand snugly in his. Then she kissed him softly on the lips, emboldened by the memory of his quick peck on her lips when she had gotten into the car and how his hands had felt her shoulders and spine languorously throughout the drive. Anand responded, softly at first, then surely, and gradually fervently. Aparna reciprocated with candour, tilting her head slightly sideways to savour his lower lip passionately, then kiss the upper lip slowly and imaginatively with her eyes closed. She allowed his tongue to probe hers longingly for a while, sensing his mounting passion with the surging force of his kiss along with the tingling sensation of her acute need for him.

"Hmm … So the girl likes to kiss!" Anand teased.

They had steeled themselves to looking ahead serenely at the waves now slowly growing rough and noisily crashing on the shore.

"Yes, she does," Aparna answered shyly, realising that this was his way of acknowledging he liked what he just got.

"So how many men would you say you've kissed yet?"

"Perhaps, four," she laughed.

"Okay! Would that be four including me?" he persisted.

"Yeah…." she said, not about to give him the real count, "but why do you ask?"

Anand looked at Aparna and smiled. She smiled back, flushed. His hand was now sensuously tracing her waistline, lingering on the slight swell on her sides over the trousers. Then Anand moved his hand, over her hips, caressingly up her middle back, and then intimately over the swell under the elastic of her bra. Aparna felt like he wanted to familiarise himself with every part of her, especially the imperfections. Suddenly he put out a leg playfully in Aparna's direction, and as if on cue, she entwined her left leg around it. Then, slipping her left foot out of her sandals, she slowly stroked his leg over his thin black linen trousers. He brought his hand up over her lap now and she instinctively clung to it, as if to keep from drowning in the wave of passion that was washing over her. Anand felt like electricity was passing between them just as it had in his tracing her body over the fine material of her blue t-shirt.

Anand now bit her ear passionately, shocking Aparna. Then

he grabbed her left hand, lifted the forefinger to his mouth, and playfully bit the top of it, all the while looking at her amusedly. She smiled back indulgently at first, and then suddenly winced with the stabbing pain his teeth digging into the side of her forefinger induced, that melted away with the pleasure it aroused in her heart. Aparna pulled her finger away laughing, with an 'Ahhh!' She noticed the two marks his teeth left, as he promptly pulled her finger towards him and kissed it lovingly as one would a child's that was hurt. She grimaced cheerily, her eyes sparkling from the sheer joy of his playful lovemaking.

"So don't you think we should have just checked into a hotel after all?" Anand grinned, as he took a few large gulps of his beer straight out of the bottle.

Aparna picked up her glass that a waiter came by and topped up just then.

"There will be plenty of time for that," Aparna replied, her head light now, from all the kissing and the copious amount of beer she had consumed, when she hardly drank.

Anand thrust his little finger in her direction hesitatingly, but on cue she gingerly held and brought it up, and took it gently into her mouth. She sensuously sucked on it, but could not help thinking that in addition to his enjoying the sensations her mouth was inducing, he was testing her desire for him, her propensity for passion, their chemistry, and her lovemaking skills. As if in proving her assumption correct, and her having passed his test satisfactorily, Anand tenderly pulled his finger out of her mouth, as from a child's who has fallen asleep sucking it. Aparna's hand accidentally brushed his lap. She felt his hardness, she thought, or perhaps she imagined it. But it sent her into a frenzy of emotions, as if pulled into the rough waves, but trying her best to stay afloat, fighting against the tide of desire that threatened to consume her. She took a deep breath and held it, in slowly floating back into a calmer state, to swim back to the shore of reality with firm mental strokes from the sea of passion, but dripping wet from the core, her heart beating madly.

The soft breeze felt cool now on Aparna's damp face, as she looked squarely in the direction of the sea, the white foam atop the approaching waves shining in the moonlight. She wondered

     Shuvashree Chowdhury

how she had allowed herself to fall so madly in love with her boss, a married man with two children. But now it was late for such contemplation. She had fallen for him hook, line, and sinker. Perhaps he had fallen for her too, though he must still love his wife. Anand turned around, and waved to a waiter to get their bills. He put his arm protectively around Aparna's shoulder as he had done several times in the course of the evening. She felt a fierce desire mounting in her again, and as she turned towards Anand, he returned her intimate gaze with longing in his eyes. She spontaneously sought his lips. This time, he kissed her passionately, his tongue probing, tasting, his desire at first flustering, then elating Aparna. But her mind soon sent out an alarm, not to be pulled back into the vortex of yearning she had just about retrieved herself from, by frantically swimming ashore mentally.

Aparna gently withdrew from his kiss, leaving Anand breathless, wanting more, and bewildered at her withdrawal. She kissed his upper lip languorously, to his surprise, and then the lower lip swiftly. Then she pulled away, suddenly consciousness of the waiter coming up behind them with the bill.

"No, this girl does not like to kiss!" Anand said sullenly, "I thought she did."

Aparna remained quiet for a while, immersed in thought, looking at the beach which was now deserted. Then she softly asked, "Why do you say that? … You just said that I like to kiss, which I do."

"Well, I thought so when we kissed earlier," Anand replied. "But the way you just pulled away, I don't think so."

"I'm very conscious of someone watching us. We are right out in public view, aren't we? And then the waiters are around … Just look behind and see."

Anand turned just in time to notice a waiter walk up to them with the bill folder. He settled the bill, and by the time the waiter returned with the charge slip, they had drained their glasses, leaving half a bottle of beer on the table and were ready to leave. On their way out, climbing the stairs back up to the poolside garden, Aparna excused herself to visit the ladies room. When she came back out on the stairway, she found Anand some way up the stairs in the garden. She went up, slinging her handbag cross-body, gaze fixed on him. He languidly assessed her, his look arousing a sensuous and cosy feeling in her from the intimate moments they had shared. Once she reached him, Aparna instinctively held out her arms. With just a moment's hesitation, Anand engulfed her in a bear hug. He crushed her body to his, as she felt him right down to her soul. They stood like that a few moments and Anand kissed Aparna lightly, then playfully bit her left cheek. She winced in painful delight, laughed, and teasingly jerked her face away from his hankering lips.

They climbed the rest of the stairs together. Anand's hands lingered over her shapely behind. She delighted in his touch, in the realisation that he couldn't keep his hands off her. Once in the car, seated on his right side now behind the driver, Aparna moved closer to Anand. She marvelled at her level of comfort with him, as he placed his right hand over her shoulder.

"Don't you think we should have just checked into a hotel this evening?" Anand asked softly, for the third time yet, turning to look into Aparna's eyes.

She nodded, looking away, for it was all she could do to prevent herself kissing him right then, after seeing the look in his eyes with the flaming desire for her in it.

"So then let's talk about how we'd please each other when we meet. What would you like me to do to you … and I'll tell you as well."

"It's better not to talk of it, so we may be spontaneous when we do meet again." Aparna replied. With a shy smile, she added, "I'll like everything and you will too, I am sure of that. So, don't worry."

"Hmm … so I will?" Anand asked playfully.

Suddenly, she felt his hand caress her shoulder, then slip down her shoulder to her breasts. A lingering stroke of her right breast, driving her mad, and he moved his hand back up to her shoulder. Then with a look at the rear-view mirror, he signalled to Aparna with his eyes that the driver would see them through it. But wanting more, she placed her bag upright over her lap, covering her up till her throat. Then she took Anand's hand and placed it on her breast. Anand looked at her and smiled, then abruptly slipped his hand into her top and inside her bra. His forefinger and thumb

    Shuvashree Chowdhury

encircled the taut and erect peak of her nipples, making all her senses tingle. He removed his hand just as abruptly.

Anand wanted to see if Aparna was ready to go all the way with him. Now that he knew her desire for him, he was willing to wait. Half the pleasure was in the anticipation.

Chapter 9

Love and Alcohol are Potent Analgesics

Shekhar Ravindran had fallen in love with Sujata, as he always told her, over their first meeting at his office in Mumbai. It had been five years. One thing had led to another since their first meeting, till he had become too involved with her. Sujata's vulnerability, youth, and troubled marriage had made it impossible for him to resist her. But there was no denying his love for Aneesha, his wife of over thirty years. He had never denied his love for Aneesha either to himself or to Sujata. He had, however, preferred to maintain a dignified silence about his marital relationship in his interactions with Sujata. Aneesha's breathing her last in his arms had shattered him, crushed his soul, and left a brutal wound in his heart.

After Aneesha's death, Shekhar had sent Sujata a group text message, unable to bring himself to talk to her so soon. He felt guilty towards Sujata, just as he had about his liaisons with her, and was miserable. In time, he would tell her all, but not now. He was glad that Sujata was not inundating him with a deluge of calls and text messages right now. She respected his need for space and time to mourn, and yet had conveyed to him she was there for him when he was ready and needed her. His two sons, along with his mother, were still with him at his residence in Mumbai, but the sprawling apartment still felt empty. They had all come for Aneesha's last rites, and would stay a couple of weeks more. But in spite of their presence, and with Sujata still occupying his mind, he felt a vacuum.

It was now that Shekhar perceived how love tends to remain pigeonholed in one's heart, each niche unique. When one slot is perforated and emptied, its hollowness hurts sharply. Then love from other slots cannot overrule the pain radiating from the wounded one. One has to suffer the emptiness left by that lost love till it heals with time, and the void fills with other existing or a new love and the pain wanes. Shekhar had never discussed Aneesha with Sujata, because he could not bring himself to dishonour what they had shared for thirty years. Moreover, how could he tell Sujata of Aneesha's acute drinking problem? It would have been so unfair to Aneesha. Shekhar had never believed Aneesha would actually succumb to her drinking, so much so that it would kill her one day, for she had been a strong woman physically. He had not considered the possibility that she would allow the tunnel of illness she had walked into deliberately to close in on her finally. Her sudden illness, the acuteness of it, her death, all in a few days, had left him broken.

* * *

Shekhar's family trip to the hills in Northeast India last October had been the beginning of the end for Aneesha.

She had been so happy and excited, when their younger son called to say "Mom … Anna (elder brother) and I, along with our wives, have planned this trip. It's been such a long time, since the entire family has taken a vacation together."

Then they had all met at Kolkata, where they spent a couple of days reminiscing the good days of when Shekhar had been posted there. From Kolkata, they had taken a flight to Bagdogra, from where they had hired a car for the five-hour drive to Darjeeling. On the drive uphill, Aneesha had felt slightly breathless and queasy, so they had stopped a number of times for her to catch her breath over cups of tea. She had also used these breaks to satiate her craving for the brisk puffs of cigarettes she had ironically made her emotional lifeline, in spite of her damaged lungs.

Shekhar had given up trying to restrict Aneesha, as hers was an advanced case of alcohol abuse, much worsened with endless smoking. His efforts to save her from physical decay only infuriated her lately, and led to heated quarrels between them. Aneesha blamed Shekhar, for his long absences, either out of town and even the country, for her dependence on the soothing companionship she had found in alcohol. Once their sons had grown up and were at college, Aneesha's reliance on alcohol took over her need to be needed. Shekhar, overcome with worry about his wife, unable to bear the stress, conversely started avoiding Aneesha. Her binges, followed by drunken brawls with him, frazzled him out. Helpless against the vicious circumstances, liquor wheedling Aneesha away from him slowly but surely, he began to wish her problem away by feigning its non-existence. They shared the house, even a bed, but love became a casualty, alcohol and smoke eroding the bond steadily.

A family trip is exactly what would invigorate Aneesha, Shekhar had thought, as he had promptly confirmed their going on the vacation their sons had planned. Watching Aneesha, as she sat flushed, the cool wind on her face, seeming happy and relaxed, Shekhar was happier than he had been in a long time. By now, his interactions with Sujata, which initially felt like tiny bursts of fresh air in the putrid stuffy room of his life, had settled as if into a cool and steady breeze coming in through a seaside house window. Yet there was something missing in Shekhar's life, like you miss sunshine during constant rain in the rainy season. As much as you love the rain and enjoy its earthy smell and watery landscapes, comparable to his associations with Sujata, you soon miss the equilibrium in your life along with the secure warmth that sunshine provides—as his steady equation with Aneesha had been.

Shekhar's inability to fully enjoy the light from the newfound prism in his life through Sujata, was from his fear that the light was steadily fading out of Aneesha's life. It was not that Shekhar felt guilty in the conventional way, now that his feelings were steadier than ever for Sujata. He merely felt regretful that life had shown him a fresh rainbow after a long deluge, while leaving Aneesha's flooded with murky water, steadily clogging her lifeline. Aneesha was physically strong, had always been ever since they met at a tennis training academy in Mumbai when they were in college. She had also been a horse-riding enthusiast. But even the strongest gutter walls corrode with a continuous flow of chemical refuse, as her liver and gut did due to flooding with alcohol, leading to her end.

On their drive to Darjeeling, Aneesha had felt nauseous a lot, but on the drive down to Bagdogra on the return trip, she was

    Shuvashree Chowdhury

horrifically sick. They had to halt a number of times. Yet Aneesha insisted on taking the flight to Kolkata, and then the longer flight back to Mumbai the same day. This was in spite of Shekhar's suggestion that they halt in Kolkata. At the airport, he had insisted that she see a doctor. But Aneesha, strong-willed as always, persisted in returning to Mumbai that evening, as planned. And Shekhar allowed it, as after taking pills for nausea, she seemed strong enough to board the flight. She barely ate anything on the flight and slept right through from the effects of the medications, her two sons seated on either side of her. In Mumbai, she seemed fine the night they arrived, except for the weariness which was expected. Shekhar thought it had only been the high altitude that had affected Aneesha's health.

But the morning after, Shekhar was woken early by the sound of Aneesha wheezing noisily. Then even before she could sit up, she started vomiting. This was accompanied by acute breathlessness. Shekhar sprang up, alarmed. He held her up, supporting her with both arms. Then promptly freeing one hand, he dialled their family doctor from the bedside phone. By the time the doctor arrived, Aneesha was wheezing uncontrollably along with sporadic vomiting. Their two sons, awake by now, had rushed to Aneesha. They hovered around her, alarmed and helpless, not having ever seen her so sick, in all their lives. Shekhar was advised to rush Aneesha to the hospital, as her condition was critical. He quickly called for an ambulance.

Aneesha was detected with pneumonia, and treatment was started promptly. She had been diagnosed with liver cirrhosis a year back and that complicated her recovery. The cirrhosis was much aggravated by her refusal to stop drinking or take any precaution. Aneesha would not even change her eating habits. Shekhar, as he kept watch at her bedside, now recalled how rotund she had become over the years since the children came along. But in the last few years, she had lost a lot of weight, and developed a dried-up, yellow look. The skin of her neck had become loose and wrinkled and her old *kurtas* that she normally wore at home, hung about her loosely. Their collars seemed three or four sizes too large. Lately her hands trembled continually, even when she tried to light her cigarettes and he was forced to help her at it. Shekhar had helplessly watched

Aneesha killing herself over the years. She was too adamant to listen to his admonishments, rather was defiant, as if they propelled her to rebel against him. Perhaps it was her deep-rooted anger at his neglect and the time Shekhar had spent away on work lifelong that had led to the loneliness she had tried to allay with drinking. It was as if, in desperation, Aneesha had made a wild dash to the finishing line of her dark, maze-like race of life. She had added many hurdles herself by smoking, drinking, and unhealthy eating habits, that had challenged her, even though kept her humoured in life's lonely race. Aneesha breathed her last, tired, weary, and gasping, but in a state of peaceful happiness from the last burst of energy she had spent on the vacation with her family, collapsing on the finishing line of her life's race in Shekhar's arms.

* * *

It was late evening when Sujata waited in the parking area of Amethyst, a popular resto-café in Chennai, not far from her office in Nungambakkam, for Shekhar's call. After work, she had just met up with a few of her ex-colleagues over coffee. They had all sat at a large table on the sweeping verandah overlooking the garden. Shekhar was to reach the Gymkhana Club where he was staying the night, then call her. She would then drive over to meet him, and only then return home. It was already late and so she would meet him only briefly. His flight had landed at its scheduled time, but the drive from the airport in the office hour traffic, amidst all the construction work of flyovers on the way, was causing this delay. Sujata, restless by now, called Shekhar a couple of times. Two of her friends waited along with her, so she would not have to wait by herself. The three women strolled on the pathway overlooking the garden and chatted.

Sujata had called home earlier, and told the children she would be late and that they must finish dinner and go to bed. She spoke to her two maids to ensure that everything was under control. Anand was, as usual, out of town, so she owed him no explanations. Even as she tried to concentrate on what her friends were saying, Sujata's mind raced to Shekhar with a mixture of excitement and trepidation. This was the first time she would be meeting him

                    Shuvashree Chowdhury

since receiving the text of his wife's demise a few months back. She had first waited for him to call her when he felt ready. Then they had spoken extensively and he filled her in on the details leading to Aneesha's sudden death. After that, Sujata made it a point to check on him every other day and had helped him grieve.

The next time Sujata called him, Shekhar told her he had just about reached the club and she could come over now. Sujata politely eased herself out of the company of her friends and signalled to her driver waiting nearby in the car. She got into the car and instructed him to take her to the club. At the Gymkhana club, she had just got out of the car at the front porch, after the long gravel-path drive, when Shekhar walked up to her briskly. It was an awkward moment, as they first shook hands, then he gave her a light hug followed by a peck on her cheek. Then as they walked down the lobby, on the way to his room, Sujata could not help thinking of what Anand would think of her going to Shekhar's room. Then she recalled the text messages she had seen on Anand's phone while they were holidaying in Munnar. The acute pain and betrayal she had felt rushed to mind. She felt more resolute now.

Sujata followed Shekhar up the steps. He had lost weight, she noticed, and this made him look much younger and more athletic. She sized him up as he walked with purposeful strides ahead of her, marvelling at his agility at his age. She took in his salt and pepper hair, the upright shoulders tapering firmly to the waistline and his taut buttocks that were emphasised with each stride. It struck her again how attracted she felt to him. She followed him into his suite. Inside, the lights were soft and Shekhar asked her to make herself comfortable on the sofa. He walked across to the next room, and, from the bedside table, lifted the telephone off its cradle. Sujata sat down awkwardly on the sofa, looking around, wondering how she should behave. This was the first time they were meeting since his wife's death. Should she say some words of condolence or talk casually as she always did before?

While Shekhar spoke on the phone, Sujata decided she would use the washroom. So, signalling to him, she walked across the large bedroom towards it and pulled the door shut louder than she intended, behind her. She used the toilet seat, keeping in mind to put it back up, then washed her face and wiped it dry with a paper napkin from a box. As she brushed her hair, Sujata noticed, lined between the mirror and washbasin, a Ponds talcum powder container, a small jar of Nivea cream, a white comb, and a black bottle of Polo eau de toilette. Beside these, there was a glass tumbler containing a razor, along with a tube of shaving gel, tooth paste, and a tooth brush. Sujata noticed every item minutely. She felt closer to him as she stepped out, as if she knew him more intimately now. Shekhar had completed his call, perhaps to his mother or his sons, Sujata assumed, and was standing beside the bed. Sujata walked up to him and, in spite of her awkwardness, the loss of appropriate words, feeling emotionally closer now, she flung her arms around him. She hugged him tight as she often did her Alsatian Pamela or her sons and no one else—not Anand for sure, not even Manas whom she had been intimate with. After a few moments of her holding him close quietly, Shekhar pulled away slowly. He walked over to his laptop bag on the study table. He retrieved a large laminated photograph and, with a sad glance at it, handed it to Sujata.

"This is Aneesha," he said softly, "when she was younger."

Sujata was awed by the radiance in Aneesha's fair-complexioned face and eyes, emphasised by the sky-blue silk *kurta* she wore. She noticed the short crop of thick, black hair over the sharp features, and the sturdy build held upright by the firm set of her shoulders.

"She was really pretty ... and smart too," Sujata said softly, still looking at the picture closely, surprised she did not feel the slightest tinge of jealousy, yet there was a constriction in her chest as her heart went out to Shekhar.

Shekhar nodded and continued to look at Aneesha's picture. Then abruptly shifting his gaze away, he took it and replaced it in the folder of his bag. He now signalled to Sujata with his hand to follow him as he walked briskly over to the adjacent room. They sat down on the sofa. Sujata noticed Shekhar's face was still a mask of pain. She felt overwhelmed by her own emotions now as with his. It was a culmination of the last weeks of texting Ponds talking to him, absorbing his pain. Unable to stop herself, Sujata leaned towards him and hugged Shekhar tight again. She clung to him in a bid to steady her overwrought nerves. After a few moments, he

       Shuvashree Chowdhury

hugged her back with equal fervour, his face nestled into the groove of her shoulder for a few brief moments. Then she was jolted when he disengaged himself and placed his hands on her waist. They moved upwards, seeking her breasts, caressing them ever so gently through her *kurta*.

Sujata felt her breasts jump into alertness, and their tips tauten and thrust prominently against the limp silk. She pulled back with a gasp to look into Shekhar's eyes questioningly, but not so far as to forego the wild sensation that his hands continued to arouse inside of her. She noticed the burning desire in Shekhar's light brown eyes, even as she stared back awestruck and excited by its ferocity. The fire he had kindled burst into flame, consuming her with desire. Sujata leaned towards him, seeking Shekhar's lips hungrily. He took her mouth, melting it with the tenderness and brutality they sought in unison. His tongue probed deep inside Sujata's mouth, as if searching her soul for the passion that was in his. She helped him discover her desire, pushing her tongue hard against his and then hungrily devouring his lips. Shekhar's hands, from caressing her breasts over her *kurta*, had slipped under it, unbuttoning the top front buttons. He took firm possession of what he felt was his under the bra that he had flipped over upward. The tips of her breasts were so taut by now, like buttons under Shekhar's fingers that rang the bell to their passion now commencing.

Slowly stealing his mouth from hers, Shekhar moved his head down to her left breast to take the tip in his mouth and suck it gently, before shifting to the other one. Sujata gasped aloud at the onslaught of pleasure, having allowed his mouth to leave hers reluctantly, his lips more pleasurably engaged now. Shekhar adroitly sucked and rolled his tongue over the tips of each of her breasts in quick succession. She wanted to cry out to him to never stop, each time that he peeled his mouth away to move it to the other breast, or bring it up to her mouth in turns. Sujata had never felt like this, this rise of what felt like hot molten lava from her body and soul. She hadn't even known she was capable of feeling like this. It takes the right man, she thought ecstatically, to find and ignite a woman's passion.

Shekhar slowly retrieved himself from her, looking at Sujata fiercely, his flaming desire scorching him by now. He sat down on the adjacent white sofa, unbuttoning his shirt, as she looked at him curiously, the flame in her eyes so strong that they could set him ablaze. He drew Sujata by hand and gestured to her to sit on his lap, even positioning her on top. She sat facing him now. Shekar gently peeled off her beige silk *kurta*, over her hands that she extended upwards, and then his lips locked on hers. He kissed her bare breasts, after nearly ripping off its lace black hood, unhooking it from behind, making her spine tingle and her whole body quiver like a leaf in the wind. Shekhar lifted her off his thighs slowly, holding Sujata at the waist, and gestured to her to pull off her black silk *salwar*.

After she stepped out of it deftly, leaving it in a heap on the carpeted floor, he gently peeled off her black Lycra panty. He then gestured to Sujata to sit back on his lap. To her amazement, Shekhar manoeuvred himself right into her centre through his already unzipped ribbed grey trousers. Sujata shuddered at the shooting thrill inside her now, as she clung to Shekhar, her arms around him, grappling with the excitement of the sensation inside of her. Then caressing Sujata's bare breasts with his shirtless taut chest, Shekhar gently lifted himself on and off the sofa, moving inside her rhythmically. He pushed her upward gently with both his hands at her waist, her legs now wrapped firmly around him, to move with him to his tempo.

Their bodies were in perfect synchronisation, for what seemed only a few moments, till they reached the culmination of their passion simultaneously, in a quick shuddering burst. Sujata hugged Shekhar, clinging to him as if she were trying to retrieve herself from a whirlpool of sensations and emotions. Then slowly disengaging, she got off Shekhar's lap to stand. He stood up too, and stepped out of his trousers. Shekhar, drawing her by hand, with not a thread between them now, they quietly walked to the bathroom together holding hands. Shekhar ran the shower and they stood under the warm water, clinging to each other under its force. Then they gently lathered each other with shower gel. After wrapping themselves in two large white towels, they stepped out of the bathroom. They quietly dressed, picking up their clothes scattered about the room.

Sujata, quickly drying off her damp hair in spite of using a shower cap, reapplied her lipstick and did her hair as it had been before. She consciously tried to make it look as if nothing had happened between them. The driver should not find anything amiss, though she was definitely not the same Sujata who had walked in. She was profoundly changed in ways she could not define. Shekhar, with his damp hair plastered to his head, dressed in his nightwear, a white *pyjama* and *kurta*.

"Hope you're not getting late," Shekhar asked suddenly, sounding worried.

"I am, but I can wait some more," Sujata replied, "Perhaps another fifteen minutes."

"Would you like me to order dinner or perhaps some snacks or a drink?" Shekhar asked somberly, his tone surprising her. "I have a bottle of Scotch here that I'm going to help myself to. Would you like some, with soda?"

Sujata nodded, "Scotch would be good, but I don't have the time to wait for the snacks."

After Shekhar returned to her with two glasses, he handed one to Sujata and sat down beside her on the larger sofa, not the one they had just preferred to the bed. They quietly sipped their drinks now, two people who did not find the need for words of companionship after the deep intimacy they had just shared. The Scotch slowly steadied their nerves, relaxed somewhat by the warm shower, quelling their awe over their lovemaking that established how much they had hungered for each other.

This was the first time that their bodies had been in unison, in spite of their souls already being so since long. It had been the build-up of passion since being connected deeply through prolonged dialogue. It had been beautiful, as love making is when not merely a physical act, but a connection between two souls. Sujata's and Shekhar's intimacy was unique now, in that two people, without reservation and inhibition, had resorted to share their pain through their bodies, too overwhelmed for words to suffice.

Sujata, knowing what she did about her husband's involvements with other women, especially the current one Aparna, squashed any guilt she might have felt over her intimacy with Shekhar now. When a woman seeks a union outside of her marriage or steady relationship, she has assuredly, prior to such a breach, dispelled her guilt by justifying her hurt, whether perceived or real from her partner. Men, on the other hand, may transgress without any trace of a lack of devotion from their partners, even shouldering the burden of their guilt they might try to unsuccessfully squash.

Shekhar's face was like a mask now, as he looked penetratingly into Sujata's eyes. She could sense that the most intimate last half hour of her life was now clearly pitched against Aneesha's ghost, with Shekhar's guilt and grief. Sujata realised this powerful burst of passion in him was in reality the zenith of weeks of pent-up emotions, his loss, and pain, not merely Shekhar's hunger for her.

Sujata did not regret a moment of what had happened between them. Shaken at first by the raw power of his passion so soon after his wife's death, she was mature enough to comprehend that its pulse was steeped in his pain that can be a potent aphrodisiac. Pain releases endorphins from the body, which try to block the signal of physical distress to the nervous system. The same kind of endorphins are released during exercise and after sex, creating happy and positive feelings about life. Shekhar had found an outlet for his grief, through his undeniable attraction for Sujata. She did not grudge him an outlet for his agony, rather had given in wholeheartedly to the bodily pleasure denied her in the last years of her marriage. Sujata stretched out her hand and took Shekhar's. She squeezed it in a bid to reassure him, then placed his clasped hands on her lap, looking into his sunken eyes. His face looked older now, haggard, with dark circles under his eyes, the crow's feet more pronounced. Perhaps his physical weariness at the end of his long day in his current grieving state had heightened from the frenzied burst of emotion and passion.

Shekhar had by now finished one drink and was on to the next, while Sujata was still halfway through the first. As Sujata continued to look at him, she noticed his face contort afresh in pain.

"She's gone away," he said abruptly, and then a steady flow of tears rolled down his cheeks to her amazement. "And she is never coming back. I never believed till the very end that she would give up. Aneesha was such a strong woman."

Sujata was shaken to her roots by the visible outpouring of his grief that he made no attempt to hide, allowing the tears to roll undeterred. She had always known him to be strong and emotionally tough, though he was proving her right on her belief that the tougher one is perceived to be, the softer they might be at the core. He was the one she had depended on emotionally, who had become her anchor, her sense of balance and well-being. Now she took on his role, even though she felt unequipped to handle his powerful emotions and felt emotionally fragile herself. But Sujata reminded herself that she had just reciprocated the stronger physical outpouring of his sentiments in equal measure, remarkably and with ease, so she could handle this too. She had never met a man letting down his guard, displaying emotions as Shekhar was doing. The fact that he was so much at ease with his feelings and his grief, that he did not find the need to hide it, gave him in Sujata's mind a newfound respect. Strong, confident men have the ability to demonstrate their feelings without fear of being judged or ridiculed.

"Aneesha was physically very strong ... from the start," Shekhar repeated, then added ruefully, "She played tennis in her younger days and basketball too. She was always athletic and had a strong constitution, but then allowed alcohol to get the better of her. She died panting for breath in my arms at the hospital, the morning after we admitted her. I called for the doctor, when she started puking and gasping for breath, after she seemed fine the evening at the hospital. But by the time the doctor got to us, she was gone. I thought she would pull through ... never imagined she'd succumb, and breathe her last right over my shoulder that I did not quite lend her through our years together. It might have made a difference, you know."

"But how did she take to alcohol?" Sujata probed softly.

"You see, it was always easily available at home, though I wasn't," Shekhar replied in a deeply regretful tone. Sujata's gentle probing and attentive listening, both skills she had honed from being a headhunter, encouraged him to spill his heavy heart to her, as he continued. "The liquor cabinet was always well-stocked as we entertained a lot at home, a lot of it work-related. After our sons left home for college, she had a lot of time on her hands. We had excessive domestic help for the two of us. Then she had a close girlfriend who drank a lot too. Whenever the two got together, either at our place or hers, they went into drinking binges. The friend passed away from an acute condition of liver cirrhosis years back. But Aneesha could not control her urges in spite of seeing what alcohol had done to her dear friend. On the contrary, since the friend's death, she relied more heavily on alcohol for companionship, instead of finding a constructive creative pursuit."

"Couldn't you have taken her to a deaddiction centre ... or done something?"

"I did suggest that but she never agreed to it, insisting she was in control. I feel very responsible for not being around and not giving her more time, but then work was that demanding and I travelled so much."

"You mustn't hold yourself responsible for what happened."

"Aneesha was such a strong-willed woman," Shekhar said, then continued sullenly. "We should not have gone on that trip to Darjeeling. She was physically very weak, but still insisted on going. The excessive cold, especially as she was not used to it in Mumbai with its coastal climate, got to her lungs. It caused the infection for which high doses of antibiotics were required. Her liver could no longer withstand this bout of contradictions it was confronted with and refused to cooperate. Finally, it gave up on her, like she had given up on me, this time irrevocably ... leaving me with guilt and regret."

Sujata looked on at Shekhar's agony, torn by it herself. It surprised her that she was not jealous that he had loved Aneesha so fiercely till the end. She comprehended here and now that it was possible to love two people equally, just as she had never stopped loving her husband Anand, whatever his transgressions. As you grow older and more mature through experiences and exposure, you realise that life is not all black and white, rather much is grey. You understand that what you considered in early life as farfetched is, in fact, plausible. And that love can be compartmentalised, but it can be unique and insulated in each slot, if you allow it to. She noticed that Shekar was looking rather tired and sleepy, but he was calm. The two drinks he had had assisted her efforts to soothe his nerves by allowing him to speak his heart. Sujata stood up and looked at her watch. She was startled to see that it was well past 10.30 p.m.

Shekhar rose too. Sujata hugged him, trying to infuse her

            Shuvashree Chowdhury

strength in him. Then they walked out the door together. Shekhar walked Sujata downstairs and waited till her driver showed up. After she was seated inside the car, Shekhar kept looking into Sujata's eyes through the glass window, as though he might never see her again. He abruptly knocked on her window urgently, signalling to her to roll it down, and then he looked into her eyes with his piercing gaze.

"Call me when you reach home," he said softly.

Sujata could almost see his heart reach out to hold her back as he spoke, and she realised that he was finding it rather difficult to let her go now after the intimacy.

On the drive back, Sujata could not help hoping the driver had not the slightest idea of what had transpired in the time that he was napping under the spread of trees in the parking. He had seen Shekhar in his *kurta* and *pyjamas* and had heard the alcohol and tears-induced tender and intimate tone of voice he had used with Sujata and had been unable to hide. But surely in all these years, from proximity to her family, the driver knew the lives of the rich and reputed were not necessarily as happy and contented as one might imagine.

Chapter 10

Making Love versus Sex

Aparna hurriedly walked into the lobby of Savoy Hotel, on Cathedral Road, handing over her car keys to the valet. She was late coming from Nungambakkam which was just down the road, where she had been interviewing a reputed writer at the Park Hotel's Leather Bar. His book had just been launched at the banquet hall in the hotel's basement. Anand was to meet her, first over drinks at the Bamboo Bar at Savoy Hotel, after his regular workout at the gymnasium. He had opted for the one here over the Park Hotel's this evening, as it would be more inconspicuous. Then their plan was to go up to the room he kept reserved all year round for unplanned official guests.

Aparna knew Anand was already at the hotel, as he had called when he drove in to say, "I'm late too, so I'll skip the workout and wait here at the bar."

Aparna walked to her right, past the reception area. Then crossing the room elevators to the left, she sauntered past the florist and the South Indian restaurant Malgudi to the left of the corridor, and walked right into the Bamboo Bar. Then casting a furtive glance around, she was surprised to see that Anand was not there. She dialled his mobile number hurriedly, trying not to allow dejection creep into her, after the weeks of elated anticipation towards this meeting.

"Come on up to the room," He said. "I've ordered the drinks here."

Aparna walked back towards the lobby, took the elevator to the eighth floor, and walked down the corridor. She identified the room, after asking a passing waiter. Anand answered the bell. Then, as Aparna stepped inside feeling rather anxious, he gave her a casual hug. Anand then led the way to the sofa at the far end of the room, by the window. In front lay his half glass of whisky on the round glass table. Aparna followed him, feeling somewhat self-conscious. There was a kind of formality even now, she thought, as though they were in his office.

"I've ordered a gin and tonic for you," Anand said in a serious tone, as she sat down facing him. Then noticing the unease etched clearly on her face, as with every passing emotion that he could usually detect, he added, "I hope that's alright. The waiter should bring it up any moment now."

Aparna nodded, feeling nervous and rather awkward, wondering why she should feel thus after the beautiful evening they had spent together at the Fisherman's Cove. They had been so close then and he had not kept his hands off her, Aparna recalled.

When the doorbell rang, Anand promptly got up and walked over to answer it. The waiter came in, balancing a tray with two glasses, each of small pegs of gin. There were also two cans of tonic, and there was a glass bowl with lemon wedges. Anand knew Aparna abhorred drinking, but since she seemed so uptight, he thought he ought to coax her into a drink or two to get her to relax. Over several conversations, he had managed to convince her that a few drinks would not make her a raging alcoholic like Nikhil.

Aparna got up and stood looking out at the view enclosing the garden, through the window. Once the waiter left, Anand poured a can of chilled tonic into a glass of gin on the tray kept on the side dashboard, squeezed lemon wedges into it, and handed it over to her. He returned to his sofa seat and picked up his glass, while she took a large sip of her drink, still standing. Its stiffness burned its way down her throat, infusing mental strength in her immediately. After a few more gulps of her drink, Aparna felt a sudden surge of calmness. Yet it was awkward being here in the room with Anand this way. He looked at her contemplatively, his eyes boring into hers, as if to gauge the intensity buried in its dark well. It was similar to the way he tended to gaze at her penetratingly, while she kept chattering, seated behind his office desk.

"Come, let's sit on the bed," Anand said spontaneously, getting up and sitting on the bed comfortably, with his legs stretched out in front of him.

Aparna followed him quietly, obediently, taking her unfinished glass, which she placed on the bedside table on the other side of the bed. It was as though he were the boss even here and now. She then climbed atop the bed and sat alongside him over the white sheet, with her legs folded under her. They looked ahead quietly, Aparna unseeingly, at the television on the front wall. The CNN news reader, an attractive young lady with blue eyes, filled their awkward silence with her rendition of the news. Anand put his hands around Aparna's shoulder instinctively, with the ease which he was used to by now, and in which she found such a cosy sense of security. A warmth emanating from her heart or maybe her body, Aparna was not really sure of its origin, rushed to engulf her now. This was obviously also because of the potent drink she was still working her way through diligently at his behest. Aparna turned to face Anand sidewards, as she sat in the groove of his arms resting casually over her shoulder. She was unable to gauge from his staid expression what he might be thinking.

Anand turned to her. His look was charged with desire and Aparna instinctively arched to offer him her mouth. He kissed her at first with a tentative deep peck right into her lower lip, and then slowly he withdrew. Aparna, the potency of the drink making her bold, moved closer to him. She placed her arms around Anand's neck and, tilting her head slightly upward, her lips softly curled round his upper lip. Anand, stunned at her initiative but pleasantly so, promptly took his left hand off her shoulder and, turning towards her, wrapped his arms tightly around her. He returned her kiss with as much fervour, and then more, his tongue probing hungrily into her mouth, seeking hers, and then devouring it. Aparna reciprocated with all of the longing she was capable of, even as she fought not to melt into oblivion with the sheer pleasure his tongue was wrecking on her. This is what Anand had imagined the day she had burst into tears in his office, and he had kept that dream torch burning steadily, till it was now a blazing fire in both of them.

Aparna kissed him with a burning desire, by now sitting astride his thighs. Then abruptly she kneeled beside him, her hands going up to gingerly touch and then run her fingers through his thick black hair, greying on the sides. Anand pulled her closer, her breasts now squashed against his broad chest. She peeled her mouth away from his, to gently kiss his left eye and then more tenderly the right. Aparna peered at Anand curiously. She felt she knew him better than she knew anybody on earth, and she belonged to him in some way.

"I feel as if I've known you forever," Aparna said softly, in surprise, "I can't believe it is the first time I'm so close to you. I feel it's always been like this with us."

Anand listened to her silently. Then noticing the calm and relaxed expression of his face now, Aparna bent and kissed the base of his throat and then gently moved her lips up the side of his throat. She felt his hands squarely on her breasts, where they had slipped under her black and red low-necked sheer top. She sat up and pulled her top, along with the black slip she wore under it, over her head. He reached behind her to unclasp her black lace bra. She undid the clasp herself, pulled it off and out of her arms, and slid naturally into a lying position beside him. Anand bent over her gently, placing one hand over her right breast, as he gently took the tip of the left into his mouth. He tentatively tasted its tip with his tongue delicately, and then started sucking it with an unsatiable hunger, his lips warm and moist.

As Anand bent over her, he gently fondled one and then sucked the tip of the other of her breasts. He then alternated between her breasts, sucking and fondling. Aparna arched back, moaning with pleasure. She ran her hands all over his bare back, caressing the smoothness of his skin. She longingly ran her hands over the back of his arms and his sides, then down his spine to the waist, feeling the width of his waistline, wanting to explore and caress every bit of him. As Aparna ran her fingers gingerly through his luxuriant hair, Anand brought his mouth up to take hers possessively. She met his mouth hungrily, their mouths and then their tongues devouring and exploring each other's. Aparna reached to unclasp his belt, tugged at the buckle a little consciously. He shifted on to his side, then reached down and unclasped the belt deftly. He unbuttoned his trousers and wriggled out of them, still lying on his back. Aparna, by now emboldened by the potent gin drink, inflaming her longing, propelled by their last intimate meeting, after months of his blowing hot and cold with her, reached below to feel his bursting desire. She felt dazed with pleasure by his arousal under her touch.

Anand's hands reached down and peeled off her black lace panty, even as she helped him ease them off her legs. Then he quickly ripped off his own briefs and, just as he lay back on the cool white sheets, Aparna climbed over him, her mouth grabbing his. She kissed him with abandon. Anand lifted himself slightly, to kiss her just as passionately, amused and pleased by her boldness. He could not help recognising the working of the potent cocktail he had made her in the breaking of her apparent prudishness. Anand had turned off the lights earlier after seeking her consent. In the dim light, Aparna kissed her way down his neck to his stomach. She lingered around his navel before cautiously venturing further. She kissed the inner side of his thighs, severely setting ablaze his need that grew visibly firmer. When she had teased his manhood enough, to the point of his inability to wait longer, Aparna took him in her mouth, making him gasp with raw eagerness. Then she adroitly worked her mouth to peak his desire to such a point that when she moved her mouth away, he pleadingly whispered, "Please don't stop, baby." And Aparna loved him then with all her heart and with her mouth.

After having demonstrated to Anand how deeply she was in love with him, which Aparna could not have expressed better even with the choicest of words, Aparna climbed on top of him. Then sitting astride him, she intuitively aligned him by hand to her epicentre. She shifted her body weight to the left, so that the left side of her vagina and clitoral shaft could get maximum stimulation. Aparna had been reading up on the best kissing and sex techniques on the Internet, so as not to disappoint Anand. But she had concluded that for a fulfilled sexual experience for a couple, a woman has to take the initiative to concentrate on her own needs rather than only focus on pleasing the man. As he watched her in a dazed stupor, she took him into her core possessively. After a few seconds to familiarise and register the sensation of him inside of her, Aparna tilted forward to urge Anand to take the tip of her left breast in his mouth. She brought his hand firmly over the other breast, before she started to move in rhythm over him, her mouth passionately seeking his. Anand, even in his most frenzied fancy

     Shuvashree Chowdhury

over the last months, had not imagined this display of passion, love, and longing that Aparna presented to him now. He was as if atop a Ferris wheel, viewing the dizzying world below in spasms of desire, as she now sat upright on him in a kneeling position, and rhythmically gyrated, sending them both into chasms of pleasure.

Anand slapped the sides of her thighs a few times in a burst of uncontainable passion, muttering "Baby, baby … oh baby," and spurred on by it, Aparna continued to ride him zealously. Then suddenly, she rolled over sideways and lay on her back, urging him to get above her. He obliged her right away, unable to bear being restrained even for a moment. And with his eyes closed tight from the sheer potency of his desire, Anand thrust inside of her, as Aparna held him as close as possible, wanting to feel him right through her gut to her heart and soul.

"Kiss me here," Anand said abruptly, indicating his chest with his chin, and Aparna lunged upward to take his left nipple gently into her mouth. She kissed it tenderly and lovingly, just as she liked to be kissed there herself. Anand muttered in an approving tone, "Hmm yeah, yes there … mmm."

Then Aparna reached up to kiss his eyes, his cheeks, and his forehead lingeringly, lovingly, feeling him right in the depths of her heart and her body. It was as if both of them might just explode into a mass of molten lava. Aparna watched with wide-eyed amusement at how Anand stretched his mouth sidewards with his eyes shut, like in a forced smile, in a bid to control himself from screaming in ecstatic agony. Anand, oblivious to anything else as he was concentrating on the task at hand, continued his swift thrusting inside of her. Aparna, with a surge of passion, placed both her hands over his buttocks and caressingly pressed him down and moved up to feel Anand tighter inside her.

"Can I come inside you, baby?" Anand muttered suddenly, his face cast in a mask of agony, sweating profusely, like one gearing up to make a final dash at the end of a marathon.

"Yes, yes, please, darling … it's safe now," Aparna gushed in a feverish voice.

Suddenly, Anand pulled out of Aparna. He put his forefinger gingerly inside her, fingering her tenderly. She felt as if he wanted to kiss her intimately but was too shy. It was as if he was assessing how she felt at her core, at the zenith of her deep love for him, so as to store the memory of the sensation that stuck deep in his heart, to reminiscence with pleasure. Aparna would have loved for him to kiss her intimately, she thought, his fingering propelling her to crave the moist softness of his mouth next. But that could wait for their next time together. Then, just as abruptly, Anand mounted her again and, with a final burst of vigour, Aparna felt him throbbing, filling her inside. With the feel of his blazing release inside her, the pulsating sensation set off inside Aparna, as she clutched him fiercely like he was her lifeline.

Aparna looked up at Anand kneeling between her raised and parted knees. Looking into her eyes, he came up close towards her. With what was remaining of his vitality before she thought he might collapse, he stroked deep between her legs and Aparna pulled him fiercely down over her. Anand let his full weight fall on her now, as they hugged tight, their arms and legs wrapped around each other, feeling each other's thumping heartbeats. Aparna was drenched in Anand's profuse sweat, and as their bodies melted into one, she loved him more than ever, more than she had ever imagined herself capable of loving anyone. They stayed enjoined like that, their hearts and minds racing, their souls in unison for what seemed a long time. After their heartbeats gradually stabilised, as if slowly coming out of a trance, they fell apart.

"You're so sweaty," Aparna giggled, breaking the hypnotic spell.

"Obviously, all you had to do was lie back and enjoy!" Anand replied.

"I allowed you to be on top," she laughed, "thinking you might want to be."

"I need a shower," Anand said firmly, sitting up abruptly on the bed.

"Let's take one together," Aparna replied, sounding enthused by the idea.

"Now don't be so greedy. We will have more opportunities soon."

"All right, you go ahead," she replied, a tad disappointed by his abrupt tone.

But she mentally brushed it off as his wry and moody sense of

  Shuvashree Chowdhury

humour surfacing again. Aparna now felt secure in the awareness of how much Anand desired her. Moreover, he just might be self-conscious of his body, in spite of his workouts, she thought amusedly, for he had wanted the lights out before undressing. Perhaps he was shaken by their electrifying physical vibes, after the mental and emotional connection they had shared but wanted to take their relationship slow, what with the uncertainty the liaison entailed. Anand got off the bed, and walked briskly over to the bathroom. Aparna lay back on the bed, feeling the cool sheets about her, smugly going over all the events that led to the deep fulfilment she now felt. She reflected on her own movements, feeing shy now of how passionately she had kissed and made love to every part of him. Anand must know now how crazily she was in love with him. Her body could not have faked it.

There are stark differences between merely having sex and making love, he must know that certainly. There is something so sensual and beautiful when two people have chemistry together and are in love. But that isn't the case when people have sex merely to satisfy their lust. The first time with someone can be awkward and it takes time to get to know their body and pleasure points. But when you are in love, the time you invest in getting to know each other's bodies is intimate. You take pleasure in ensuring you know what pleases them, and makes them tick. Making love is not just having sex, it is an integrated mind-body-spirit relationship, and having sex without love is just a physical drill and not nearly as emotionally fulfilling. Women tend to enjoy watching passionate lovemaking in the movies, but are often disappointed by their personal experiences that don't come close to being that beautiful. But, in Aparna's case with Anand, being in love with him and their deep emotional connection ensured even their first time was surprisingly far more gorgeous.

Once Anand was out fully dressed, he walked over quietly to the sofa by the window and sat down. Aparna got out of bed now, gathering up her clothes, after fishing out her underwear from within the crevices of the sheet.

"Let's go out and get some dinner," Anand said, as soon as Aparna stepped out of the bathroom, "I'm ravenous. I skipped lunch today, after a heavy breakfast."

"Where would you like to go?" Aparna asked. Then walking back into the bathroom, she added, "I'll just do my makeup, I wouldn't want to look any different from when I walked in here."

Aparna emerged from the bathroom looking fresh, her lipstick and eyeliner in place, her handbag tucked under her arm. She asked Anand, who was waiting by the door, "Do I look just as I did when I came in?"

"No, you don't," Anand replied in a flat tone. "You're all flushed."

Aparna smiled in response. "So where are we going for dinner?"

"Let's go to the South Indian restaurant they have down here, Malgudi, if that's alright with you. I don't feel up to going anywhere outside now."

"That's absolutely fine with me," Aparna replied, as they got into the lift.

At the entrance to the restaurant, which was flanked by small, ornate dome-roofed pavilions, one occupied by an astrologer replete with a parrot and other paraphernalia, they were greeted warmly by two lady hostesses. They stepped into the traditionally decorated interiors, to soft sounds of the *tabla* and *mirudhangam* played by musicians seated on a pavilion at the far end of the restaurant. A young suit-clad man, the maitre'd, briskly walked up to them. He shook hands with Anand very warmly, after which he bowed politely to Aparna, escorting them to a table near the musicians on an elevated plane. Anand sat facing the musicians, Aparna across him. A waiter promptly brought them two menu cards. After a cursory glance, they ordered a portion of grilled lobster and fish as starters, along with beer. It was recommended by the restaurant manager, who lingered nearby attentively, throughout their meal. Aparna looked at Anand's usual mask-like, sulky expression that had returned right after he got out of the bed, curiously. She wondered what was on his mind. He looked back quizzically.

"So how would you rate my escort services? Do you think it will do well?" Aparna said laughing, picking up the thread of conversation she had started in jest, on arriving at the room, to make light of her sheer awkwardness.

                    Shuvashree Chowdhury

"Yeah, I would think it'll do rather well ... though there is scope for improvement," Anand replied, playing along with her joke now, though he had sharply said, "shut up" when she had grinned mischievously and asked him at the peak of their lovemaking, with him atop and inside her.

"Ah! Improvement, and how so?" Aparna laughed, though her face fell at the seriousness of his voice, though she knew he was only taking her up on the joke she had made of their genuine intimacy. In a playful tone, she added, "That's okay, as I would not be the primary service provider you see. I will have younger and more beautiful and proficient women, while I coordinate the business module."

"I only said that, as one cannot say only good things always," he smiled affectionately, then as she smiled back pleased, he added "One must leave some room for further improvement, isn't it?"

"So it's just like the way you would appraise my work, right?" she grinned. "But then, what else was I really expecting out of an association with my boss?"

After two bottles of beer shared between them, along with the grilled lobsters they had devoured, followed by a spicy baked whole fish, and a plate of chicken kebabs, both in Kerala style, they were served the main course. They had ordered mutton stew and fish in coconut gravy, along with *appams*. Both of them had a penchant for Keralite cuisine.

"I'm so hungry today I could eat all of this and more," Anand said, tearing a portion of *appam* from his side plate and dipping it into the small bowl of mutton stew the waiter had placed over his plate, along with another bowl of the fish broth.

Aparna followed him, dipping into her mutton stew with a portion of *appam*, though she felt full from the snacks and the beer.

"So how is it you eat non-vegetarian food ... would you eat beef too?" Anand asked suddenly.

"If I'm outside of home or travelling or something, I do. And yes, I'd eat beef too." Aparna replied in a casual tone, "But, of course, not at home. My family is strictly vegetarian."

"By the way, who are all these old people you've befriended ... the ones you keep mentioning? How did you meet them?"

"Oh! Them? They are all my readers," Aparna said laughing, taken aback by the abrupt question. Then enthusiastically, she continued, "You will be rather surprised to know that I have got some savvy and well-placed admirers. There's this one gentleman who wrote to me a few times, said he was from Mumbai, and then, one day, requested my telephone number. One afternoon, he called asking me out to lunch and, when we met, he turned out to be a very senior corporate official who has been reading my poems in my blog and likes them a lot."

"You write poetry too?" Anand asked, looking at her, surprised, "And you never told me that you had a blog!"

"Well, I don't usually talk of it, as it's personal stuff I like to write in it," Aparna replied sheepishly. "I wouldn't want that to affect my journalism."

"Hmm, interesting," Anand nodded. "Forward the link to me, won't you? I'd like to get to know more of this 'personal' Aparna and what it is that makes her tick."

Just then, the waiter came up, to serve them a portion each of the coconut dessert that Anand had ordered on the manager's suggestion.

"I'm too full for this," Aparna said, grimacing at the chilled white cream in the silver bowl placed in front of her and then up at Anand.

"You don't need to finish it," Anand replied. "Just try it, you'll like the taste, or so I think." And then turning to the waiter, he said, "Get our check please."

They walked out of the restaurant hand in hand, contentedly chewing mouth fresheners. Once outside, Anand shook hands with Aparna as he would a colleague or business associate. Then he returned to his room. He didn't want to go home and ruin his mood with his wife's tantrums or sullen silences. Aparna drove home in complete rapture, at what she considered was the best evening of her life. But then again, on second thoughts, the evening at the Fisherman's Cove was better still, she concluded. There was a better thrill in anticipation.

     Shuvashree Chowdhury

Chapter 11

The Marriage at a Crossroads

Sujata had always been rather conscious of Anand's average looks, and his lack of elegance and charisma at public functions. She did not bother with his intelligence, as it was not a factor she considered attractive, as Aparna did. She tended to remind Anand often, how he and his family lacked sophistication compared to hers. From the start, it was Sujata who stole the attention from him in any gathering, due to her confident personal style, sense of fashion, and charisma. Her overall attitude towards Anand, since they married, had been condescending, as if he had done himself rather well in marrying her. A man can hardly forgive this constant squashing of his ego, however well it is ensconced in a mask of placidity. Anand tended to laugh off and humour all Sujata's jibes, overriding it with maturity. But his soul craved for adulation from his wife, as he got from other women. This had now begun to come to him easily of its own accord with success and power.

Sujata's attractive personality tended to make an immediate impression on people, and her easy demeanour and ability to charm anyone with ease made Anand insecure. She did nothing to pamper his typically male brittle ego, even though she was a responsible wife, who fulfilled all her duties. Thus, whenever another woman did pay him devotion, Anand's marital attentions tended to waiver, till he now sought to invoke the devotion himself, just to test his prowess. A man craves constant attention from his partner, as does a woman, and finding it lacking makes them prone to seeking it elsewhere. Both sexes may feel claustrophobic with a partner's excessive attentions and drift away in a bid to be free from emotional clinginess. Aparna, as did many other girls in his office, fulfilled Anand's deep need for affection and adulation and he had had a series of flings even before her.

Anand had not discerned what he truly wanted out of his relationship with Aparna. This was even after having taken it to an intimate level, unlike with any of the girls in his office before. He did genuinely like her and did not want to lose her affections, while he figured out what to do about it. Aparna was a prodigious worker and would be more committed to her work now because of her sincere feelings for him. Anand knew he was better off harnessing the power of her feelings for him to a good end professionally. Women tend to give all they have got, to excel at their work, especially if their heart is entangled to it too. The way Aparna had made love to him, with every ounce of her being, was validation to Anand of her sincerity. He remembered how his aloofness at dinner afterwards had visibly saddened her. Anand had tried to draw her out, but she had remained somewhat reticent. She did not seek to use him merely for means of her advancement, Anand knew, as is not uncommon with either sex, especially when in relationships with successfully powerful people or bosses.

But the circumstances of his marriage prevented him from taking any stances in his relationship with Aparna. He was not going to risk losing the children, as he surely would, if Sujata and he separated. His marriage was intolerable to him lately, with Sujata's long periods of stony silence when she just would not talk to him, in spite of all his efforts. She little understood that, like many men, her husband often had no clue why she was upset and sulking to begin with. So how was he going to make it up to her, or stop doing the same things repeatedly that offended or hurt her? That he did not understand upset her further and was their gravest bone of contention, as far as she was concerned.

Then when her iciness thawed, Sujata might fly into such an instantaneous rage, that anyone but those close to her would not believe her capable of, flooding him with a volley of accusations. Anand would then dodge or avoid her, to keep the peace he needed to concentrate on his demanding work. He would stay out late, often till it was past Sujata's regular bedtime, especially the children's, to avoid a confrontation with her in front of them, and risk being further distanced from them. The children tended to support their mother and Sujata was fiercely possessive about them. It was so that Sujata's dispositions would not wash out his own splendid mood,

          Shuvashree Chowdhury

like after that evening with Aparna at Savoy Hotel, that Anand had spent the night there, when home in T-Nagar was barely a ten-minute drive away. Why women will not speak precisely, define what they expect, instead of sulking, or worse skirting the issue in rage, Anand often wondered in exasperation.

On her part, Sujata sensed that telling Anand anything was rather useless. Was it so difficult for him to understand what was expected of him? But wasn't this the crux of most relationship problems? Women want their men to understand them without being told, which in their view would prove their love. Some women, reticent like Sujata, tend more to need an assurance of love, a display of sentiments and emotions, to feel comfortable in demonstrating their own feelings, or they tend to freeze up. But then, both women and men can be alike in that way, in the need for demonstration of love, in order to be able to reciprocate, and yet often tend to misunderstand each other's need. Sujata had over time forgiven, and was in mental acceptance of, Anand's neglect of her, but what truly infuriated her was his attitude towards the children. It was like they were not even his.

Anand was particularly harsh on the elder boy Varun, who tended to avoid him, out of a deep-rooted inhibition, since early childhood. The boy's early experiences were reinforced continuously by Anand's callous behaviour towards him. It was few months back that Anand had returned home early one evening, on Sujata's insistence. She had organised a family get-together for her uncle, who was visiting from London. Anand had walked through the open, heavy wooden main door, to find a large group of people in the living area. Varun was playing cricket with a plastic bat and ball there, around the guests. Anand raged at Varun so violently that he sent the boy scuttling to his room in shame and fear. Sujata was so enraged that she had had a good mind to subject Anand to the same humiliation in front of their guests, but better sense prevailed. Then she remained icily silent for days after.

Then there had been the instance, a few weeks back, when Anand had taken Varun along to the Crossword bookstore at Alwarpet. It was a Sunday and Anand liked to spend part of the early evening there, browsing and buying books. He did not like reading or buying books online. At the billing counter, when Varun handed him a few books, Anand was displeased with his choices, so he refused to pay for them. He paid for the ones he had selected himself, and chiding and ridiculing Varun on his choice in books, they left the store. Sujata, on hearing of this from the flustered boy on their return, was furious.

"How dare you ridicule my son yet again in public?" She yelled. "Is this your way of destroying his voracious interest in reading forever?"

She promptly took the child back to Crossword and bought him the books he had selected. After each such incident, Sujata would not speak to Anand for days, even avoiding his presence. She hated his insensitive callousness. It was almost like he did all this to spite and to hurt her. In fact, most of Anand and Sujata's antipathies towards each other had been spearheaded by the birth of their first son and Anand's absence at that time. It was then that Sujata had become obsessed with the child, and would sulkily ignore Anand's wish to spend time alone with her, just as before the child's birth. Anand thus began to find the child an intrusion to their couple time, and began to avoid him, becoming resentful of his coming between him and his wife. Anand had liked to go to the movies or to meals alone with Sujata, and on international holidays, as they had before the child came along. But Sujata had turned him down, not wanting to leave the child behind. Worse still, she would insist on taking the child along, much to Anand's vexation. Anand did relent sometimes, after much fuss, and they took the one-year-old child on a number of trips even to Europe and Russia, but Sujata tended to be mentally and emotionally engaged with Varun, leaving him out in the cold.

If Anand tried to draw her attention, demand it even, insisting they leave the child in the hotel with the maid, as they always took one along for him, she would get upset. Sujata just could not understand how a grown man could be jealous of his own child. Her insistence to let the child sleep between them at night, at home or at a hotel, rather than in his room with the maid nearby, irked Anand to no end. It was Sujata's excessive attention to their son, as is usual for new mothers who often neglect their husband's needs, that resulted in Anand's drifting further away, then holding the child responsible and thus disliking him. Also in later years, once

Shuvashree Chowdhury

she was working, Sujata was not able to find energy reserves to give attention to both father and son.

Then Anand's not standing up to his parents and his family for Sujata was another cause for the rift between them. Anand did not want to project to his parents and brother that he was controlled by his wife. Thus, he would be stand-offish with her in front of them. There was an instance, etched in Sujata's memory, when out for lunch with the family one Saturday at their favourite restaurant, The Wharf, at the Radisson Blu Resort Temple Bay, on ECR, she was the only one who was not yet served by the waiter. The mixed vegetarian *tandoor* platter that they had ordered as starters had run out before Sujata's turn to be served. The rest of the family, including Anand, much to Sujata's shock, began to eat, without even offering her some out of their plates, or waiting till the waiter got another platter. They did not, in fact, bother to order another portion of the same dish, moving on to another item, as though she was inconsequential. Sujata had looked out at the sea and tried desperately to control her humiliation, along with the raging tears that had erupted in her eyes.

Whenever Anand's parents derided Sujata, then telephoned her parents and spoke offensively of Sujata's defiance—as they referred to her silent withdrawal—Anand would not speak up for her in defence. He sported a nonchalant attitude to his family's attitude towards his wife. His mother, jealous that her son no longer gave her the attention she still sought, increasingly detested Sujata, in spite of all her subservience since her marriage at an early age.

"I know that I love my wife," Anand would then justify to Sujata's taunts at his timidity. "So why would I have to go around proving anything to the world?"

What eluded Anand was Sujata's dire need for him to stand up to the world for her, to prove his love, thus giving her assurance and security of his presence in her life. How else could he expect adulation in return? Over time, the debris of varied issues had created a boulder between Sujata and Anand, becoming so largely out of proportion that it blocked their view of the other's viewpoint completely. They loved each other, but were not able to keep their loyalties rooted any longer, and might have considered a separation with relief, but they had the children to think about.

It was after the birth of their second child Vishal that things between the couple had gotten worse than ever before. But ironically, Anand had made all attempts to connect with the younger son, who was by nature much friendlier and lovable. Perhaps this was from seeing how the older one avoided him altogether now and was fearful of him, while closer than ever to his mother. Anand realised he could not allow the children to be taken away, as Sujata would surely do, in the event of a separation. There was no way she would not fight tooth and nail to take the children with her, away from him.

Sujata knew well how aloof Anand was with them and that he did practically nothing towards their physical or emotional growth. Anand did not deserve them, in Sujata's view, and they did not deserve such a negligent father. How could a father possibly be so cold to his children, Sujata wondered desperately? She was afraid they would grow up emotionally deficient, because of Anand's detached attitude towards them. Her worst fear was of them turning out just as insensitive like him, as grown men. Due to her anxieties, Sujata went overboard to compensate Anand's lacking affections in the children's lives. They grew increasingly closer and dependant on their mother, while more distant with their father.

Sujata did not help with regard to fortifying the father-son relationship. She highlighted Anand's absences and negligence, and made it clear to the boys that she was all they would ever need and could depend on in life. Even the younger Vishal tended to avoid Anand now, in spite of all Anand's efforts to draw him out with gifts and attention, seeking to take him on outings. He was four years old now, and tended to follow his elder brother, about eleven years old, who was his real hero.

"What kind of a man cannot even earn the respect, love, and admiration of his own children?" Sujata would rage at Anand, if Vishal refused to go out with him.

"The boys will understand one day … once they grow up and inherit everything, the business especially, what their father has done for them." Anand always smugly replied. "And then they will respect and love me … you will see."

"You think money can buy everything, don't you?" Sujata

          Shuvashree Chowdhury

would say bitingly, "Including the love of your children? We will see how they'll respect you … They are my children after all."

Anand had no intention of leaving his marriage, as he still loved Sujata whether she believed it or not. But under the circumstances, he could not help toying with the idea of separation, as a way of earning his peace of mind. He wanted their sons to take over the business someday. After all, he was working hard to fortify the *National Daily*, to take its circulation to smaller towns all over India. And all of it might one day be lost, if his sons didn't step in to uphold it. There was no way he was going to jeopardise the slim bond he had created with the children, even though he was more connected to the younger one. Who with his father's exaggerated attentions, was getting audacious and defiant, contrary to the older Varun who was shy, uncomfortable, apprehensive and avoided Anand totally. Anand had to take it casually with Aparna, he knew, even after understanding the connection they had, both mentally and physically. This was at least till his children were older, and could independently have opinions of their father and their equation with him. He would have to allow circumstances to take care of themselves, Anand decided.

* * *

Sujata had no close friends, except for the two men in her life, Shekhar and Manas. The first she trusted implicitly, and discussed every aspect of her life with. With Manas, it was more an alliance that entertained her immensely and boosted her self-esteem. It was her colleagues, past and present, and also the mothers of her son's school friends that she socialised with. There was a cousin, a few years older, with whom Sujata was very friendly, but didn't reveal everything to. She would only hint to her about events and people, but then hold it all close to her heart. It was like she wanted to say so much, but dared not, in fear of damaging her reputation, but more so because she was risking her husband's and his family's. Her sister Ramya was the other friend Sujata had, but then she could not talk to her heart-to-heart any longer, as their wavelengths increasingly differed. Ramya had led a sheltered life always, a housewife whose focus was her children and husband, in that order. She could not relate to Sujata's working life.

Over and above, Ramya was always in awe of Anand's success and power, and found him the ideal man and husband. She tended to blatantly support him in every respect, over her sister. This irked Sujata immensely, as even her parents tended to support Anand over her. Ramya had become close to Anand over the years, and they chatted often, over the phone or meeting sometimes at a café. He often confided his grievances and Ramya always took his side, blaming Sujata for everything. Anand was shrewd and knew that if he had Sujata's family's support, he had control over her. He often gave Ramya expensive gifts—a designer bag from Ritu Kumar or a Satya Paul *sari* or scarf, sometimes a watch or piece of jewellery. Sujata, when shopping for herself in Chennai or abroad, often bought Ramya and her family clothes, household gadgets, also pieces of jewellery to add one by one to her daughters' trousseau in the far future. But still it was Anand whom Ramya always supported over her sister.

Sujata, in turn, considered Ramya's husband Prashant the ideal husband and father. She had admired his good looks and charming manner from the start, but now appreciated his doting manner to his kids and wife. Anand did not match up to Prashant in looks and charisma. But in addition to that, he was an inattentive husband and, the worst crime in Sujata's eyes, a negligent father. All this made Anand's success, money, and power inconsequential to Sujata. While Prashant, over time, had become her friend, confidant, and advisor. To him, other than to Shekhar, Sujata confided issues she faced with Anand and his family, and received a sympathetic ear and smart advice. She had even disclosed to him, on his probing, her non-existent sex life with Anand, to which Prashant sympathised. He even volunteered, much to her shock, to be of help.

"I passed it off as a joke," Sujata confessed to her cousin, laughing, after she blurted out to her involuntarily about Prashant's sexual advances. "What could I say to him? I know it was just an involuntary reaction to his empathising with me. Also, he might have meant he would find me a guy … I didn't wait to find out what he meant."

Prashant was aware that Anand tended to neglect Sujata, not

                    Shuvashree Chowdhury

merely physically but emotionally. Anand would not stand up for her to his family who still treated her as an outsider.

"You recall how Anand was not even there during the birth of both his sons," Sujata had said to Prashant, her voice faltering with pain. Then icily, she had added "Even now he does next to nothing for his children, other than upset them. And yet your wife and my parents think he is the coolest man alive."

"Yes, I gauged that." Prashant had replied sympathetically, adding in an irritated tone, "If one focuses on too many women, it's bound to happen."

"It is immensely hurtful, when I think about it now." Sujata continued, her eyes dewy, "Anand never did fall in love with me, as I'd presumed in my naivety from his hours of phone calls, romantic poetry, and the emails. For him, it was merely a challenge as I was not easily won. You must remember him, don't you, at the time of our marriage … which girl would marry him?"

Anand's current entanglement, of which Prashant knew first-hand from their conversations at the Savoy Hotel's gym, was a woman in his office who had come from Mumbai, called Aparna. Anand was much taken with her, her apparent helplessness adding to the allure. Sujata too was sure of Anand's involvement with Aparna, from her sources in Anand's office. She knew many there disliked her, due to Aparna's perceived arrogance due to her closeness to Anand. Sujata had met Aparna a few times at official parties, and had been traumatised by her overconfident, smug projections of her proximity to Anand. Even though she had ignored her, Aparna's attitude humiliated Sujata immensely. She described these encounters to Prashant, also filling him in on a string of women before Aparna.

"There was the time when, on a holiday at Munnar with Anand, sitting by the fireplace with him, I happened to come upon a text message from this girl Vasudha from his office." Sujata confided in Prashant, over one of their chats. "I then compelled Anand to show me his mobile phone, and discovered a trail of romantic messages between the two."

"Where's this girl now? She's still one of the entourage?"

"No, Vasudha left his office a few years later, a year after Aparna's joining. She got married. But there were his numerous other flirtations. I learned of them from people we know in common. Initially, it seemed unbearable. But I survived."

Prashant had listened to Sujata, seemingly enraged by Anand's callous treatment of the innocent starry-eyed girl he married. Then he had solemnly advised her, "You must be strong, Sujata, and deal with Anand firmly from now on. No more sulky silences and teary tantrums, due to which he takes you for granted. But first stop worrying about the other women, including Aparna. They will soon be things of the past, you will see. Anand will lose interest in each of them, at worst later, if not sooner. They are not worth your emotions and tears, I tell you."

"It's all so humiliating. I feel everyone is laughing at me, especially these women" she had replied, sounding helpless. "It's not as if they are better than me."

Looking into Sujata's eyes, Prashant had added resolutely "You are his wife, not they. Always remember that. They are merely his flirtations."

"Yes, but that does not absolve him," Sujata had replied irately. "Anand is too self-centred to really love anyone. Don't I know that by now?"

"Then you need not worry that he might leave you someday for another woman. He is merely enjoying all the attention coming his way. You lead your own life—enjoy yourself and be happy, without rocking the boat of your family's security. You concentrate on your personal welfare and that of your children's."

"Just give me a good reason, Prashant, why I should not leave him … really?" Sujata had retorted. "I am financially and emotionally capable of bringing up the children myself, more now that I've gone back to working, am I not?"

Now it was not that Prashant was learning of all this for the first time. Prashant knew Anand well and they were friends in a sense. They not only went to the same gym and were often together at family functions. They also went out to movies and for long drives to Mahabalipuram and Pondicherry. Prashant did not worry about Anand ever leaving the marriage. He had even advised him against it. But he became worried now, at Sujata's awareness and mention of it. In fact, Prashant was one of the men who advised Anand how to get Aparna's attention. He became aware now, from the

 Shuvashree Chowdhury

chat with Sujata, that it had worked rather well. Prashant recalled how excited Anand had been about Aparna. But he decided not to share the details of his own involvement in the matter with Sujata. He had just not thought of her perspective, or considered Anand would be so callous as to allow Sujata to find out about Aparna.

Prashant had always been a ladies' man. His good looks made it easier than it had been for Anand, who was also reserved and shy in his youth—qualities that Sujata had initially found charming. But now Anand was endowed with money and power, both more compelling to women than mere good looks and charm, changing him unrecognizably.

It was true that Anand had relied on Prashant's advice to try and hook Aparna. He hadn't realised that she would be attracted to him for his personality and intelligence. By the time Aparna met him, Anand was more urbane and elegant. He had an improved physique, from working out at the gym and playing tennis at the Presidency Club and Cosmopolitan Club. Now he got his hair styled at premium salons like the one at the Park Hotel, in addition to dressing elegantly ever since Sujata had started shopping for his clothes. He had more exposure now, from his work and extensive travelling, and from meeting influential and powerful people. Thus, Anand's use of Prashant's tactics had only brought to the fore and then cemented what Aparna felt for him from the start— an immense adulation for his mind and professional expertise. It is quite common for young women to have crushes on their male bosses, established and powerful in fields they aspire to join and excel in. In Aparna's case, journalism had become her lifeline and Anand was its soul.

When Sujata confided in Prashant about Aparna, describing the late-night hysterical calls to discuss her marital woes, endless text messages, and video calls, Prashant was rather amused. But he tried to look grave for Sujata's sake. Then his anger and jealousy for Anand surfacing, he fuelled her insecurity glibly.

"Be careful, she may get herself pregnant to entrap him," Prashant said, much to Sujata's shock. She had hoped that he would refute her words but he was confirming that there was a dalliance!

"That would serve him right, wouldn't it?" Sujata retorted

venomously, seething with rage. "Quite a scandal that would be."

"You know well, Anand is a good catch … he is affluent and powerful. Any woman, especially one like this Aparna, will make a play for him. You need to act judiciously to save your marriage and your family. Yet, as I keep insisting, you must lead your own life, Sujata. Enjoy it as Anand does. Don't be such a stick-in-the-mud."

Sujata's pride was hurt. She imagined Anand and Aparna together, laughing at her plight. She defiantly took her relationship with Shekhar to the next level. She had been close to Manas too and had indulged in flirtatious petting, but she had not gone all the way. Before this conversation with Prashant and the stinging insult she felt from his conviction of Anand's latest affair, along with his taunts of her baseless devotion to him, Sujata might not have slept with Shekhar. Prashant was right. She must not be such a fool and allow Anand to keep hurting her. He claimed to love her, but that was clearly a lie. Theirs was a marriage of convenience and she had better accept that.

It was through his chats with Sujata that Prashant was kept updated on the details of Anand and Aparna's relationship. Anand, after a point, had stopped discussing Aparna or any other woman for that matter with Prashant. He had become aware of Prashant's growing closeness to Sujata, and the risk inherent in that. Also, the equations between Anand and Prashant had starkly deteriorated, from Anand's steady success and Prashant's business failures. Prashant was angry about his circumstances and frustrated that his wife Ramya constantly nagged and badgered him. It didn't help that she was always praising Anand and his capability, intelligence, and success. Why could his wife and her family not see, Prashant thought angrily, that he hadn't inherited a legacy like Anand?

Ramya and Prashant lived with her parents now. They had moved to the bungalow in Nungambakkam a couple of years after their marriage. Ramya had constantly been in friction with her mother-in-law. She had been dissatisfied from the beginning with the circumstances of Prashant's family's small apartment, their standard, and ways of living, as compared to what she was used to. Though his mother-in-law showered him with affection and supported him over her own daughter, Prashant forced to be grateful, found himself doing household chores and running

                    Shuvashree Chowdhury

most errands, thus he felt taken for granted. Ramya, considering this was her second marriage to Prashant, having eloped to marry the first time, made no effort to boost his often flagging ego. She even hurled at him, when angry, how her ex-husband had been better, more caring and responsible, and had been better in bed too. Though in reality, she had divorced him due to his being a compulsive womaniser, and yet she seemed to be in love with him still.

On the other hand, everybody was all praise for Anand and he was consulted on all family matters. Whenever Anand visited, it was like an event to celebrate. Prashant was then lectured on how he had to, like Anand, be more responsible towards his family. Anand's cheerleader, ironically, was his wife Ramya, followed by her father. All this had resulted in a frustration for which Prashant now found an outlet. Criticising Anand, along with Sujata, made him feel better, in knowing Anand's life was not so perfect after all. And he did all he could to fan Anand's marital discord and distance Sujata from Anand. At times, Prashant could not help wishing Anand and he had been married to each other's wives. Sujata was always supportive of Anand in his business dealings, if he were in any trouble, in spite of all her personal problems with him. She was level-headed and knew how the world worked. Unlike his wife, she was not lazy. Ramya would not take up a job, though he was struggling to make ends meet, preferring to spend her time hounding the children and nagging him.

Prashant had a lot of bad debt due to him from clients because of the current global recession, in addition to the large sums he owed vendors. But what was crucifying was that his wife was not his ally, worse still, she threw insults at him in front of the children. He ran a business of manufacturing tools and parts for heavy industry. Prashant had asked Ramya to lend him money, perhaps mortgage her jewellery which she had inherited in abundance, but she flatly refused. Ramya was advised by her parents not to forfeit her personal security. Prashant had not proven worthy of their respect, in terms of handling his business judicially. He had also made grave misjudgements in the handling of his father-in-law's business, when he had been trusted to overlook it. He was now hounded by debtors. They even landed up at home unannounced, looking for Prashant. They were unable to get him on his mobile phone, since he kept changing numbers often to avoid them.

With no support from his wife or her family, and his own parents not having the ability to help, Prashant was now a wretched man. He had borrowed about four lakh rupees from Sujata, who had given him that much and no more, as she had mentally written off ever getting it back. Anand did not know of this, as Sujata did not want to humiliate Prashant. But the amount was too little to save Prashant, and as Sujata rightly assumed, he was to never return it. Prashant in his loyalty to Sujata, and his deep annoyance towards Anand, by being a ready listener to her woes and joining her in maligning him, became persuasive fuel to their marital woes. But Sujata and Anand had no way of knowing that he thrived on their differences.

Anand had become wary of Prashant for quite another reason, in addition to his wife's friendship with him. Their sons were in awe of Prashant, as were Prashant's own children. Whatever else he did or did not do, Prashant was a doting parent and uncle, demonstrative of his affections too. He hugged and kissed the children and allowed them to ride on his shoulder or back, and the children loved all the fun and games when he was around. This was contrary to Anand's distant demeanour with all the children. During yearly family holidays at their summer houses in Kodaikanal or Munnar, this disparity between the men was very obvious. Sujata would make it a point to draw Anand's attention to Prashant's affection for the children and how they enjoyed his company.

Ramya would then promptly defend Anand and say, "He is running such a successful business. You cannot expect him to run after the children too, can you? He is providing everything for them and for you, isn't he, Sujata?"

"You're always expecting too much from your husband." Sujata's mother would join in. "He works so hard for all of you."

Anand was thus the hero to Sujata's family: He could do no wrong, as after all, he more than fulfilled his basic role as husband and father, that of a provider. His wife and children were never in want for anything materially. Anand also helped his in-laws financially, especially with his father-in-law's business when

                     Shuvashree Chowdhury

needed, in addition to sponsoring family holidays and meals, often at expensive places. How could Sujata explain to her family, who were so in awe of Anand, that material provisions did not compensate for his emotionally distant attitude to his wife and children? They were dazzled by the halo effect money creates and would not risk Anand's displeasure in the least, lest his generosity to them waned.

Anand's success was a matter of immense pride to Sujata's family, especially socially. They looked upon him with rose-tinted glasses, thus stealing from Sujata the support they owed her, making her feel alienated. It was her own family's attitude towards money, in addition to Anand's negligent attitude, that had driven Sujata to building her career and becoming financially independent. She was now capable of planning an exit from her marriage, with the strength of her conviction that she could bring up her children on her own. They could well do without a father, as she could do without a husband, especially one who was missing more often than not from their lives. But Sujata was in no hurry to leave. She had better let the children grow up while she consolidated her career.

Anand made it a point to attend all of Sujata's family's functions. He basked in their adulation, affirming his conviction that her family's support of him would prevent Sujata's ever leaving him along with the children. Thus, to Sujata's chagrin, it was due to her family that Anand took her more for granted. He knew her family's power over her, especially her mother's. And he was smug that his money and social position gave them all a sense of security they would not risk, by giving wind to Sujata's declarations of his negligence, and her whims to leave him.

By this time, Anand was increasingly distanced from his own family too. His brother Murali, who had bare business acumen, did not have with it the lack of ambition one might presume he would, to keep himself happy by a mere hefty allowance. He wished to be as much a part of their business's decision-making process as Anand, on the editorial board of the newspaper. Then after marriage, he was also egged on by his wife's ambitions. Murali took the issues pertaining to Anand's lack of support of his business ideas and not giving him the importance he sought at work to their mother to resolve. This was since the death of their father. His mother blamed Sujata at first for trying to bring a rift between her sons to malign her. What she didn't quite fathom was it was actually the handiwork of a college mate and long-time friend of Anand's named Balaji. He had been hired as the head of finance, and had become Murali's mentor, influencing his dissent for Anand's authority.

Balaji relished in fuelling the differences between the two brothers. He had always been jealous of Anand. He hated the fact that, even though he had been the better student, he had to be employed under his friend. Balaji was also close to Sujata as they all frequently met. The three sometimes went out for movies and meals together. Sujata and Anand also hosted him at their home. Sujata now had him as a source of steady information on the proceedings at Anand's office. Balaji updated her about the women that caught Anand's fancy and those who had a crush on him and found some excuse or other to knock on the boss's door.

Sujata did not guess Balaji's jealous motives in the information he supplied her with. Even if she did, she chose to overlook it. He made a good spy, whatever his intentions were.

Sujata found solace only in talking to Shekhar, telling him the twists and turns of her marriage. She had poured her heart out to him, of how humiliated she felt by Anand's affair that was now public. This was before the death of his wife Aneesha, when he was not so broken himself. Shekhar, in all his maturity, had never criticised Anand. After listening to her woes, he tended to take Anand's side, just to give Sujata a male perspective and calm her. Perhaps if he had been critical of her husband, she would not have liked it, and would have grown resentful of Shekhar. That is why she avoided Balaji and Murali now, as they were a reminder of her humiliation.

It was Balaji who had apprised her of the games Anand was playing to get Aparna's attention. When Aparna had called Anand late at night, Sujata had known they had bonded well by now, for her to feel free to do that. Sujata clearly understood that Aparna's emotional reliance on her boss and the liberties she took was proof of their liaison. It highlighted that Aparna had opened up to

　　　　　　　Shuvashree Chowdhury

him, trusted him with her personal problems, and was assured of Anand's support.

"Why the hell is this woman calling you so late at night?" Sujata had erupted, looking at Anand angrily, able to hear Aparna's voice through his mobile phone, as he had sat up in bed, beside her. "… That too howling as if someone has died?"

Anand had signalled to Sujata with his eyes to be quiet, and then said on the phone "Please calm down, Aparna, he cannot take away the child like that. We will discuss this tomorrow at the office. Yes, and I will give you the best lawyer's contact."

Since that night, Aparna had become the most tangible wall between Anand and Sujata. The updates Sujata had got from people of his office, on their interactions, including that from his brother Murali and friend Balaji, had served to fuel this raging fire already.

Women tend to criticise those they love when upset, more so their spouse. They may vent their anger and frustrations, but might not take well to even friends criticising them. Shekhar was a confident man, and he did not find the need to undermine Anand to gain prominence in Sujata's life. Moreover, the stress and anger she lived with and complained of often, made him worried about her health. She had a nagging, often unbearable lower back pain, and sometimes a throbbing headache caused by overwork and anxiety, the doctor had diagnosed. Shekhar always had her welfare in mind, for he truly loved her and was her only true friend. Thus, even as Anand's relationship with Aparna grew and he became a source of emotional support to her, the fumes of this fire propelled his wife to frantically seek an anchor in another man.

Chapter 12

The Handsome Englishman

With the soaring popularity of her Saturday column in the *Urban Plus*, also her WordPress blog, Aparna now received a steady flow of Facebook friendship requests. Many of these were from westerners as well. She would accept a couple of invites, while others she didn't accept would begin to follow her posts which she kept in the public mode. Aparna was rather pleased that westerners liked her writing too. It motivated her to write more thoughtful status messages on Facebook, in addition to posting the links to her latest columns and blogs on it. She also posted inspiring quotes by authors or iconic personalities, always adding her own viewpoints, for a personal and unique touch. In time, her posts became as popular as her newspaper columns, if not more, and her friends and followers on FB kept increasing. It was the morning after her dinner with Anand at the Savoy Hotel that Aparna noticed the friendship request from a young white man from Manchester, UK.

She had woken early, though it was a Sunday, her heart aflutter, senses alive in vivid recall of the previous evening, playing uninitiated as if in a slideshow, in her mind. It was after her son Kartik had left for his painting classes with her father, while resting on the mat after her yoga, that Aparna saw the notification on her mobile phone. This was along with invites from two other men from India. She had been receiving a stream of invites from men in Manchester, she recalled. Were these people all connected, she wondered fleetingly? Her mind and soul were too enmeshed in the intimacy of the previous evening to engage further with anyone or anything else right away. She would have to scan these profiles as she tended to, if she were to accept them as friends. It was only later in the evening, as on days after work, that she would spend

Shuvashree Chowdhury

time on FB. Aparna had seen the notifications—in silent mode, on hearing the loud beeping of an incoming text message. She had decided to check on the beeps, as it was not often she received text messages this early, that too on a Sunday

The message from Anand, had read, "It was a lovely evening."

After reading the message several times, smiling to herself, Aparna had been flushed with spasms of longing, as she replied, "The best I've known yet."

That evening, Aparna accepted the FB invites of two of the three men, after she scanned their profiles. One of them was the man from Manchester, by the name, Stephan Shedrack. He was a gorgeous young man, Aparna noticed admiringly, from the ten or so pictures posted. His profile picture had been changed a few times in the last six months, which added to those on his timeline. Most of his close friends, Aparna deduced from their gushing comments on his pictures, had oriental appearances and names. There were, both men and women, many from East India—Sikkim, Manipur. And a few from Chennai as well, much to Aparna's surprise.

Stephan Shedrack was white, with dark wavy hair, a broad forehead, intense piercing black eyes, a straight sharp nose, and shapely lips. He was stylishly dressed in the pictures, both in formal suits as well as casual wear, in expensive-looking, impeccably tailored, or branded clothes. He had a regal bearing about him, Aparna conceded, and looked somewhat arrogant even. Seated in a plush office, amidst majestic teakwood furniture, or posing by an expensively stocked ornate bar at a residence, Stephan came across as a rich and suave young man.

After accepting Stephan's invite, though not in the least drawn to him in spite of appreciating his dashing good looks, Aparna posted two Shakespearean quotes to her timeline. She had spent the day at home, helped her mother in cooking, and then later taken the family to the beach at Besant Nagar. They had had dinner there, and then returned home tired but happy. It was after everyone else was in bed that Aparna had sat at her desk. But her intimacy with Anand last evening came to her in flashes, distracting her, as she tried to write. She recalled every word, expression, and movement, every whirl of her feelings.

"Thank you so much for such a beautiful evening," he had texted her this morning, after she responded to his initial message.

"Whatever I did was genuine, and from the heart," Aparna had promptly typed, lying on her yoga mat, smiling to herself. "It was not to impress, but to please you. There's a big difference between the two."

"Of course, I know it was all from the heart," Anand had replied, "I don't doubt that."

After she had got her column started, the first paragraph in place now, Aparna distractedly switched browser pages on her laptop. She noticed the alert of a message on her Facebook account and clicked it open. It was from her new friend Stephan Shedrack.

"Thank you for accepting me," he wrote.

Aparna noted curiously, also somewhat suspiciously, that he had not said "Thank you for accepting my invite or my friendship invite," but "for accepting me." She thought, perhaps it had the ring of an ulterior motive, but replied "You're welcome."

She realised it was futile to work on her writing further. Her mind was too fancy free, for her to rein it in to concentrate. So she logged out, and picked up a book to read. But then she could barely focus on it either for more than a few paragraphs. It was best to just go to sleep, she decided, that is if it would come at her behest.

Aparna's interactions with Stephan on FB were to increase gradually—spaced over a few days, then months. It was usually on her phone that she interacted with him. This is how the conversation commenced.

"So what do you do?" he had messaged a week after they became friends on FB.

"I was hoping you would have checked my profile details by now," she replied crisply, irritated. "I'm a writer and columnist, and everything about me is on my profile."

After half a day of silence, he had replied, "Very impressive. So how many books have you written so far?"

"Well, I have not written a single yet, but plan to, soon." She typed, wondering why she bothered interacting with someone so callous, who clearly had no interest in her, for he had not even gone through her profile well yet. "Now I write newspaper columns and magazine articles. So what do you do?"

 Shuvashree Chowdhury

"I'm the director of a construction firm—J&W Construction Company."

"What kind of construction?" Aparna enquired, even as she quickly googled the company's name to come up with a list of websites named thus. "Do you build residential houses, or commercial complexes like malls?"

"Both kinds, residential homes, commercial malls, also highways," he wrote, and then promptly posted a photo image, which before she could open on her phone, he added, "this is a picture of my car."

By now, she had scanned the list of companies found on Google. There were two or three listings by the name—J&W Construction Company—one in California and two others in UK. She now retrieved the image of the car he sent her, noticing he was indeed trying to impress her. But to her surprise, it was not a swanky car but a black back-open wagon, in the foreground of a construction project. She decided to ignore her niggling suspicion of his motives, and deduced he was merely trying to be friendly. Thus, it would be safe to continue to chat with him on FB messenger.

"So, do you drive this car yourself?" Aparna enquired, chattily.

"No, my driver does." He had replied promptly, as he was still online.

"Do you have to travel a lot on work … I mean, to the locations?"

"Yes, I do, but not always, only to oversee the work sometimes."

"So where's your office and is it far from your home? Is it a long drive?"

"I live in Manchester … my office is in Liverpool, so about an hour or so."

"Do you have a male or a female secretary? Is she possessive of you?" Aparna continued in her usual chatty manner, used to it by now due to her job.

"Hahahaha … Yes, why do you ask?"

"Just like that … I've always known woman secretaries to be possessive of their bosses," Aparna replied, beginning to enjoy this distraction. "When I need to get an interview, I have to befriend the secretary first and keep her in good humour so she will put me on to her boss easily."

"I'll tell you soon, you will learn all about me very soon. You're really pretty, in fact, the prettiest woman I have come across in a really long time."

"You can't be serious? The women in London and UK that I have seen are so beautiful, well-dressed, and above all so slim and well made-up. I once went on a junket—it's those all-paid-for trips we journos get to go on to write about."

"Yes, they are slim alright, but not pretty like you."

"So then you agree I need to lose weight, right?"

"Hahahaha, a little only, but that's okay."

"So how did a gorgeous guy like you just land on my roof? You are really gorgeous, you know? I don't believe you're for real."

"Hahahaha, not more gorgeous than you and you're real. You're so so pretty, the prettiest woman I've come across, and your heart is of gold."

"Now don't be smart with me. Where have you seen my heart, Mister?

"I've read your blogs—your poems and short stories."

"Ah, so you read too … what else do you read?"

"You are so beautiful and so intelligent. I love the way you dress, and above all, I love your smile … You are so so pretty. I have honestly never seen anyone more pretty. In fact, I love everything about you."

"I'm married, you know, and have a son as well."

"That's alright. Nothing can make me stop admiring you. I'm not doing anything wrong, am I? What can I do to you anyway, from so far?"

"Well, considering we are at such a distance, why would you want to chat with me in an unreal world, rather than be out on a real date with a real woman? I'm sure with the way you look, you have women at your doorstep all the time."

"Yes, you're right, I do have women chasing me. But I have had enough of UK women. They cannot be relied upon at all. My ex-wife, she taught me such a big, bad lesson, a really bad woman she was. Then the two girlfriends after her, they were just like her, never satisfied with one man."

     Shuvashree Chowdhury

"So you were married as well? How long? Do you have children too?"

"Yes, a daughter, who is six years old. I got divorced six years back."

"Ah that is sweet! So how old are you really? Your FB profile says you were born on 28 September 1978, but you don't look anywhere above thirty years, well twenty actually."

"Hahaha, you must be joking, I'm older than you, and you look twenty."

"Well, according to your profile, you are thirty-seven years old. So you can't be older than me. How can you? I'm forty-three years old."

"Hahahaha, I don't want to lie to you. I was born on 4 April 1973."

"Well, why did you change your details, to find younger prospective partners? Are Virgo men better marriage prospects that you changed your birthday too? Anyways, by this account, you're still younger than me and with the two years that I've lived more than you, I can teach you a lot, haha."

"You are actually my coach in all respects, and I have so much to learn from you. To start with, your English is excellent."

"Thanks," Aparna replied. "But then how is your English so poor, when you're British and are living in the UK?" Then in a bid to tone down her impoliteness, above all to not seem shallow, whatever the reason for his poor English, she added "Anyways, now be a good student. Okay, read me for homework. The rest you will learn through our interactions here."

"I was in Vietnam till two years back, completed my studies there in Vietnamese. My mother is from there."

"Ah, that explains your oriental gorgeous looks … and also the poor spellings … I mean the way you spell is the way you must speak. But it's all very cute actually, adds to your exotic charm."

"Thank you so much, for accepting me the way I am."

"Now come on, you are so gorgeous, why would I not … I can't help repeating all the time how gorgeous you are. Then your simplicity of heart is very appealing."

"No … no, you're preeeety … very preeety!"

"So why would you be chatting with someone online rather

than going out on a real date now, more so, why someone from remote India?

"I'm enjoying chatting with you online, much more than I have enjoyed talking to someone real in a long time. My friends recommended Indian women to me, after all the pain I have gone through. 'They are loyal,' my friends said to me."

"So you're not dating anyone now?"

"No, not in the last six months. I haven't been with a woman since that long. I'm not in the habit of online chatting, if that's what you're thinking. It's just that, seeing your picture, I knew I had to have you."

"Have me … Now what's that supposed to mean … how can you have me? I'm married and that too at such a distance, haha. Anyways, I get it … it's your queer English that makes you say funny things. In spite of whatever you say, I cannot help wondering how a gorgeous guy like you literally lands on my roof … seems too good to be real. Are your pictures and profile for real? What's even stranger is that you find me gorgeous in comparison to all the beautiful women in UK … it's so funny, really."

"Hahahaha, don't keep saying that. You're the one who is truly gorgeous and much more than me. So tell me little more about your work."

"I work for a leading newspaper in Chennai—ever heard of the place? I have a weekly column, and I also write more as and when required or if I get a good lead. I enjoy my work immensely."

"Good … as long as you like what you do, you will be good at it."

"So what do you do outside of work? You must have friends, who you hang out with? Are your friends married? Do they have children?"

"Yes, there is Chris and there is Ben. They all work with me. We hang out together, go to the club, or for a game of football sometimes."

"Are all your friends British and what about their wives?"

"Chris and Ben are British and their wives too, but my other friends are married to Italians and Spaniards too. They all saw your picture and are impressed as to how I managed to befriend

        Shuvashree Chowdhury

someone as pretty as you. This picture." (He posts Aparna's earlier profile picture in a pink knitted top)

"What, they all saw my pictures?"

"Yes, they were here a while back and wanted me to go out with them … but I didn't feel like going, so they left after a drink. I'd much rather be with you. After a really long time, I feel like talking to someone."

"I'm surprised at myself that I'm chatting with you. I never chat online, rarely ever with friends even. Over the last months, I've received friendship invites, men trying to send inane messages to chat me up. Somehow it has never moved beyond a few sentences, and here I'm chatting with you so long and so effortlessly."

"Hahaha, that's because we have a connection. Our friendship is a gift from God and destined really. I like you very much."

"You mean we have chemistry? Well, that may be the explanation. But how did someone as gorgeous as you ever land on my roof, I'm increasingly curious, as I do believe in God but not really in miracles. Why don't you spend this time over a real woman? It will do you much good."

"Stop saying that! You're not a ghost! You are so pretty, the prettiest woman I have ever seen, and especially your smile and your eyes are so beautiful. I will see you someday for sure, whenever that may be."

"Okay, we'll see, now I've got to go. I have to take my son and parents for a movie. Perhaps you should catch up with your friends wherever they are."

"I don't feel like going out. I will just stay home now."

"Watch a movie or something then. Bye!"

"Bye, my pretty darling … you have a good time and think of me!"

It was another Sunday. The week had gone by really fast in her newfound contentment. That evening, Aparna felt really happy, happier than she had been in a long time, as she strolled about the recently opened Express Avenue mall, built on the ground of the Indian Express offices, after they moved to Ambattur. She loved hanging out here, as much as her son did. She recalled how the meetings with Anand had been far better than she had ever imagined. It was the best romantic outing she'd had yet—the one at Fisherman's Cove with the moonlight, the sea breeze, and a candlelight dinner, the beer and the atmosphere intoxicating her. The images ran through her mind as vividly as if she was still there. The feel of his lips still felt alive on hers. Yet through these warm thoughts that she was encased in, she could not help smiling at the effortless, casual chat with Stephan. She had got drawn into the web of flirtation with him, even though her heart and mind were securely with Anand. Was this a signal her soul was sending her? Was she indulging in interactions with Stephan to extricate her emotions from the web of those she acutely felt for Anand, which were really scaring her now.

Stephan was sweet. His simplicity of thought, the open and straightforward attitude, was refreshing. Aparna usually met men who tended to play games and beat about the bush in their interactions with women. She had never encountered a man as openly appreciative of her as Stephan. But then, men in Chennai were relatively reserved, as compared to those in Mumbai whom she had met while working there, after her marriage. Her interaction with Stephan today had certainly distracted Aparna from Anand, taken her mind off her acute feelings for him, since last week, that scared her. She recalled nervously how, that evening at the hotel, she had felt reluctant to go down for dinner, expecting the intimacy between them to last longer. Aparna had cursed herself for involuntarily breaking the passionate spell they had lain in, in each other's arms. This had driven her suggestion to shower together, only to lead to disappointment when he turned her down. She had also hated leaving Anand that night, hated how they had to shake hands coolly as if they were just business associates.

Aparna wondered how Anand could have been so detached right after what they had shared. She could never see sex and love as mutually exclusive concepts. But then, she knew from her marital experience, men can become detached right after sex, even remain so through a bout of physical intimacy, however difficult a woman may find it. That is, unless she braces herself for it. Isn't this one of the reasons why sex workers do not kiss their clients? These recurring thoughts distressed Aparna, as she realised how fervently involved she had become with Anand, and how that put

		Shuvashree Chowdhury

her at a huge risk of having her soul crushed from the onslaught of the rough wheels of the horse-cart of unrequited love her heart had drawn and nurtured. She felt alarmed now, thinking about Anand's marital status and reputation, not to mention her own situation. Though she was divorced now, her son spent his vacations with his father, and they were still a family—however dysfunctional it may be. In such circumstances, what was she expecting out of this relationship with Anand that she had allowed to develop to such intensity?

This man Stephan Shedrack had appeared just in time, to distract her from getting further caught in the muddy ditch of her entangling emotions from where it was going to be extremely painful to haul her heart out, even if she were to do so right away. This was because, in spite of her fears, she still nursed the two exquisite attitudes that perched on the human mind, called hope and optimism. The next day was a Monday. At work, Aparna felt flustered just crossing Anand's cabin, on returning from an outdoor assignment. In a flash, the intimacy she had shared with him had rushed to her mind, disarming her again. Aparna had marched on to her desk, resolute that she was going to avoid him unless absolutely necessary. She had to gauge his feelings now, see if she meant anything to him beyond the physical chemistry they obviously shared. More so, she had to calm down and rein in her feelings, before it destroyed her completely. Radhika, her boss, was in her cabin, concentrating on her laptop. Aparna decided to go and have a chat with her, to distract herself from the thoughts of Anand and the unrest she felt. She left her bag at her workstation and walked over to Radhika's cabin.

"Good morning, Radhika," she said from the doorway, "May I sit with you for a while?"

"Yeah, sure, how did your breakfast meeting with the three expat hotel general managers go? Did you meet the three of them at one of their hotels, or what?"

"It went off rather well, Radhika, and they were fun to talk to." Aparna started enthusiastically, her eyes twinkling with the excitement of the interlude she was narrating. "We met at the Marina beach over a morning walk. I got the photographer to take some good pictures of them with the backdrop of Mahatma

Gandhi's statue and the rising sun. The three men had turned up in their jogging suits and shoes."

"Looking dapper, I'm sure." Radhika smiled conspiratorially, with a wink. "They must all be very fit, not to mention handsome men."

"Yeah, you can say that again!" Aparna grinned. "They looked debonair, and you know how charming hoteliers are, French ones at that."

"Hope you'll have the write-up ready soon, for Friday. This is a busy week."

Aparna returned to her desk, settled in, and started transcribing the interviews with the French general managers of three reputed luxury hotels.

She heard the alert of an incoming text message on her phone from a colleague and, after she replied, she checked the FB icon that indicated a notification to a message in her inbox.

There was a message from Stephan, that read, "Good morning, the prettiest woman in the whole world."

Aparna smiled, as she was much amused, even flattered, by his outrageous flirtation. She looked at the wall in front, and it was nearly 12 a.m. on the clock. Stephan must have just woken up, she noted, as it would be about 7.30 a.m. at his end.

"Good morning, gorgeous," she replied.

"Hahahaha, good morning, my pretty. So how was your evening? Did you sleep well?"

"Evening was good, but I didn't sleep too well," Aparna typed slowly at the thought of how it was not easy to fall asleep anymore. "I was awakened by strange thoughts very early and could not get back to sleep."

"Why, my darling, what thoughts? Why is it you didn't sleep well"?

"I guess it was the stress over the early assignment I had this morning—you know I interviewed three French national, luxury hotel general managers."

"Ah! That's very nice! You must get all the exposure, so you will shine in your field. I want my princess to be the best in the world."

"So what are you doing now, gorgeous?"

     Shuvashree Chowdhury

"Hahaha, I'm not gorgeous, you are!"

"No, you! I still cannot get over how and from where you landed on my roof … Anyways, I'm working now and you must have to get to work."

"Alright … You have a good day. Muuuuaah!"

Placing her phone back into her handbag as she preferred, so as not to misplace it, Aparna tried to concentrate on transcribing the interviews. But she could not rein in her thoughts, slipping into recalling the ease with which she was engaging with Stephan. Perhaps it was what she needed now, this easy friendship, she reminded herself, to distract her from Anand. Her heart was as much with Anand as before, but Stephan gave her hope, an emotional support, moments of simple happiness that Anand would not provide. What she found refreshing about Stephan, and looked forward to, she realised now with a smile, was his simplicity, his modesty actually, the way he liked everything about her. He seemed much in awe of her—though she discerned a lot of it was his natural congeniality and flirtation. More than Stephan's temperament, what attracted her, now that she was growing more aware of it, was his Greek-god appearance. His intense eyes, innocently engaging smile, his suave style—perceptible from the photographs—had arrested her and now held Aparna's interest.

Physical inclination plays a vital role in relationships, even if platonic, definitely gaining significance in love—thus the phrase 'love at first sight'. Aparna was flattered that a man as gorgeous as Stephan, warm, charming, successful as well, who owned a construction company left to him by his father, would find her beautiful, and be so sensitive and adoring. Though she attributed most of his attentions to his acute loneliness and sense of mistrust from the bad marriage that she could relate well to, however different their experiences.

Aparna decided on continuing the friendship with Stephan, however strange his sudden appearance in her life seemed. It would certainly help her recoup and deal with her feelings for Anand, going forward. She looked up from her desk just then to notice Anand walk into Radhika's cabin. He would have crossed her, she realised, and noticed her staring at her computer unseeingly. The thought flustered her. She didn't want him to think she was not as committed to work as before. Aparna knew well that it had been her dedication and efficiency at work that had drawn Anand to her, not just his physical attraction. He was not about to tolerate a lackadaisical attitude, whatever his personal equation with her now. He had a professional work culture, and this was the primary attraction Aparna felt towards him.

For Aparna and Anand, intellectual stimulation and the passion they brought to their work was a mutual turn on. Though they had been drawn to each other from the start, it was really over work, their views at meetings, discussions, and also their writing—Anand also wrote a Sunday column—that they had started to really feel their mutual attraction. Their ability to trust and confide in each other about work and their personal lives was the fundamental and primary elements to the growth of their intimate relationship. But Aparna was scared. Now that the initial attraction had given way to the thrill of covert lust, what was to happen next? Was this liaison going to go past being a casual affair, a messy short-term relationship perhaps, or lead to something more meaningful?

Aparna pulled in the reins of her thoughts and spurred her mind back to the interviews. She decided she had to complete this article by the end of the day. Anand must have walked past her again, Aparna gathered, on his way out of Radhika's cabin. For when she looked up, Radhika was alone and peering into her laptop with a stern expression. After a few more moments of vicarious pleasure from being unable to withhold snatches of the evening at Fisherman's Cove flashing to mind with the thought of Anand having just passed by, Aparna vehemently steered her mind back to the article she was writing. This was not before realising she priced that evening more than the culmination of their passion at the Savoy hotel. Aparna left office for that day, only after filing the story of the French general managers with all the determination she could muster in reining her errant thoughts.

It was much later that evening, reading a book after the family had had dinner, with her parents watching television and son tucked into bed, that Stephan knocked on her door—in the virtual world on FB. In his charming tone, he wrote, "Good evening! How's my pretty lady? Did she have a good day?"

                    Shuvashree Chowdhury

"Hi, gorgeous!" Aparna promptly replied, "So you're back from work?"

"Hahahaha, you always say that! You're the one who is so pretty, intelligent, pretty pretty pretty! The most beautiful lady I have seen! Now take a look at this picture… (Shares another one of Aparna's profile pictures in a black georgette top) isn't she pretty? My friends still don't believe I'm chatting with this woman!"

"What, your friends, are they with you again now? I hope they're not a part of our chat too?"

"No, no, I would never show them our chats, how can I … it's just between us and I treasure it. They just dropped in to have a drink with me … they're saying 'Hello' to you. There's Ben and Chris."

"Hello, guys! It's nice to meet you!" Aparna typed, feeling a bit edgy.

"They look forward to meeting you someday, very soon, they say!"

"Now that's quite a far-fetched idea, isn't it, gorgeous?"

"No, it's not that difficult … I can come to visit you as soon as you invite me. Then you can come over here—I'll take care of everything for your visit. You won't need to worry about a thing."

"We'll see about that! Now tell me, how did your day go? Did you visit locations or were you in office? Ah … but your friends are waiting for you, aren't they, please go on … Are you guys going to the pub or where?"

"No, I'd much rather stay here chatting with you! They're leaving now, going to a football game in Manchester."

"You must go! You need to be spending time with your real friends even if you're off real women, not stay home alone chatting online with me."

"You're as real to me as anyone can ever be … and I am so happy to chat with you…After a really long time, I feel so happy. I don't want to go out with my friends now. I will see them over the weekend."

"All right then, gorgeous, if that's what you wish. So tell me about your day. What was it like? Did your secretary bother you today?"

"Hahahaha, no, no one bothers me. It was a regular work day, nothing special, though I was very busy all day. Returned home by 4 p.m."

"What is the first thing you do once you get home ... take a shower or have tea? Do you prefer tea, coffee, or a drink?"

"I have tea first. I prefer tea. Then shower later."

"You like it with milk or cream and sugar?"

"With milk and a little sugar"

"Ah! I prefer tea too and that's exactly how I like mine."

"We have a lot in common. That is why it is clear that it was God who brought us together. And it is his wish that I find you."

"Well, if God drops someone as gorgeous as you on my roof out of the blue, I must certainly be privileged."

"Hahahaha, you always say that ... but you're the one who is so pretty. I am truly lucky to have found you, more so because you are so intelligent, so good in English—that really impresses me—but above all, you have a beautiful heart, of gold. There must be some reason God brought us together."

"Now ... together is quite a far dream, you see. We've barely just met online."

"I like you very much and no one is going to stop me from getting you ... not even you yourself. I know exactly what I want. It's you!"

"Hahaha, now we'll see just how you go about achieving that."

"You will see. I know God has brought me to you and I must follow his plan. He wants me to be happy; that is why he has found the best woman for me. My friends are going to be so jealous when they see you."

"Now wait, let's not rush things here ... I understand you like me, but you cannot rush something if you want it to last forever."

"Haha. You're right. See that's why I say you are my coach. I have so much to learn from you. It's just that I know you are right for me ... It is God's wish and he has brought you to me. I can be happy now, finally."

"Tell me, how did you come across my profile? How did you find me?"

"I told you, I will tell you everything about me, including this, when we meet ... when I come to visit you in your country. You are going to invite me someday, I hope?"

                    Shuvashree Chowdhury

"It's just that I can't help thinking you're somewhere around here and playing some prank on me ... you're too good to be real."

"Hahaha ... I keep telling you, it is God's hand in all of this. He brought us together. When we have so much in common, don't you see God's hand at work in getting us together? How can we defy what God wants?"

All of this conversation between Aparna and Stephan had taken place in snatches, in the course of a couple of weeks and was to follow. Aparna was slipping into an anaesthetic web of comfort with Stephan, with Anand apparently receding to the back of her mind. She basked in Stephan's warmth. His simplicity was endearing, and the attention he showered her with was sweeping her off her feet. This was in spite of the controlled façade she still held with him. Stephan was right; she felt happy, truly happy after a really long time. Could this then really be God's wish at play—was he leading her to her destiny? A palmist friend, whose predictions of her life had been accurate so far, had told Aparna that she would marry again, a rich man at that. And have a big and beautiful house, and settle in the West—Europe perhaps. She had never taken his words seriously. But now, she could not help but wonder if he might be right again. Was it then divine providence acting upon her, in that Stephan had dropped on her out of nowhere?

Stephan was rich. Added to this, being in the construction business, he could build her dream home for her someday. He had built himself a new house recently, moving out of the larger one his father had built, where he had lived with his ex-wife. He had told Aparna he would not consider moving back to his father's old house, as it had bad memories of his ex-wife. Aparna had not liked his new, rather plainly built house, from the pictures Stephan had shown her recently. It had no elaborate front garden as she imagined of her dream home, and was quite like the house of a bachelor. But he had shown her pictures of the residences, commercial complexes, and chapels, all at various stages of construction by his company that she had liked.

It must surely be her destiny unfurling before her, Aparna thought as she remembered the strange events that she had been going through. Thus, she felt powerless to resist Stephan's charms, his gorgeous looks, and undeniable bait. It was in recall of these astrological predictions that Aparna opened up her heart to Stephan consciously, allowing her feelings for Anand to be superseded forcibly. It was far from easy, as intimate moments with Anand would flash to mind abruptly, with a shooting pain in her chest—the type you might feel in extricating a sharp object. Then consciously, she would steer her thoughts towards Stephan—his smile the easiest memory to evoke.

This was the most difficult period emotionally, in Aparna's life, much more than the trauma she had undergone in marriage, and then the separation from her ex-husband. She had not been so in love with Nikhil as with Anand now. That must be the reason, Aparna concluded. But however difficult it was to detach emotionally from Anand, she was determined not to lose herself, as she did naively in marriage. She would keep Stephan on her radar, continue focusing on her career, and working alongside Anand.

    Shuvashree Chowdhury

Chapter 13

An Unwarranted Guilt

Sujata opened her eyes to the loud crowing outside her open window. It was still dark. She pulled the light floral-printed duvet up around her neck, even as she tried to make sense of what time it was. January nights in Chennai can be somewhat chilly and the day rather pleasant. The crows making a racket was an indication that it was still the wee hours of the morning. Was it their loud crowing that had jolted her out of sleep, sleep that had been late in coming the previous night? Not likely, she thought, closing her weary eyes and relishing again the comfort of her warm bed. Usually, she slept soundly till the alarm set for 7 a.m. startled her awake. Even then, she would hit the snooze button and stay in bed a while longer. Then what could possibly have awoken her so abruptly this morning?

She turned on her side and opened her eyes slightly, but Anand wasn't there. He was away on work in Mumbai, she remembered, and had been gone the whole of last week. That's why the door was bolted from inside. As Sujata attempted to get back to sleep again, an image from the previous night pervaded her consciousness. It was of her sitting on Shekhar's lap, her arms wrapped around his neck tightly. They had kissed deeply as if their souls were in unison. She could feel the moist warmth of his mouth even now, the throbbing heat of his nude body that was pressed to hers. She gasped suddenly, every bit of her body awake now to his touch.

Sujata sat up in bed, as the events of the previous evening rushed to mind. She felt restless and shaken to the core as she thought about every touch and move. The impact of their sensual yet passionate lovemaking after years of yearning had had a deep impact on Sujata. But more than that, it was the strength of the man she had always known and counted upon, melting away with the tears of grief over his wife's death that he had felt no qualms in exhibiting, which had grabbed Sujata's gut, churned her heart, and blown her mind to smithereens. She had come home last night, emotionally and physically totally spent, even though she was calm.

But now, her desire to reach out to Shekhar grew into a desperate longing for him. Sujata looked at the bedside clock. It was close to 5 a.m., but still too early to call him. He needed a good rest more than her urgent need to hear his voice, to hug him in comforting him as well as herself, and make love to him again languorously and gently. Last evening, Sujata had absorbed Shekhar's pain spontaneously, as if it had been inflicted on her personally, as he spoke of Aneesha, after he had made love to Sujata somewhat distractedly. It was as if the act of making love had unclogged his heart, and warmed it from the acute coldness it had been dumped into by Aneesha's sudden passing. His pain had melted into tears of molten wax from the burning candle of his being, the light emanating from which Sujata had quietly absorbed.

Perhaps his ease in talking, letting his emotions flow, was heightened by the two drinks Shekhar had in quick succession. But whatever the cause, the events had pulled Sujata further into the whirlpool of love, and entrapped her in a way that it was perhaps impossible to extricate from. She had developed strong feelings for him over a while now. But it never felt as powerful, as all-encompassing, as it did right this moment sitting up quietly on her bed looking out of the window, waiting for the the breaking of dawn. The crowing had died out, or was it replaced by the clamour in her head, Sujata wondered. The faint light of day creeping upon her now meant she must have been lying awake in bed for over an hour and a half and it must be nearing 6 a.m.

Sujata pulled her thoughts together and got up. She felt wrapped in the warmth of love, with her heart aflutter and mind cottony. She stepped out of her room to check on the children. They were snuggled cosily into bed in the adjacent room. She bent down to kiss their heads one at a time, but her heart felt too covered with a blanket of romantic love at this point to really feel the deep love for them which was always ensconced in its core. If it had not been for the events of last evening, Sujata would have slept with them,

	Shuvashree Chowdhury

as she tended to when Anand was away. But last night, she had needed the time to herself. Shekhar's touch on her body had made it his and she wanted to savour that.

Sujata went to the kitchen and asked one of the maids to make her tea. She preferred it green with lemon and honey, first thing in the morning, though she opted for coffee in the course of the day. Feeling too restless to even read the newspapers till she spoke to Shekhar, Sujata decided to shower and get ready for the day. By the time she emerged from her room in a floral printed pink and white silk *salwar* suit, her mid-length hair leaving a damp mark on the back of her *kurta*, tea was served. The tea-tray, as she had requested, was placed on the centre table in the large drawing room. She had recently had it refurbished and she took in the new chandeliers, paintings, and finely engraved antique rosewood furniture including a rather large wall-to-wall book case with pleasure. Sujata took great pride in her home, which was an extension of her tastes and personality, even if she could not say the same for her marriage. Since her in-laws, including the brother-in-law and his family lived on separate floors, hers was a self-sufficient apartment. She now did not have to feel restricted to her room.

Over the tea that made her calmer now after her shower, Sujata distractedly flipped the pages of the *Hindu* and the *Times of India*. She simultaneously kept a watch on the time on the large clock on the wall. The children would have to be woken by 7 a.m. and would be readied for school by the maids. But Sujata would overlook their breakfast, eating only after them. They would leave home by 8 a.m., along with Anand's personal driver who was a trustworthy man. But when in town, Anand preferred she use her own driver, as his one worked late shifts and came in late.

Sujata had just about finished her tea, from the dainty floral, white, pink and gold bone china cup, when the alarm in her bedroom went off, followed by one in the children's room. After turning the one in her room off first, she went to the children's room and sat down on their bed. As usual, the boys continued to sleep right through the alarm's loud ringing. Unable to bear the shrill sound, Sujata pressed down the clock's lever and stopped the alarm. Then she lovingly ran her hands through the hair of both the boys and stroked their foreheads tenderly, before firmly shaking their arms.

"Now enough, boys, get up … right now," she said forcefully. "We have to get ready for school. Or you will be late and the gate will be shut."

The maid, after making Sujata's tea, now persuaded the boys off the bed playfully, one at a time, and got them standing groggily. Then she thrust their toothpaste-topped brushes into their hands, which she quickly brought out of the adjoining bathroom. Sujata, knowing the boys were in good hands, walked to the privacy of her room. She could call Shekhar now. It was well past 7 a.m. and he should be up by now. But when his mobile went unanswered, Sujata held the phone till it stopped ringing. Then, she hung up, disappointed at the delay in reaching him. After a while, since Shekhar did not call back, she dialled again. There still was no response at his end. Where could he have gone without his mobile, she worried, or was he still asleep? But then he would have woken to the repeated ringing of his phone, unless of course it was in the silent mode. Sujata felt a wave of restlessness wash over her, along with the urge to go over and meet him. But what would he think? Would she like to see her so soon again, she wondered? It was strange, thinking this way, after their closeness over the years. But before last evening, she would have never hesitated with him this way, Sujata thought dismally. Everything was changed now.

It was only after Sujata had had breakfast, ensuring the boys ate their toasted and buttered multigrain bread with poached eggs and *upma* followed by Bournvita milk, that her mobile phone rang. She grabbed it from over her wood-carved tablemat she had hand-picked, and answered, signalling to a maid to get the boys to rinse their mouths. To her dismay, it wasn't Shekhar on the phone. It was her husband Anand's routine morning call to check on all of them when he was travelling. Sujata's disappointment immediately turned to guilt on hearing Anand's voice.

"Hope all is well at home?" he asked, in a soft, caring voice. "How are the children, are they ready for school? Have you all had breakfast?"

The scenes of the previous evening flashed in Sujata's mind uninitiated, unsettling her feigned calm. She had not allowed

                    Shuvashree Chowdhury

herself to feel guilty over her relationship with Shekhar, or even with Manas. But after last evening, she could no longer justify the new physical equation with him, even to herself. After her stilted responses, when Anand hung up, Sujata consciously decided to deal with and crush what she considered her unwarranted guilt. She convinced herself that, knowing what she did of Anand's activities and flings, she had as much right as him to enjoy herself. Moreover, who knew where he really was now, and with whom? Was this trip even work-related as he claimed? Sujata felt more vexed with herself now at these thoughts than with Anand. She no longer cared, she had thought, or questioned him on his whereabouts.

Later in the day, when Sujata met Shekhar in the lobby of the Taj Coromandel Hotel in Nungambakkam, she thought he looked rather tired and much older. She had been waiting for a while, looking towards the imposing gate each time it was held open by the liveried guard, thinking of the conversation with him that morning. After the children had left for school, Sujata, too restless to go to work, had called Shekhar yet again. This time he had picked up the phone, sounding muzzy and quite unlike his usual self.

"You know what ... I continued to drink long after you left last night." Shekhar admitted in a guilty voice, "Then I fell asleep, with my mobile on the silent mode. I'd forgotten to change it back to normal after a meeting last evening."

"That's alright. I was really worried about you. Especially since I saw how washed out you were last night." Sujata said anxiously, then in a chiding tone, she added, "But I didn't think you'd drink more. You had already taken more than you should have when I left."

"You are right, my dear. I really overdid myself last night. Hope all is well at your end and you reached home without a hitch. I did see your message last night that you'd reached home safely. I had the phone in hand till you reached."

Sujata, her need to see him accelerating on hearing his voice, setting aside her pride, abruptly said, "I need to meet you, Shekhar ... today ... before your return to Mumbai."

He sounded worried at her urgency, as he promptly replied.

"Yes, my dear … of course … but hope nothing's wrong. You don't sound alright."

And now she was waiting for Shekhar at the Taj. They had decided it was the ideal place to meet, due to the proximity to her office. It was not far from the Gymkhana Club where he was staying either, and convenient for him to go to the airport afterwards, via Mount Road. After a few hours at the office, Sujata had excused herself for an early lunch meeting and had driven here, with a mixture of anticipation and unease. As she waited, hoping not to meet anyone she knew, Sujata felt comforted at the prospect of meeting Shekhar shortly.

Sujata felt dependant on Shekhar now. She had never felt like this in all the years of their friendship. She was still caught in the sudden whirlwind of last evening's passion, and was finding it difficult to extricate herself mentally. She hoped that meeting him now would calm her somewhat and help her get a grip.

It was Shekhar's steady walk, with his shoulders back, chest out and head held high, that Sujata first noticed as he walked towards her. Then she met his piercing light brown eyes, set off against the salt and pepper hair. As Shekhar came up close, Sujata got up and walked towards him. They exchanged warm glances. Then she led him back towards the hotel's entrance to the bar on their left.

"I have only an hour or so before I leave for the airport," Shekhar said, as they walked into the bar. He looked as serious as he had been looking last night when she left him. "I had a rather late and heavy breakfast at the club … A beer would be great."

Sujata nodded, and even as they strode into the baroque bar, the manager approached her. He knew her well as Anand's wife.

"This is Mr. Shekhar Ravindran." She crisply introduced Shekhar to the manager. "He's a much-valued client from Mumbai."

Sujata met clients and senior candidates here who couldn't come to her office for reasons of confidentiality. It was not as if this meeting would draw any undue attention. The manager led them to four seats at a round table at the centre. They sat overlooking the bar counters. When the waiter walked over to them, she ordered a beer for Shekhar and fresh orange juice for herself. She suddenly noticed Shekhar looking at her piercingly, as though he was trying to perceive her thoughts. Sujata looked back at him solemnly, held

    Shuvashree Chowdhury

his gaze steadily for a while, and felt the restlessness inside her ebb and a sense of calm take over. It was as if the boat of her flailing emotions had found anchor, after being tossed around in a storm at sea.

Sujata felt Shekhar's gaze touch her soul now, more deeply than their physical proximity of last night. It felt like a bear hug that embedded his emotional strength into her. A gaze is sometimes more powerful and intimate than words or physical touch, as his often seemed to Sujata, making her believe in its potency from the time they first met. Shekhar now seemed like the composed man she had always known, and Sujata felt the familiar sense of security about him. Even though he lived in Mumbai, just knowing he was in her life was comforting. On his part, Shekhar now drew from the glow of strength Sujata reflected, as the sea reflects moonlight, illuminating its tumultuous water and shores magnificently, more than what the moon can light up of its own accord. Sujata was comforted in Shekhar's presence and her guilt over their intimacy waned.

As they chatted, Sujata opened up her heart to Shekhar afresh. She told him, as she had over the years, the circumstances of her life. Perhaps he would understand how she had got drawn into the physical aspect of their relationship last evening, after all these years. He was mature and, above that, non-judgemental. So he would put her unease to rest with his reasoning, she believed. Sujata detailed Anand's associations with a number of women again, particularly with Aparna. She elaborated without holding back, how it still hurt and affected her emotionally. In her mind, she was alleviating her guilt, which she could not help feeling due to her childhood conditioning of the propriety of a married woman's behaviour. Also, she was justifying the same to Shekhar and safeguarding her image to him. She didn't care what the rest of the world thought of her.

"You won't believe it, Shekhar, someone left a horrible message last week in my FB inbox ...." Sujata said. "I was so rattled by it, traumatised even."

"What message, what about ... you didn't tell me about this before?"

"I didn't know how to tell you. I was so overwhelmed, and I

didn't want to bother you with my problems, what with your own grief over Aneesha.

"Come on, tell me now … go ahead. You know you can tell me anything."

"I have a strong hunch this message was from Aparna in a bid to rattle me." Sujata started passionately, and then looking about her, she cautiously continued. "But the name of the sender, whose FB profile was recently created, was Shivani."

"What did it say?" Shekhar asked impatiently, in a firm tone.

"This is how the message read roughly: 'I tried reaching you before, but you didn't see my messages. It's to tell you about your cheating husband—with not one woman but many. His phone is your Pandora's box. The password is 2510—your birthday. Lewd WhatsApp messages, pictures, and what not of his sexual jaunts. Be careful, he is very smart. If you let it out, he will cover his tracks. Anuradha, Sakshi, Aparna, Ritika, he claims to love them all. There are many more. I had to tell you. Was my duty."

After a few minutes of silence, looking vexed, Shekhar thoughtfully said: "So you think Aparna added her own name to the list of women to take away suspicion of it being her message? Hmm, you're right … Also, what if you were to check Anand's cell phone and find her messages? So, she was telling the truth to prove her point."

"Yes, that's what I think … I was shocked when I saw it. And I just felt horribly humiliated." Sujata replied, looking crushed. "The whole world must know of my husband's character by now. And I must be quite the laughing stock."

"Don't beat yourself up now, Sujata…." Shekhar promptly said, and then his eyes taking on a suspicious look, he added. "But then … you're not one to just let it go like that. What exactly did you do?"

"Well, you know me rather well, Shekhar, don't you?" Sujata laughed aloud. "What do you think? I gave Anand a piece of my mind. I rattled all the names of the women in the message, much to his shock, without disclosing my source of information."

"What did you do to the woman who wrote the message?" Shekhar pressed.

"Well, I gave her the larger piece of my mind," Sujata said, her

          Shuvashree Chowdhury

eyes shining in cynical mirth. I replied to the message something like this: Thanks Aparna (yes, I used her name) for fulfilling your duty, which is evidently self-serving … You've not told me anything that I didn't know … Sorry you found out you're no more than another casual fling. And I've shared your message with him too. But then you should not complain, he gave you your own column. That's what you were after, weren't you? So stop acting like you've my interest at heart and don't overestimate your bird brain! I've saved your IP address too, along with the message, till I figure out what to do about your identity."

"Good lord! This is so like you," Shekhar said, smiling affectionately at Sujata. "But honestly, if you ask me, this message is not from Aparna … That's what I think. It just does not make sense for her to write this, considering all you've told me about her closeness to Anand. This is some other mischief maker, someone from his office or another woman who has a crush on him, but whom he does not indulge."

"Well, whoever it was, did manage to rattle me all right … Though the real aim might have been to get even with Anand through me."

"Forget this, Sujata," Shekhar said firmly. "Just focus on your work, on the children … but the most, on yourself. Don't waste emotions and guilt over a man who does not know how to treat a woman as special as you. Also, don't curse your destiny. It is because of the way your husband is, due to your dysfunctional marriage, that you were forced into becoming self-reliant and earning an independent identity. In fact, you must thank God—he gave you the fortitude to gear up for the success you are today, Sujata. And you know well, I am always here for you … so never feel alone in life."

"Yes, Shekhar, you are my rock of Gibraltar," Sujata smiled affectionately. "What would I ever do without you? I know you're in a lot of pain now with Aneesha's passing, and how I truly wish I could do something to lessen it for you…."

"You have made it bearable, my dear girl, by sharing my grief. I must say, it was beautiful last evening. And though I understand your guilt about it now, just as you understand my underlying pain over my wife's passing, we both know our love for each other is sincere."

Sujata nodded silently, looking into Shekhar's eyes meaningfully. His look was caressing and intimate. There was nothing more that needed to be said between them after that. Shekhar sat up, downing the last of his beer. On noticing Sujata's finished glass of orange juice, he waved to the waiter and signalled to him to get their check. They made their exit from the bar in silence, nodding to the manager in passing. Each of them called their respective drivers on their mobile phones, after a formal handshake in the hotel's lobby, as if they were business associates. Shekhar got into the car that had pulled up on the porch to take him to the airport, and looked at Sujata intensely. She returned his look with matching intensity, then walked over to her car parked just behind his, to take her back to office.

          Shuvashree Chowdhury

Chapter 14

You Cannot Run Away from Love

Because of Aparna's growing lenience with Stephan, dropping her guard in flirting with him online, unaware as he was of her feelings for Anand, Stephan heightened his charms on her. She thus got drawn into a whirlpool of confusing feelings for him as well, as their FB chats increased in frequency, duration, and also intensity. Aparna, trusting it was her destiny that brought Stephan to her, went with the flow. Moreover, any attempt to alter her position now might tilt the boat of her emotions dangerously back to Anand. The fluidity of her feelings for him might flood her again, possibly capsizing her now. Aparna thus quashed her feelings for Anand, hoping with time all that would be left was a residue of the all-consuming passion she could look back upon in warm reminiscence. So, she avoided Anand as much as was possible at the office, and remained unusually quiet at meetings at which he was present. Anand, on his part, kept a reserve with her, unaware of the digression of her feelings for him, but keeping an eye on her from afar.

In the few weeks of their interactions, it had become routine for Stephan to come online every night well after 11 p.m. and chat with Aparna on Facebook messenger. This was after he returned from work after 6 p.m. in the UK. Aparna, by this time, would have finished dinner, and her son and parents were usually asleep. She would sit with her laptop at the desk in her room, illuminated by a table lamp, as it was inconvenient to type long or fast on the cell phone. Also, if her son or parents awoke, they would consider she was working late as she often did to complete her stories. Stephan sometimes also messaged her in the morning before he left for work, by which time she would already be at work, ready to take a coffee break at the canteen. So she would chat with him briefly on her phone. It was not long before, it became a practice for Stephan, like they were a couple, to check on what Aparna was doing, what she had worn to work, where she was going on meetings or interviews. She indulged him as well.

"Hello darling, so how was your day?" Stephan asked, the first thing when online early one Saturday evening "So what is my pretty lady doing. Forgotten me?"

"Haha … How can I possibly forget you, Handsome?" Aparna replied, smiling. She now awaited his messages, looking forward to his coming online, to ward off thoughts of Anand that still threatened to envelop her, having usually seen him at work. "My day was rather good. So how was yours … was it hectic?"

"Yeah, visited two construction sites. It was busy at office too. But all day, I looked forward to being with you. It is what keeps me going now, you know. I am so happy that I've met you. God is great and I have all faith in his direction."

"By the way, as we're talking of God, are you a Catholic or a Protestant?"

"Haha, Catholic, why do you ask?"

"I'm almost a Catholic myself and know a lot about it, though I was born a Hindu. I did my schooling at a convent school and went to church every Sunday along with my friends, and was often a part of the choir at school. You won't believe, I even said the rosary—Hail Mary— daily, and also Our Father."

"Really, what is your religion—Hindi?"

"It's not Hindi, silly, it is Hindu. I am a Hindu by birth, but I have for long been a Catholic by faith, though I was never baptised. So, do you go to church every Sunday, Stephan, and for confession regularly?"

"Yes, I go to church every Sunday, but not so often for confession."

"Why not for confession? Don't you need, for example, to confess to loving a married woman? You know I am married, don't you?"

"I am not doing anything wrong in loving you. I have nothing to confess. It feels most right. Moreover, it is God who brings us together."

"Isn't that too convenient? You do what you please and how

     Shuvashree Chowdhury

you please. Then even make God your ally. So you're not really devout?"

"Well, I don't know the meaning of devout, but I am true to Jesus."

"All right then, so who else is there in your family? What about your parents, any siblings? I know you have a daughter, but where does she live, with her mother?

"I will never allow my daughter to live with that wicked woman."

"Then where does she live—your daughter?"

"She lives with my mother, in Manchester."

"With your father and mother?"

"My father passed away in 2010. My mother is from Vietnam, and I lived there with her most of the time. After my father's passing away, we moved here to the UK, so I could look after the business from here."

"Now is that why your English is so shaky, gorgeous, and you misspell so many words? I've been meaning to ask you how come your English is so poor."

"Hahahaha, yes, I used to speak only in Vietnamese till I came to the UK. I am trying to learn English fast, but it is not alright yet. But thank you so much for accepting me the way I am, with my poor English."

"But tell me, your profile says you were educated at Oxford. And you also told me that it is true, and that your course of study was civil engineering, right? Are you in touch with your friends from college now?"

"Yes, it is true … but it was a long time back, and I am in touch with some of my college friends. We used to be a large group back then."

There were things about Stephan that did not add up logically in Aparna's mind. But she decided to let it go for now, as her heart had accepted the simplicity of his heart without any reservation. Perhaps his English was good enough for a course in civil engineering—even in Oxford, but how was she to know, Aparna justified to herself. She would have plenty of time to get into the details of his life chronologically, in due course.

So, Aparna, continuing their conversation, replied, "What's in a language anyway? I will teach you English in the course of our chats and you will soon be proficient. I do not see why people, even my friends, make so much fuss about the knowledge of English. It is necessary, but not something to judge a person by surely. What's important really, is that one is a good human being. You are simple and warm-hearted—perhaps that's what you imbibed being in Vietnam. As you mention, people in the UK are just not trustworthy."

"You are so kind and sincere and genuine, that's what I love about you."

"But all that pales to your good looks, gorgeous ... doesn't it?"

"Hahahaha, you always say that, but it is your kindness and enormous heart that accepts me just the way I am. Also, perhaps by now, you know how much I love you. I will never let you go. And nothing can stop me from having you here with me. It is God who brought us together."

"Perhaps it is!" Aparna typed, slowly growing convinced about that. "Tell me about your ex-wife ... you said you've been divorced for six years. But your daughter is also six years old, isn't she? Did you file for divorce while your wife was pregnant?"

"Yes, almost around the same time, you can say. I will tell you everything in good time. Now I just don't feel like talking about that wicked woman. Let's talk about you, about when I can come and visit you."

"Well, there's not a lot of interesting stuff about me, other than that I'm just out of a bad divorce, and a tedious custody battle over our son who is now nine years old and lives with me and my parents here in Chennai."

"So see, you're not married ... I knew it! I just knew God would not be so unkind to me again. But how did it reach this stage? I mean to the stage of filing for divorce to bring up a son singlehanded ... What did the man do to you?"

Aparna, finding a good listener and a sympathetic ear, by now smug in Stephan's adoration, went over with him the entire saga of her marriage. She started with the newspaper search for a groom by her parents, to locating the perfect one, much to Stephan's amusement. She told him all about Nikhil's drinking right from the honeymoon and how it only got worse, and then the difficult

Shuvashree Chowdhury

times in Mumbai. Stephan became angry, very angry with Nikhil, at the way he treated Aparna.

"How can he behave that way with you and the small child … of only a year or so? How can anyone behave like that, however drunk, with his wife? Then you are one of the best human beings I have encountered."

"Well, Nikhil, my ex-husband, is a nice person and a good father, when he is sober. But then that is very rarely. He is always either drunk or in a hangover."

"It's absolutely unacceptable, darling! How the hell could he treat you like this? You did the best thing to get away."

"I had to leave, and I took the firm stance for the sake of my son. I could not allow him to be brought up in such a horrifying atmosphere, always in fear, watching his mother subjugated to constant humiliation. What would be the effect on his impressionable mind? What are the values he would grow up with—among other things? Would he respect women? Would he value the need to work for his living?"

"I'm horrified at all that you have undergone, darling. But it's all over … All your unhappiness is in the past now. I'm here for you. And you must come here to be with me in the UK. We will have a good life here, you will see."

"Will I fit in there, in your society? I've heard and also felt that racism is not extinct there yet. Also, what would I do there and what about my son?"

"Many of my friends are not British and some of their wives aren't either. We even have black British people here a lot. They are all happy here. And then you are so friendly, everyone will love you … you will see."

"We'll see about all that, darling … for now, let's just get to know each other." Aparna replied smugly, though the seed of interest to be with Stephan in the long term was sown in her mind, from where it would flourish unhindered.

"I just don't get it, how can someone be so cruel, that too to his own wife and child? I am so angry on hearing your story, darling."

"You see, people who drink so much are not in control either of their drinking, certainly not of what they do after they drink. It is useless making judgements of them, other than to say that they are ill … very ill."

"It's almost like you're defending your ex-husband. That man did so much harm, hurt you really badly, not to mention the damage to your son. And you still have it in your heart to defend him? I just don't get it. Are you still in love with him or what … wait, tell me, do you still love him?"

"I'm not defending him. And I'm not in love with him either. But sure, I do care about him," Aparna replied, noting the anger and jealousy in Stephan's words.

She was rather pleased by it and realised how easily she had begun to read his emotions only through his written words. They leapt right off at her, even in the absence of a clear physical picture of him in her mind yet, let alone a view of his facial expressions to the emotions. It was as a blind or a deaf person assesses the world through senses other than the one they are missing.

"I'm angry, very angry with that man, and he is still troubling you, harassing you with his calls and threats, of taking the child away, if you don't return to him."

"After all this while, I'm not even angry with Nikhil anymore. He is ill, and doesn't know what he is doing. So I feel sorry for him. In fact, I went to great lengths to understand alcoholism, in order to understand if any of this was my fault, if I could possibly help him, save our marriage perhaps for the sake of our child. I had to do that, to save myself the regret of giving up on my marriage, to ensure I would not regret my decision, before I took the firm stance of seeking a divorce."

"So what are your findings? As for me, I just don't understand this—'it's not in his control' theory! How can one not have control of what one does—as in control over whether one drinks or not? If alcohol does not suit you, then just stay away from it altogether. I can understand that a person after drinking is under the influence of alcohol and thus loses control of his thinking and behaviour. But then, if that is the case, then just don't drink at all. There is absolutely no defence for a lack of control."

"I agree with you on that. Some of us are strong enough to stay away from temptation and others are not. That's what it really is. Alcoholism is a chronic and often progressive disease. It includes

          Shuvashree Chowdhury

the inability to avoid and then to control drinking, to becoming preoccupied with it, then continuing to drink even when it causes problems, to having to drink more to get the same effect. It's a physical dependence, having withdrawal symptoms when you decrease or stop drinking. In fact, if you are alcoholic, you unfailingly can't predict how much you'll drink, how long you'll drink, and certainly not the consequences or what will occur from your drinking."

"I get it all, but then, such people have no right to marry and spoil other people's lives, not to mention to mess up their children's mind and life."

"Such people often do not know they are alcoholic, or worse, will not accept it. More often, in our culture, families will get alcoholics married soon, to pass on responsibility to their spouses. They tend to believe, in case of sons, that with a wife and children, they will give up drinking. Women tend to take up chronic drinking later in life. It's possible to have a problem with alcohol, even when it has not progressed to the point of alcoholism, and thus it goes undetected for a long time. Problem drinking could mean you drink too much at times, causing repeated problems in your life, although you're not completely dependent on alcohol. This is not uncommon with youngsters, whose families do not see the impending danger to them becoming severely alcoholic later. Thus, they sacrifice the lives of their young brides, at times their whole families, to the sacrificial fire of alcoholism, to burn for a lifetime."

"Just like it happened with you ... It makes me so angry, so very angry."

"It's all right now. I had to learn all these lessons the hard way, by suffering for the follies of Nikhil's parents, also mine. For Nikhil, it started with binge drinking—a pattern I was to understand only recently, in which one consumes four or five drinks in a row. It can lead to the same health risks and social problems associated with alcoholism. The more you drink, the greater the risks. Binge drinking, which often occurs with teenagers and young adults, may lead to faster development of alcoholism as it did with Nikhil, before anyone even realised it. In fact, even his brother suffers from the same problem. If you have alcoholism or even have a problem with alcohol, you may not be able to cut back or quit without professional help. Denying that you have a problem is usually an inherent part of alcoholism and other types of excessive drinking. In Nikhil's case, not only him, his whole family—especially his mother—was in denial and did not seek help, till it got out of hand. His parents expected me to handle the situation and to take care of him, but I was very young and so ill equipped at that time. Nikhil's drinking and behaviour freaked me out. And that my marriage and husband were so unusual made me so mistrustful."

"All that is behind you now, darling, I'm here to ensure that going ahead you're always going to be happy and safe. You've got to trust me on that. I am so happy to have found you that now I'm the happiest person."

"Thanks, gorgeous. I too feel the bad times are well past me now. I look forward to the good times, a bright life."

"Now can I have my second dinner, darling? Have you had yours?"

"Yes, yes, I've had dinner a long time back … it's really late here. Now you go ahead and have yours. Goodnight."

"Goodnight, darling … my pretty princess. Sleep well. Love you."

That night, as in the last many weeks, chatting with Stephan till late, Aparna hardly slept. It was past 1 a.m. when she fell asleep, as soon as her head touched the pillow, from the exertion of the day. But she was coerced awake by 4 a.m., with the distress she was under, over her heart tumbling rapidly between Anand and Stephan. At times, it was a bit of a conscious effort to keep her emotions on track with Stephan, but he was steadily displacing Anand. Now Aparna had begun to worry about her racing relationship with Stephan that was all but breaking her emotional shore and washing her out, causing her turmoil and anxious sleepless nights.

Stephan made demands on her time and emotions, which Aparna welcomed and looked forward to. But he was expediting plans to visit Chennai, which made her somewhat anxious. She herself had invited him, looked forward to meeting him, and to set realistic expectations of him and their relationship. But now she became increasingly tensed by her own decision in rushing it.

	Shuvashree Chowdhury

Also, her feelings for Anand still tugged at her heart, making her wonder, if she was running into Stephan's arms, just to get away from Anand, in fear of getting hurt. It was during their plans of Stephan's visit that he asked about the financial investment opportunities in India.

"I would like to invest in property in your country," Stephan abruptly wrote one evening, after their initial loving exchanges. "Where would it be a good place to do so?"

"But why would you want to invest in property in my country?"

"So there will be some security for you there, and we can visit whenever we want, even after you move here to UK."

Aparna was taken aback by Stephan's declaration on her moving to the UK so firmly and definitively. They had talked about it, but in doing so, she had merely been considering the idea aloud. It was not like she had made up her mind yet. Though she should not be surprised, she chided herself. As by now, their conversations had evolved to become personal and binding, as in a real relationship, rather than a virtual one. Stephan had even telephoned her a few times, on her cell number that she had readily given him on his asking. To her surprise, contrary to his assertive body language, arrogant and flamboyant looks in his photographs, even the confidence in chatting online, Stephan had a soft low voice and his tone was gentle. Aparna could barely hear his words, which came across as bare whispers, the first time he had called during her lunch time at work. This was in spite of pressing her phone close to her ear, then walking outside to a quieter place.

The way Stephan spoke to her, lovingly and firmly as if he had a right over her, endeared him further to Aparna, over their online chats. It was only over a few more conversations that Aparna got accustomed to his soft low voice and his heavy British accent. After his first call, Aparna had fished out her mobile earphone from her desk drawer at home and placed it in her handbag, for ease of retrieval on his next call. She had been right in using it, as the earphone increased the audibility of his voice, thus bringing him closer. Even while talking, he would laugh as frequently as he typed the "hahahahaha" in their Facebook chats, along with every other thing she said. Aparna knew from his laughter that he genuinely liked her, to be so delighted by her and her sense of humour.

It was through their telephone conversations that Stephan came further alive. Also, on their online chats, Aparna now tended to keep his varied profile pictures she had copied to her laptop in the background, to feel his physical presence. She had discovered this way of feeling physical proximity after Stephan had posted one or other of her pictures on the screen in the course of their chats, to make it seem like he was in her physical presence. Thus, often in each other's company now, in varying degrees of proximity through their pictures, sharing their lives, aspirations, and disappointments thus far, their conversations became more intimate. Aparna felt emotionally close to Stephan in just over a month. It was more than she felt with anyone, even Anand, after their exchanges of months and the intimacy they had recently shared. But Aparna was not sure whether this closeness to Stephan was their chemistry and a natural progression, or an innate defensiveness to run away from feelings for Anand. If it was so, she had succeeded rather well.

Aparna now slipped into consent with Stephan's plan of her moving to live in Liverpool, now that they were a couple. In her current mental state, after the trauma of the divorce, along with fear of losing her son, and then fear of her feelings for a married man, her boss at that, Aparna might have been lured by anyone. She could hardly trust herself not to do anything drastic, to escape the walls caving in on her emotionally, crushing her. That Stephan wanted to invest in India, for her sake primarily, so she would feel rooted, confirmed his love and seriousness in their relationship. It sealed Aparna's conviction of staying firmly on the lifeboat she had set foot on inadvertently with him. And she was prepared for setting sail, to however unprecedented and unknown a future with Stephan.

"So what kind of an investment are you considering here and where?" Aparna asked Stephan when he came online, late one evening.

This was after they had exchanged details of their day with romantic endearments that no longer seemed affected to Aparna as before. Stephan referred to her as "darling", "my princess", "my life", "my soul", "sweetheart", "the source of my happiness"

          Shuvashree Chowdhury

and such blandishments. Though she could not herself drop her inhibitions, or feel the deep emotions she needed to call him anything more than "gorgeous" or, on rare occasions, "darling". Aparna was trying to cope fast with his culture, social manners, and fluid expressions and was surprised at how well she was faring in his way of dating—online though it might be. As for Aparna's feelings for Anand, she had them in control, and was by now able to squash it to the back of her mind, in a remote corner of her heart, where it would perhaps remain forever.

The thing with desire is, it might bloom well in freedom and crumble in rigid possessiveness and restrictions, as happens in many marriages and long-term relationships. But conversely, it withers with too much air, as a fire might in an open space, if neglected. Like a fireplace, you have to tend to desire recurrently, feed it with logs of love and devotion, to keep warm the chamber of your heart, to keep you cosy. If spurned, if lacking a secure heath, even a robust love, as in Aparna's case, might relinquish and find another shelter to burn in. This might leave the primary recipient of love out cold, as would be with Anand, once he figured his own true intentions and stance on the desire he had ignited in Aparna's vulnerability. After their intimacy, he had been avoiding Aparna, or so she perceived. This led her to warm her sore heart with Stephan, where it was more likely to stay lit steadily.

Stephan by now had gained a firm ground in Aparna's mind and heart. They spoke every day, with their conversations getting longer—running into hours now, over discussing Aparna's life primarily. She would try to finish her writing, before Stephan came online and also do much of it in the office. Even after their chats ending at 1.30 a.m. or 2 a.m., Stephan would message her in the late morning, early at his end—after he was ready to leave for work. By which time, Aparna was at work, but would steal a few moments to converse online with him. Stephan now took interest and was allowed access to every aspect of her life. He would ask about her new hair style right after she got one, for example, or comment on what she wore to this outing or that party. Then he would make suggestions on the outfit she might wear to another event, insisting on a selfie, to demonstrate her appearance for his approval.

"You look great in that black outfit, with the black leggings, my love. I always want my wife to be the best dressed, everywhere, at all times," Stephan would say to her. "You must have the best of everything, my princess … and now you will."

Aparna thus became more and more emotionally dependent on Stephan.

In turn, instinctively, she worried about Stephan's health and affairs:

"So what did you have for breakfast, darling?" she would ask every morning, after Stephan once told her he had buttered toast with tea, and had then been unwell that very afternoon. "I hope your cook is getting from the market what I told you—yoghurt and eggs to go with your toast along with muesli. I keep telling you that you must eat well, and take care of yourself."

"Now you come here, and tell him yourself, my princess … This house and I need you here soon, to make this home."

"Yes, that I will. But you have to eat well and be healthy till then, darling. You seem very pulled down in the picture, the one you sent me last evening, as compared to your earlier robust-looking pictures."

"You really think I seem pulled down now, darling?"

"Yes, you're not sleeping enough maybe. You're feeling unwell often and tiring out easily at office, as you mentioned. Only on my insistence, you called the doctor and he advised you only to take a break and stay at home. But I recommend you improve your diet immediately, or mere rest is not going to make you healthy."

"I will, baby, now may I go to work? I will catch up with you in the evening."

"Go now … but I insist you eat well or I'm not going to stop nagging you. I will ask you every morning what you've eaten, till you're bored with it."

"Hahahahaha, you do that, my pretty, pretty princess … but don't worry, how can I not listen to my life, my heart, my soul? Now, aren't you forgetting something?"

"Muuuuah! Now go, run along and let me get back to work."

"Muuuuah, darling … just cannot wait till you're here with me."

"Bye now … we'll talk in the evening," Aparna wrote.

			Shuvashree Chowdhury

"Can I call you sometime in the afternoon … Your lunch time, maybe?"

"Sure … just message before that, so I can take my earphone and step outside."

Later that evening, when Stephan came online on FB, having spoken to Aparna over the telephone in the afternoon, Aparna was watching television. She liked to flip news channels, mentally engaging in the debates on NDTV, Headlines Today, and Times Now. Her choice of channel depended on the topic of debate and guest speakers, whoever the anchor might be—Barkha Dutt, Rajdeep Sardesai, or Arnab Goswami. She preferred Rahul Kanwal over the rest, due to his coming across as more level-headed, and not being unduly impassioned as the others. So she tuned into Headlines Today more often. These debates were intellectually stimulating, Aparna thought, and they offered different perspectives on current pressing topics. She liked to listen to a variety of viewpoints, however vociferous and stressful it got at times, as it allowed her to exercise her own thinking judiciously. But she first listened to the news on the varied channels, before tuning into debates, including BBC and CNN.

It was at the end of a rather noisy debate on Times Now, moderated by Arnab Goswami, that Aparna noticed Stephan's message on her phone. It read, "Hello, darling, I'm home now … where is my soul, what is my princess doing?"

She smiled—he always brought it on with his endearing words—and then replied, "As usual waiting for you, gorgeous."

Aparna turned off the TV, walked to her own room passing Kartik's and her parents' larger one, noticing they were asleep. At her desk, she turned on her laptop. It would be a long chat as usual. And she was as yet more comfortable typing on the larger laptop keyboard, viewing its larger screen, than on the cell phone.

"So did you check on the investment options I might have in your country?" Stephan asked. "As you suggested, I had a chat with my investment consultant here and he said India, currently in 2016, is surely a good place to invest in."

"Well, in fact, I did check as well…" Aparna replied. She had discussed this with a friend—a senior executive who had recently retired from Larsen and Tubro, and on his advice, she now enquired of Stephan, "But what is the exact type of investment you're planning on? Do you want to buy residential or commercial properties ... or are you considering buying land and constructing here? If so, it would be difficult for a foreign company like yours, but you could outsource the job to a local company."

"No, no, I want to buy ready property ... for a school perhaps, or a hotel. You must tell me where—in which city, I should buy it in, and also help me go about it."

"A school or a hotel should be interesting. My country could well do with both," Aparna replied, enthused and more certain of the sincerity of Stephan's intentions. "But if you ask me, I would suggest a school. As for which city—Delhi or Bangalore would be good. But I'd recommend Chennai as well, as that's where I live."

"Alright, a school in Chennai is what we will set up then ... And, of course, a house also, where we can stay, when we visit India— which we will quite often if we have business interests there."

"I would not know about properties, but I could suggest a few leading property portals that deal in such transactions." Aparna had already checked a few, since Stephan first showed interest in property in India, but had not brought it up with him yet. She did not want to seem pushy on the idea of his investing here. "You could check the sites directly, or ask your property consultant to do that. Then you can contact the agents here, after viewing and identifying some prospective properties."

"That is my sweet darling ... always so intelligent and efficient."

"Thank you! Now why don't you give me a job as your secretary, hahaha, I could organise your work and life—both at home and the office—pretty well."

"Hahahaha, a brilliant idea that is..."

"So when are you planning to come here to meet me?"

Aparna, considering the speed, at which her relationship with Stephan was progressing, with their plans for the future, decided it was high time they met. Uppermost in her mind was the plans for her son Kartik, that would need to be made. What if Stephan and she did not like each other when they met? Physical chemistry might just be missing, even though they had seen each other well in pictures and felt they had known each other for a long time.

Then the future of their relationship might just remain a pipe dream. So they had to expedite a meeting to know for sure.

"As soon as you wish me to and invite me, I will be there … I'm just waiting for you to call me. In fact, why don't you tell me where I should stay?"

"How about coming here next month?" Aparna replied promptly. She had given the matter much thought by now. "My son will be spending his winter vacations with his father and grandparents in Mumbai … So I would have more time for myself and you. I could take leave from office, to show you around or maybe go out of town."

"Now that's a plan … I just cannot wait to be with you, darling."

"I look forward to meeting you too, gorgeous … to ensure you're for real, hahahaha … as I keep saying you're too good to just land on my roof like that."

"So you still don't trust me fully, do you?"

"My heart does in all totality, and that is why it has opened up to you. Moreover, I've even told you all about myself with no reservations. But my mind keeps sending out warning signals … What if you're not the one you claim to be?"

"Just trust your heart, baby … Listen to what it tells you. God has brought us together and given us another shot at happiness, don't ruin it with doubt."

"I cannot help it, darling … This afternoon, a friend was narrating an incident of how a girl met a guy online and their relationship flourished right up to planning their marriage with the minutest of details online. They even made all preparations for the groom to be here from UK for the wedding ceremony. It was only at the end that they learnt that the guy's Facebook address was fake. It was all a big hoax."

"So you go around believing all these stories? Do you?"

"Well, it is very scary after all. And truly I have no clue who you really are."

"What … What did you just say? You don't know me? That you don't know your heart and soul, your Stephan? After all this time, you still don't trust me?"

"It's not that I don't trust you … But it is true that your FB profile is somewhat wishy-washy. All the details don't match what you tell me, and then you even have so many friends in India, especially in the northeast like in Sikkim, Manipur … even a few in Chennai actually. Though you claim you have never been to India. You know what, it scares me to think you're somewhere right here and this is all one big prank."

"My God … my God … my God! I just don't believe it is you … my own heart and soul, the one I trust more than myself, that is telling me all this. I placed all my faith and happiness in you, our future, and you don't trust I am for real?"

"Now don't be angry … of course, I trust you … or how would I be chatting so long, up to planning a future with you? But doubts crop up, especially listening to stories like this. You must understand how scared I am. As I'm putting my whole life on the line for someone I'm not absolutely sure really exists."

"Till this morning, you were fine … then you go and talk to your friend and she shakes the very basis of our relationship. Is it her you're going to spend your future with? Why have you told her about us? I told you, didn't I, not to discuss our relationship with anyone, not even your close friends … And to have faith in God, for he is masterminding the whole thing. He is the one who brought us together and now you don't have faith in him or in your heart? Trust your heart, that's the only thing that's real. You know how people are jealous and will go to any length to burn a good thing if they see one. Don't let them spoil our happiness."

"I didn't tell her in detail about us, just that I was chatting with a guy and we get along so well. The next thing I know, she tells me this story about the fake ID and all my doubts on your profile's variances flash in front of me. I think of all the friends on your profile, how you all must be having a good laugh at my expense from somewhere close and I freak out."

"Alright then, now let me go … I will talk to you later. I'm not in the mood to talk now. I am so upset."

"What happened? Why are you getting angry with me, instead of trying to pacify me of your real entity and identity?"

"After all that we've exchanged, shared our lives … everything, if you still doubt my very existence, need clarifications, we have nothing to talk about really."

     Shuvashree Chowdhury

"But look at it from my point of view. Understand how scared I am … As a woman, with a child and all else I've been through, in a conservative society … making all these plans, when I'm scared of your very existence and authenticity."

"Well then, Aparna, let's just call it a night … I'm really very tired and want to have my dinner."

"Good night, Stephan," Aparna typed, as she was angry too and more scared of him now. Was it not his duty to put her fears to rest, if he had nothing to hide? If he was not going to do that, she had better reconsider this relationship.

Aparna shut her laptop in a frenzy, frantic now that her doubts were not unfounded after all. She lay down in bed, but was awake, going over every minute interaction with Stephan. Even with her eyes shut tight, she lay awake till dawn—in disturbed thoughts, and the immense pain it generated. Now over and above her own desperation and stupidity, she also blamed Anand. What a mess she had got into, in trying to run away from her feelings for him. Love comes knocking at the most inopportune times, Aparna had heard, she thought dismally. But in her case, not just one, to her gravest fear, she found herself loving two people—both at the same time.

Chapter 15

A Lonely Marriage

Anand and Sujata were seemingly reading the book of life in divergent ways, so how could they possibly find a common plot? The first year of their marriage had been difficult, as tends to be with many couples, in spite of the control of the body at this time over the mind. After the initial months, Sujata and Anand had begun to perceive themselves as living with people they did not know, who were practically strangers to each other, dissimilar in their values and outlook to life. There were all the adjustments to make on either side, more so for Sujata in fitting into a new household, a new family, and a different lifestyle. Sujata had made her displeasure known to Anand often enough then. But he was too set in his ways to care to change. His equable temperament also did not allow him to rock the boat of his equation with his parents. How could he possibly display a leaning towards his new wife over them? Then again, he began basking in a newfound self-importance, from the prestige and attention from the responsibilities as chief editor of the *National Daily*, his family's newspaper. This created further rifts between him and Sujata.

An inevitable disillusionment began to set in for the young couple, within the second year or so, having become a constant appendage of the other. They went everywhere together and did everything together, as was expected from a newly-wed couple. The tiny fissions that appeared in the marriage now, left to fester, would take on grave proportions, and differences between them would grow. As neither was convinced the other was doing their part to accommodate their partner's preferences, to alleviate adjustment problems, the crack went deeper. They had walked into marriage with high expectations, from a conviction on the love they felt for the other over mere tele-conversations and letters.

                    Shuvashree Chowdhury

Little did they realise that being in love is only the pretty gateway leading to the steep climb up the imposing castle of a successful marriage. The hurdles they faced after marriage, but more in viewing each other's reactions to these obstacles, disillusioned Anand and Sujata of each other's love, even of their own. But they adjusted and came together emotionally on and off, finding a common ground, however diverse their psyche.

They lived in a joint family then, and their moments alone with each other gained a sweetness only by their comparative rarity. But in a few more years, when they were to live on their own, after differences with Anand's parents and his brother that aggravated after he married, they began to look forward to their future together with something like dread. Every marriage has its periods of despair, but Sujata's and Anand's also had interfering bystanders—their families, both immediate and extended, who by paying much attention to the discordant chords of their marriage, had stepped in to render their difficulty permanent. The blow to their individual pride, when their respective familial prestige was under threat by differences between the two families, brought Sujata and Anand on opposing sides often, aggravating disputes between them. Thus, they became lonely souls stranded on a stony island of marriage. They fought for their own survival, as best they could, yet amiable to the other for self-sustenance.

Then with the coming of their first child, Sujata had exalted, finding recourse from lying between the tracks of her powerful and disillusioning emotions, waiting to be run over by the train of Anand's negligence. This had been the most trying period of her life, as her emotions were unstable, as she waited to give birth, and more so right after the birth. Ironically, in case of the births of both sons, Anand, who did not want children just yet, was to be out of town. An extreme weakness overtook Sujata in longing for the support and sympathy of her husband during these emotionally and physically trying times. But not finding it, dejection made her spurt bitterness at him. Anand was at first shocked, and then amused, till the time Sujata's acrimony became too much for him to bear, so he simply distanced himself from her. All she had wished at such times, that would have set Sujata's balance, was for Anand to take her in his arms, saying he loved her. But Anand never realised that her rancour against him was actually from her craving for his attention.

Sujata was too proud to employ any other way that might be decipherable to Anand, so as to get his attention, other than coldness or tantrums. Though even now, just as in the initial years, there was not much needed to bring on sporadic changes in sentiments in Sujata, to spark her dying affection for her husband. She would, in sudden bursts, want Anand's help and support, as in the early years of their marriage, when she could not live without his love. Then his aloofness and her disenchantment with him would take over, and bring on a fresh tirade—which became more frequent and vicious over time.

Anand did not make the slightest effort for her or the children, Sujata consistently complained, not realising that her criticism was nurturing his resistance. Some appreciation of his little efforts might have motivated Anand, but Sujata did not have the capacity to lower her pride in doing so. Neither did he have the maturity to understand the need for it. On his part, Anand often genuinely did not know what to do, or how to please his wife. He came to the conclusion that whatever he did was never good enough. All his efforts, frail as they seemed to Sujata, were met with nitpicking and protests. Worse still, Sujata would randomly blame his parents' strained and formal relationship with each other for his attitude to marriage. Also, she would bring up that both his parents, especially his father since his own childhood, had been on psychiatric medication, without which he was prone to temper outbursts. His mother often threatened to commit suicide when she didn't get her way and even locked her room and acted like she was going to set herself on fire.

"You will never do anything for the children or me if it interferes with your own likes and dislikes." Sujata raged one evening, when Anand returned from work, with his driver bringing up tubs of vanilla ice cream. "You don't even care that we, especially the children, don't like vanilla ice cream! You would not even buy Varun the books he chose at Crossword, but paid for ones you picked and then got him back home."

"Don't I know what's best for the children? Don't I?" Anand retorted in his usual soft but bitingly condescending tone, leaving

     Shuvashree Chowdhury

Sujata frustrated for having initiated any dialogue on the matter with him again.

Thus, Sujata was unable to get her displeasure across to Anand, due to his arrogance and complacency. This exasperated her but not for herself any longer, but in worrying that all this would have an adverse psychological impact on the children, from growing up with an emotionally distant, and negligent father. Anand's indifference towards them and his condescending attitude to their mother might tarnish their own perspectives of love, relationships, marriage, and view of women in general, for life. Her stress and anxiety had also heightened over the years due to the emotional harassment— the constant monitoring and interference by her in-laws, where Anand never stood up for her. Sujata had been nursing her wrath diligently, thus now it had come to a stage where she could only be near him with difficulty. She could hardly bear even his casual touch and withdrew far from him emotionally.

Anand still slept on the same bed with her. He made it a point to do so when at home, as he had always. But Sujata would now turn her back on him and fall cosily into the dream haven of Shekhar's arms, leaving Anand to his preoccupation with his devices—laptop or tablet. Sujata assumed he was chatting with Aparna on Skype, as she did from her office with Shekhar and sometimes from home too. She no longer felt the outrage from her wounded pride, over Anand's association and his explicit support of Aparna, when people in his office randomly mentioned it to her. Her relationship with Shekhar now buttressed the neglect, the perceived public humiliation, and the dent to her pride over the years. Yet she was intrinsically unhappy about her dysfunctional marriage, as she truly craved her husband's love and a healthy familial relationship. With Shekhar, it was a deep friendship and emotional dependency that Sujata was using to laminate her hurt and disillusionment with life.

Sujata's love for her husband had with time become a bitter heart-ache. She still loved him, having once loved him well and passionately, but she felt that he had merely been fond of her in his placid and calm way. It made her furious to think even now of how she had married Anand with such conviction that he had truly, passionately, and deeply loved her. His soft-spoken words had sounded so earnest when wooing her, over the long phone calls, even from outside the country. It had shortly turned to the cynical jibes so inherent to Anand's personality, much to Sujata's horror. She was tired of always giving way, of humiliating herself, and was sick and tired of being made a convenience by him. She was too proud to be treated like he always preferred the company of any other woman, however badly she might fare in every respect as compared to Sujata.

It was as if everything Anand did was to show his contempt for her, Sujata thought. Back home in the evenings from work, he began to lock up their bedroom for over an hour, saying he was working. If she happened to be in the room when he walked in, he would curtly ask her to leave and shut the door behind her. What could he possibly be doing inside closed doors, Sujata concluded, but having sex chats with a woman or watching porn and possibly sharing his arousal with the woman at the other end of a video chat. His gall to take her for granted thus, and to face his hostile attitude that included threatening gestures when she objected, was a deep shock to Sujata, and yet she adjusted to this abuse. She didn't feel strong enough or self-sufficient to leave him, along with the children, and she had never considered leaving them with him.

Anand didn't even care that his behaviour was making her acutely unhappy, treating her as a sort of fool the world could laugh and sneer at. It was on their last anniversary, the tenth year of their attempt to stay together, that recorded the worst of his demeanour towards her, in Sujata's view. This was at the lavish party at the Taj Coromandel for a large number of people that consisted of the crème de la crème of Chennai society. The party was not just their anniversary party, but more a public relations and brand-building exercise for his newspaper, now among the top four English language dailies in Chennai.

Sujata was circulating among the guests, when her eyes fell on a slender and pretty young lady, a westerner, in an ankle-length white chiffon dress. She had just walked into the banquet hall. Even as Sujata looked on appreciatively at her striking good looks—her blonde, shoulder-length hair framing her chiselled, luminous face, accentuating her grey-green eyes—she noticed Anand striding across the hall towards her. After exchanging introductions in

		Shuvashree Chowdhury

his lately acquired charming manner, he led her further inside by her hand. Soon he was walking around the hall with this lady, her arm wrapped in his, as all starry-eyed and giggling, she hung on to his words. Sujata noticed Anand's elated face and his overstated mannerisms, knowing everyone was noticing him. He looked at Sujata a few times, smiling smugly each time, as if enjoying her discomfiture. She looked back at him sternly in exasperation. It was embarrassing her to see how Anand, who was a little tipsy now, was making a fool of himself and his wife.

Sujata tried to act normal and keep a straight face, while interacting with the guests. But she seethed with rage internally. When it was beyond her endurance, she strode over to Anand with her head held high. Ignoring him, she looked at the woman.

"May I please borrow my husband for a while?" Sujata said to her resolutely.

The young woman looked visibly flustered, and, in silence, nodded repeatedly, stepping away from Anand after disengaging her arm. Anand looked at Sujata enquiringly, but the angry glint in her eyes made him quietly follow her aside.

"Even on our anniversary, you cannot restrict your urge to embarrass me in public, can you? Sujata said to him in a low voice, looking into Anand's eyes viciously. Then, not mincing her words, "The way you are going about stuck to that woman is shamefully pathetic, especially at your office party."

"What, what are you talking about?" Anand replied nonchalantly, "She is Amanda, a distinguished guest and is one of our director's daughters. Her mother is German, and she goes to college in London, so you've never met her. In fact, I'm doing what you ought to be doing, taking care to see she is comfortable and enjoying. Instead, you embarrass yourself and me by your sullenness. Now go on, smile and meet the rest of the guests, instead of standing around with your friends who can do without your personalised hospitality."

Anand walked away, but Sujata strode out of the hall, trying not to meet any eyes. People would notice her eyes welling up. This was a public confirmation that their marriage was a sham. Sujata became angry with herself now. She should have controlled herself better. By now she should know well, all her husband would do is trample over her sentiments at any display of possessiveness. Aparna too was at the party, Sujata knew, as their paths had crossed a couple of times. But Sujata had ignored her outright, when Aparna said hello to her.

Aparna would be keeping an eye on her surely, and would not have missed the scene. He just didn't understand anything, Sujata thought furiously, as she marched into the ladies' washroom enclosure purposefully. Then she frantically tore the wrapper off a Ferrero Rocher chocolate she retrieved from her handbag and shoved it whole into her mouth. Sujata proceeded to chew it fast, almost choking on it with the powerful rush of anger, hurt, and humiliation she had suppressed on the walk from the hall, right through the corridor. Once she swallowed the chocolate, it would overpower the bitterness she felt inside, Sujata knew, and then sweeten her mood enough, to allow her to even smile at people on her return to the party. She tended to use chocolate rather than alcohol as many do, for downing her sorrow, but only when compelled to.

After swallowing one semi-chewed chocolate, even as she felt it slowly dissolve her anger and hurt, Sujata looked into the mirror, smiling cynically at her dishevelled look. Suddenly thinking of Shekhar now, of what he would say if he had to see her this way, and gaining strength from the thought of him, she retrieved another chocolate from her bag. But before she ripped off the wrapper, she took a selfie—ensuring it captured the melted chocolate over her mouth that had gushed out as if with her emotions, also her smudged eye makeup. Then forwarding the picture to Shekhar in a WhatsApp message, she placed the phone back into her bag. Sujata enjoyed the flavour of the chocolate bite by bite, and then wiped her face clean with a wet towel from the tray. She refreshed her makeup, and combed her hair. Then she sauntered down the corridor to meet the world head-on.

After this incident, there had been stony silence on Sujata's part with Anand for months. During this time, she had got steadily closer to Shekhar, basking in the stability, understanding, and security he provided in her life. Anand's sentiments were consistently drawn towards Aparna by now. Sujata's silent treatment irritated and then enraged him, as he didn't quite get the cause of it. In his mind,

    Shuvashree Chowdhury

he had done nothing really so wrong, well not as yet. It was her vicious treatment of him after this anniversary party, followed by her ignoring him completely, that had led to his guiltless pursuit of Aparna.

What really infuriated Anand was that Sujata's behaviour with him influenced his image in the children's mind and his equation with them. They also tended to avoid him and to treat him suspiciously. Conversely, at this time, Aparna's warmth, her emotional dependence on him and its generous projections rather pleased Anand and made him feel needed. The contrast with Sujata's coldness, her wild temper tantrums, and her hurtful jibes further propelled him towards Aparna. Aparna was forthright and stated her thoughts, needs, and displeasure in precise words, not with accusatory, deprecating coldness like Sujata whom Anand just did not understand.

A typical conversation between Anand and his wife went like this: "You're absolutely selfish." Sujata would yell at Anand when she was angry and anxious. "All you care about is yourself."

"Aren't you selfish too ... aren't we all?" Anand would retort smugly, with his imperturbable grin that frustrated and infuriated Sujata more.

Then she had to rein in all of her control to prevent the urge to fling something sharp at him, to wipe his smug smile off his face at her agony, that chilled her bones.

"You think that you can charm women into thinking you're such a great guy. If they knew you as well as I do, they'd realise it's a mask you wear. In reality, you're perfectly indifferent to people and so you can be nice to everybody. You treat everyone as if they are your close friends at the start, and then when they're gone, you've forgotten all about them."

"What ... you can't really mean this?" Anand replied, sounding dejected. "No one has ever accused me of the things you do. All you do is try to show me how you and your family are so superior to me and mine. You are shallow. Have you ever shown any respect or value for me?"

"Oh! No one's told you, no one's shown you the mirror, have they? That's really where the problem is! Someone should have told you all this much earlier, in childhood, and it would not be so late to change yourself. Even your own parents and brother don't trust you, do they? Doesn't that show how selfish you truly are? And the worst part is the children and I are no more to you than anyone else is. You never sacrifice even your slightest whim for my sake or the children's desires, not even something as basic as choice in ice cream flavours, the places you take us for meals, the toys and books for the kids, and, least of all, the gifts for me."

"That is … because you never appreciate anything I do or anything I bring of my own accord. Would I not know what is good for my wife and children? Don't I try to provide the best that money can buy for all of you?"

"You don't get it, do you, Anand? It's not only and always about money. See how useless it is to even talk to you? If you really loved us and cared about our likes and dislikes, you'd not be asking if the things we want are reasonable. How I wish now I had thought of a good enough reason when I decided to marry you!"

Anand, in complete exasperation, would not reply any more, which invariably aggravated Sujata. She would just walk away, leaving him more perplexed.

"Where are you going?" Anand would call after her, but Sujata would pull the door shut loudly behind her.

The conversation, would just hang there frustratingly, like it can be when withdrawing abruptly in the middle of the sex act. Then they would be left with all the raging miscommunications and misgivings of their hearts and minds that further widened their rift. This is what tends to happen with couples after a period, once they think they know each other too well. They are no longer willing to communicate openly, thus raising a wall that with time gets higher and impenetrable. Such couples then rarely have the time or the inclination to listen to each other; also they stop trying to really talk. They tend to merely hear each other based on past experiences and assumptions and are then quick to judge and retort. This is because real listening doesn't leave as much room for incongruity, as mere hearing does.

The bitter scornful tone, added to the violence in Sujata's voice lately, only drove Anand further away. While he had no way of understanding how humiliated and neglected Sujata felt, she became deeply conscious of the world laughing at her predicament. People

          Shuvashree Chowdhury

surely thought, why as a smart, beautiful, and intelligent woman, she could not stop her husband's roving eyes—usually women who didn't measure up to her in anyway. Little did the world care to understand that these women provided in their averageness an adulation Anand craved for, and she didn't provide. Moreover, just as you cannot really judge a book by the cover, how can you judge a man's character by his wife's capabilities and intent? Why didn't Anand realise that all it would take to vanquish Sujata's demons, to take away her fretful bad-tempered behaviour, was a little kindness, love and concern? It would ally her insecurity and fears that first manifested during her children's birth and deepened.

The awareness of her pregnancy, in the case of both their sons, had brought Sujata immense joy. She had never forgiven Anand his disappointment at the news. Then his callousness about her feelings was reinstated by his casual attitude towards the children right since their birth. His disinterest in the children was in sharp contrast to Sujata's passionate and blinding love for them, even now that they were grown. The primary cause of contention between Anand and Sujata was the disparity in the love and importance of the children in their lives.

Another crucial difference between them that existed from the start was their inherent variance in passion. Sujata had found Anand's slack sexual interest, and their few and far between encounters even as early as on their honeymoon appalling. He had, time and again, rejected Sujata's shy advances in bed, in the early years. This hurt her pride and augmented her feeling of being undesirable to him. This was more so because he didn't seem to stop paying attention to other women all the time, even watching porn, she noticed. Was he so dissatisfied with her, for such outright neglect? Sujata was unable to reconcile to Anand's not heeding her needs, not caring to satisfy her in bed or out of it. When in later years, on those rare occasions he initiated sex, only at his need or suitability, it left Sujata's pride outraged. Added to everything, the suspicion that Anand was using sex to control her made Sujata withdraw completely. She would not even meet his friendly touch, let alone his sexual advances, even though they still slept on the same bed. This continued till it reached a stage that it was now over two years since they had had sex at all.

To Sujata, as tends to be for many women, love and marriage was supposed to be an all-consuming fire that absorbed the rest of life. But for Anand, it was a convenient and necessary institution, with no real need for exhilaration. Sujata's initial passion for life had for a while masked her husband's lack of ardour, and she would not see that it was really his temperament to blame. But she accused him of not loving her, and had for long wondered how to gain his affection and attention. Then her pride became humiliated, in the ripening of the awareness that her own love and desire was so much greater than his. In the early years, Sujata had loved Anand blindly, until a cold fear gripped her that he neither loved her nor had he ever loved her. She had then swung uncertainly between her old passionate devotion and an equally, perhaps a more passionate hatred for him. Then Sujata realised she could not do things in halves, and she could either love or hate, in both cases passionately, and opted to hate Anand with all her heart. She channelled her capacity and need for love into loving Shekhar, as she had done Manas. But her children remained the centre of her universe and nothing was too good for them.

                    Shuvashree Chowdhury

Chapter 16

An Internet Love Affair

Aparna ran a search for 'Stephan Shedrack' on Google that morning at the office. This was after the spat with him the previous night, about her friend's warning her of fake profiles on FB. She was anxious and curious to find other people with Stephan's surname. It might ascertain if he was really British as he claimed. To her surprise, those she found by this name were mostly black, thus she got an inkling his name might not really be Stephan Shedrack after all. Then Aparna ran a search on his company's name 'JW Construction' and it threw up a number of small, medium, and large companies in the UK and US. She went into each of these websites at length, but even with expert manoeuvres from her experience as a journalist, she could not trace his name to any of them. Aparna sat staring blankly at her computer, quietly pondering over this web of lies she might be caught in. There was a sudden flipping of her heart now in Anand's favour, in fear and a desperate need for comfort.

At least, with him, Aparna was sure where she stood—on firm even if parched ground. But with Stephan, she had jumped off a cliff, on a paratrooping mission. Then she had been gliding in air, desperately trying to enjoy herself, with the fear of crashing strapped to her shoulder, bearing heavily on her. Yet she carried in her heart the strong wind of hope—of landing upon the paradise of her dream life. Aparna forcibly snapped herself out of her doubts of Stephan now, as out of a parachute. As she knew, fear tends to weigh heavily on you, and would pull her down in this precarious trip she had undertaken with Stephan, though it had been exhilarating.

Aparna got up and walked over to Radhika's cabin. As chatting with her, would instantly drive away her thoughts on the tough decisions Aparna was on the brink of taking in life. Radhika warm and chatty as always, unplugged Aparna's professional thinking, got her into the mood of the interview she had later in the day. They discussed her research for it and the angle of the story she would seek. Aparna's uneasiness on Stephan was shoved under her mental carpet, much to her ease for now. It was work that was Aparna's haven, where she could come home to mentally.

After lunch, Aparna walked past Anand's cabin on her way out to the meeting with a veteran theatre artist from Mumbai. With a sudden urge to meet him, mentally bracing herself, she strode into the foyer of Anand's cabin. She asked his secretary Rose, a good friend by now whom she often lunched with, if she could meet Anand. It was an instinctive, involuntary step, as she had not consciously thought about meeting him. In fact, Aparna had been avoiding Anand as much as she could in the last few months. Meanwhile, he was watching her curiously from a distance, giving her time to align her thoughts and feelings, after he discovered her true feelings.

Anand had been concerned that Aparna might hurt herself all over again, as there was not much in terms of emotional security he could offer her right away. In spite of reciprocating her feelings, he was keeping a distance from Aparna. She was trying to seal and store their passion away in a recess of her heart. When Aparna knocked on his door and walked in, she felt calm, and Anand looked up at her curiously.

"Anand, I just came to discuss the meeting I'm on my way to now, with the veteran theatre actor from Mumbai—Mahendran" She said coolly, surprising herself more than she did Anand, by her casualness. "Radhika says he is a friend of yours."

"Yes ... well, as a matter of fact, he is. We went to engineering college together, and then see how differently our lives turned out."

As Anand went on to elaborate his friendship with Mahendran, he felt relieved that Aparna had taken the initiative to ease the awkward situation that had developed between them. He was tempted to ask her how she was doing, to enquire about her son, if her ex-husband was still harassing her, and to talk about their last two evenings together. But he decided not to step on intimate

          Shuvashree Chowdhury

territory so quickly again, from where it would be difficult to extricate himself. Aparna was impressed by her own display of calmness, when, in reality, she recognised that her feelings for Anand were as intense as ever.

On her way to the meeting, Aparna thought about Nikhil. He wanted Aparna back in his life, as he was lost without her and would often call in a drunken state. At first, he would be cajoling, then he would threaten her asking her to return along with their son. With Anand's support and security at her job, she had kept her chin up, in getting through the divorce, and the custody of her son.

At the interview, while Mahendran took an urgent call on his mobile phone, his glass of draught beer unattended on the table, Aparna watched the fizz of the soft drink in her glass. They were seated across each other on the sofa seats of the bar of the Presidency Club. Mahendran was staying here, through a reciprocal membership of his club in Mumbai. After a few sips of her drink, Aparna looked about her distractedly. There were just a few men at a table at the far end, and two waiters at the bar counter. It was just after 4 p.m., too early for the crowd that would descend here later, it being a Saturday.

Aparna's gaze fell back on her glass. Having met Anand on her way here, she could not help but think of just how like a fizzy cola drink love is. Only the bottle perceives the pressure inside till you open it, though the world sees its perky colour. Then once you uncork it, it keeps fizzing for a while and is unsettling, gushing out and over, till it slowly settles down to allow you to enjoy it. It cools you, then drains away completely to leave an aftertaste, bitter or sweet. If you've enjoyed the drink, you'll crave for another one, perhaps similar. If not, you'll avoid it for a long time to come, perhaps forever. That was just the way relationships progress.

Aparna's first tryst with love—in her case, with marriage—had been so traumatic, it had left her with a putrid aftertaste, along with the fear of trying it again. But falling in love with Anand inadvertently, from seeing his commitment to work and family, his sense of duty, in admiring and trusting him, she had realised how different two men can be, how different their love. In spite of it, Aparna could not allow herself to get scorched again, knowing

Anand's marital and parental status took precedence over her. She had just about healed from the emotional burns she almost succumbed to in marriage, so she dared not test her immunity on another unhealthy love. Aparna did not blame Anand, but rather respected and loved him deep in her heart, and she would continue to. After all, it was her experience of love with him, like a whiff of perfume sprayed on her wrists that still lingered on her senses.

As she thought of Stephan now, the doubts of the evening before rushed to mind. She felt a jab of pain in her chest, followed by a sudden bout of anxiety that she took a slow deep breath to dissolve. Mahendran looked at Aparna quizzically, guiltily raised his hand, signalling he would be with her right away. It unplugged Aparna's present stream of thoughts, and mentally braced her for the conversation ahead. But before she pulled the carriage of her personal thoughts to a complete halt at the door of her professional duty, Aparna briskly reiterated the decision she had arrived at this morning, after a sleepless night.

She was going to trust her heart with Stephan, just as he had insisted last night. Perhaps he was rich and well known, Aparna thought, so didn't want to disclose his real identity, till he was sure of her feelings. Her instincts told her Stephan—whatever his real name or his occupation might be, was a sincere and good man. Her heart had adjudged his humility and sincerity, much more than his love for her. With regard to her marriage, Aparna had followed her mind, validating Nikhil's family, qualifications, and references and where did it all lead her to? This time around, she was going to go with the flow, follow the signals of her heart and destiny, and see where they led her. This thought gave Aparna renewed strength and vigour. After the meeting, Aparna had returned to office and briskly transcribed the interview from her notes. She had felt too drained to do anything beyond that. She had not slept a wink last night.

That evening when Aparna returned home, she did not wait for Stephan to message her as she always did, but left a message for him herself: "How's my gorgeous, still sulking, is he?"

Why would he not download WhatsApp? Aparna wondered. She had reminded him a few times, that it would be so much easier to communicate with.

 Shuvashree Chowdhury

"You can download it for me, when I'm with you, hahaha," he had replied every time. "I'm not good with all those applications."

It was a few hours since Aparna's first message, yet there was no response from Stephan, even though she noticed her message had been read.

She left another message, "I'm really sorry about last evening ... I should not have mistrusted you, Steph, but try to see my point of view ... I was really scared."

"I'm still in shock...." he typed promptly, "that you, the person whom I trusted with all my heart, more than myself, called you my God even, have no trust in my very existence. All this after the time I spent in trying to show you how much I love you."

Aparna, relieved to see his reply, briskly replied, "I am so very sorry ... I really am ... I should have trusted my heart, the way you trust me, Steph. But I was just so shocked by the story my friend told me and so very frightened ... I was looking to you for revalidation of your own existence. I really did not mean to hurt you."

"But how can you even doubt my very existence after all that we've shared and the way I love you?"

"I'm sorry, very sorry ... can you ever forgive me?" Aparna typed, feeling desperate now, as if Stephan was giving up on her, on their future and her dreams they had built so far. "It's just that I was really scared."

"I'm still in shock ... I didn't go to work all day, just lying in bed thinking how could I have gone so wrong, that too to trust a woman so much? It makes me so physically ill, you know, so sick."

"Don't say that, baby, don't speak like that. I hate to think I caused you to suffer so much. You're so sensitive and I've really hurt you now. It worries me so much that you react like this to my impulsive outbursts ... I can be quite temperamental, you know, how will you ever deal with that going ahead?"

"It was a big shock, but I'm recovering slowly, give me some time. That you don't trust my very existence, while I've gone all out with my feelings for you, makes me rethink our future now."

"Oh Steph, now don't do this, stop talking this way. I know I've really upset and hurt you and I'm really very sorry ... but nothing has changed, trust me. Don't make me feel so horribly guilty. You know well that what I said was not because I don't trust you. It was my desperate fear, since I've been planning to give up my entire present and secure life to be with you … I have so much at stake."

"I'll just go now … we'll talk later."

"But where are you going? Are your friends there, are you going out with them? You know I'm very disturbed too. Didn't sleep all of last night.'

"No, I'm not well. I just want to lie down … I'm still in shock."

"All right then, go ahead … but just try and understand my point of view and how I must be feeling too. I know so little about you anyway. Yet I've been planning to go away with you and you're acting so difficult."

"I understand, and you must be tired too after the long day. You go now and rest … we will talk tomorrow."

"No, I cannot rest until we resolve this matter and till I know that you're okay. I'm really worried this disturbed you so much that you didn't even go to work."

"You have no idea what I've been through, so how can you understand why I feel so let down by my destiny all over again? I was so happy, so very happy to have found you and then you give me this shock."

"I have repeatedly told you how sorry I am. Must you still hang on to what I said, knowing in your heart I didn't mean it."

"Would you fight with your husband on every small issue, would you abuse your mother-in-law … then would you sleep with your husband's best friend? If you were in my place and you caught your wife in bed with your best friend … Would you not be angry, really angry, humiliated, and hurt?

"What! What did you just say! Are you serious? Oh my poor baby, how and when … Oh my God! Why didn't you tell me this before … why didn't you tell me all this while we've been chatting. I had no idea you'd caught her in bed and that too with your best friend … how horribly cruel is that!"

"I just couldn't tell you … how could I tell you … how was I possibly supposed to tell you my horrible past? I tried telling you a few times, when you repeatedly asked me, but just couldn't say it all."

     Shuvashree Chowdhury

"But you should have, darling ... if for nothing else, it would make you feel lighter, much better, just as I feel better from having told you my circumstances."

"But I just don't like to talk about that wicked woman ... the way she finished me, robbed my peace and happiness, and humiliated me."

"What really happened ... how did you come to know, then walk in on them?"

"One morning after I had driven a distance on my way to work, I had to come back home, as I realised at the gas station that I had forgotten to take my wallet. I saw my friend's bike parked in front of my house...."

"Now which friend ... I mean how did you know this guy?"

"We worked together. Neil was one of my construction contractors ... so he came home often. We even hung out together a lot."

"Then what happened after you came back home?"

"I had the key, so while my driver waited outside in the car, I walked through the back gate and up the driveway ... I walked straight to our bedroom, pulled open the door, and there they were together in bed—that wicked woman and the man who was my good friend. I pulled out my mobile phone to take their picture, but the man jumped at me, tried to grab the phone which fell off, and he ran out."

"Oh my God! What a horrible sight. I can imagine how shocked and angry you must have felt at the betrayal by your closest ones. But I must say, the scene seems so much like an English film or serial ... I've seen this kind of stuff somewhere before."

"So how do you think I could tell you such a nasty and humiliating story that is part of my life, without fear of what you will think of me?" Stephan replied, ignoring Aparna's reference to how unreal it sounded—surprising her.

"Why would I think badly of you? What is your fault in all this? But no wonder you keep insisting that UK women cannot be trusted at all ... so you're looking to find a partner from India."

"It was a humiliating, hurtful experience that I never want to talk about to anyone, especially about that wicked woman."

"But was this after your daughter's birth or before...?"

"I just don't want to talk about all this now. It makes me so sick and so tired … that is why I have avoided it for so long. I thought to telling you once we met, to ensure you would not think any less of me and leave me on learning of this story."

"But why do you insist I might think less of you … I don't get it?"

"You might think I'm not good enough to satisfy my wife; that is why she has the need to go to someone else. In any case, that is what the friend has told everyone since then—that my wife is the one who went after him and it was not his fault."

"How horrible … First you betray your friend and then go about bad-mouthing him, showing him down. So, are you still in touch with him?

"No, I don't work with Neil anymore, but obviously he knows a lot of the same people I do. And I feel everyone is laughing behind my back. But due to my position and influence here, no one will say anything to me on my face."

"So where is your ex-wife now … does she live nearby?"

"I have no idea where she is now. I had to give her a good amount of money as alimony, to get rid of her."

"Alimony, for what … Why would you need to pay her alimony, she is the one who cheated on you."

"Yeah, but my mother thought it would be best to pay her a good amount of money, so as never to be in our lives again, especially our daughter's."

"What's your daughter called?"

"Angel."

"That's really sweet, just cannot imagine you—gorgeous—as the father of a six-year-old girl … You are such a child yourself."

"Hahaha now you always say that … you're the sweet and pretty, pretty girl and you call me a child. I don't know how relieved I feel to have told you about my life and you still accept me. Thank you so much for accepting me just the way I am."

"We were talking of trust, weren't we? You keep insisting you were scared to tell me about your life, wondering how I would take it … You cannot trust me to like all of you, on hearing your past, even though I have told you everything about myself."

"How could I tell you? It is so humiliating, that your wife

          Shuvashree Chowdhury

goes around sleeping with your close friend. It's as if she was not satisfied with me … but then, she is like all UK women … they are never satisfied with one single man."

"I am really sorry and really shaken hearing your story. How I wish I was there with you now, to give you a real big hug and remind you that it's all over … in the far past. And now I'm here for you and will always be. You need never worry about such situations with me."

"Yes, I am so happy…God is really kind and has given me another chance at happiness … You are the best thing that ever happened in my life. Now do you understand why I'm so sick and shaken by your mistrusting me? When I'm just about trusting myself all over again … to be let down?"

"I understand. Now I will never bring up this topic again, so you need never recall it … Forget it like it was from a past life."

"Thank you so much! Thank you, darling! I don't know how I can ever thank you enough for accepting me just the way I am with all my flaws and my past … You are the best!"

"Now don't spoil me, gorgeous … I have my large share of a murky past as well. So will you think it was my fault that my husband was alcoholic and abusive?"

"Never, darling! You're an angel—the sweetest and most innocent. Now don't remind me of that husband of yours, makes my blood boil. Now my heart … my soul, may I please go for my second dinner? Have you eaten?"

"Yes, it is very late at my end and no, I haven't eaten … How could I eat when I was so worried about you? Mother called me a few times when they were having dinner, but seeing me engrossed on the laptop, she thought I was working on an urgent assignment. So they've all eaten and gone to sleep."

"Ah! My darling … how can I ever have doubts on you, knowing how deeply you care about me … I'm sorry … so very sorry … now go and eat … I will catch you in the morning as soon as I wake up …. Bye, my soul!"

The next morning, when Aparna awoke, having slept well—now that the spat with Stephan was resolved and also having been worn-out—her mind was decided on him. She felt a renewed optimism and energy, as she woke up her son Kartik, prepared his lunch box, and got him to drink his milk with Bournvita. Then she sat him through his breakfast of *upma* with mint *chutney*. While she saw Kartik off at the bus stop, waving to him as the school bus rolled away, it struck Aparna how his life was soon going to change drastically, with her choice of a life with Stephan. Her move back to Chennai and then the divorce had not impacted him so much, as Kartik was too young then to perceive the changes. But then this upcoming change would be good for Kartik, Aparna convinced herself, as he would have a premier education at universities abroad, also a varied choice of careers. She began to dream of his going to Oxford. Over and above, she justified, he would be far from his father's influence.

Back home, practising her yoga this morning was a spiritually uplifting experience, for Aparna. Her life seemed to be getting more enriched now than ever before. She was going to talk to Anand and Radhika, she decided, of continuing to write for the *Sunday Magazine*, perhaps travel pieces from the UK and all the new places she would visit. The thought of the sense of security it would bring to her life, in writing for the same paper, retaining connection with her ex-bosses, what with all the changes moving to the UK would entail, was reassuring. Stephan had told her he would love it if Aparna travelled with him on his work. Then during the day while he worked, she could explore places to write about. In fact, she had even excitedly broached the topic of writing a novel. Stephan had encouraged the idea.

"Yes, darling, that would be great!" he had replied promptly, "And for my part, I will use all my influence here to help you find a publisher. I was quite unaware till you told me of how difficult it is to find one."

Even as she recalled Stephan's supportive words, Aparna felt a fresh surge of guilt for ever doubting his intentions in befriending her. What was worse was her impulsive doubt on his very existence, after the emotional intimacy they had shared. How excited he had been over establishing her as an author, after curiosity on her dreams, then the plans he had made for her and with her.

"You will have plenty of time to write and I love the idea of a novel, darling." Stephan had said to her. "I am so happy now, even to imagine having you with me all the time. And don't

Shuvashree Chowdhury

worry about Kartik; he will be safe with my mother and daughter Angel, continuing school. Moreover, Angel will have a companion growing up."

As she got ready and rushed to work, Aparna felt a compelling warmth towards Stephan, an urge to hug him—and she did mentally. He was the kindest person she had met and so sensitive. It upset her, recalling hurting him so acutely that he had been unable to go to work. And she knew by now how passionate Stephan was about his work. His sensitivity and his emotional dependence on her worried Aparna. She was, at times, rather impulsive and haughty. With her temperament, she would be hurting him often, if she did not control her spontaneity, though her reactions were usually quite short-lived. As Aparna deftly manoeuvred her maroon coloured Maruti Suzuki Ritz car into the steep underground parking of her office, she decided she would make it up to Stephan, when he messaged her. The next day, as Aparna sauntered to her desk distractedly, she nearly bumped into Anand coming out of Radhika's cabin from an early meeting.

Aparna mumbled a meek "Good morning." Anand, noting her preoccupation, looked her in the eye quizzically and nodded, adding "Have a good day … will see you at the meeting I've called at 11 a.m."

Aparna sat down at her desk, perceiving how Anand still had a sweeping impact on her, mentally and physically. She felt relieved reminding herself she now had Stephan in her life, to cushion her emotional surges. And she would soon be free of Anand's overwhelming control over her. With this thought, Aparna felt blessed by Stephan's love, more so his loyalty. She smiled now, at his seeking her approval, on whether he could go out with his friends, if they happened to come over when he was chatting with her. Then when she amusedly gave her permission, he would insist to stay home chatting with her. Thus, Aparna was completely charmed.

After leaving her bag in the desk drawer, Aparna switched on her computer, and walked across to Radhika's cabin. It was just after 9 a.m. She had good time to prepare for the meeting with Anand, if required, after finding out from Radhika why he had called for this sudden meeting. Aparna hated to go unprepared to any meeting, more so with Anand. She was sensitive to his scathing remarks to anyone who did not answer when he asked questions. She had become used to talking back to him, standing up to his caustic remarks, but now with the odd situation between them, it was best to be out of his line of attack.

"I liked your theatre guy Mahendran's story," Radhika said warmly, on seeing Aparna, making her beam and lifting her mood. "It was an intimate chat and you've done well to draw him out the way you did with pertinent questions." After a brief chat with Radhika, Aparna returned to her desk.

Aparna decided to message Stephan. It would be when she was at the meeting with Anand that he would wake up and then message her. She didn't want his messages to go unanswered today, with the way he was upset about her doubting him. He still needed more assurance, due to his hurtful betrayals in life, about her trusting him. One thing was certain, that it was the recent emotional tussle with Stephan, the fear of losing him, that made Aparna sure of her own feelings for him. So she was pleased now for it, as it reinstated her faith in his intentions, confirmed her own resolution on a life ahead with him. It was like a sign from God, assuring her that Stephan was the path for her, and so she could tread confidently now. It was time to take their relationship to the next level, and to meet him soon.

There was a time when Aparna was naïve in thinking that a mental and emotional connect was all it took for a successful relationship. It was with this idealistic view that she had plunged headlong into her marriage. On the basis of Nikhil's fervent answers to her questions, he had fit snugly into the picture of the ideal husband she had carried in her immature mind. But Aparna knew better now, how important the physical connect also was, to stay in love, even if two people were already mentally in sync. When she had pondered over her dysfunctional marriage, she realised that it wasn't only his drinking that was the problem. They were not compatible, either mentally or physically, as their values and outlook to life were on a tangent. Perhaps they had lacked chemistry. Aparna wondered if that might be why her husband, even in the initial months of marriage, loved alcohol over her.

Nikhil would disappear for long periods, to go out drinking

Shuvashree Chowdhury

with his friends. Even at home, he had little desire to spend time alone with Aparna, as couples newly in love do. They were not drawn to each other, except perfunctorily, beyond the initial days. They might have fallen in love over time, as happens in arranged marriages. But in their case, love did not find conducive circumstances, perhaps due to Nikhil's alcoholism. At their first meeting, it had taken Aparna more than a few moments to attune to Nikhil's physical presence, even after prolonged email and telephone conversations. Aparna had imagined him darker, taller, and more athletic from his photographs, while Nikhil had expected her to be slimmer on seeing her pictures that were professionally taken at a studio.

But with Anand, meeting him in person from the start, there was no disappointment or reduced expectations. Aparna further grew to like him as a person, and to respect his thinking and values, all of which led to her falling in love with Anand so passionately. It is quite common for people to be physically attracted to each other and then fall apart over mental disparity. Whatever the situation, it is best to meet one's love interest as early as possible in the association. As the sooner expectations are set right, higher the chances of love growing steadily and sustaining. Physical chemistry and intimacy may then be considered akin to a lock which binds lovers, while a strong friendship is the key to adjustment and a fulfilling relationship. Thus, now with all the understanding of love and life she had, Aparna had decided to expedite meeting Stephan, so any unreal expectations and insecurities from both sides would be quickly grounded.

"What if you don't like me in person," Aparna had said to him several times.

"Darling, I have seen everything I need to, in detail … hahaha … from your numerous photographs, and you can check me out," he would reply. "And then our souls are one. So there is nothing to stop us from liking each other in person."

But Aparna worried about their meeting. As she had begun to mentally plan for their future, with Stephan's initiation and encouragement, she could not keep fear of disappointment at bay. It weighed upon her to carry the nagging doubt that this illusionary fire of love they had built and were feeding the flames of, with a steady flow of emotional timber, might be doused by a lack of physical allure for each other. Small things can make a difference, between seeing photographs and meeting in person. So she was going to insist upon Stephan to visit her as soon as it was possible for him to get away from work. He could stay at the Park Hotel at Nungambakkam, which would be convenient for her due to the proximity to her office on Mount Road. Having made up her mind on the need to meet Stephan shortly, their Internet affair gone far enough already, Aparna messaged him she would be away at a meeting. Then she steadfastly stopped thinking of him, to mentally prepare for the meeting with Anand in an hour. Radhika had asked her to retrieve some relevant data online, to discuss with Anand. Aparna hated to bring her personal moods into work, but in her anxiousness after last night, it was difficult not to. But she was able to seal her private thoughts, put her mobile phone away, after messaging Stephan, with the resolve to get him to initiate travel plans to meet her.

                    Shuvashree Chowdhury

Chapter 17

Power is the Ultimate Aphrodisiac

Sujata rushed into the lobby of the Leela Kempinski Hotel at MRC Nagar, after handing her car keys to the valet. It had been a long and tedious drive from her office in Nungambakkam in the morning rush hour traffic. As she looked around catching her breath, a young lady employee approached her.

"Good morning, ma'am," she said, bowing slightly, "where would you like to go?"

"I'd like to go to the ninth floor to room no. 931 to meet General Tejinder Singh. He's expecting me."

"Ma'am, please come to the reception desk. We will call him and let him know you're here." She then asked politely, "Who may I say would like to meet him?"

"It's alright. I'll find my way. Thank you!" Sujata replied, walking briskly in the direction of the elevator.

She would call the general on the way up herself. Sujata was impatient, as she was already late for her meeting with him. He owned and headed a large real estate company based in Dubai and India. He lived in Dubai and Delhi mainly, and visited Chennai sometimes on large work projects. He had called Sujata twice, when she was on her way to the hotel to find out how far away she was. The second time, he had asked her what she would like and had already ordered lunch in his suite, as he would have to leave for the airport by 2.30 p.m. Sujata was a little hesitant to meet him in his room, but then the man was over seventy years old, and was a friend of her husband. She had met him a few times, along with Anand, on his Chennai visits.

Anand had known Lieutenant General Singh since he had been in service and had been posted in Chennai decades back. Now they played golf or tennis at the Gymkhana club sometimes, when the general was in town. The charismatic, good-humoured general was now a friend of Sujata's too. When he learned of her headhunting venture, he was interested in her firm's services. Then on his last visit a month back, on his invitation, she had lunched with him at the coffee shop here, to discuss the possibilities of doing business. They had sat at a table overlooking the sea through large glass windows, as they chatted over the mutton *rogan josh* he had ordered with *tandoori roti*. Sujata had ordered a platter of fish and chips on his suggestion.

Now as she hurriedly strode to the elevator, Sujata encountered two smart young men in uniform and asked them, "This lift will take me to the ninth floor, right?"

"Ma'am, you will require a room card for entry to the ninth floor. Why don't you come to the reception? We will call the guest and then someone will escort you up."

"That should be fine, thank you!" Sujata said in haste, stepping out of the lift. "I'll just call him myself."

"Wait, I'm coming down," Tejinder said, when Sujata breathlessly explained his privileged security status on the ninth floor, due to which she could not come up without a key.

As Sujata looked around at the stately décor, casually pacing the area in front of the elevator, the general came down to the lobby. He hugged her warmly.

"How long does it take you to come?" he thundered in his usual booming voice, sounding almost like it was a threat. "I've been waiting in the room so long, and then going round and round here looking for you downstairs."

"I'm really sorry! I was held up by a client who dropped in at the office without any warning. Then the traffic was so tedious at this time. My driver has taken the day off, so I had to drive myself."

"Why couldn't you just ask Anand to send you his driver?" Tejinder replied abruptly, in his commanding voice but in a good-humoured tone, and then walked towards the elevator, "Come this way."

"I avoid taking his driver." Sujata replied crisply, following him into the lift. "The children and I use one driver and when the guy is busy with their duties—school, tuitions and their numerous extra-curricular activities, like tennis, swimming, theatre, and

 Shuvashree Chowdhury

violin classes—I drive myself in my spare car, a Maruti Swift. It gives me a sense of independence not to rely on the driver all the time."

Sujata walked into the large plush room after him. It was an overwhelmingly bright room, lit up by the sunlight streaming in through the large glass window that overlooked the sea. The view was spectacular. The white sand beach, shining silver in the sunlight, was speckled with green shrubbery shooting out of breaks in the sand. There were numerous shacks with tiny boats tied to them. Sujata crossed the room and stood by the window, looking out keenly. Calm enveloped her. The sea had that effect, in spite of the anxiety she felt at being in the room here with Tejinder that had sharpened with one look at the plush bed behind her.

She took a deep breath and, still looking outside, exclaimed, "It's beautiful out here!" and then she turned around, and sat down on the sofa by the coffee table.

Tejinder sat with his back to the window, behind the large study table, facing Sujata on the sofa. Then he looked piercingly in her direction.

"Should we just call for lunch and chat over it?" he asked casually, and as Sujata nodded spontaneously, he telephoned room service.

When the doorbell rang sharply, Sujata looked at Tejinder to see if she should get up and open the door. But he promptly rose and let the waiter in himself. The young man, with a jovial smile, marched in behind the trolley bearing their lunch and laid the dishes out meticulously on the coffee table. There was a plate of mutton *rogan josh*, and one of yellow *dal*, along with another of *tandoori rotis*. Sujata recalled he had ordered the same dishes last time too, so they must be his favourite. She could not help attributing his immense weight now to the excessive red meat intake. There was also a platter of green salad, and a bowl of curd. Sujata smiled as she noticed a small blueberry-topped mousse-cake on another dish, through its glass cover.

"The dessert is all yours," Tejinder announced in an affectionate tone."

By now, Sujata was as relaxed as was possible in the circumstances, sitting across the gregarious—to the point of even being outrageous—general. He regaled her with his encounters with women even as young as nineteen years, in Cambodia and Bangkok on his numerous visits.

"They were so eager and keen to have me as a partner." He stated, and then narrated an incident. "One girlfriend, a cashier at a bar in Cambodia, who I spent the last fifteen days with, would not even take any money from me … she refused to, saying she could not, as she really liked me! Yet I left her two hundred dollars before leaving."

Sujata was rather uncomfortable, in spite of trying to be cool, with his explicit stories on his conquests of women. Anand's escapades had taught her how power and money could be a big lure for young women. Tejinder's attempt was to impress upon her with his last story that he was still appealing to young women, irrespective of his money and clout. But Sujata ensured that her disinterest, annoyance even, did not show in her tone or expression. She had heard similar stories from him in Anand's presence.

The general loved to brag about his escapades and the younger men, including Anand, were much amused and awestruck by his stories. So his narratives now were not shocking to Sujata, in spite of her conservative upbringing. The years since her marriage to a media baron, especially her own working years, where she met such a variety of successful people, had given her exposure to many such situations. It was the same every time she met the flamboyant general along with Anand. His conversations were invariably composed of ingredients such as booze, women, parties, sports, and even dope. To hear him, one would think he had never done anything serious in his life. Yet he had been a valiant soldier who had won many accolades. But each time Sujata brought up the topic of their proposed business alliance, Tejinder jovially waved it off, continuing his banter.

"I know you're a great business woman…." he joked, "But what is the hurry in getting to work so soon … we have time."

After they finished eating, Tejinder asked Sujata, "Would you like coffee?"

"No, I'd much rather not, after the awesome dessert."

"I ordered it especially for you … I knew you would like it." Sujata smiled and he asked her casually, "So how long have you

     Shuvashree Chowdhury

been handling the headhunting for real estate companies?"

"It's been over ten years since I started as a researcher, and then went on to become a consultant with the same multinational firm. Then I started out on my own."

"I will ask my HR director to get in touch with you," Tejinder abruptly said, and then shocking and confusing Sujata, added, "You must come for a holiday with me sometime." Even as Sujata wondered what he might really be implying, Tejinder continued in a warm voice, smiling at her, "It will give you a break from all your stress here. The choice of place will be yours ... wherever you choose, we can go. Just let me know and I will have everything organised."

"Why would I go on a holiday with you?" Sujata blurted, laughing shakily, registering Tejinder's sexual advance in horror. She attempted to pass it off as a joke. "I'm not interested. Moreover, I'm not a nineteen-year-old Thai or Cambodian girl who is fascinated with you."

Sujata now regretted mentioning her problems with Anand the last time she had met Tejinder over lunch at the coffee shop. He had probed and she had admitted to Anand's interest in various women, also his involvement with Aparna. Even today, Tejinder had asked her how things were between her and Anand.

"What can possibly change in a month? She had replied, in a dejected voice. "I'm surviving and making a damn good effort to do so well."

Sujata became aware that what she had taken to be his genuine concern had actually been Tejinder's strategy to establishing a liaison with her. She felt a revulsion towards him for his duplicity, that she fought to hide, but more for her own naivety.

"We could go on a trip, just for companionship. It would be great to just sit and chat." Tejinder replied, ignoring Sujata's feigned amusement. Then getting bolder, he added, "If you're interested, we could get to know each other a lot better and have sex too, but if not, it's all right. I will be giving you my business after all, and so we are associates, aren't we?"

Sujata stood up firmly, as she sharply recalled Tejinder's random statements on life's wisdom, that he frequently made in a deep-throated-drawl: "Everything comes for a price." And the other one was, "A position at the top is always a lonely one." She was shaken by his direct sexual advance. At his age, it felt like a breach of her trust. As a woman, she felt violated by a man she might consider a father figure. The implications of his suggestion hit her hard. He wanted her companionship in return for his business. Sujata decided it was better not to get into any discussion, but to just promptly leave. After all, he was a friend of the family and she couldn't end their association on a sour note. Then also, if she handled this tactfully, there was the chance Tejinder might not change his mind about doing business with her. Sujata picked up her bag and trying to sound as causal as possible, stepped in the direction of the door.

"Thank you for the lunch. I'd better leave now," she said, walking quickly.

"Don't run away now." Tejinder said firmly, with an urgent ring to his voice. Sensing her anxiety, he added pleadingly, "Wait for a while. We can leave here together as I'm also leaving for the airport."

"But you must leave now or you'll miss the flight," Sujata replied without turning around, "It's a long drive from here and the traffic is heavy on that route."

Tejinder abruptly strode over to Sujata and she was forced to turn around. He gave her a light hug before she could step away. Then trying to appear unruffled, she allowed him to kiss her lightly on the cheek as he always had before. But it was when she tried to turn around and leave that Sujata found she was held tight in one of Tejinder's arms. She tried to move away with a jerk, but he held her tighter now.

"Tell me, when are you coming on a holiday with me?" he cajoled. "It'll be your choice of place, wherever you want to go."

"You leave me now. Just let me go. We can talk later," Sujata ground out irately, alarmed now. She felt violated and humiliated. Pushing against him with all her might, she added sharply, "Just let me go now."

"If I leave you, you will run away," Tejinder stated, holding her more firmly instead. "I want to only talk to you. Tell me when you'll come on a holiday and I will leave you."

Then before Sujata could say anything, even think of a way

 Shuvashree Chowdhury

out of this trap, Tejinder abruptly brought his lips down firmly on hers. This forceful display of his desire and desperation shook Sujata to her core, frightening her and making her incapable of fighting him back. But she held her face and lips firm to show her resistance. Tejinder lifted his lips off hers, just as abruptly as he had kissed her.

"Just kiss me once, once kiss me nicely, and I will let you go." He muttered hoarsely, still holding her tight, now pressing her body close to his.

"Leave me, Tejinder," Sujata thundered, with all the force she could summon from the pit of her stomach, scared when she noticed him look in the direction of the bed.

The implication of his looking at the bed made her freeze in fear. She felt desperate, imagining the worst—that he might rape her now. She pushed harder to extricate herself from his powerful grip.

"We're only kissing now, so what's the problem?" Tejinder said nonchalantly, before crushing her lips with his over again. To her fury, she realised that he was too physically strong for her to wriggle out unless he let her go himself. Then he lifted his mouth slightly and pleaded, "Just kiss me once … just once nicely," even as he pressed her firmly closer to his chest with one hand. With the other hand, she felt him thrust himself closer by holding her derriere.

Sujata did not feel the slightest desire or the least bit of attraction towards Tejinder as he had so confidently expected to arouse. Considering he was still a handsome man, with his sharp facial features, piercing light brown eyes and charming smile. Quite the contrary, she was repulsed, and she wanted to hit him on the head. When he let her go finally, as abruptly as he had grabbed her, she quickly pulled herself together both mentally and physically. Sujata decided firmly that she would not allow him to see her discomfiture.

"I'll just use the washroom," she said, making a dash for it, in a bid to freshen her lipstick and hair, but more to compose herself.

She had rather not leave his room dishevelled, she thought, who knows who she might walk into. There were CCTV cameras in the corridors. She did not want this to become sensational news. It was her identity as the wife of a media tycoon that would provide fodder for the gossip mills.

When Sujata came out of the washroom, looking as fresh as when she had come up here, Tejinder said to her, "Let's go down together. It's time for me to leave."

Sujata nodded quietly, her mind a whirlpool of raging emotions that she was fighting to control. She picked up her bag, and had barely turned to walk briskly out of the door, when Tejinder came up close behind her. When she turned in surprise, he took her hand in his. To her horror and bewilderment, he abruptly pulled her hand down and placed it over his manhood with a purposeful flourish and held it there.

"Here see, do you feel that? I can still get it up, if you thought otherwise."

Then laughing, as Sujata jerked her hand away in repugnance, seething with rage, Tejinder added, "I'm almost seventy, but there is no decline in my ability in bed. If you wish, I can prove it to you."

Sujata did not reply. She firmly clutched her handbag close to her chest, and walked in the direction of the door. Tejinder pulled his stroller bag with a duffel bag strapped over it and followed her. She walked with all the dignity she could summon under the circumstances, as two waiters crossed their path and she nodded politely at them. It was pointless fighting Tejinder now. It would only cause more embarrassment, so she allowed him to fall in step with her, as if nothing askance had happened. She was not going to create a spectacle here, where they could bump into anyone either of them knew. Then there were the CCTV cameras. She had her husband's and her own reputation to protect from unwarranted maligning. Sujata got into the lift in silence. Tejinder followed her in.

"Why don't you come with me to the airport?" Tejinder said casually, exasperating Sujata by his pestering, as they descended. "You leave your car here, and then when you return in the hotel car, pick up yours to go home."

"No, I must get back to work right now." Sujata said casually, in a bid to show him she was as cool about the whole matter too.

Her pride now overriding the wretched humiliation she had

     Shuvashree Chowdhury

suffered, Sujata decided she was not going to allow Tejinder to see how he had crushed her dignity. If he wanted to act as if his misconduct was normal, she would play along and instead make him feel trivial for her rejection of him. Though in reality, she was too flustered and confused to think what would be the best way to handle him and this situation now. It was different from anything that had happened to her. Then there was Tejinder's association with Anand and the number of people they knew in common for Sujata to worry about.

Would Anand believe her if she had to tell him the whole story? Or would he blame her instead for this incident—starting with why she had gone to his hotel room in the first place. What would she say to Anand in her defence? Would she tell him she was stupid enough to think a man of seventy, one who knew her husband and his family well, one who was a father figure to her, had seemed safe? What a profound lie she had lived for long, Sujata thought dejectedly, in her opinion of men. There are good men and not so good men, but age surely has nothing to do with it.

At the reception lounge, Sujata acted composed and at ease. Why would she allow him the sadistic pleasure of knowing he had rattled her to her very core? The world need not be party to her humiliation either, from gossip that might erupt at any time later. She waited for Tejinder to finish his check-out formalities and they walked out of the hotel's exit together. Then they waited in the porch for the car to pull up.

"Come with me to the airport. You can always call your office...." Tejinder insisted again "And ask your colleagues to look into things at office till you're back."

"No, I must go now," Sujata said firmly, shaking Tejinder's hand formally in the presence of half a dozen hotel employees as if after a fruitful business meeting. "The traffic will be heavy later in the evening, and I will be really late returning."

Tejinder stepped into the hotel's car that had pulled up in front of them. A concierge had taken his baggage and settled it into the car's trunk already.

"Come with me to the airport," Tejinder repeated, seated in the back seat of the car.

Was this childish persistence from being rebuffed, Sujata

wondered incredulously. Or was he so aged that he did not remember that he had asked her many times? She was aghast at his surety and confidence that Sujata would come around to an affair or whatever he was hoping for, if he persisted. Didn't he see how repulsed she was? Sujata firmly, without replying, waved goodbye. She then left for her office in her car.

Once on the stretch that led to the MRC Nagar main road, Sujata was relieved the traffic was still not heavy. She continued to drive with the car's windows down, craving fresh air after the raging turmoil she had felt in the chilled hotel room. Going over the events that had just transpired with Tejinder, Sujata wondered if there was anything she could have done differently, to prevent this revolting fiasco. After much thought, she concluded that there wasn't, except for not going to his room alone. Whether it is sexual harassment, rape, or attempted rape, they are all about asserting power that demeans and threatens the victim's self-worth and crushes their soul. It then leaves the mere ghost of the victim's former self, to deal with the world's accusatory fingers, and frail attempts to nail the culprit. This explained Sujata's attempt at normalcy of behaviour in public, even after Tejinder's atrocious outbreak.

Often, one will come across a man in power, chasing a woman whom he thinks he can win over with his seasoned charms, but if not, he will resort to persuasion and bullying. Such men cannot take 'no' for an answer, as it hurts their fragile egos. They have usually got all they've desired in life, and are used to having their way with women too often. And thus, they do not understand that when a woman says 'no' … she means so. A man who then stoops to sexually harass and bully doesn't realise an unresponsive woman is not flattered by his interest, neither will she succumb however powerful or affluent he may be. She might be ashamed, humiliated by his undue attention. It takes moral strength and the nerves of steel to ward off a man with immense social power, more so if he is her superior at work or even her husband's. A woman then cannot even easily talk about her predator to anyone, as she is blamed for how she looks or dresses, and might have acted to allure him.

Then even the law will ask a woman for physical proof of having been sexually harassed, which is more humiliating in recounting,

   Shuvashree Chowdhury

let alone proving. Thus women, often in saving their dignity from further abuse, after already having had it crushed, tend to be quiet on the matter. How would they go about proving it, and who would believe them, they fear. Their well-meaning friends and families too will advise them not to take on such a powerful and socially respected man. Thus, Sujata was afraid no one would believe her! To make matters worse, in her case, she was not even sure if she could relate this incident to her husband, for fear he might blame her instead and make her feel cheap. How could she relate this to her parents or sister either? They would surely say it was her fault for going to the general's room, knowing how he bragged of his escapades with women. Little would they understand that she had never imagined being the victim of a family friend who was seventy years old.

Sujata went over the last two meetings with Tejinder, when she had met him along with Anand. There was no way of telling he would turn out this way. She cursed herself repeatedly now for going up to his room. But this could have happened at any other place—in her office or his. You cannot be suspicious of the world at large, of all men all the time, Sujata judiciously concluded. Yet she was convinced that such issues need to be dealt with severely when they do arise, in an attempt to reduce the sureness and guts of such people. She would talk to Tejinder firmly. It's just that she would first allow herself to heal from the blow and the resulting emotional fragility before doing so.

Sujata needed more time to get back her composure before she could return to her office and deal with people. She decided to fill her car's fuel tank at a Bharat Petroleum pump on the way and also to kill time at the store inside it. As Sujata pulled out of the pump fifteen minutes later, feeling much better after the brisk distraction and retail therapy, her car now merging slowly into the traffic, her phone rang inside her bag. She retrieved it briskly, thinking it might be her children, who would have returned from school by now. To her amazed exasperation, Sujata saw Tejinder's name flashing on the screen. Though she detested even hearing his voice, she forced herself to take the call, as she had decided to be strong about this.

"Why didn't you come to the airport, with me?" He said, on

hearing her say 'hello' and then added, "It's such a long drive, and we could have easily chatted on the way." Then even as she remained silent, he added nonchalantly, much to Sujata's rising dread on his psychotic, egotistic whim not to give up on the seemingly latest toy that had caught his fancy, "Never mind, but you must come on a holiday. I promise you, we will just be friends. Promise me you will come."

		Shuvashree Chowdhury

Chapter 18

Expensive Gifts

"**G**ood Morning, gorgeous, I'm off to a meeting with my bosses," Aparna had messaged Stephan from office, the morning after their tiff. "I just want to say again, I'm really sorry for hurting you so much. You know well it was unintentional, and it was my own fear that made me become doubtful of you. But now I can't wait to meet you … we'll chat at night over the details. You go on to work and have a good day."

"When do you want me to visit you, darling?" Stephan had replied on waking.

Aparna returned to her desk from the meeting with Anand and the Sunday magazine team. At the meeting, held at his office, after they discussed routine matters, Anand announced the proposed launch of a Friday lifestyle magazine supplement in a month's time. What took Aparna by storm was his announcement that she would be heading it, with two members from this team right here and a few new recruits. After she had recovered from the shock, Aparna looked curiously at Radhika, who was calmly smiling. This meant she had known of this decision and was a part of it. Aparna turned to Anand next, with a confused expression, but the look in her eyes was one of firm refusal. It was her intimacy with him that impelled her instinctive defiance, even in public. She was about to blurt out that she could not accept this responsibility, however grateful she was to be given the opportunity. But Anand's grave expression and the authority in his stare cowed her defiant look and froze the words in her mouth.

All Aparna could do now was shut up and think about how the other members in the team had taken this news. After all, Aparna was one of the last among them to join this team and to be given this significant responsibility so soon was so unfair.

They attributed this selection to her closeness to both Radhika and Anand, not to her diligence and proficiency. On her part, Aparna could not help but worry. She would now have to come up with a justifiable explanation as to why she wished to decline this responsibility that others clamoured for. Anand would otherwise see this as sheer negligence on her part and be rather disappointed in her, which she could not bear. Aparna realised that she had been given this crucial job because of Anand's immense faith in her. He knew how sincere her feelings were for him and that she would do anything for him.

Radhika had figured out the personal dynamics between Anand and Aparna by now, though she never spoke of it to either. But she understood Anand's choice. She agreed wholeheartedly that Aparna was the best choice, as in addition to her diligence and efficiency, she genuinely liked her. The meeting ended shortly after the announcement. Anand left the plans and preparations for the new magazine for a subsequent meeting. He knew the proclamation he had just made would need to first percolate down the minds of the team, with inspiration by Radhika, before acceptance came about. Anand recognized that the team's approval was crucial to the success of the magazine.

This delaying of further discussions on the magazine was just what Aparna needed, to break the news to Anand and Radhika, of her plans to go away to UK. But how was she ever going to explain to Anand about Stephan's entry into her life, just after what transpired between them? What was he going to think of her? Not as if he would ever be convinced that she had fallen in love with Stephan, after what they had shared. Anand was going to conclude, Aparna reasoned, and perhaps rightly so, that she had been indulging and convincing herself of her feelings for Stephan in a bid to run away from him. He would realise that she was, in effect, running away from the eventuality of the emotional trench she envisaged herself drowning in, if she did not make her getaway in time.

As Aparna sauntered back to her desk thoughtfully, looking about her, she suddenly realised everyone else had walked up way ahead. It was a kind of protest and a way to show their indignation at what they perceived as an unfair promotion. Radhika noticed

    Shuvashree Chowdhury

this, and reduced her pace to walk with Aparna. She had quite a task ahead, Radhika knew, in holding the team together and motivating them for the challenge ahead. She turned to Aparna, looking at her curiously.

"Why do you look so hassled … as if you're just coming in from a storm?" She said cautiously. "I would expect you to be elated, and enthusiastic to start your new assignment. Well, if it's what you've been thinking—I didn't tell you earlier so that it would be a pleasant surprise when Anand broke it to everybody at the meeting."

"No, Radhika, it's not like I'm not happy," Aparna blurted, in a fix now whether to open up to Radhika on her plans, but deciding to talk to Anand first. She added smiling, "I sincerely appreciate and value the faith you and Anand have in me. It's just that … I'm still getting over the shock of the announcement. Soon I will bounce back with all the enthusiasm and grit you expect out of me … you will see."

Even as Aparna sat at her workstation, she realised how it was not a good idea to mention Stephan to anyone right now. Definitely not before she had met him and was convinced she had a future with him. What was she thinking, considering talking to Anand now—it might cost her everything she had worked so hard to achieve, not to mention the fall from Anand's grace. Aparna was now more determined she would have to get Stephan to visit her as soon as possible, or be left in a web of confusion and conflicting circumstances. Till then, she would just have to put her mind and soul into preparing for the launch of the new magazine. In any case, this was the most crucial time, when Anand needed her most. Also, it was time for her to repay his kindness, more so, bring about a closure to her feelings for him. After the magazine's launch, she would tell Anand her UK plans and then hand its charge to someone else. He would then not feel let down by her, as he might now.

Aparna retrieved her mobile phone. She hoped Stephan would have woken up and replied to her message. She needed to know he was there for her, after her mental commitment to a life with him. And to her relief, he had messaged.

"I want you here right away, darling…" Aparna replied, smiling to herself, on reading Stephan's message. "You go ahead and make your travel plans. I will talk to you at night ... it's a busy day at work today."

Aparna put her phone away, along with thoughts of Stephan and their future. There was quite the chance of Anand walking up this way, and he would be watching her, she knew. Anand had seen her confusion, the unwillingness in her expression, to take on the new assignment, and he had looked at her sharply—both surprised and curious. Aparna decided she had better go into Radhika's cabin for a chat, and show enthusiasm for the new magazine, initiating its preliminary planning right away. Radhika, noting Aparna's enthusiastic expression and her interest in the magazine's details, was relieved. She would have to only deal with the lack of motivation of the other staff now. In a while, Anand walked in to talk to Radhika, very casually, just as Aparna had envisaged. He was relieved and pleased to hear their animated discussion on the new magazine's first issue cover.

It was only on her way home from work that evening, when driving out of the parking area, that Aparna allowed her mind to steer back to Stephan. When she reached home, her parents and Kartik were in the living room, laughing over a cartoon show on TV. It warmed her heart to see them so cosy together, and how her parents, in indulging the child, were happy doing whatever made Kartik happy. He was so emotionally secure in their love. It was almost like her parents were Kartik's parents and she his sister and buddy. Aparna was pleased with the equation they had all fallen into over the years. She liked how Kartik had come to look upon her as his best friend, his co-conspirator in hoodwinking his grandparents, on matters of importance to his childish mind. He would wait for his mother to come home, to relate all the fun he had had in school, what his friends and teachers did and said, and share his life with gusto. Aparna's father looked at Aparna warmly, and her mother briskly got up to go to the kitchen as Aparna left her bag on the floor and plonked on the sofa beside Kartik. He nestled up to her and Aparna sat cradling his head on her shoulder, even as they sat looking ahead at the TV.

"Mom, this show will get over right now..." Kartik said to Aparna distractedly. "And then I'll tell you all what Piyush and I discussed on our plans for our future."

   Shuvashree Chowdhury

After finishing the coffee and snacks served by her mother, Aparna stood up, picking up her bag.

"Kartik, get to your study table." She said firmly, "I'll join you after a shower. First, we'll take a look at your homework and then we will chat about school."

"But Grandma and I have already completed all the homework."

"That's all right," Aparna replied. "Wouldn't you like to show it to me too, so I'm also clued in on where you are at school? Then we will talk about your friends and all your plans for your future."

It was only after her parents and son had gone to sleep that night, after all had dinner together, that Aparna sat down at her bedroom desk. At first, she checked Facebook messenger on her laptop to see if Stephan was online yet. He was usually the one to message her first. She still preferred to wait for him, as she hesitated to intrude on his work. Also, she would be sure he was truly interested in her. Somehow, she still needed that reassertion continually. But after the previous evening, Aparna was still anxious she had upset Stephan, so she should take the initiative to make it up.

"Are you home yet, gorgeous?" Aparna messaged him.

"Yes, my darling, right here waiting for you." Stephan replied promptly.

"So did you initiate your travel plans or not? I must meet you soon, darling. After last evening, I feel compelled. It is like the incident has brought us much closer to each other. I am in no doubt now of my feelings or of yours. It is like God created this situation to test our feelings, more to show us a mirror to them."

"I cannot wait to meet you too, darling. I'm happy to know that my soul is now convinced she is mine. I had no doubts whatsoever about us. I did talk to my travel agent. He has applied for my visa already, and I can come to meet you in a month's time … is that okay?"

"Perfect … but wait, first let me tell you what happened at work today, over the meeting I mentioned in the morning … Our paper is launching a new lifestyle magazine, a weekly one, a Friday issue. And you just won't believe this … they've declared me as the editor. I almost fell from my chair on hearing this announcement.

But then I became worried over my plans of going away to the UK with you."

"Now wait, wait, darling! Our plans can wait … I'm right here for you! You must accept this marvellous opportunity. It will give you so much exposure and experience. It will make me the happiest man, so proud of my wife."

"Really, you really want me to take this up? I thought you might suggest I let it go, as in any case I'm going to move to the UK with you soon."

"There is no doubt that I need you here with me at the earliest, darling, but I want you to prove yourself to your family, your son, your colleagues, and above all to yourself. As for me, I have no doubt in you whatsoever. I'm ready to wait till you've finished all businesses in your current life."

"Alright, good then … you've helped me with that decision. I was much confused and about to relinquish the role, in an impulsive haste, right at the meeting after it was announced. You know nothing means more to me than love."

"No, my love, you will do no such thing. I will come to see you right after the launch of your magazine … You must concentrate on working, proving yourself for it. In the meantime, I am getting my travel plans set. I have to travel to Malaysia first. I will spend a week there, and from there come over to see you in Chennai. How many days can I spend with you, my soul … and where will I stay?"

"Darling you would need to stay at a hotel, I hope you understand. I cannot bring you home, not yet … Yes, for a meal perhaps, and to meet the family, but not to stay here. So will you stay about ten days to two weeks perhaps? I will make room reservations for you at the Park Hotel?"

"Hahahahha … No, my sweet darling! I cannot stay away from work for that long, I can at most spend 4–5 days. But I'm sure that will be more than enough … I won't let you leave my sight for even a second."

"Alright, 4–5 days then … we will make the most of it. I'll take leave from work at the time and tell them at home I'm going on some trip with my friends."

"Hahahaha, I knew my love was the smartest! Now there's

some work we need to get done before I can come. Remember I asked you about the investment options in your country and the links you sent me of the property consultants and prospective commercial properties? I got my consultant here in UK to talk to two consultants in India, on a few properties that we've shortlisted. They want us to pay them an advance in Indian currency."

"Now how are you going to do that? Why didn't you tell them you are coming here in a month or so, and then you will talk?"

"It's not a problem, darling ... they are not ready to wait and moreover, they want it in Indian currency only. So, I'm going to send you some money and you keep it very safely, till I get there."

"Alright, will do, Boss! I cannot wait to see you, darling ... I'm so excited."

"Me too, my sweet darling ... And by the way, please give me your sizes for clothes, shoes, underwear. Also ... wait ... which make of mobile phone do you use? Do you have an iPad?'

"Why, baby ... I don't need anything, you just come here!"

"Now don't argue with me on this ... just do as I tell you! I want to give my darling everything, dress her up to my taste. Don't I have the privilege?"

"Of course you have, my love! But first you come here ... I only want you."

"I want to send you stuff to my taste that you can use and wear when I visit you. It will make me so happy."

"Alright then, Boss ... just as you say. I will message the details soon."

"Now that's like my good girl! My soul, may I go out with my friends now? Two of them just came over."

"Yes, darling, you go ahead ... even though I would have liked to chat with you a while more. I'll go to bed early instead, didn't sleep well last night."

"Then darling, I'll stay right here to chat with my soul ... I'll ask my friends to carry on. I will never go anywhere without your permission, my love."

"No, baby, you must go ... you must spend time with your friends. Even when I'll be with you, you must make out time for your friends, for yourself. I'll come along sometimes, but at others I will stay home and write or read a book or something."

"You are the best, my darling, so understanding … what did I do to deserve someone as perfect as you? You make me so happy. The past is all far behind us now. And I will never ever let you go, ever. That husband of yours is such a big fool, he has no idea he is losing you forever. But then, how would God send you to me otherwise?"

"Yes, we've both been through a fair share of unhappiness, trials and troubles. But now we've found each other, all will be well … Now you go, go on."

"Alright, baby, I'm going, but I don't feel like leaving you and going."

"Run along, baby, but I want to hear every detail of your evening, tomorrow morning. I will be happy to share your life and happiness through your telling."

"Good night, my love … you sleep well and look even more pretty for me."

"Good night … Have fun, darling!"

Aparna awoke refreshed the next morning, ready to take on the world. She had her life right on track. Indecision, the most painful obstacle in life's race, had been crossed. It was now a matter of garnering all her faculties and resources, in pushing to the finishing line—in the start of a new life. In the course of going about her morning's chores, Aparna decided she would speak to Anand today, to confirm her enthusiasm in the new role and also convey her gratitude to him. She was not going to tell him anything about her plans with Stephan though, till after she had met Stephan. This would be well after the launch of the Friday magazine. Aparna served Kartik, who was seated between her parents at the table, his breakfast of *upma* and *chutney*. It being a Saturday, he did not have school, but would shortly be leaving for his painting classes, along with her father. As she indulgently watched her son eat, Aparna messaged Stephan on FB, from her cell phone.

"Darling I don't need you to get me anything, but since you insist and if it will make you happy, my shoe size is UK 38 and clothes a size 10, but I need a size 12 for all lower wear like trousers and skirts, as we Indians are bottom heavy, hahaha. It's going to

                   Shuvashree Chowdhury

be a busy day at work, so if you don't hear from me … we'll talk at night."

Aparna walked into office early that morning, with a sense of assured calm. She went over to Anand's office, after settling into her work station—leaving her bag, switching on her computer, checking her email—and left word with his secretary Rose to call her in when Anand was free to meet her. It was only after lunch that day that Aparna was called into Anand's office. On Saturdays, he had several meetings.

After she was seated across him at his desk, Aparna started promptly, on a polite and formal note, "I'm very grateful to you, Anand, for offering me the role of editor of the proposed Friday magazine." Then looking him in the eye, after the initial hesitation, she added crisply, "I wish to convey that I am honoured to be given the opportunity, and pleased to accept the same. I assure you, I will give it my best."

Anand looked at her curiously, but her face now was a masterful mask of professionalism. He was hesitant to look past this shield that she seemed to hold against him. But this was his opportunity to break the ice that seemed to be developing between them after the intimate warmth they had shared.

"How are Kartik and your parents?" Anand said casually, looking into Aparna's eyes, with warmth and tenderness like the earlier days.

In his mind, there was no reason for them to be so distant with each other. He liked her as much as he had earlier, and it was just that he had decided to take it slow due to certain circumstances. So why was he allowing this fence to grow between them?

"They are all well," Aparna replied, moved by his look and the tone of his voice. But she was not going to fall for his charms over again.

"Is Nikhil still troubling you?" Anand blurted, thinking it was a justifiable reason for her to be acting so preoccupied and strange lately.

"It's just the usual … random drunken calls intermittently."

"Well, things with me are worse than ever before," Anand said dismally, in a bid to prolong their conversation, "In fact, the relationship with my mother and brother is worse than it has ever been. And my father is rather ill. He has been detected with lung cancer. He is undergoing chemotherapy and the doctors give him a few months to a year at most. As for Sujata, you know how things are with her. I've discussed it at length over the years. But now she's too busy at work to give me much attention and that suits me just fine."

Aparna remained silent for a few moments, then abruptly and firmly said, "I'd really like to talk about the magazine, Anand. That's what I came here for. And you should not be discussing your wife with me. It's rather disrespectful, don't you think?"

Anand was taken aback by Aparna's abrupt, crisp remarks, and the firm cool detachedness in her tone. What he did not realise was that it was his mention of his wife so casually, knowing he could never leave her, that had made Aparna acutely angry. But Anand chose not to press his intention to cement their relationship at this point, as he was trying to do. He switched tracks promptly, took on a professional approach.

"You know how important this new magazine's success would be, to prove my personal merit to the board of directors, since taking on the role of chief editor." Anand was ardent. Then looking imploringly into Aparna's eyes, he added, "And thus you know why I cannot trust anyone else with its charge other than you."

"Yes, Anand, I understand completely. Don't worry … you can trust me to give all I have into making this project successful."

"I'm planning a really big high-budget launch. We'll have a meeting shortly to discuss everything, starting with a chic name for the magazine."

It was only late that evening, on her laptop, Aparna checked her FB messages for Stephan's reply to her morning's message over breakfast.

"Knock, knock! I'm home, darling." Stephan promptly wrote, seeing her come online. Then after a few seconds, before she had replied, he wrote, "Where's my soul … where's my darling?"

"I'm right here, darling … waiting for you." Aparna replied. "Now would you like tea first or to take a shower?"

"A long kiss first, darling, with a big hug … and then tea over a chat with my life ... followed by a shower. May I, darling, my sweetest baby?"

"Yes, my love, muuuuuaaaah ... a bigggggg hug! Now tea with little milk and sugar ... right?"

"Yes, just the way I like it. I cannot wait for you to get here, darling. I will be the happiest person ever. Guess what, I got a new contract for the company today."

"You did, darling? That's just great, baby! Where is this new assignment?"

"In Paris, my love ... I will be going early next week. My people have already done the inspection of the site, and only then we submitted a quotation. It got approved and the client's representatives visited us here a few days back ... then after much discussion, this morning we finally signed the contract."

"That's just great, darling! I'm so happy and proud of you."

"So now I have more reason to go shopping for you, baby. I noted your sizes. Do you have an iPhone, a Laptop, and iPad ... which make of phone do you use?"

"No, no, no, darling ... Please don't spoil me silly now ... you just come here, that is all I want. I only agreed to the clothes, thinking I'd dress up the way you like when you come, but that's about it. No more stuff, definitely not all these expensive ones."

"But I want my wife to have the best of all things ... when I have everything, why should you not have all? I must ensure you are set up well in your country, even as we wait to get you here. Which make of phone do you use ... is it a good one?"

"I have everything that I need till I come there to be with you ... I have a laptop, but not an iPad. I use a Blackberry phone. It serves me well enough."

"Alright, darling, do you know what I'm doing tomorrow? Chris and his wife are taking me shopping. They are so excited to hear you're coming, and that you'll be living here with me. We've all been planning what we'll do when you are here. And speculating what you will like and what you won't."

"That is really sweet, darling ... but it makes me so embarrassed that you are spoiling me silly like this. So tomorrow no work ... It's Saturday? They come home and take you out, or what?"

"Just be happy for my happiness, darling ... I'm doing it for myself, so please let me. I'm so happy. Which colours do you like, my love?"

"Alright, if you put it that way, about your happiness, how can I refuse? I like bright colours, darling … pinks, mauves, reds and blues."

"The bright colours really go well with you. I was thinking … for our son Kartik, instead of clothes, I could get a camera, also an iPad, and a good watch. Wouldn't that be nice? I wouldn't really know what clothes to buy him … So I'll leave that choice to you always, and going ahead also for our daughter Angel."

"All this is too much now, darling. Don't spoil him … he doesn't need any of this yet. He's too young, and moreover let him learn to live within his current resources and what his mother can provide."

"Come on, darling, now he has a father as well, who can give him the best in life. So why should he not have it all when Angel does here? What she lacks is a mother's love and guidance, just as Kartik needs a father to spoil him."

"Kartik's father here and grandparents already spoil him, darling, so I'm strict. Just thinking, I'll make no distinction between our children … from now on, Angel is as much mine as she is yours, baby … So you don't worry about her anymore."

"Ahhhhh that's the best thing I've heard in the longest time …. Darling, you will do that? You will love Angel as your own? So she may never know she had any other mother before you?"

"Yes, darling, you just see … perhaps God wanted a mother for her much more than he needed you to find a wife."

"Perhaps so, baby, I'm so happy … what can I say or ever ask of God again?"

The next day, a Sunday, Stephan messaged Aparna in the afternoon. He had just returned from church.

Along with a "Hello, Darling", he posted the picture of a gorgeous-looking, purple, green, and maroon Furla handbag.

Aparna had seen it in a magazine recently, so knew it was the latest design. She also knew that Furla was an expensive and aspirational brand.

Stephan's message along with the elegant bag read, "Please keep this bag very carefully, darling, it has pounds. You must keep it very safe, till I come. It has the money we will need, while I'm visiting in your country, as well as some for your travel expenditure to the UK later."

Then one at a time, Stephan forwarded pictures of more of the things he had bought Aparna, over the shopping trip with his friend's wife the day before. There was a pause after each item, so she would register it to mind, and he could gauge her reactions to it. After the handbag, there were two pairs of the most elegant shoes Aparna had ever seen. One was in brown patent leather, the other in a greenish-blue. Both were high-heeled and trendy and seemed to be in size 38 as she had mentioned. They both went rather well with the Furla bag, Aparna noticed. It reflected Stephan's keen eye for design and colour, his sensitivity to fashion, along with his refined taste. He had seen a number of Aparna's pictures on FB and had often commented on Aparna's fine taste, noticing how she tended to match her accessories well. She was enchanted by all the lovely things, and overwhelmed by his love for her.

Next, Stephan forwarded the picture of a tiny brown leather case, with its cover open. There was a slender platinum ring imbedded into its navy-blue velvet base, on which was mounted a queen-cut diamond. Viewing it made Aparna emotional.

"It's so lovely, darling … so exquisite, really, just like you!" she typed spontaneously, with her heart in her mouth in happiness.

"No, it's like you, my heart! You're pretty, really beautiful like this diamond."

"I'm very touched, darling. But I must say you are really spoiling me."

In response, Stephan promptly posted the picture of an iPhone, and before Aparna could even register it, there was one of an iPad, followed by an Apple Mac Book-Aid. A set of two watches followed shortly, even as Aparna looked on in silence. All items were pictured, with their respective packaging boxes as props.

"Darling … this really is too much!" Aparna stated, coming out of her blinding stupor. "I cannot accept all this … you must understand that. Even though I'm immensely touched and so overwhelmed! No one has ever done so much for me in my whole life. No one ever got me so many gifts, regardless of value … even though since a child, I loved assortment of small gifts, rather than one single big thing. It's like you read my heart, love, before my asking, and place its desires before me."

"You are so precious, darling, and all these things don't match up to you, not in the least … I really want to show you that. You've got to take all this to please me, if for nothing else. It will make me the happiest man. I'm sending all this by courier, so they will be reaching you shortly."

"But why are you not bringing all this with you … when you come here next month? It will be so much safer and easier to bring it yourself."

"I don't travel with so much baggage. In fact, I usually carry hand luggage only. And I forward any other baggage just before my travel, to the designated place."

"Alright, I see … my gorgeous spoilt brat. I will keep everything safe till you come. When you are here, you can open and give me the things yourself. It's the thought you've put behind each and every item, much over their costs, that is so special, darling … You have no idea just how overwhelmingly touched I am."

"I don't care for any of the things really, it's only you who matters, my soul. But you must keep the bag very carefully … It contains a lot of money. We will need it when I come, and the rest will be for your visa and other stuff."

"But how much money is there?"

"8000 exactly … pounds."

"All right, I won't open the courier box, but will keep it exactly the way it is."

"So how was your day, baby? Did you go to church alone, or with your friends and their families? What did you do after that?" Aparna asked, changing the topic.

"I usually go alone but tend to meet my friends there … they come by too. After church, we had a parish meeting. I am actively involved in church work. Then I came home quickly, as I was excited to show you my purchases. But first I had my lunch, as I was starving, as I had a very small breakfast."

"Now, Darling, didn't I tell you that you must eat well at breakfast? It is the most important meal of the day. I've told you so many times, that you must eat eggs, cereal, and yogurt every morning. Now I must talk to that cook of yours, mustn't I?"

     Shuvashree Chowdhury

"Hahahahaha, now you talk to him when you come over here, and then you can fix everything around here. It's your home and so you make the rules."

"Did you see the doctor as I asked you to … You've still been feeling weak?"

"Yes, I did and he said it is nothing, only fatigue. He advised complete rest for a couple of days, not to go to work."

"Now see, didn't I tell you, you must eat well, a nutritious diet and not just any meal. You cannot help the work pressure and fatigue, they're all expected. But if you eat well, your immunity will be high and you'll have strength to withstand exertion."

"Yes, my pretty, pretty baby, I will do as you say … Now you just come here soon. I will listen to everything you say, once you're here. So how was your day so far?"

"Pretty much the same as every Sunday. After breakfast with the family, I took Kartik for his violin classes. Then we all had lunch altogether. I will take the family to the Express Avenue mall later … I showed you the photos of the place I had my haircut in last time, at Tony N Guy. Then we'll go to a movie and dinner at the food court."

"Sounds perfect to me … So you go ahead, my love, my friends have just come over and we're going for a football match. I will catch you at night perhaps, or if not, tomorrow morning. My friends are so excited to meet you, darling!"

"And I am excited to meet them … to come over and be part of your life."

"Bye, my love … you are the heart of my soul."

"Isn't that so sweet … heart of my soul … I quite like that. You always come up with something new to make me smile. Bye for now, gorgeous … and have fun!"

In the following days, Aparna was rather busy at work. She put all her energies into planning the new magazine, in collating articles that would go into the launch issue. Also, along with Radhika and the team, Aparna culled out a comprehensive guest list. They kept adding to it, as and when they recalled having missed someone of relevance. All the influential and affluent people of the city would be invited. After all, the magazine would need a steady supply of advertisements to fund itself. It was slated to be a mega launch.

The new team for this magazine, almost in place now, would be operational in a week. As yet, the *Sunday Magazine* team worked on the planning of the new magazine as well. They had, by now, accepted Aparna's selection as editor after consistent motivation by Radhika.

"I could not spare all the good workers from the *Sunday magazine*, now could I?" Radhika had told the team at a meeting she called, the day after Anand's announcement. "We had to make a choice, and it just happened to be Aparna … It might have been any of you, who are all just as proficient and sincere."

Aparna concentrated well on work in the next days. But she could not dislodge the unrest in her chest, of how she was going to break the news of Stephan to Anand. She was not over Anand, Aparna realised dismally, as she had hoped. It was the impracticality of the situation with him that had sent her scuttling to fall headlong in love with Stephan. Her bid to extricate herself from the emotional web she anticipated being stuck in, if attached to Anand longer, had propelled her.

Aparna continued chatting with Stephan on FB every night. Their interactions kept reassuring her of their life together, of the promise of an everlasting happiness that was gifted by God. After all, had he not already given them both more than their fair share of miseries? Stephan was in touch with the property consultants here in India and they awaited his arrival, to proceed with the deal he planned. It was decided then that Stephan would be here in the first week of November, which was now only over a month away. The new magazine's launch was scheduled for the end of October, so Aparna was at her wit's end with all the arrangements.

A few weeks later, one evening, suddenly in conversation with Aparna, Stephan wrote: "Darling, there's one big problem—the parcel that I sent you, the courier company here, FedEx, they say I cannot pay for the taxes at my end. You will have to pay at the time of delivery. I realise I should have told you earlier, when I sent it. I insisted I would pay it here, but they would not accept, and firmly stated the recipient will have to pay taxes. It is a sum of 300 pounds, but would you be able to pay that amount, darling? Would it be a big problem? Do you have the money?"

"It is a little strange, I would think, in that the recipient has to pay," Aparna typed. Then in her mental calculation, she assumed it would only be approximately Rs. 3000 and so cheerily added, "But then that's okay, 300 pounds is not that much. I will give it to them when they deliver. You don't worry, gorgeous. But then, I hope you have with you a comprehensive list, with pricing and pictures, of all the items you've sent. This is just in case the courier gets misplaced in transit, and then you will have to prove the sending of each of those goods."

"Yes, I've got a list, duly signed by FedEx. Just keep the bag very carefully, darling. It's a lot of money and all for our future. We would need it to spend when I'm with you, but more for your visas and travel here."

The next morning, when seated behind the steering wheel of her car at the parking of her apartment building, Aparna received a call on her cell phone from a number she recognised as coming from Delhi. It had 011 STD code prefixed to it.

"Ma'am, I'm calling from the Customs office in Delhi," the female voice at the other end, with a heavy north-eastern accent said. "We've got your parcel, from your husband Mr. Stephan Shedrack of the UK. You will have to deposit Rs. 34000 into our account in the State Bank of India to have the parcel delivered to you."

"But why so much," Aparna blurted in shock, "wouldn't it be around Rs. 3000?"

"No, ma'am, it will be Rs. 34000. And you must deposit it today." She stated politely, "For us to deliver immediately, or you know how it is, there's a huge number of parcels we get daily."

"So which account do I pay it into? Could you please text me the details, so I can deposit the check?"

Stephan called Aparna immediately thereafter, much to her surprise, due to the early hour, and without preface, he urgently said: "I've just received a call from FedEx; they say the Customs department at your end has seized the parcel due to the size, and nature of the contents. Please, darling, make the payment today. I'm very worried about the money … and don't forget to keep the bag safely once you get it."

Even though Aparna was getting late for work, she decided to get the check deposited at the State Bank right away. She first called

Radhika and excused herself for coming late. Radhika sounded sullen, as she was already stressed in planning for the new magazine they had named *Elite*, after much collective brainstorming. She already had her regular work on the daily *Urban Plus* and the Sunday magazine. But Aparna had to do what she had to, and though peeved at this new bother now, at a bad time, she went back up home and retrieved her check book.

On the way down in the lift, Aparna's phone beeped with the account number texted to her, along with the name and address of the bank, which to her surprise was in Uttar Pradesh. Aparna drove straight to the State Bank of India, a branch on her way to work, where she had an account. She took the queue token, wrote out the check standing by the slim wooden desk-stand mounted on the wall, and awaited her chance to be serviced. The money would have to be transferred by today, so it would have to be a direct transfer her branch would make to the payee branch, so she could not just drop a check and go away.

After Aparna had the money transferred and the check deposit slip was signed and duly returned to her, she headed to office. There she scanned the deposit slip as instructed by the Customs lady and emailed it to her. Aparna messaged Stephan, updated him on the proceedings. She could not help smiling, in spite of her frustration, at him going to such lengths to send all the items he had for her. It was sometime after lunch at the office canteen that the lady at the Customs office called Aparna again. She was very polite and had a softer, kinder voice now.

"Ma'am, we've received the money you transferred," she stated, then sounding sympathetic, she continued, "But there is one small problem. Just when we were going to dispatch the parcel, we had it scanned as is usual and found it contains a hand bag that has a big sum of money, 8000 pounds. Do you know of it? Has your husband told you of it? It is a really big sum when converted to Indian currency."

"Well, yes," Aparna replied hesitantly. "I am aware. Is there a problem?"

"Ma'am, we're unable to have the parcel dispatched to you." She said bluntly now, taking Aparna by surprise, but more so striking her with renewed anxiety. Then before Aparna could reply, she

 Shuvashree Chowdhury

added "You will have to pay a service tax on receipt of this parcel, as it actually amounts to money laundering. You could get into big problem for this. I hope you understand it is illegal to transfer money this way."

Aparna was alarmed, but holding a steady voice with difficulty, she replied: "You see my friend did not know these formalities. He is travelling to India next month, so he forwarded the money for me to keep safely till he arrives. He wishes to invest in property here, a house perhaps, along with commercial assets, for which he will require money as advance. That is why he sent the large sum of money."

"That is fine, but you will have to pay a sum of Rs. 57000, in view of taxes on the 8000 pounds you received. The previous amount was for all the other items."

"Can't you reduce the charges please?" Aparna pleaded now, her mind in a dilemma, on how she was going to come up with this money. But then, she had to, how could she allow it to be forfeited? "I'm a simple service person, how can I afford to pay this amount of money? And my friend will be coming only after a month."

"Ma'am, I'm really sorry," the woman said very gently, and emphasising her heavy north-eastern accent further, she added "It is not in my hands. My boss will not agree, as the amount is really large and it is a risk on his part also to let it pass."

"So what must I do?" Aparna asked, sounding exasperated now.

"I'm sending you two account numbers, with the account names and the branch addresses. Both are of ICICI bank. You will have to deposit the amount in them, in two parts."

"Why two parts, why not into the same account that I deposited in earlier? I have all the details already, so that will be much easier."

"No, no, you must not put the money into the same account. I'm giving you these account numbers of our employees ... We do not have such high limits, so it has to be divided into a number of accounts. I will call you back in a while."

In a few seconds after she had disconnected, Aparna's mind, trying to grasp the circumstance, concluded this was an illegal transaction. It was something like a bribe she now had to pay to retrieve the parcel. She was contemplating on how murky this matter was getting and risky too, when her phone rang again. It was Stephan. She was surprised at the timing of his call, being right after the Customs lady again. But then he was worried, she thought, and also must be in touch with them.

"Darling, you must get that bag. The money is really very important for us," Stephan said, sounding calm, and then in an assertive tone, he added, "I'm trusting that you will do the right thing to get that bag."

"I am doing all I can, baby," Aparna replied earnestly. "But this is really at a very bad time for me. You know how busy and stressed I am with the new magazines launch and over that this added pressure."

"How would I know things in your country would be so complicated? These people have seen all the money, while scanning the bag, so they are blackmailing you to get a share of it. But baby, please give them whatever they ask. I hope you understand we need the money. It's for our future."

"But you should have told me before you dispatched the parcel, not after. Are you so naïve, darling? I thought you would be smarter. How could you send so much money just like that, by courier? When you told me of the amount in pounds, I didn't figure out the value in rupees immediately."

"Darling, my sweet, intelligent princess … from now on, I will leave everything to your wisdom. But for now, please recover the bag. I hope you know that once that bag is with you, you can keep more than the money you are paying now; so don't worry about the money you're losing."

"Yes, gorgeous, I will have to get that parcel at any cost … How could I allow them to take away all the precious things you put much thought and time into buying for me? I will do whatever it takes, darling. But I insist you're still far from worldly smart. But don't worry, as from now on you have me to watch out for you."

"Thank you, darling … what would I ever do without you! It is not for nothing that God has found you for me."

"Bye for now, baby … I really must get to work." Aparna said briskly, hanging up, "There's so much to be done before we can be together."

Aparna placed her cell phone in her bag, to return fervently to her work.

Chapter 19

A Pillar of Strength

"You men are all the same … aren't you?" Sujata wrote to her friend Shekhar in a WhatsApp message, a few days after her atrocious encounter with General Tejinder.

She was unable to keep the episode to herself any longer. With Shekhar, the bond they shared meant that Sujata didn't need a prologue to pick up a conversation, whatever the matter. He was her most trusted friend and she would always love him. She had tried to keep the incident with Tejinder bottled up inside as there really was no one in Chennai she could talk to about it. But it caused her a lot of unease. It was like lava inside of her, waiting to erupt. This was from the deep sense of humiliation she had felt, but more so because of the difficulty in handling the mental pressure Tejinder created. He still called, and texted her randomly, the way he had on her drive back from the Leela Palace hotel, after her lunch with him. It was as though everything was as normal between them, as before the appalling occurrence. She did not take Tejinder's calls, but every time her phone rang with his name flashing on the screen or she saw his text message, Sujata got all wound up in panic and anger.

Shekhar, with no clue what Sujata meant by the random message, pertly replied, "What has Manas done to you again now? Some cheeky fellow he is, I tell you. How dare he kiss you in the car at the parking lot of the Presidency club? And then you say you'd thought to make out in the car there that morning?"

"Hahaha, no, it's not about Manas," Sujata replied, laughing and typing.

She fondly reminisced how Shekhar had been livid for months after she told him over one of their telephone chats that she had reconnected with Manas. But then, slowly, better sense had prevailed. And he was resigned to the fact that Sujata was so much younger than him, and with her children still so young, leaving her husband was not a judicious prospect. So how could he think of a future with her? Also, they lived in different cities. A long-distance steady relationship was impractical. Abruptly, her mind returned, with acute revulsion and rage, to her problem at present, the menace Tejinder had turned out to be after their meeting. She sent Shekhar another message, typing angrily.

"It's that General Tejinder, you know him. He's been harassing me. And I'm so distressed. I just don't know what to do … I haven't told a soul yet."

"What the hell … what has he done now … the old man's still up to his tricks?"

"Yes, it was also my fault. I met him at his room at the Leela Palace for lunch. I thought he's such an old man, so what'll he possibly do? I also reasoned that no one will even imagine anything to gossip, so I'm safe. But how wrong I was! How horribly stupid of me … Age perhaps takes away one's inhibitions."

"So what did he actually do? Tell me in detail, will you? You're just hinting at things. You mentioned your first lunch meeting with him at the coffee-shop … that went well, didn't it? Just wait, I'm calling you on your mobile. Don't risk typing all this."

As soon as Sujata heard Shekhar's voice, she burst out in continuance of their conversation, "Tejinder kept making passes, inviting me for a holiday with him to any place in the world. Even though I tried to laugh it off, he kept insisting the place would be of my choice. In spite of being uncomfortable, I continued laughing off his suggestions of places as I thought this was another of his outrageous jokes. Then on the pretext of goodbye, he grabbed me and kissed my lips brutally. He just would not let me go, and he pressed me hard against him. I was so scared, as there was the bed just behind us. I thought he might rape me. After all the drama, when we came down to the lobby, he kept insisting I see him off at the airport. I obviously didn't. But he kept calling me on my drive back. It was so obsessive."

There was silence at the other end for a while and Sujata knew Shekhar was outrageously angry. He did not know what to say to her though, so he was quiet. She proceeded to tell him more details

		Shuvashree Chowdhury

of the incident, followed by that of the text messages she received now. Shekhar still remained silent.

Then firmly, he rejoined, "Block his number. Bar all the incoming calls."

"I've done that. But I can see the incoming calls … I mean, his name flashes … before the call drops. It agitates me so much. Also, there are his text messages, wherein he keeps asking me where I am, why I am not picking up the phone … as if nothing has changed. He's driving me crazy. But I don't know why I've become so paranoid at my age after all my exposure. I've been thinking. Perhaps it's a deep-rooted childhood fear I still have of few similar situations I've been through with older relatives. I was so terrified then though I understood their intent only later."

"Just ask him to go to hell. Pick up the phone and tell him that or reply to his texts and say it. Don't be afraid, he can do nothing more. Just face him and tell him off."

"I will do that … I must do it." Sujata replied shakily, but with a surge of mental strength now. "Thank you so much, Shekhar. I really needed to get this out of my system. I've been so troubled." Then, as the anxiety she had felt slowly dissipated, she added in an affectionately jovial tone, "What would I do without you, Shekhar?"

Sujata, as always, was grateful for Shekhar's mental strength and his continued presence in her life. They had slipped with ease from a romantic liaison to that of a rock-solid friendship. This had been possible because Shekhar, in his maturity, did not hold it against Sujata that she had moved on romantically. This was bound to happen with the physical distance between them, he had reasoned. He was now much stronger emotionally and had recovered from the sudden blow of his wife's untimely death. It was perhaps Aneesha's passing and his ensuing guilt over neglecting her in her last years that had also caused him to detract from the relationship with Sujata, even after the intimacy they succumbed to from his emotional weakness at the time and her empathy. Shekhar had not met Sujata since their meeting at the Taj Coromandel bar, the day after, and had made no effort to. But he valued their friendship immensely and always would.

Sujata felt much better and stronger, now that she had shared all the details of her harassment to Shekhar. She knew her words and her predicament would always be safe with him, just as everything she had shared with him over the years. She used to once chat with him on Skype all the time, from home and office, in the early years of their friendship. The chemistry between them was fierce then, but now she had shifted to regular and constant WhatsApp messages and phone calls every once in a while. One night, when chatting with Shekhar on Skype from their bedroom at home, Sujata had gone over to the children's room on hearing an abrupt shriek. Anand had walked over and taken a look at her open laptop screen. Shekhar's images, with their romantic and sexually charged messages, had enraged him. Anand had swiftly saved their chat history on a pen drive to read in detail later. He still had it though it was unknown to Sujata.

Anand had felt smug, feeling justified even, of his own relationship with Aparna and his dalliances with other women. They gave him the love and attention Sujata had never shown him from the start. And now she was even involved with other men. She did not find him physically appealing or mentally attractive as Aparna did. But Anand was never to tell Sujata he was aware of her liaison or that he had seen her explicit and sexually charged messages. He had read several times with much irritation the one where she had written "I love you. I cannot live without you". But the silence suited him fine, to feel guilt-free in every way. What did it matter to him, if he could justify his ways, that Sujata had got involved with another man, only out of his neglect of her both physically and emotionally. In his mind, she was having fun. So why should she complain now of what he did? Both of them were in a marriage of convenience, as many a couple are, from societal, parental, and familial benefits.

As Sujata continued to chat with Shekhar late into the night, she felt better. With his moral and emotional support, she felt ready to deal with the Tejinder issue confidently.

"I'll give Tejinder a piece of my mind the next time he calls, or I'll reply very stiffly to his next text message." Sujata said decisively, "You are absolutely right. I need to deal with him resolutely or be destroyed by my own rage."

"But why are you so intimidated by Tejinder? Is it also because

                    Shuvashree Chowdhury

you feel alone in this? And are sure you want to keep your husband and parents out of this?"

"Yes, Shekhar. You know well how it is. Whenever I have complained to Anand about anything, he always manages to turn the tables against me. When I've told him of my run-ins with traffic cops, like once when a car hit mine from behind on Cathedral road and the cop started shouting at me, Anand blamed me. Then our neighbour was harassing me—parking his car too close behind mine on the road, blocking my way in the morning, so I would be forced to interact with him. Then too, Anand repeatedly asked me, 'But what exactly is he doing to you? Tell me, what's he doing?'"

"Yes, I remember those incidents. You'd called me about the neighbour later and I had given that fellow a piece of my mind, saying I was your lawyer. Then he didn't trouble you again."

"Yes, such a male chauvinistic society here, what can I tell you? And what hypocrisy too! They don't project what they truly are. But it's certain we women have little say in matters of importance. We are to just keep quiet, act dumb, follow all the rigid traditions, and worship the men who supposedly know everything. You know how Anand keeps telling me 'It's your aggressive attitude that gets you into trouble. How does all this happen only to you? No one has these issues in Chennai. People are so polite here. They address everyone as sir or madam. Why can't you just be quieter and more patient?' But tell me, how can I possibly be quiet on seeing such strange practices? When we are invited anywhere, they will always serve the man first. Once Anand was invited as chief guest to a reputed college, and after the event, over high tea, a waiter served me first. You won't believe it, but the learned male professors, and to my surprise, the principal asked him to pick up the coffee cup and serve it to Anand sir first. This sir-sir business really irks me, especially when they look over your head like we women don't really exist. But they will ogle at you outrageously, so you don't have to worry about missing that."

"Yes, I know what you mean. I can quite relate to it." Shekhar laughed heartily at Sujata's dramatic monologue, then continued, "Unlike in North India where male chauvinism is often aggressively flaunted, in the South—especially in Chennai—it is usually under wraps of politeness. But it is just as prevalent, if not more.

Women are to remain in the background and be quiet on matters of importance. Also, at public functions, women and men don't mingle freely. It is a rather conservative society out there, on the face of it, with hypocrisy that camouflages sensual excesses. But as for you, Sujata, it's only because you've started travelling to Mumbai and elsewhere that all this is now odd to you. Having been born and brought up in Chennai like I was, you should be used to it all."

"Yes, that's true. Working and travelling widely has definitely broadened my perspectives on life, and even alienated me from my family and my own people. Nowadays, when I stay over at my mother's place, there is little space for me there, both mentally and physically. I feel like a total outsider. Our views are so divergent. My room is used by my sister Ramya's children as their play room and they really mess up the place. I don't like going there much anymore."

"How are your parents, by the way?" Shekhar interrupted, easily switching the track of the conversation.

"I haven't met them in a while," she confessed, rather abruptly.

"But Sujata, you all live in the same city, don't you? In fact, isn't your office just a few blocks away from your parents' home? So why don't you go to meet them?"

Sujata was silent for a while, and then she said "I'm very upset with all of them. That's why I don't go over. They're always busy with my sister Ramya and her family."

Ramya, a few years older than Sujata, had been living at their parent's house along with her husband Prashant and two children since a few years after her marriage. Her husband's house was small and cramped, but more than that, Ramya found getting along with her mother-in-law an impossible task and they had fought relentlessly over trivial matters. It had thus come to the point where she and her mother-in-law would cook separate meals at different times in the one kitchen the house possessed. Even this arrangement where they were living merely as housemates did not ensure a peaceful cohabitation between the older and younger couples. The best option then was for Ramya to move to her parent's house, as there was ample place for her family there. Also, her children would have plenty of space to run about and play.

Shuvashree Chowdhury

Sujata, in a sharp contrast to her sister, had married into an affluent family, with a large house. She had been bestowed every physical comfort, if not emotional. When her relationship with the in-laws was no longer pleasant, she and Anand had moved to a separate floor of the same house. This way, they lived near and with his family, but had their personal space as a couple. Sujata had then refurbished her new apartment tastefully. For this, she used the services of her own family's carpenter and construction contractor, so it was the way she wanted it. Anand would go upstairs to his parent's home for breakfast, also read all the varied newspapers he did habitually there, in order to justify spending time with his parents. He had dinner at his home downstairs with his wife and children. They all got their lunch packed for school and to work. Sujata could easily have lunch at her mother's house, but she avoided it to save her mother the added trouble.

"Ramya is so much a part of our parents' home. In fact, even her husband is more at home there than I am." Sujata confided sadly to Shekhar. "Mom and Dad go all out to provide for everything for her and her family."

"They live together. That's the way it should be! That doesn't mean they don't love you," Shekhar replied in a placating tone. "Your parents know they can depend on Ramya and her husband for anything at any time. In the same way, Ramya can take a breather from tending to her children, knowing your parents can mind them. For her husband, it is in all ways a win-win situation. On the one hand, Ramya is grateful for his living with her parents and leaving his own. On the other, your parents are grateful to him for living with them and letting them keep their daughter close. So your parents go out of their way to be nice to them."

"That is your take on the matter, Shekhar, and it's a sound perspective. But why must I be made to feel like a guest in my own home?" Sujata said sharply, frustrated by Shekhar always keeping a balanced view. "I want my childhood room back, the one Ramya has adopted in my absence. It's always a mess now with her children's stuff. I want it to be a place I can come home to sometimes—a mental refuge."

"Well, your parents know you have everything you could want or ever need. You have a luxurious house and the money to buy whatever you want. It's possible they feel they have nothing much to offer you anymore. But they feel responsible for your sister due to her deprived circumstances. They are protective and indulgent to her."

After a pause, Sujata sighed audibly, and, in a resigned tone said, "I suppose you are right. They think I have no problems at all. To them, no trouble is comparable to the financial troubles Ramya faces, as her husband is always in and out of a job. He could not even manage my father's business efficiently. Prashant, though a great husband and father, is unable to hold on to his jobs. Anand, who was never around for me since our marriage, is professionally adept. He inherited his family business, no doubt, but he has steered it to greater success. I have had to make a career for myself because of the circumstances of my marriage. But Ramya has it easy, as our parents support her. She just does not want to work. She spends the time fighting with her husband and children, who are exasperated by her pestering."

"You are right. Your parents do indulge your sister excessively, which will be rather detrimental to her in the long run. But you mustn't allow that to weigh you down, as you are better off independent. I really think you need to communicate your feelings to your parents, Sujata. They see you as a strong, self-sufficient woman who needs no one. And so, they feel they have nothing much they can offer you. They know that you are not likely to ever live with them. I know you help them when you can, and also give your mother money every month. You parents know Anand will never go and live with them or give them the importance Ramya's husband does, whatever the problems you may have with his people or at his house. You see, it's all about mutual understanding."

"Life, love, relationships—it's all only about convenience then, isn't it?" Sujata stated dejectedly. "And you cannot even depend on your parents to love you unconditionally and without partiality?"

"Maybe not entirely so, but yes, convenience does play a big role," Shekhar replied ruefully. "In our country, the family system contributes immensely to our emotional stability and well-being. Here, marriage and family are not for the purpose of romantic love only. In fact, for women, the fear of loneliness is a factor, in addition to the quest for economic stability. For men, it is a need

                    Shuvashree Chowdhury

for emotional security and the convenience of a well-managed home that protects marriage vows in our culture. We compromise and live as a family, cohabitating in mutual dependency. If your husband was poor, in addition to not having time for you, you might have moved out by now with the children to your parent's house. But now, you can justify staying in the loveless marriage for the lifestyle it offers you—trips abroad, five-star hotel stays and meals on holidays and also in Chennai, the diamonds, the parties, fancy cars and the houses you have on ECR road and Kodaikanal. You've told me all this yourself. You see, you cannot afford all this as yet with only your personal earnings, can you? Then why deprive your children?"

"Yes, it is true, often money compensates for the lack of personal time and company of a spouse and a parent," Sujata said resignedly. "I get your point. If there was nothing to it, I might have long left. There is no denying that ours is now a marriage of convenience."

"That is why I would never woo you out of that marriage for my own selfish motives and purposes." Shekhar replied, laughing aloud, "Even if that means losing you forever. But then you clearly don't understand, nor do you value my feelings for you or my intentions either. Instead you go and renew your passion for that stupid thug Manas."

"He is just a friend." Sujata promptly replied. "There is nothing more to it. I keep telling you about him to make you jealous, so you take a bold step about us."

"Don't give me that, Sujata. There is no need to justify anything to me. I know well how lonely and unhappy you are in your marriage. And Manas provides the physical companionship and support I am unable to. But I just want you to understand that and be careful. He's using you as a ladder to climb the Chennai social and corporate ladder. As for me, I would be happy to just come home to you and the children as Anand has the privilege now. Who but me would know its importance ... the value of family, now that I live alone? But I would not cheat your children of their real family and a lifestyle rightfully theirs, as they are still young."

"Why can't you just think of yourself, think of me, and of us?"

After a brief silence, in a sad voice, Shekhar replied, "It's been a rather long chat, Sujata, but let me conclude by saying that maybe once your children are grown and ready to leave the house, you might consider a life with me. Till then, you know I will be there for you whenever you should need me."

"Yes, it's been long indeed. I have an early meeting tomorrow. Thankfully, Anand has been out of town or he would have added to my stress over Tejinder." Then before hanging up, in a teasing voice, Sujata added, "And as for waiting for the children to grow up, you will be far too old by then, won't you? Ok, bye for now!"

As she lay awake in bed after hanging up, Sujata could not steer her mind away from Shekhar and their conversation. She noticed how much it had lifted her spirits and given her so much strength and self-assurance. It was his inspiration and support that had gone a long way into building her enterprise to where it was today, Sujata recalled warmly. She had not seen her goals clearly and yet had set out alone on a rock-strewn track. But Shekhar's professional and personal guidance, his mentorship, and timely assurances, had been beams of moonlight that propelled her to trudging uphill in the seemingly acute darkness of her life.

                    Shuvashree Chowdhury

Chapter 20

The Price of Love

After lunch at the office canteen, of lemon rice and *appalam*, Aparna was trying to concentrate on work. She was screening resumes to recruit additional staff for the new magazine. Some would be taken from the *Urban Plus*, also the *Sunday Magazine*, but they still needed more hands. She would next have to draw up a list of ideas for the launch issue. This situation about the payment to the Customs department this morning had been an unnecessary bother. The joy of receiving the varied gifts from Stephan felt reduced now. Aparna felt exasperation at his mismanagement of even such a small issue, more so when she was so busy. Here she slipped into thinking how efficiently Anand might have handled this similar situation. It was obvious to Aparna the money they were extracting, was going into the personal accounts of the Customs employees. This is how they made extra income as a team, which was a bribe that they then divided among themselves.

What could Aparna do now in this circumstance? If she did not pay the money, she and Stephan had so much to lose. Much over her aversion to be exploited, and be a party to illegality and bribery, was Aparna's fear of being implicated for money laundering. That too in collaboration with a foreigner whom the lady from Customs strangely kept referring to as her husband. As a journalist working for a reputed newspaper, how would she ever explain or justify all this mess to anyone? Anand would lose respect for her and what of the trust he had reposed in her for the new assignment? What would her parents think of all this illegality and what about Kartik? They would all be devastated. Then would this lead her to a probable jail term or entanglement with cops at the least? Her relationship with Stephan would stumble out like a cat out of a wheat flour bag, in a reproachful manner smearing everyone. The thought of it all sent a chill down Aparna's spine.

She would lose face completely, Aparna thought. Stephan was safely away and would not face the indignity of this situation like her. So, rationalising the circumstances, added to the emotional pressure from Stephan to retrieve the large sum of money, Aparna decided on buying herself out of trouble. She would stop by the bank again on her way back from work, and ironically have the charges for the varied gifts of love transferred from her meagre savings of the last few years. Her salary account was in ICICI bank but she had put aside money every month into this State Bank account. She had refused to take an ATM card, so she would not be tempted to withdraw from it or use it impulsively. Now, to pay a bribe from this account that had her hard-earned savings was indeed a test of her faith and trust in Stephan. It was not that she was greedy for the gifts, but how could she let go all the time and sentiments he had lavished on her, in choosing and sending them?

On her way home, Aparna was able to transfer the money, equally into the two accounts, the details of which had been texted to her. She was relieved after she had taken a picture of the receipt on her cell phone and then emailed it to the lady at Customs as she had insisted. They would dispatch the parcel tomorrow morning from Delhi and it would be delivered to her by day end. But what if she was not at home then? Aparna was nervous, as she would have to explain the parcel to her parents and answer Kartik's queries about it, whether or not it came in her presence. But she had an idea. What if she didn't open it at all and told all at home the parcel was for a friend who would be collecting it from her in a month? That seemed like a reasonable excuse and then she would not have to explain the contents to anyone.

That evening, when Stephan came online on FB, Aparna updated him she had transferred the money and the parcel would hopefully be with her by tomorrow.

"You're the best wife, darling," Stephan replied. "You are so pretty, loving, kind and over and above all that, so efficient. I knew I could rely on you blindly. I'm really sorry to put you through so much trouble, baby."

     Shuvashree Chowdhury

The next morning, Aparna left home rather early for work, getting ready quickly — after seeing Kartik off at the bus stop, followed by a few quick rounds of *surya namaskar*, instead of the entire cycle of her yoga practice. She told her mother about the parcel and how she was to just keep it in a corner of her bedroom, and that it belonged to a friend. At office, it felt good to walk into an empty hall and not have to greet or talk to anyone for a while. The bearers were still dusting and cleaning the corridors. It was the best time to get some serious work done. In a while, the others would be trickling in. Aparna was about to switch on her computer, when her phone rang. It was the lady from Customs.

"Good morning, madam, there is a problem," she said sounding rigid and business-like, and then after a dramatic pause, added cautiously, "Ma'am, if we send the money to you the way it is in the handbag, it will get intercepted at the airport by the police department officials and at other points of transit. It may either get lost or confiscated or, worse still, lead you to a lot of complications."

"So what are you suggesting I do now?" Aparna replied impatiently, perceiving that they were really trying to blackmail her now, thus becoming anxious.

"Don't worry, madam; the money will reach you safe and sound, without any hassles. My boss has instructed me to route it to you through the Reserve Bank of India. They will transfer it to your account."

"What … Why would RBI do that?" Aparna blurted out, feeling fearful now, doubting where all this was leading her to. "I've never heard of such a thing."

"Don't worry, madam," the lady said in a placating tone, "We would just like to ensure that the money your husband has sent you reaches you safely."

"But he is not my husband," Aparna said resolutely, wondering why the woman kept calling him that. "He is a friend."

"When I contacted Mr. Stephan at the time when we got the parcel, he said you were his wife. But anyways, that is all right. It does not matter if he isn't."

"Well, he might have said it to justify sending the money, in fear of any problem coming upon me," Aparna said, but was irked at Stephan's naivety. Did he not envision how deep a trouble she could get into, with all this?

"That's okay, ma'am, you don't worry. It is our responsibility to get the money to you. I just require you to give us your account number, for RBI to transfer the money into."

Aparna, thought quickly, perhaps this was better, and she would keep the money intact till Stephan's arrival and not have to worry about it. The thought of the money getting intercepted and then having to deal with police agencies and others was daunting. She would give them her Standard Chartered account number, which she hardly used and had the minimum balance of Rs. 10,000 only. Stephan's money would remain isolated from hers there, in case of any further problem arising from it.

"I'm emailing my account details to you," Aparna said, quickly recalling that she had the details in her old digital diary that she carried in her hand bag always.

By the time Aparna emailed her account details and then returned to the resumes of the new staff they had shortlisted to recruit, Radhika walked past her desk with a chirpy "Good morning." She was on her way to her cabin. Soon others trickled in and the work stations were occupied one by one. Aparna had lost out on the solitude of the morning before anyone else came in, the time she liked to kick-start her day's work, and for which she often came in early. This business of the parcel was distressing Aparna immensely, and stealing the pleasure of receiving all the gifts. What was worse, it was unsettling her tender feelings for Stephan, making her annoyed at his impulsive naivety that might as yet get her into much trouble. Then it was the worst time now, with all the pressure at work. Aparna was having a flicker of doubt again, on her relationship and future with Stephan, when her cell phone rang.

"Ma'am, I'm calling from RBI," the polite male voice said, in the same familiar north-eastern accent as the Customs lady. "We have got your bag with the 8000 pounds from the Customs department. Also, we have your account details to transfer the money into. But you will need to pay a small service fee for this transaction."

"What! Again, a service fee?" Aparna retorted, "But I've already just paid Rs. 55000 to the Customs people into two SBI accounts."

   Shuvashree Chowdhury

"You will have to pay a fee for the conversion of the pounds to rupees, before we can transfer the money to you" the man said in a business-like, but soft voice. "The amount you have already paid was to the Customs department, for the receipt of the parcel containing a number of high value items, I was told."

"I don't have any more money to pay now," Aparna stated flatly, vexed. "I am an ordinary service person; how can I keep paying this kind of money? I am only receiving this money on behalf of my friend who will be coming to India next month."

"I'm really sorry, ma'am, but you will have to pay the fee in order to receive the money into your account. It is a rather big amount."

"Well then, let me think about this. How am I ever going to come up with this kind of money again?" Then after a pause, wherein the man on the line much to her irritation firmly repeated, "I'm really sorry ma'am," Aparna added in an exasperated tone, "Let me think. Please call me in a while."

Aparna had just disconnected, and placed her phone back into her bag as she tended to, to avoid misplacing it, when it rang again. It was Stephan.

"Darling, I am so sorry," he said briskly, in a disturbed and sympathetic voice, "I am so sorry to put you through all this trouble, but all will be fine, as you should get the parcel by this evening. I had called the Customs lady."

"Oh, thank God you called, baby," Aparna said, happy to hear his voice. "I am so disturbed by all this, above all when there's so much work out here. I just got a call from the RBI... don't know how they all sound so much like you, I mean the oriental accent. It's very strange ... Anyways ... They will not transfer the money, they say, till I pay them charges for the conversion from pounds to rupees."

"My God, darling, this seems like a huge problem we've got into. These people are trying to blackmail us now. I am so worried for you. But you do understand that we must get that money, right? We cannot let them take it away. So, you must pay the charges. The money is worth a lot more than the charges, so don't worry about the money you pay now. You borrow it from someone for now, if necessary."

"Yes, gorgeous. I know, baby, but I'm scared … really scared now. Anyways you don't worry, let's see how I can resolve this soon."

When the man from RBI—he had said his name was Vikas Sharma—called again, Aparna said to him "Why don't you just deduct the amount of Rs. 48000 from the pounds you have, and transfer the rest to me. Won't that be so much simpler?"

"No, ma'am, I'm really sorry, that is not possible." Vikas replied politely but firmly. "The procedure is that you will have to transfer the fee money directly into our account, before we initiate the transfer of your money to you online."

"Isn't that too rigid a policy, and uncalled for? But anyways, you please text me the account details and I will transfer the money."

"Yes, ma'am, I'm forwarding two account numbers with the details. And please ensure that the money is transferred right away, so I can start the online transfer process, which must be completed before the close of day today."

This time, the account numbers Aparna was given were of ICICI bank. Since she was carrying her SBI check book in her hand bag, she walked over to the ICICI branch close to her office at lunch time, and deposited the checks. Aparna had her salary account in this branch of ICICI, but she didn't have much money in the account to transfer directly from it. She returned to office, and emailed the scanned copy of the two check deposit slips of Rs. 24000 each to the address she was given. Aparna promptly received an automated receipt for the same. It was after she had her lunch at the canteen, as she had no further intimation yet, that she called Vikas—the RBI man—whose number she had saved just as she had the Customs lady's.

"Ma'am, we have received the scanned copy of your money transfer receipt," he replied to her sharp inquiry. "I will call you within the next ten minutes and then email a link. You need to click open. It will lead you to the RBI website. After you log into the site, you can yourself monitor the transfer of the money into your account."

Aparna logged into the RBI website on her desktop computer at office, Vikas still holding the phone line with her. She was awed by the sheer grandeur and professionalism of the site, overwhelmed

          Shuvashree Chowdhury

at the immense advance in technology. The details she had given them: her Standard Chartered Bank account number, passport, and pan number, along with the scanned copy of her driving licence, with three passport-size photographs, were all uploaded into the account created in her name. After she logged into her account with an initial password they provided that she was advised to change later, Aparna could view onscreen the transfer of the money. This was on a bar slowly shifting from left to right, depicting the percentage accurately. Aparna watched the bar move slowly in the transfer progress, thrilled as a child.

She looked around her to ensure no one was approaching her desk, to take a peek into her computer screen. Then she would have to justify her association with RBI. As it is, Aparna was hesitant to use the office computer, as its IP address would get logged as would the RBI's at this end, but she had little choice as RBI wanted it done immediately. Just as the bar depicted a completion of 65 per cent of the money transferred, it abruptly stopped moving, and an alarm flashed furiously on the screen—"Error Encountered." Then in a few seconds, another message below it said, "Please log in fresh and check the actual status of the money transferred." Aparna quickly followed the instructions, but she could not log in. She was then instructed by another message on the screen, "Please call the RBI representative, if unable to renew viewing the transfer process." It was after repeated failed attempts to log into her personal account again, that Aparna called the RBI employee Vikas Sharma.

"Oh, my God! What have you done?" he exclaimed, after patiently hearing Aparna's dilemma, "How did you manage to make this blunder? Now it's going to be near impossible to restart the transfer. It has got stuck midway, and it is a very difficult process to restart, almost impossible in some cases."

"But I didn't do anything," Aparna blurted anxiously, rather shaken by his words. "I was following instructions perfectly, just as I was instructed to, by the site."

"You have obviously done something…." the man said rather rudely now, sounding agitated and vicious, much to Aparna's shock. "It rarely ever hangs midway like this. Now I will have to talk to my supervisor, to reinstate your password, if possible. But the problem is the money was to get transferred by day end today."

"Now please, please do something, talk to your supervisor," Aparna pleaded, feeling dejected, after having got her hopes up on the completion of 65 per cent of the transfer, in assuming the ordeal was almost over.

"Alright, I will call you back and tell you what to do."

Aparna, guilty over neglecting her work over this personal issue, got up leaving her phone in her handbag, so as not to be disturbed for a while. Also, she wanted to get her mind off this stressful mess she had got into unwittingly. She went to Radhika's cabin, and they discussed the work in progress on the new magazine. Aparna was thus able to display her seriousness on the new project to Radhika, who would obviously be updating Anand with the details of the headway they were making. When she returned to her desk, seeing a missed call from 'RBI Vikas Sharma', Aparna called him back. He instructed her to reboot the link and try logging in afresh now, while he held the phone line as she attempted it. But to her frustration, and Vikas's impatience as she reported it to him, Aparna was unable to log in to her account and an alarm flashed onscreen "Unknown Error, please contact RBI supervisor for further assistance."

"I don't know now if the transfer of the money is at all possible," Vikas stated, sounding outraged, grinding his words menacingly. "What have you done?"

"I have very accurately done only what you have asked me to," Aparna replied emphatically, irritated now. "I have followed the step by step guidelines in the link."

"Alright then, let me see what can be done now. I will call you back."

Aparna was quite rattled by Vikas Sharma's anger at her, by his overt frustration. But then, perhaps it was his sincerity in wishing she receive the money by day end that made him react thus, she justified, thus feeling a burst of gratitude towards him. He must be a friend of the Customs lady, Aparna thought, as they spoke in similar accents and tones, and both were quite kind and supportive. The lady had perhaps handed over the money to Vikas on a personal level, so as to ensure transferring the same quickly. It is always much easier when you have friends in an agency that you have to get your work done through. The Customs and RBI were

   Shuvashree Chowdhury

separate government agencies, but working in Delhi, the lady and Vikas might be friends, Aparna concluded.

There were a large number of people from the Northeast, studying and working in Delhi. The Customs lady too had sincerely organised the hassle-free delivery of her parcel. It was due to reach Aparna by day end. Her cell-phone rang, cutting through Aparna's charitable thoughts on the kindness of the two strangers from the Northeast. It was Stephan. He was calling her frequently now. She was by now accustomed to his soft voice, with the heavy and odd mix of an Oriental and British accent. He tended to speak deliberately and gently.

"Hello, darling! How are you? I hope things are sorted out by now? I am so worried for you, that you are taking on all this pressure. I'm really sorry."

"I'm alright. But it is highly stressful indeed. More so, that I'm doing all of this from office, when there is so much work now."

"So where is the bag with the money now, darling? Have they delivered it to you or not? What about the rest of the parcel?"

"The parcel will be delivered by today, but I don't know about the money … it's all so complicated."

"What do you mean by you don't know, darling? Where is the money now, and who has it? When will they deliver it to you? I'm banking on you!"

"It's a rather long story now, baby and I can't get into it just now. The Reserve Bank of India has your money. They were in the process of transferring the money electronically, when the link hung. Now they're asking me what I have done …I haven't done anything."

"Darling, you must get that money … you know how important it is."

"You know what … this seems like a well-oiled wheel of corruption," Aparna said, sounding exasperated now. "In fact, I get this feeling you're all in one gang, out to fool me. It's funny. I have this nagging feeling since last evening, but now it is so pronounced. Isn't it strange that all of you have a similar oriental accent and speak in a similar deliberated, slow manner? But the funnier thing really is, that I've been thinking since morning, even if you were to be a team of crooks, I'd still love you. And

I'd help you to get out of this ring, change yourself, and become a good person."

"Hahahaha, you always make me laugh so much, darling," Stephan replied after a pause, as if registering Aparna's implication. "You are so funny. But I know you will love me in spite of it all, as you're like that, a really good person. But don't worry, baby … why would someone of my status have to join a group of crooks?"

"I don't know … I get this vague and nagging instinct. Like I am in a movie or what? Perhaps it is God's way of showing me how much I really love you."

"You are so sweet, baby … the best, darling. Whatever did I do to deserve you? I know I can trust you completely, with my life."

"Anyways you go to work now, baby, I will keep you posted."

It was more than an hour later that the RBI man Vikas Sharma called again.

He said, excitedly, "I've managed to convince my supervisor. He in turn spoke to the manager to get you a fresh password for your account on the transfer link."

"Thank God! So what do I do next?"

"You will have to pay a sum of Rs. 65000 as service fee, for the password. It is restricted, available only rarely. The last time you paid the fee by check, isn't it? Though you had to transfer the money by day end, you gave a check, which will take a few days to encash. Now this amount, please transfer directly and not by check."

"What, 65000?" Aparna exclaimed in shock and then in immense anger, she added, "Is this a joke or what … So much money for a password?"

"It's because it is very difficult to get this link reinstalled. You made some big error in following instructions for the transfer to complete … And the technical department and our supervisor have been working on this for so long."

"But I don't have any money to pay…." Aparna said firmly, then recalled the conversation with Stephan and conceded, "But then I don't have a choice really, do I?

"Okay then, I'm texting you the two ICICI account numbers that you need to transfer the money into."

"It's ICICI bank and there are two accounts again?"

    Shuvashree Chowdhury

"Yes, but not the same account numbers. I'm sending you two other account details, and you will have to transfer the amount immediately. Only after the money reaches our account and we get the intimation, we continue the transfer. The process will have to be completed by day end or it will pass into a waiting list and take ages."

"Fine, please text me the details, I'm just going over to the ICICI bank across the street, to transfer the money right now."

Aparna wrote out the two checks to the accounts she had to deposit into, after she received their details from Vikas. As there was not enough money in her ICICI account, she chose to ignore Vikas's directions on the direct transfer part, in spite of his insistence. On her return from the bank, Aparna quickly emailed the scanned copies of the deposit slips to Vikas. And he called her on receipt of it.

"The amounts that you paid in the morning ... have you transferred the money to the accounts, or have you dropped checks? We haven't received the amounts."

"I dropped SBI account checks. They will be transferred to your ICICI accounts for sure. I don't have sufficient money in my ICICI account so could not initiate a transfer directly. Also, the SBI branch is far from here, to withdraw."

"It will take another day or two for the money to get transferred to us and only then can we reinitiate the transfer of your money into your account."

"Well then, so be it, as I cannot do any better," Aparna snapped, exasperated with all the pressure and anxiety, angry at Stephan for causing it, and at Vikas for his excessive and undue concern. "I will just have to wait till tomorrow or the day after for the money to get transferred."

"Why don't you talk to the bank people, they may find a way of expediting the transfer, by day end perhaps. You can call them now, maybe talk to the manager."

"What do you think ... I'm such an important and high-value client that they will have my check encashed immediately?"

"You can try, at least call them or better just walk across and meet them. The money will reach us by today is what I had communicated to my manager. So he had asked the technical guys to work on your account to reset it today. Now he is going to be very upset with me."

"I understand, and I'm very grateful for all your initiation and help, but this is all I can do, the best. So the transfer will just have to wait. I'm in office, and with taking on this added stress and distraction, my boss is going to throw me out of work."

"But if the money does not reach us today, I don't know what may happen to your money. It had to reach us by day end to close this account."

"Alright then, wait. Why don't you call my branch of ICICI bank? They will take your words seriously," Aparna said emphatically, worried now Stephan would be really upset at her irresponsibility over the money. "After all, you are from RBI. They will understand the technical issue you're talking about and take you seriously."

"Okay, I will talk. But once you are there and have already spoken to them," Vikas answered with an air of authority, convincing Aparna of his clout at being an RBI employee, with the ability to convince the ICICI bank staff.

At the ICICI bank, Aparna requested the lady at the front Customer Service desk that she would like to meet the manager. After some explaining on the cause for it and why the lady herself could not herself help, Aparna was led into a small cabin. Across the desk sat a young lady, with a dusky bloated face, shoulder-length hair, her eyes beady but alert, head held upright over a plump body clad in a red cotton *kurta*.

"Ma'am here would like to talk to the manager." The lady assistant who had brought Aparna inside said to the lady across the desk, and then she left.

"Hello, I'm Sabita," the manager said, indicating with her hand for Aparna to take a seat in front. After Aparna was seated, she added, "How may I help you?"

"I would like a prompt money transfer into an ICICI account. It is very urgent. And I have the check here with me. How soon do you think the money can be transferred from my SBI account?"

"It will take about two days. The check will go for clearance to your bank tomorrow and then it will take another day for the money to get transferred."

"But it is very urgent. Isn't there some way you can get it

          Shuvashree Chowdhury

transferred immediately?" Aparna pleaded, then for impact, she added, "It is to accounts of RBI."

"To RBI?" the manager said, looking at her curiously, "Is it some charges?"

"Well, it is. For the transfer of a large sum of money sent to me by a friend in the UK, now in the possession of RBI. I have already paid charges for the conversion from pounds to rupees. Now I have to pay more, as service charges for the transfer."

"But why do you have to pay conversion charges? I don't understand; it all sounds very strange. Who are you in touch with from RBI?"

"There's a guy named Vikas who has been calling me. In fact, would you please talk to him now on the phone? He says it is very urgent that I transfer the money into their account right away, so they can complete the pending transfer by day end."

"But I'm still wondering why you would need to pay conversion charges at all? At most, even if it were required, why don't they deduct it from the principal amount, that is the money they have … How much is it anyway?

"I don't know…." Aparna replied hesitatingly, but her mind was alert now. "I've asked them to do so but they won't. They insist I pay additional charges separately."

Aparna's mobile phone rang just then and on the screen flashed—RBI Vikas Sharma. She promptly took the call and, feeling flustered, meekly said "Hello."

"Hello! What happened? Did you talk to the manager?" Was the sharp, brisk response in the heavy oriental accent. "I'm waiting to finish your transaction."

"In fact, I'm sitting with the manager at ICICI bank. She says they cannot transfer the money today, that it will take a day or two. Why don't you speak to her?"

"All right, give it to her," Vikas said firmly.

Aparna held out her hand to the manager eagerly, who took the cell phone from her. That Vikas was talking to the manager validated his authenticity to Aparna's mind, also certified the service charges she was asked to pay. Aparna now reconsidered the amount being a bribe, for if it was really so, Vikas would not have agreed to talk to the manager.

"We will not be able to transfer the money today, as it is too late for banking transactions now." Aparna heard the manager Sabita say politely into the phone. "The check will go for clearance tomorrow."

Once she was handed back her phone, Aparna said to Vikas, "Now do you see, I have tried and it is not possible to transfer the money today. This must also prove I'm serious about paying up. But I'm not in a hurry to receive my money. So please wait till you get my payment into your account, and then we can reinitiate the transfer."

After Vikas hung up, Aparna, more from the sheer anxiety over this matter than on the manager's prodding, blurted out the whole story to her, but withholding her actual relationship with Stephan. She related her encounter with the Customs lady, then in detail about the RBI website she had logged into, with the moving bar depicting the money being transferred to her account, till the site abruptly hung.

"The whole thing sounds kind of strange to me," the manager stated, looking confused, "As you've already paid a lot, through the checks you paid this morning."

The manager dialled and spoke on her telephone extension, and a young lady appeared at the door of her cabin. She then asked Aparna to give the lady assistant the details of the checks she had deposited this morning, to find out if they had already gone for clearance. After taking the deposit slips from Aparna, the young lady left and then reappeared shortly with her checks in hand. On recognising the checks she had written out and dropped here this morning, now handed over to Sabita, Aparna promptly decided she would take them away with her. If they were still here, that meant they would not get cleared in the next two days. She decided she would go to State Bank, withdraw the money, and deposit it directly into the accounts in ICICI bank. So RBI would expedite transfer of the pounds into her own account.

"Are these even valid accounts … let me just check," Sabita said doubtingly, and then viewing the checks one at a time, briskly she typed their account numbers into her computer. After a pause, looking with concentration at her screen, she continued "Yes, they are indeed valid accounts, but all with addresses in UP, and recently

 Shuvashree Chowdhury

opened—which is quite strange." Then looking up at Aparna, she abruptly added, "Ma'am, could you please give me the deposit slips? I will have them copied, in order to verify the authenticity of these accounts through our head office."

The immense stress of the last two days, along with the doubts in Aparna's mind regarding the Customs and RBI operations, returned to the fore. She realised now, there was something really wrong about all of these people and transactions. Her mind had been warning her, but her heart would not consume the suspicions it was trying keenly to feed it. Aparna's instincts suggested there must surely be some connection between the Customs lady, the RBI man Vikas Sharma, and Stephan. It's just that she could not decide what it was, other than that they all had an oriental accent, though Stephan's was also British in a way.

Aparna recalled, as if in a trance now, her telling Stephan how she had instincts he was one of a team of frauds out to make a fool of her. Aparna recoiled at the thought of how naively she had told him, that even if it were so, she would still love him, try to make a good man out of him. So he would leave this criminal group to get into a moral line of work. The lady staff returned to the manager's cabin, with a copy of the four receipts, on the checks Aparna had deposited today. She asked Aparna what the RBI website she had logged into looked like, and what was its link address.

"Perhaps it is a hoax link, one used for phishing," the young lady assistant announced, looking resolutely at her manager Sabita. "These things are very common now. These fraudsters operate in a group. They target vulnerable people who they can manipulate into disclosing all their personal details. Then they hack their emails, send phishing links to crack their bank accounts, clear out their money."

Aparna looked at the young lady—she must still be in her early twenties—marvelling at how sure and aware youngsters today are. Then an acute pain shooting out of her ribs, as if a dagger was wedged in the region of her heart, Aparna turned to the manager who looked back at her concernedly. So far in denial at what might have been happening to her, Aparna stared back silently, clearly perceiving it all now.

"But the RBI website was so authentic, so sophisticated and

advanced—it even had the Askoka Stupa and Chakra as on the Indian Rupee," Aparna blurted dejectedly, cursing herself at how she had been fooled, "Then the money transfer was so graphic that the whole web experience seemed so authentic."

In spite of her doubts, the nagging fear on the authenticity of her dealings in the past two days, talking aloud now made Aparna see the whole drama in a fresh light. She realised how she was being systematically duped, swindled of money. She was now really irritated, angry, at Stephan's naivety in putting her through this ordeal. He was stupid to send that parcel, and get her embroiled in these scandalous transactions. What if all this was ever to get out, she would be in so much trouble, let alone the immense loss of face and reputation.

As Aparna walked out of the bank angry and dejected, she ran the incident of the last two days over in her head. She realised she had allowed herself to be plummeted into this well, cushioned by a hope for love and a new life. She firmly clutched the four checks in her hand of about a lakh and a half rupees. They gave her a sense of security, as she realised how lucky she had been to recover this money. As she strolled back to her office's parking lot to collect her car, her phone rang. Aparna distractedly took the call and said "Hello" without even looking at the screen for who it might be.

"So you've deposited the money?" The familiar, oriental voice of Vikas asked.

"I will deposit the money first thing tomorrow," Aparna replied firmly.

She realised it was best to say so, rather than foolishly let on she had caught on to their game, that they were a group of thugs, and make herself prey to further harassment. As she navigated out of the parking area, Aparna's phone rang again. She stopped the car and pulled it out of her bag. This time, it was Stephan on the line.

"Hello, darling" he said, in his usual, soft, mellow, cajoling voice. "I hope everything is taken care of and you have paid the money they asked for?"

"Give me a moment," Aparna replied, relieved to hear his familiar voice. Then she drove her car out to the side, to prevent blocking the way of other cars and said in a low voice, "Hello, Steph ... are you there?"

"Yes, baby, I'm right here," he promptly replied.

"I was just there at the bank to deposit the money into the RBI's accounts they'd given me. But on narrating to the manager the sequence of events since you sending me the courier, she and her staff feel I'm being taken for a ride. They think that the money is now in the wrong hands. This is a group of frauds, some in UP and others in Manipur, who are trying to swindle me of more money. This is over the pounds, also after all that I've already paid to get it. They are really scaring me."

"What are you saying, darling, really?" Stephan replied in an alarmed tone, but which sounded pretentious. "Now what happens to our money? How do we get it back from them? You should not have told the manager the story. Instead just paid up to these guys and got our money from them, even at the cost of little extra money."

"But Steph, I didn't want to go to talk to the manager. This RBI man Vikas insisted I talk to her. In fact, he also spoke to her directly, so as to expedite the money transfer into their accounts. They wanted our money to get transferred by day end."

"Yes, I get it, but there was no point in telling the manager and staff the whole story, was there? ... It seems like you are in love with this manager, to trust her so much now, instead of listening to me and getting this matter resolved as soon as possible. You know how important the money is to us. It is all for our future."

"What do you mean, Stephan ... you know that I'm trying my very best here." Aparna replied sharply, livid, also weary now, "And you know how busy I am right now, and then to be running out of office, leaving my work?"

"Alright, my wife, I understand. I am so, so sorry, baby. It's just that I'm worried about the money and don't want anything to spoil our future plans. You go home now and we will talk again at night."

On the drive home, Aparna distinctly evoked again her FB conversation of the previous evening with Stephan, of how, when she told him of her intuition of his being with a criminal gang, and if so, she would still love him.

"Hahahahaha, I know you will do that, because you love me like that," he had replied after a long silence. "But with my status, why would I need to do such trivial things? Don't worry about such things, darling."

Aparna next went through the conversation she just had with the bank manager. She went over every point, up to her realisation that she was surrounded by a radical criminal gang, who were intelligent, resourceful, and could be dangerous. The months of interactions with Stephan seemed as if in a dream to Aparna, from which she now seemed to be waking to this harsh reality. Her head, her instincts, had kept indicating to her, that Stephan must surely be involved with this group, what with the strange Oriental accent they shared. But her heart had rebelled to accept it. How could he possibly be involved with a criminal gang? He, who was so caring and respectful, and also genuinely loved her.

In Aparna's mind, there was now a clear dichotomy. On one hand, she didn't trust him and was really scared of him. While on the other hand, she believed he was simple and naive, so she decided she would have to look out for him as for her son. Aparna recollected how Stephan was becoming increasingly possessive of her, lately following her every move on FB. She was beginning to feel restricted, anxious, that this tendency might get worse with time, especially once she was with him in UK. And she would not even be working at the start, so she would be controlled by him completely. It was about a month back that Aparna had told Stephan about a man in UK who had sent her a FB friendship invite and that she had accepted. After that, this man had asked her about the investments one could possibly make in India. Stephan had become very irritated, hearing of it.

"Am I not good enough for you? Do you need to have more friends?" he had threatened, "I'm happy to just be with you every moment, but you are surely not."

Aparna had been very prompt in pacifying him then that the man she befriended was much older. And that she was only responding to his queries, if it might help him in any small way. In view of Stephan's experiences with his ex-wife and the ensuing mistrust he had of women in general, due also to those he met

    Shuvashree Chowdhury

in UK, Aparna though apprehensive, had been empathetic of his possessiveness so far.

But last evening, to her surprise and annoyance, he had come online quite early in the morning—by his time—to abruptly ask her: "Who are you chatting with?"

"Who would I be chatting with?" Aparna had replied promptly, unsuccessful in hiding her irritation, "It's a strange question to ask me so early, isn't it—when you know I never chat with anyone other than you, not even my close friends."

"But you have been online on FB for quite some time," Stephan insisted.

"I was reading my friends' posts and updating my status. Go and see the picture quote I just posted. This is why it is showing the online signal. But wait … are you stalking me or what?"

"Hahahaha, no, darling … how can you think that? But then, you are my wife and I want to be close to you always. I just woke up and saw you online, and even after showering and getting ready for work, I find you still online. So I wondered."

This was the second time, the last being a few weeks back, that Stephan had asked Aparna who she was chatting with. He was beginning to make her anxious, with his tabs on her. Now as she was almost home, waiting for the traffic signal to turn green at the crossing near her house, Aparna's mind went back to the issue at hand—the gang of crooks in whose net she was enmeshed. It was a worrisome matter, as they had her contact details. And now from what the staff at the bank just told her, perhaps even access to her email, and FB accounts, the bank accounts for sure. Luckily, she did not have much money in the Standard Chartered Bank account they might have access to through the phishing link they had sent via the RBI link. There was no easy way out now, so she would just lie low for a while, Aparna decided. Later that evening, when chatting on FB Messenger with Stephan, Aparna decidedly wrote to him to take charge of the situation:

"Steph, I will stay out of all this from now. You better be the man and find a way of resolving this matter, any which way you can. I cannot take any more of this."

"Alright, darling, I understand you are very busy with your

work. I'm really sorry to bother you with this. I will handle it now, and do whatever is necessary to get the parcel safely to you. I'll speak to the Customs lady tomorrow, and resolve it."

"Good night, Stephan. I'm very tired tonight. I'd like to just go to bed."

Shuvashree Chowdhury

Chapter 21

The Compulsive Womaniser

"I will jump off this bridge. I swear I will, if you don't promise me that you will sever all connections with that woman," Sujata shrieked into her cell phone.

She was standing on the Adyar River bridge in Chennai, along with her sons.

"What drama is this now? I'm at work, in an important meeting," Anand said curtly. "You know very well that I'm in Delhi."

"Oh, then well, she must be there too! Now I'm telling you, I'm damned serious. I'm not going to tolerate this public humiliation any longer," Sujata stated violently, and then shoving the mobile into the tiny, trembling hand of the four-year-old Vishal, she added "Here now, talk to the kids."

"Papa, papa, please save us. We are with Mama over the big bridge. She wants us all to jump off." Vishal lisped breathlessly, and then started sobbing. The older boy looked around embarrassedly to see if anyone was noticing them.

Sujata hugged the children, taking both together in her embrace, though Varun rather tall now at eleven years, tried to resist.

Then taking the phone from Vishal, she shrieked into it again, "So you know now that I'm serious."

"Are you crazy or what? How can you take the children there and involve them in your drama?" Anand yelled back. He immediately thought better of it. It was pointless trying to talk sense into Sujata, when she was in such an adamant mood. So promptly putting on an earnest voice, he now cajoled, "Ok, please, please calm down, Sujata. I promise you I will not talk to her again directly or alone. I swear on the children. Now for heaven's sake, get back home."

But Sujata was not appeased. She had been taking on far more than she could bear and suddenly realised she could not take the stress any longer. She had to lambast Anand, as he deserved that at least. So what if he was out of town on work? The mood struck her here and now, so she must act on it. Lately, she was having excruciating pain in her lower back, and could hardly stand straight sometimes. She also felt nauseous a lot. On insistence from her friend Manas, driven by him last evening, she had visited her doctor. He prescribed bed rest for about two weeks along with mild doses of an anti-depressant, as she was also suffering from insomnia. He attributed her ailment to an anxiety disorder. Her blood pressure was alarmingly high. But there was no way Sujata could afford the rest now, though she had taken the first dose of antidepressant last night. Perhaps the good sleep gave her strength to deal with Anand, as she should have done earlier.

Sujata now said menacingly, "Anand, I'm the one who was visiting your father in the hospital twice daily in the last many months. I have been taking care of your mother and her household, along with ours, even though I hardly have time to breathe from my work and the children. I made all arrangements at your father's funeral last month. But you have all the time to gallivant, to go and cry on Aparna's lap, and on the shoulders of all your stupid women at office. I ensured that everything went smoothly, right up to taking your mother to the hospital after she had a nervous breakdown after your father's funeral. After that, I've been checking on her upstairs several times daily, even though I was in much need of medical aid myself. And what do you do, you go and romance that witch Aparna in public, and make a fool of me. I've just learned that you go to the Marina beach for morning walks instead of the gym, and she also comes there. Then what audacity! You took her to dinner at Fisherman's Cove? Someone saw you there."

"It was just a coincidence that Aparna came to the Marina one morning, when I was there on work," Anand blurted in shock and perturbed at Sujata's awareness of all this, even the Fisherman's Cove incident. He wondered how she knew all this and whether she had hired a detective to follow him around. In alarmed defence, Anand added, "She was doing her job. I did not plan any meeting with her there. You know, I go to the Marina after my workout sometimes. And what has gotten into you now? You know I am ever thankful for everything that you do and you're everything I have.

 Shuvashree Chowdhury

Especially now, with Father gone, Mother even more distant with me, and a brother who is more an enemy, I have no other family but you. These women do not mean anything. How many times have I told you that? At Fisherman's Cove, it was a conference and I just stayed longer, talking to Aparna after that. That's all there is to it. You have friends too, don't you? Do I make such a big fuss? Do I throw tantrums? And now of all times, when you know how devastated I feel after Father's death."

Sujata had no reply after Anand's mention of her friends. It was like a shot of guilt that he had injected into her by the mere reference.

She ended the conversation abruptly with, "Look Anand, I'm just so sick now and so tired of all your meticulously derived stories. I'm going home."

Sujata then got into the car with the boys and drove off without a word. She turned the music on loud for the boys, so they wouldn't question her erratic behaviour right away. They had been headed home, after Sujata had picked up the boys from Shishya School, as she did when she could get away from work. It was while crossing the Adyar Bridge that the idea of threatening Anand had suddenly struck her. He was becoming increasingly defiant in his position on Aparna.

Sujata had heard of her friend, an ex-colleague, threatening her husband similarly over the Howrah Bridge in Calcutta about his mistress. And though she had been horrified at learning of a working, sensible woman's capacity for such theatrics, the idea had stayed in her mind. The friend's husband had been so shocked at the involvement of their children that it had jostled him into terminating his affair with an office colleague—an intern in his firm. He had not wanted his children to lose respect for him, even though the wife's esteem had been of little concern so far. In Anand's case too, though aloof with them, he would not want his children to learn of their father's infidelities and lose all respect for him, even if they did not show their love for him demonstratively.

After Sujata got home with the boys, she was not in the mood to return to her office. She avoided the children's questions on what their father had done anew to bring on her wrath. Sujata shut herself in her room. She spent over an hour in an attempt to hack

Anand's email. She tried all permutation and combinations to open his Gmail account. The thing that was bothering her acutely since she awoke this morning, making her physically sick, was not a sudden and renewed suspicion about Anand's dalliances, not even his affair with Aparna. It was her own guilt and confusion over what to do with her life. Shekhar's words had left a deep impact on her. And for weeks, she had been thinking of his marriage of convenience theory, concluding dejectedly, that it was not how she envisaged living the rest of her life.

Sujata had as yet to reach a comfortable level of financial security. But she wanted to make up her mind now, whether to remain in this marriage or get out of it sooner or later. She was hoping to scan Anand's emails as they might have notifications from his FB account or throw up other signs to give her concrete evidence of his disloyalty. Then she would take it as a sign from God to move on in life, without the raging confusion she was fighting now. It was going to impact their children too, so she must be certain.

So far, Sujata was only going by Anand's emotional absence—extended time spent on his iPhone, tablet, or laptop late into the night. Then there was the office gossip, and the hysterical calls from Aparna, also the random text messages when they were on holiday, from some women, to prove his dalliances. If only she found some hard proof, it would assuage the guilt of her relationships with Shekhar and Manas. Even now, she wished for a loving marriage and family, willing to give up interest in any other man for it. The reason she had slipped into physical and emotional entanglements outside of her marriage was to ward off the deep hurt, negligence, and humiliation she felt. If Anand would make a renewed effort at reconstructing their marriage, Sujata decided, she would be happy to remain wholeheartedly and loyally within its boundaries.

Once she cracked Anand's email password—a combination of both the children's names—Sujata scanned the emails at random. Most of them were as she expected, work-related. She searched for Aparna Nikhil by name in the sent box and found a long line of emails with official subject headers. But Sujata persisted. She had to confirm for herself Anand's infidelity, instead of relying on mere fragments of her imagination and gossip. She soon found what she was looking for. Anand's responses to Aparna's official

                    Shuvashree Chowdhury

emails even were with endearing words. Scanning one email after another thoroughly, the raw passion on either side in some of the emails tore into Sujata's heart, with claw-like savagery. She could not recall when Anand had last made love to her. She tried to think. But it seemed like it was not in an eternity.

Sujata had attributed Anand's lack of interest in sex with her to his basic lack of passion. Later, she ascribed it to his work stress and then even to all the female flirtations that were offered to him on a platter, with his success. What a fool she had been, Sujata now thought painfully. It was her he was not drawn to. Even his early letters to her, also his lovemaking then, had lacked the passion she had sought. While with Aparna, he was evidently intellectually and physically much attracted. Sujata felt sick now. The pain shot through her like someone had set her on fire alive. She felt unable to bear it. She had assumed that her own extramarital affairs would cocoon her from this hurt. But to her dismay, they did not suffice to check the feeling that she had been cheated into this marriage in the first place, and then too right from the beginning of it, Anand had never fulfilled her as a woman.

Sujata looked around desperately, looking for something to help her stop feeling this way. She spotted the bottle of whiskey lying on Anand's bedside table. She quickly pulled off the lid and took a couple of brisk swigs. The burning liquid felt milder than the stinging in her heart, Sujata thought. The alcohol burned her tongue, her throat, and then slowly flowed down to allow the volcanic emotions in her gut to dislodge. She broke down in tears, sobbing her heart out. Luckily, she was alone in the house. The children had left with Anand's driver for swimming lessons at the Presidency Club. And the cook and maid had gone out to the grocer's, while another maid had taken their Alsatian Pamela who was much too weak now, for a walk.

Sujata got up and walked to the door, bolting it firmly. She would hate for the boys or the servants to see her in this state. Then she sat with her feet up on her side of the bed, with the bottle now on the floor. It was only after her heart-wrenching sobs had satiated the raging in her belly, ignited by the Scotch poured on the firewood of her pain that was doused with gasoline of the emails she just saw, that Sujata began to feel a deep calm. She decided that she would not tell Anand anything of the emails. It was pointless talking to him further on any matter. He seemed more distant now to her mentally than ever before. Anand spent a lot of time at their Delhi office lately.

To Sujata's immense surprise, Anand returned home late that evening. He usually tended to avoid confrontations and she had not expected him home that day. After Sujata's outburst, Anand sensed something unusually amiss. He also had to figure out what else she knew, other than the Marina and Fisherman's Cove jaunts. But Sujata was on her calmest behaviour, even though her eyes and face were swollen. What more could she really say to him anymore, after what she had found out? So far, she had not really wanted to believe that Anand would be involved beyond a few flirtations. The indisputable proof that she had found had shattered her illusions. She had taken her dose of antidepressant and felt rather calm.

Anand apparently did not notice anything amiss about Sujata's appearance, in spite of the reddening of her eyes and her swollen and puffy face. He hardly noticed anything about her anyway, Sujata thought dejectedly. And to her amazement, he did not bring up the topic of her threatening call of the afternoon. Anand, on his part, was rather tired, and only too glad that Sujata did not bring it all up either. He was not in the mood for allegations and tantrums. Luckily, the boys were asleep by the time he arrived. Anand had had his dinner on the Jet Airways flight, traveling in Club Premiere, as he had anticipated a showdown at home. They slipped into an outwardly peaceful sleep on the same bed, but they were miles apart mentally.

In a few weeks, the children's school would close for the summer vacation. The next day over breakfast, Sujata suggested to Anand that they all go to Kodaikanal once vacations started. She had decided she was going to be as natural as possible. It was as if she was cleaned of all emotions by the torrent of tears yesterday. But she was not up to taking the European trip the boys had been insisting on and had convinced Anand of. Sujata could not afford that much time away from work. More so now, since she decided it was her earnings that would have to sustain her and her children. She had to work much harder from now to ensure their lifelong financial security. There was no more Sujata could do about her

          Shuvashree Chowdhury

marriage. Anand's emails had been the final nail in the coffin and only the carcass remained.

Sujata realised that she had uselessly had her self-esteem crushed, from the idiocy of her threatening call to Anand yesterday and thought about the lies he had placated her with. How easily he spun a web of intricate lies, cover-up stories, and false alibis, to sustain his double life. Now he would coolly convince her of his integrity, in spite of the emails, if she told him she had herself seen them. Sujata mentally went over the numerous years of marriage to Anand over the day. She was sure that sex was not necessarily what he sought from women. But it sure was the ultimate form of female acceptance. Anand, like all womanisers, was more a validation addict than a sex addict. People like him are insecure about their worth and personal appeal, thus desperately need repeated reassurances of many women to validate their desirability. Since this is about external validation that is unmatched by an inherent self-confidence, such a quest is unquenchable. No one woman is ever enough. Then a woman was not to be blamed for such a partner, and she should not lose her own self-worth over it.

A womaniser, like an alcoholic, is actually a tragic person who keeps creating greater and greater messes, and may never be secure except fleetingly. Wives like Sujata, remain unprepared for long to face reality, because it will devastate their trust and love for their husband, and shatter their family and life. They may be in denial because of financial dependence, a fear of abandonment, or simply the dread of facing overwhelming life-altering changes as Sujata was. They may also feel guilty about their part of this crisis, and may thus be willing to forgive the husband under promises of cessation. However, many womanisers like Anand may even love their wives. As a steady, loving, and supportive partner, she is seen by the man as the family's anchor. He may respect, admire, and cherish his wife, and be unable to see himself without her. Yet, in his weakness, he offends. This may be equally relevant with regard to women who tend to seek assurance from multiple partners.

Wives or girlfriends of womanisers are often sweet, loyal, trusting, and usually naïve women. This might also be the case with a man, of being rather trusting, when the woman is the compulsive flirt. These partners of compulsive flirts may be quite gullible initially, as they are often decent themselves; so they accept the tall tales. They cling to the flimsy thread of the possible, rather than the probable explanation. Sometimes they are in denial of the intolerable reality. Then, like Sujata, they may seek to assuage their feelings of neglect and rejection, by indiscriminate affairs. This ultimately does not satisfy them emotionally. But they convince themselves they are happy with their transformed personality and with compulsive flirtation, perhaps leading to their self-destruction.

When confronted, a womaniser like an alcoholic or drug-addict, often feels remorse, and promises to alter his conduct, only to resume his escapades shortly after the emotional storm with the aggrieved partner subsides. As such a person usually feels insecure when he is not pursuing a new love interest, it then becomes a vicious cycle of addiction for him, just as it is for an alcoholic or a drug addict.

Chapter 22

Upholding Faith in Humanity

Aparna was seated beside Kartik as he ate his breakfast of buttered toast and an omelette, chattily narrating to her the events of the day before. She made a deliberate attempt to show enthusiasm in her son's chatter, in spite of her mind being bogged down with work. Added to that was all the confusion with Stephan's parcel that she now desperately wished had not been sent at all. Aparna asked relevant questions to encourage him, as Kartik excitedly told her the details of the cricket match in school yesterday, along with nuggets of conversations between him and his friends. She had not been in the mood to talk to him as usual last evening, so had asked her mother to keep him busy, telling the disappointed boy she had urgent work to complete. It was while returning from seeing Kartik off at the school bus that Aparna received a call on her phone from a number in Delhi. On viewing the number on the screen, she became fearful.

The calls from Customs and RBI in the last few days had all been from Delhi numbers, and it was probably either of them again. It had to be Vikas from RBI or the Customs lady, calling to ask her to expedite transfer of the money to the ICICI account numbers Aparna had been given, two days back. This was as charges to transfer the pounds into her account. But to Aparna's surprise, it was a different, rather authoritative male voice, in a mix of Oriental and British accents, on the line.

"Good morning, Ma'am," he said crisply, "Mr. Stephan Shedrack has appointed me as diplomat. I will be physically collecting the parcel he has sent you, from the Customs officials in Delhi. And I will deliver it to you at your residence in Chennai. I am already in Delhi and would be in Chennai by this evening."

"That's great! About what time do I expect you?" Aparna promptly asked, relieved this problem was finally getting resolved. "This is so I may intimate my mother to receive the parcel as I may be out, at work still, when you come."

Aparna's respect for Stephan was reinstated now that he had taken charge of the situation. In fact, she was impressed by his sending of a diplomat. It proved his affluence and clout in his country, that he could arrange someone so soon. It was just the evening before last, on her visit to the ICICI bank, that Aparna was deeply shaken by the probability of being a victim in a major criminal racket. Worse, it was in government quarters, what with Customs department and RBI involved.

It was in narrating the details of her conversation with the ICICI bank manager and staff that Aparna had said brusquely to Stephan, "I'm not going to be involved in this matter any longer and you must solve it yourself."

"That's alright, darling. I will take care of everything from now on. You just don't worry about anything anymore. And you must concentrate on your work only."

Stephan had called her again only a day later, last evening, and crisply said, "I have spoken to the Customs lady, and the parcel would be delivered safely to your home. I have arranged for a diplomat to collect the parcel."

But Aparna had not taken Stephan's words seriously. In fact, she had assumed he had just used the word "diplomat" to mean a representative he would organise. But the formal call so early this morning, from a man whose voice and tone had the bearing of a real foreign service diplomat quite impressed and thrilled her.

"I will call you once I reach Chennai, so you may be prepared," the diplomat said to Aparna, in response to her query on when she should expect him and then briskly added, "But you will have to pay a service charge of 360 pounds to the Customs officials, before they allow me to collect the parcel on your behalf."

"That's alright," Aparna replied coolly, in the newfound confidence that Stephan would take care of everything henceforth. "If you pay it for me, my mother or I will give you the money, when you come home to deliver the parcel."

"No, that is not my job," the diplomat replied, tersely, shocking

      Shuvashree Chowdhury

Aparna by his tone. "You will have to put the money into this bank account that I will give you now. Only then they will deliver the parcel to me."

"Oh my God, not another of those account numbers again!" Aparna blurted involuntarily, in rapid suspicion of this diplomat also being a part of the fraud racket, even as she cautiously added in a firm voice, "I do not have any more money to pay now. I'm not in business that I can afford to keep paying money randomly like this."

"I cannot deliver the parcel in that case," the man replied viciously.

"Well, just too bad, that's not my problem," Aparna snapped back at him. She had had enough of this baloney, and this last bit of drama was as much as she could take. "You can go tell that to Mr. Stephan Shedrack, and ask him to handle it."

It was barely a few minutes after she hung up on the diplomat that Stephan called Aparna, and in his usual gentle and affectionate tone, he asked, "Darling, did the diplomat call you?"

"Yes, he did, and again he asked me to deposit money into an ICICI account," Aparna said flatly and then irately added. "What is really going on here, Stephan? I'm not going anywhere to deposit any more money. Get it? I've had enough of drama."

"Darling, please don't be angry. I know you are justified in what you say. But we don't have any option but to do as they say now, do we? We're stuck. You've got to ensure that parcel is with you and then keep it safely till I come. After that, everything will be as beautiful as we planned. Do you get me?"

"I just don't understand why I cannot pay the charges to the diplomat when he delivers the parcel to me. He can pay the Customs people that small amount, can't he? But he told me rather rudely that it's not his job—how weird is that?"

Aparna would have doubted the very existence of this parcel by now, if Stephan had not shown her all the items, the clothes and shoes in her size. This was even though he had not yet emailed to her the courier receipt as she had insisted.

"The money has to be deposited from your account directly into theirs, as your name is on the parcel," Stephan said. "Then as I've said before, just don't worry about the money. Once you receive the parcel, you can take the pounds from the bag, and keep some for me and use the rest."

Aparna sounded convinced, as she replied, "Alright, I will see to it."

But she decided to do nothing more about it. She quickly went on to finish her morning chores, after a quick round of yoga that hardly calmed her as it always tended to. It was when she was on her drive to work that the diplomat called again.

"Have you received the account details that I texted you? Please deposit the money and intimate me, so I may take delivery of the parcel. I have to take the afternoon flight out of Delhi, so there isn't much time I have left."

"Yes, I have received the account details. How much do I have to pay, about Rs. 3500, am I right? And what is your name?"

"No, ma'am," he replied briskly. "It will come to around Rs. 34,745."

"Sorry, I do not have that kind of money to spare," Aparna stated firmly, surprised at hearing of the large amount. "But didn't you say it was 36 pounds?"

"No, I said it will be 360 pounds."

"Well then, I don't have that kind of money to spare now," Aparna repeated curtly, alarmed by him over again. "I have already paid over a lakh rupees and now you want that I pay another 35000 … Do you think this is a joke or what?"

"I cannot do anything, ma'am," the man replied dispassionately, "it's the Customs department that needs you to pay the money."

"Well then, just forget delivering the parcel. I do not have the money to pay now," Aparna replied with a feigned nonchalance. "When Mr. Shedrack comes here a few months later, he can collect the parcel himself."

After she hung up, manoeuvring her car deftly through the thick office-hour traffic on Mount Road, Aparna went over her interaction with the diplomat. She was certain now that he was hand in glove with the Customs lady and the RBI man. They all had a thick Oriental accent that she recognised so well, which was making her really angry. All her life, due to having friends in school and college, Aparna had immense faith in the simplicity and goodness of those from the northeast, which this gang had

     Shuvashree Chowdhury

now shaken. As soon as she reached office, briskly settling into her work station, Aparna messaged Stephan on FB messenger.

"I'm not going to pay any more money," she typed purposefully on her phone, angry now, but more petrified. "Why do I get the feeling that the diplomat too is in unison with the gang? Since talking to the bank manager, I'm much stressed about being on the radar of this gang. The manager made me write a first-hand complaint letter about this incident, with all details of the account numbers. She is going to take up the matter with her head office. I do not want to be at the centre of a public storm. You should just wait to get here, and then collect the parcel yourself."

"Darling, are you in love with the bank manager that you believe whatever she said and are even acting in accordance? And you do not listen to what I say. The diplomat could have delivered the parcel to you, at a small cost."

"I will not pay a single rupee more, without seeing that parcel," Aparna stated vehemently, with all her suspicions on Stephan resurfacing. "And you've still not sent me that list of the items given to the courier company. Why is it that I'm not sure you're not in this too? Perhaps you're the one in charge of all that's happening?"

"Hahahaha, my darling wife, again you have started to joke? Don't you have faith in the bond between us? Don't you have faith in God?"

"No, I no longer have faith in anyone. Not in God. Last week, a picture that you sent me of your house and front garden were downloaded from the internet."

"Oh my God! What is this you are saying now, darling? You don't trust me … Why would I do something like that?"

"Well, it was a stock image that had a faint but visible Fotosearch mark on it that I noticed when I enlarged it to full size on my laptop. I thought you might have had these images professionally uploaded as advertisement for your company, but now with all that's been happening, I am not sure of anything about you anymore."

"It was the picture of my house that I sent you, the home we are going to live in after you come to UK. Darling, I don't know what is this Fotosearch that you mention. All I can say is that it is my own house."

"Alright, let's just drop it. I'm very stressed about all that's happening since you sent that parcel. Don't get me wrong, I do appreciate your intentions and all the trouble you went through to get each item. But I have lost faith in everything and everyone. You go on to work now, we will talk later. I must concentrate on work."

Alright, darling … don't let our love, our core faith in each other be shaken due to these small things. I know you are stressed … Please forget I sent that parcel. I will deal with it myself. And till such time that it is handed to you, just forget all about it."

And so, Aparna did very gratefully try to forget about it, to concentrate on her work. But it was always there, a nagging feeling that she was being monitored, perhaps online, by this group of thugs. She had no option left now, but to pretend the whole incident away and lie low, so that in time they would leave her alone. Aparna could not help cursing Stephan's stupidity though. This incident had taken away the intimacy between them, on which solely was based her plans for the future with him. Aparna also now felt numb about all the lovely gifts that Stephan had sent her. The euphoria at seeing the pictures and the eagerness to receive them was all gone. What was worse and more disheartening was that these thugs who had snatched away her happiness were from such reputed government agencies. But Aparna was relieved that there was no mention of this issue in the next two days by Stephan.

"Darling, good morning! I hope you have not forgotten me already." Stephan messaged on waking, the next morning. "Just concentrate on your work now, and I'll take care of everything."

"How can I forget you, gorgeous?" Aparna replied promptly, smiling to herself. "You too get some work done now. Let that parcel remain where it is. You plan your visit here and come via Delhi, collecting it personally."

The rest of the day passed like a breeze, in planning for the new magazine, also a meeting with Anand, Radhika, and the new team. Anand had looked at Aparna quizzically a few times, wondering at her cool composure and apparent mental distance from him. What was going on in her mind, he wondered? She had become less sensitive of his critical remarks and jibes, even smiling back at him very coolly. Aparna was proud of her control, her feelings for Anand well tucked under, even though during all the problems

   Shuvashree Chowdhury

she faced with that parcel, she had been much tempted to seek his advice and help. But how was she ever going to justify Stephan to Anand? That evening, Aparna went home in a more composed frame of mind, having pushed aside the parcel issue for now. It was rather early that evening, while the family was watching TV, that she saw Stephan's message.

"I'm home, my darling, my sweet wife ... what are you doing?"

"Welcome, gorgeous ... I've been waiting for you, baby. But aren't you home rather early from work?" Aparna typed in reply, on her phone.

This was even as Kartik cuddled up to her. She was sipping her filter coffee, along with savouring the piping hot *medu vadais* and onion *chutney*—her favourite snacks—that her mother had served on her return from work.

"I've made my travel plans to visit you, in exactly a month from now."

"That's great. I really need to see you soon," Aparna replied. "It's high time we meet, so as to remove all these miscommunications arising between us."

"Why do you put it like that? Aren't you looking forward to meet me?"

"Of course I am, gorgeous, that is what I want most now. It will also put to rest my undue fears, cropping up every now and then on your authenticity. All this is more because I am unable to see you. It's difficult to have blind faith."

"Well, just a few weeks left, my love. I'm coming there via Malaysia."

"Why Malaysia now, you can take a direct flight to Delhi, to pick up the parcel, though you have direct flights to Chennai too."

"I have some work in Malaysia before that."

"Where in Malaysia are you going?"

"I'll go to Kuala Lumpur. I have a large ongoing project there, of building public roadways. It is a government contract and a very big one at that."

"That's interesting. I didn't know you made roads too. I thought you only did buildings. I went on a junket to Kuala Lumpur recently, and also to Genting. I did see a lot of development work—a lot of new bridges, flyovers, and highways."

"Yes, now I will arrive in Chennai from Kuala Lumpur. In fact, I will be reaching Kuala Lumpur in a day or two. So I will not be available online tomorrow, as my flight is early in the morning."

"That's really fast, isn't it? Won't you meet your mother and daughter? After all, you're going to be away for quite long, if you're coming to meet me from KL."

"I don't have the time to meet them now, and they will be fine. I am just leaving now to meet my uncle, the one who will take care of them and things here in my absence. In fact, Uncle likes you a lot too."

"How does he like me ... we haven't ever met, not even spoken."

"He's met you, and spoken to you, just like my friends have, darling ... they've all met you through me. Everyone thinks you are great for me, as I've been so happy since meeting you and they can distinctly see that. Even though they just cannot understand, how I got someone like you to love me so much."

"I'm looking forward to meeting everyone soon," Aparna replied, with a sense of relief and joy, that they all liked her and would thus welcome her into their fold warmly. She had worried how his family and friends would treat her, more so Kartik. Even though not contemplating a marriage with Stephan as yet, Aparna was going to UK depending on Stephan, after all. She intended to take up a job there soon, if Stephan would help her get a work permit, to first get a sense of personal security.

Then as he had informed her, Aparna did not hear from Stephan the next day and she concentrated on her work. It was after two days, on settling at her work station after evening coffee at Radhika's desk over discussing the articles that would go into *Elite's* launch issue, that she noticed his FB notification on her phone.

"Darling, I've reached Kaula Lumpur. How is my wife doing?"

"Good to hear from you, gorgeous ... I'm very well. I'm at the office now. So how was your flight?"

"Flight was good, baby. I'm at the Hilton right now. I'm going over to the construction site again. In fact, I've been there since morning, and just came back to the hotel to freshen up. I will be in touch with you, as and when I can."

It was only late the next evening, that Aparna got a message from Stephan again. This was after her dinner, when everyone else was already asleep. She had been writing a piece, typing with speed on her laptop, at her desk in her bedroom. She had been logged into Facebook, as she always was since meeting Stephan, even though she remained invisible online.

"Hello, darling, are you there? Sorry, I could not connect with you earlier," Stephan wrote. "My phone does not have good connectivity at the construction site, where I've been most of the time. But I get the connection when at the hotel. I've just come back here for a quick shower and a change, before I return to the site."

"I'm right here, darling, always there for you. How's everything at the site?"

"Baby, I'm in a lot of trouble here … I really wish you were here with me. I need you with me now. Please help me!"

"Now what's happened, baby? What's the problem? Tell me!"

"My debit cards are not working here. I used them in two ATMs and they did not work. I then got a notification on my phone that my cards are blocked for security reasons, and that I must get new cards issued from my bank. I am unable to withdraw money to pay my workers now. They are all so upset, but more than that … I am so embarrassed, so very humiliated."

"Darling, calm down now. How did this happen suddenly? Did you call up your bank? What did they say?"

"Yes, of course I did. They said the cards will be reissued and sent to my address in UK. But I need the money here urgently."

"Why don't you talk to the hotel? The manager there can perhaps help you."

"I have spoken to the hotel, and they cannot do anything here. I have to get the card reissued. But that will take about a week. So I am in big trouble now. I don't even have the money to buy a ticket back to UK."

"Did you use the card at the hotel, at the restaurants there, or any other place for that matter? Malaysia is well known for card rackets and such, so due to some suspicious transaction, the bank must have blocked it."

"I might have used them somewhere, perhaps the airport. But

I cannot consciously recall that now. I need the money and I must get it soon."

"Why don't you call your uncle and your friends in UK, ask them to transfer some money to you at the hotel's account perhaps. They could even visit your bank in the UK and request the manager to expedite the issue of the new cards."

"Thanks, darling, for your support! But I have already done that, and my uncle and friends said they cannot help me with more money. They have already lent me as much as they could, for this new project I've undertaken. In any case, I know their financial conditions well and know they really cannot help me."

"Then talk to your workers, explain your problem. Tell them to wait and that you will clear their dues surely, and you are not going anywhere before making their payments. In fact, call a few representatives from among the workers ... Get them on your side and to convince the other workers. It's always easier to deal with a few."

"All this I've already tried, to no effect. So I have to make a trip to UK immediately. But I don't even have the money for the tickets. Baby, can you send me some money, to buy a ticket back to the UK?"

"But you know well that I don't have any money, Stephan. For months, I've been telling you how I'm tight on my budget," Aparna replied, beginning to sense something amiss over again, as she had a strong hunch of it. "Then I've already paid about a lakh to the Customs for your parcel, which I wonder now even exists."

"So you won't help me? Is that it? Is that what you're telling me? This is what your love is all about then ... in return for all my trust in you?"

"I really don't have the money ... you know that well. I've always told you about my financial condition. Why don't you have a chat with the hotel? They will certainly help you out in this situation."

"I need your help now, and not your advice. You don't think I have already tried all means? There is no option left for me, but to make a trip back to UK. So I need the money for the ticket only. Will you help me or not?"

"I can help you in any way you want, but not with money, as I really don't have any. You have to believe me on this," Aparna

		Shuvashree Chowdhury

replied, realising alarmingly that all Stephan was after now, was extracting money from her, somehow. "In any case, how would I send you the money from here? Perhaps you could do one thing … You could ask the diplomat to pay charges and take possession of your parcel in Delhi. Then ask him to go over to Kaula Lumpur, give you the money. It would take a day."

"So YOU won't give me the money? YOU won't help me out of this problem? You are a wicked woman. But now you will see what I will do."

Aparna could sense Stephan's anger, insolence, and hate, even from his written words. She was suddenly angry herself, and then felt a stabbing pain in her chest as the realisation of what had happened to her registered to mind. Was this all it really was, only for money, only a little money, really? Stephan had emotionally entrapped her over months, working diligently, and all for what— money? Aparna was shocked at the thought that any person would go to such lengths to fool another, just for money. What he and his gang had done was a heinous crime she could barely allow herself to believe was possible. Did God have to play this really cheap, mean, and rude trick on her? Had he not taught her enough lessons on mistrust, on human anomalies, already through her marriage?

"So you were after me only for money, Stephan? All this drama of love, the relentless pursuing, planning our future for months, was all for money, that too such a measly amount? I cannot believe I fell for it, in spite of your profound acting. How stupid and vulnerable I must really be. And I was prepared to throw up my whole life, leave everything, and to go away with you, a swindler."

"Will you give me the money or not? You can think whatever you want later. Give me the money, or I will post our entire chat history to your friends on FB. I have copied your friend's details and have all our chats stored."

Aparna felt Stephan's cruelty pierce her skin as a sharp knife. Then as she pondered over his words, their implication sinking in— that he had not the slightest respect or affection, leave alone love, in spite of her sincerity and love—she felt as if the knife was brutally twisting into her gut. She felt dizzy, with the acute, shooting pain of betrayal of the most atrocious kind. But Aparna was a strong woman, as she had to be now under the circumstances. So, after a momentary rest to recoup her flailing emotions, she mentally extracted the knife of poisoned love with all her might from her gut, where it would begin to rupture her heart and poison her soul. Thus, mentally and emotionally armed now, with the strength of the knife she had retrieved, Aparna decided to fight Stephan back, with similar sharpness as he had dug into her soul. Aparna was not going to let him take advantage of her vulnerability any more, to arm-wring and coerce her as his allies had. No more was she going to allow this gang to get the better of her, not even under the worst pressure or threat.

Aparna briskly recalled Stephan's verbal build up until his request for money to buy his ticket to UK. It all added up to the trap she had set foot into with the crooks, supposedly from Customs, RBI, also the diplomat. She was glad she was not on a video chat now and never had been for him to have any such records, to see her expression at her crushing disappointment on her strong suspicion of him. Aparna discerned with certainty by now, that it was Stephan who was the kingpin of this group and it shredded her heart to think so. All this drama was masterminded by him, even as he remained in the background, clawing her heart and her trust, like a child clutching his mother's apron strings. Their previous ploys to extract more money from her, with the RBI link and then the diplomat had not worked, as expected. So this new drama in Kaula Lumpur, as he claimed, was executed so Aparna would embrace it out of all her love for Stephan and thus pay more.

Stephan, or whatever his real name was, and it didn't matter to Aparna anymore, knew she had at least one lakh rupees in her bank account, as she had written the checks amounting to it, to pay the RBI. This was till before her meeting with the ICICI bank manager. So Aparna surely had with her at least that amount of money from the checks she retrieved from the bank, after having dropped them there for payment. This money is what they were after now—the lakh of rupees at least, that they were sure she possessed. This new act, supposedly from Malaysia, Stephan had enacted, as he believed Aparna was so steeped in love with him that she would do anything to relieve him of his troubles. He was right on her love, only that he underestimated her intelligence and

   Shuvashree Chowdhury

mental strength, to recover from it so soon. The last few months flashed in Aparna's mind as if in a slide show, especially the ones where Stephan's affections were at its peak. His soft-spoken voice rang as if as a distant bell in her mind. The part where she had allowed his fraudulent words to override her true feelings for Anand made her momentarily hysterical.

"You can do whatever you like. I won't give you a single rupee more," Aparna pounded angrily on her laptop, in response to Stephan's message, steering her mind and heart through the rush of excruciating pain that surged through her. "Show me what you can do. Post our chat history to my friends on FB. Do as you like. And I will do what I have to. In fact, I will have the last laugh you will soon see. I'll write this story for the launch issue of my new magazine, with all the drama it demands. I'll quote your romantic dialogues and entreaties. I'll add details of interactions with your Customs, RBI, and diplomat friends, of course. Now won't it be quite a story?"

"You are a very wicked woman. So you're going to write the story, eh! Do it if you dare! You will face the consequences, you will soon see. But before that, give me the money I ask. Otherwise you are going to be really very painfully sorry."

"I told you, I'm not giving you a single rupee more. So do what you want. In fact, writing this story, I will be applauded for busting this racket. The ICICI officials are already working on all your account numbers. Who knows, I might even get a hike for this brilliant story of love, deception, and fraud. It'll warn youngsters and vulnerable women of leeches like you and your friends. In fact, this is worse than that story my friend once told me and you did all the drama of restricting my talking about us to anyone. Oh my God! Why didn't I see through your charade right then?"

"I'm telling you I am in big trouble, stranded here in Kuala Lumpur. I am pleading with you to help me. But you cannot even do such a small thing. Now you will see the consequences."

"You really think I believe a word of what you say anymore? Do you really think I still have any doubts on your ingenuity? In fact, I'm still interacting with you, only so as to come to terms with what happened in my mind. To see you for who you truly are and to convince myself that I'm making no mistake on it. So I may never look back with regret at the loss of a love—of it being my fault in any way."

It was only a few weeks back that Aparna had learnt from watching the CNN channel, about the Dark Web and illegal pornography: wherein they send you an email link and when you click on it innocently, it activates your web cam, which then begins to film your every move. There are women who have thus unknowingly got themselves filmed in the nude or semi-nude and been blackmailed for money in lieu of the recordings. Some have also been cajoled into baring more or doing porn, to save themselves of the initial accidental recordings, thus getting deeper into the hell of blackmail. But that was done to them by unknown assailants, and though a horribly nasty thing to happen to anyone, it was not as bad as what had happened to Aparna. She had been subject to being charmed onto the carpet of love and trust over a long time. And then the rug had been pulled from right under her feet. It was as if a steady drug was infused into her bloodstream, and when her heart was joyously dependent and controlled by it, a dagger was stuck into its epicentre.

"You know well that I have all our chats saved. It has your opinions of your boss and super boss, all the details of your marriage, and intimate details of your life," Stephan wrote, as if on cue with Aparna's alarmed thoughts. "Firstly, I will send the chat history to your son, then to your colleagues and bosses, then to your FB friends."

Aparna saw she was up against the wall now, but she could not clam up. She would have to remain strong and fight this evil. Though it was killing her to see this demonic side of the man she had sincerely loved, from viewing his gentle and loving one. But blackmailers thrive on one's fear and mental confusion, she knew well. So Aparna was determined that she was not going to allow Stephan see she was really afraid, terrified of him and his gang, and in tremendous emotional pain.

"What a horrible crime against humanity," Aparna wrote, still unable to cut the thick emotional cord that bound her to Stephan and with a desperate hope he might be joking with her about all this. "First igniting, then developing and nursing, finally breaking hearts and emotional trust. Could you guys not find an easier, less

　　　　　Shuvashree Chowdhury

painful way to make money, rather than destroying people's souls? But I told you, I won't give you a single rupee more and I stick to it even at the cost of my life."

"So you won't give me the money? I know how to make you give it."

Aparna abruptly logged out of FB. She couldn't take this anymore. Then she went to bed, but lay awake, worrying about the probable consequences of her immense stupidity, and now this inanely feigned boldness. What was she to do, in any case? Should she confide in Anand and hope he would understand her? No, that would be the stupidest thing to do, over all she had so far. Aparna was able to catch a few winks of sleep, after she abruptly dozed off. She awoke startled the next morning, to the alarm, but more the searing fear of the night before, like a splash of cold water on her face. What she did promptly was log onto her laptop, make her FB friends list invisible. So the criminal gang could not access it any longer to send out group messages as Stephan had threatened. But she didn't 'unfriend' or 'block' Stephan Shedrack on FB. This way, she could track his moves, but remain quiet and unnoticed. She didn't want him to think she was afraid, thus get nastier.

Aparna decided to be absolutely inactive on FB for a while, till this whole episode died down. Hopefully it would, if only she could hold her ground bravely. The frauds would not waste much time on her anymore when they could rather invest on a new target. She was right in thinking so, as through the next day, there was no message from Stephan, and similarly the day after, there was none too. This gave Aparna time to recoup her thoughts and emotions.

Then it was after a week that she got a sudden message from Stephan again, "So are you giving the money or not? I'm waiting for you to arrange it."

Aparna did not reply. In the weeks ahead, she received a few more similar and random messages from Stephan. But she determinedly remained inactive on FB. And though she saw Stephan's incoming messages on her phone, she did not open any, as it would show at his end she had seen it. In time, Aparna believed, she could relegate this incident to the back of her mind as a nightmare. But now it hurt awfully, intolerably. If wounded, the heart does not lose its yearning for love forever, even in acute cognizance and memory of the strife. But crushed to the core by this calculated, acute treachery, as she now was by Stephan's playing up love, it just might. This incident threatened to defeat and eradicate Aparna's trust in mankind forever. But she had to be strong, she told herself. She would have to overcome this attempted homicide—it was no less than that, as it was an assault on her heart and her spirit. But she would raise her soul from ashes, Aparna decided, and heal her soul, to upkeep her faith in humanity. As to live without trust would surely mean to die.

Shuvashree Chowdhury

Chapter 23

The Wife Versus the Girlfriend

It was finally the evening of the launch party of *Elite*, the Friday supplement of the *National Daily*. Anand and Sujata reached the venue, the banquet hall of one of the best luxury hotels in the city, the Taj Coromandel, at 8.30 p.m. They walked past the ornate front lobby, then took the staircase to the banquet hall in the basement. They were greeted by a row of *sari*-clad ladies flanking the corridor leading to the hall, positioned to usher the guests in. At the entrance to the banquet hall, they were greeted by Radhika Nair who was ensuring that all the guests were warmly welcomed. As features head, she was in charge of all supplements. Aparna was busy inside, coordinating the event. It was her big day as she was the editor.

As Sujata and Anand walked inside the hall, they were transported into a world of gorgeous people, and were enveloped into the collective sound of clinking glasses and muted conversations. The crowd comprised the who's who of Chennai, as the new supplement was to be on the lifestyles of the rich and famous. There were industrialists, entrepreneurs, television and cinema personalities, and a number of expatriates. They all mingled with Radhika's team who were in full attendance. Sujata had been quite undecided on what to wear for the evening. As the wife of the managing director, there would be eyes on her. She knew Aparna would be here as the star of the event, so she didn't want to pale in comparison.

Sujata wore a white georgette *sari* with aqua blue and matte gold sequins beautifully sewn into bold sun shaped designs. She had picked it up after much deliberation from Sundari Silks in T. Nagar, which was among one of her favourite *sari* shops in the city. She had opted not to wear much jewellery, except for a pair of platinum dangler earrings, almost reaching her shoulders. As Sujata was one of the few women wearing a *sari*, she stood out. The way she carried herself with élan in the beautiful *sari* made people turn and look at her. The appreciative glances pleased Sujata and infused confidence in her. She was bracing herself for meeting Aparna. She was determined to be on her most gracious behaviour with her. After all, many here knew their circumstances and would look out for sparks between them.

Anand looked suave and distinguished in an impeccably tailored, grey-black suit by Barkat Ali on Cathedral Road. Striding through the crowd, with a smile here, a nod there, and a hello somewhere, Anand reached the bar. Sujata went with him. He tended to be unable to get into the mood of a party without a drink. But he needed it more now, as he was not looking forward to the inevitable meeting of Aparna and Sujata, that too at a public event. Though they had met before, Sujata was in a particularly volatile mood nowadays. Even as the bartender handed Anand his glass of Scotch, Sujata looked around at the crowd, making eye contact with people and smiling. She was in no hurry to get a drink herself, preferring to visually soak in the glamour and glitz around instead.

Sujata was not much of a drinker, just a social one, and would in time get herself a cocktail, a Mojito preferably. But now she looked from one woman to another, appraising their hairstyles, makeup, jewellery, their trendy designer outfits, shoes, and handbags. Sujata didn't miss the men either, rather made it a point to finish her consideration of every woman, with the man by her side. It was interesting to note the confidence and ease with which these men carried their chic attire, along with the gorgeous woman they flaunted. It was easy to gauge the man's affluence as they tended to carry their success and ensuing confidence on their persona.

Just then, in spite of all the bonhomie around her in awaiting the formal function to commence, her eyes fell on an elegant man with a glass in hand. He was standing alone, across the room from her, absolutely at ease with himself and watching her with an amused look. As their eyes met, Sujata instinctively lowered hers out of an inherent shyness. But she instantly regretted it and, taking

          Shuvashree Chowdhury

a deep breath, looked up at him. His amused look had changed now to one of admiration as he was sizing her up appreciatively. The way he looked at her was what she needed to boost her morale and to squash the demons of insecurity gnawing her. Sujata was becoming increasingly conscious that Aparna was the star of this show, a woman in her own right here, not just the wife of the MD like her.

Radhika walked up to her just then, and with her usual vivacity, grabbed Sujata's attention. She quickly plucked her out of her pall of doubt and anxiety. Radhika Nair, tall, slender, with mid-length, wavy brown hair, her wide smile accentuated by her glowing complexion, was a strikingly attractive woman, even in her mid-fifties.

"How are you, Sujata? It's been quite a while since we met, hasn't it?" Radhika said, as she gave Sujata a light hug with a peck on her cheek. "I couldn't really meet you at the entrance. You know how it is with greeting guests first."

"That's alright, Radhika. Of course, I understand," Sujata replied, smiling.

Then looking at Sujata's hand that clutched her sequined white and gold hand bag, Radhika said cheerily, "Why don't you have a drink yet?"

"I just wanted to take in the ambience for a while."

"You're looking absolutely gorgeous … the aqua blue sets off the white beautifully, doesn't it? Your taste in *saris* is just the best."

"Thank you so much!" Sujata gushed, and appraising Radhika's royal blue and gold Kanjeevaram *sari* appreciatively she added, "You look rather elegant yourself … and it's such a beautiful *sari* you're wearing."

"Thank you! Come, let's get a drink and find ourselves a good place by the ramp. The fashion show and events are due to start any minute." Radhika said enthusiastically. Looking around towards the bar, she added, "May I get you one of the evening's special cocktails? We have a celebrity bartender, especially flown in from Italy for this bash."

"Yeah, sure, why not! That'll be great!" Sujata replied.

Radhika turned to the young man behind the bar. Sujata turned too, and could not help admiring the handsome, chiselled youthful face, with the blue-green eyes and the short crop of brown hair highlighting the tattoos around his neck.

"May we try one of your specialities, please?" Radhika said aloud to him.

"Sure, ma'am. You go along and take your seats. I will have a waiter serve it to you." He grinned, his eyes sparkling, emphasising his good looks.

"It had better be good, guys." Radhika replied, smiling warmly, and then turning to Sujata, said, "Come, let's go take our seats. I've had the front row reserved."

Radhika knew the bartenders by now, including the celebrity bartender Nicco. She had got him interviewed this morning by a senior reporter to carry the piece in tomorrow's inaugural issue of *Elite* and the Sunday magazine. They would be covering the launch party extensively in the next few days in all the supplements. Sujata felt relaxed in Radhika's company, as they weaved through the crowd, smiling at familiar faces. Radhika knew a lot of people, and she introduced Sujata to some on the way, briefing her about some others. Then they settled into their seats, alongside the ramp, for the fashion show to begin. Shortly, the other seats filled up. Then a waiter arrived, with a salver balancing two tall glasses of a maroon-red drink.

One small sip of her drink and Sujata, looking at Radhika, said "This stuff is really strong. What's it?"

"Strong's okay! Strong's good!" Radhika grinned. "You have a long time to sip it gradually. Unless of course, you don't like the taste. Then I'll have it changed … How's it?"

"It tastes awesome, I have to admit." Sujata smiled back warmly.

The anchor, a celebrated television jockey known for her comic timing, came on stage. She was petite, and looked pretty in an elegant, white maxi dress and long, wavy hair. She started the evening off with practised ease. And then Anand was called on stage to thundering applause from the audience. Sujata instinctively felt her heart warm up and swell in pride, as she turned around to watch him walk towards the podium. Then as Anand was about to climb the stairs, Sujata noticed someone right behind him, an attractive woman in a flaming red dress, her thick hair falling stylishly over

    Shuvashree Chowdhury

her attractive face. It took a few seconds for recognition to dawn on Sujata.

Aparna looked radiant in red, as she smiled confidently back at the audience, and then turned towards Anand again as he walked over to the dais and stood behind the mike. Sujata's heart froze, and she felt anger shoot through her. As she looked on, awestruck at Aparna's star-like personality and the way she looked at Anand in possessive adulation, Sujata was consumed with fresh resentment for both of them. She suddenly knew why Anand was drawn to this woman. Aparna, as was obvious from the way she looked at him, revered Anand in a way Sujata knew she never had and never could, in spite of loving him.

Sujata's love for Anand had been just a warm glow from the start, never fiery and all-consuming like Aparna's. With marriage, expectations are high, and one tends to easily accrue resentment over unmet realisations of them. It seemed to Sujata that Aparna was happy with whatever little Anand gave her. She didn't know that Aparna was already upset by his aloofness. Anand was giving his speech now. His opening lines were greeted with loud applause.

Anand's speech was crisp and witty. Though he was reserved in private, he had quite a flair for public speaking. Sujata, in spite of her raging anger, was impressed and proud of her husband's impact on the audience. His speech was followed by a short and sweet speech by the new chief editor, a thorough professional brought in a year ago from another leading newspaper in Delhi. He had made a lot of changes. There was a new head designer now, who had changed the layout of the paper, uplifting its look and appeal substantially. With quite a few big players in the print media now, it was imperative to make sweeping changes to retain the fickle reader, who tended to move on fast. The new supplement was also his brainchild. At some point in the address, Sujata got distracted and looked around to see if Anand was with Aparna now after his speech. But to her relief, she found Anand sitting alone in the front row, along with some dignitaries. Aparna was standing behind, close to the bar and looked collected.

Sujata turned back to the stage, wondering if Aparna felt the same unease she felt and was merely acting calm, for surely she had noticed her too. But then, journalists tended to be arrogant, even hypocritical, Sujata had concluded, from her years of watching and interacting with them since her marriage. There were couples whom she knew personally, who put on an act of such perfect unity and harmony, of being happily married, though Sujata was aware of the man's romantic alliance with another woman. What never ceased to irk her was the appearance in social and official functions of one senior editor from a rival newspaper, with his wife and his girlfriend—an editor in the same paper as him. The two women even seemed to be dear friends, with the girlfriend making all efforts to be warm to the wife in public, even to look out for her and keep her company.

There were more such cases of two-facedness that Sujata was often confronted with. And it infuriated her as it was a reminder, like a resounding slap on her pride each time, of the pretentious life she herself lived. The man in such cases would invariably appear nonchalant, basking in the affability of the wife and girlfriend, in the former's naivety and the latter's shrewdness. In Sujata's view, journalists were a supercilious lot, sharply opinionated and critical about everything and everyone, but their own lives. She understood it came with their jobs, of years of their opinions being given public precedence and acceptance. The media were opinionmakers, in a country like India where people preferred or at least tended not to think wholesomely for themselves. How else, could one explain, the patronising commercial success of all those books and films which least taxed one's mind, whereas serious, meaningful and hard thinking work suffocated in frustrated silence and ignominy?

The common man usually took everything in the media, whether print or visual, as gospel truth. This included not only political and social analyses, but reviews on books, films, theatres, art, eateries, and all of life. Incidentally, it was on reading Aparna's review of a notable author's book she herself had loved that Sujata had become agitated on the unfairness of this situation.

"You must start a good journalism school soon, of international standards," She had said to Anand indignantly, without naming Aparna, but he understood her implication was the *Sunday Magazine* as it was still in Sujata's hand as she spoke. "And enhance your social responsibility initiatives."

          Shuvashree Chowdhury

"As if I don't have enough on my plate already," Anand had replied, laughing aloud, and then added crisply, "But perhaps you'd like to diversify your business and start this school. Or perhaps you could join us and take up the new project."

"I'm serious … I just read some wonderful reviews that got me thinking," Sujata spluttered, countering him vehemently. "And you must ensure to have a specialisation course for wannabe critics. After the basic course, those who wish to be literary, film, or any other art critic must be trained in their field of interest, if not aptitude. Then to qualify, they must submit a dissertation in that particular field. A prospective film critic must make a short documentary film, and a literary critic should write a novella at the least. It goes without saying that a dance critic had better learn varied dance forms, just as a food critic needs to taste his own culinary skills first. Wouldn't it make the reviews you print more equitable? Now it is common for those with no knowledge or experience to critique and influence the country's opinions on the works of those who have strived to attain perfection, maybe over a lifetime. Or write off someone new with real talent or establish one with none."

"That's a brilliant idea indeed! You must take up this initiative yourself, when you start this school," Anand replied grinning, to be met by Sujata's disparaging look, followed by stony silence.

Sujata mentally reiterated now that she was never going to be friends with Aparna, to adopt the smug state of associations common to their professional creed, if that is what Anand hoped for. Her dignity was of priority and Sujata would not compromise it, knowing Aparna's aspirations and her ensuing status in her husband's work and personal life well. With the current journalism schools now mostly accessible only to students able to afford their high costs, Sujata realised you had over-confident graduates, who didn't necessarily have the flair or the seriousness required, joining leading papers. They are given positions of responsibility early, unlike a decade or so ago, when one had to work oneself slowly and tediously up to senior positions.

Often in a couple of years, these youngsters may switch to another industry for the allure of more money. You no longer have the really diligent and passionate reporters whose life's goal it was to be a journalist, thereby their choice in the job, but only overly ambitious ones. Aparna must be one of those over-zealous journalists then, more in it for the glamour and prestige, Sujata concluded, both of which she must find aplenty in her inexcusable allure towards Anand.

As Sujata turned her attention back to the stage, she took another sip of her potent drink. And then she guzzled it quickly in an attempt to soothe her frazzled nerves. She noticed Radhika had also finished her drink. The speeches were over by now and the fashion show had commenced, showcasing leading designers. Sujata was wooed into the visual feast immediately. The colourful, classy ensembles and the artful movements of the models to the lilting music promptly lifted her spirits. The fashion show was followed by a high-voltage, pulsating show by the Mumbai-based well-known dancer and choreographer Shiamak Davak and his troupe. Just when the MC took over the mike again, Radhika got up and asked Sujata if she wanted to come along. But Sujata decided to stay on, so as not to walk into Aparna who now stood near the bar. It was still crowded near the bar, many watching the show, standing there with their glasses in hand.

Sujata recalled how at a party at a reputed lady journalist's house, last new year's eve, her boyfriend, who was another senior editor, came with his wife. The wife, perhaps, had no clue of the relationship between her husband and their hostess. It was her husband's birthday the next day, so in due course two cakes were laid out—one for new year's and the other for his birthday. All this was deftly organised by his girlfriend, amidst a large group of their journalist and high-society friends. The man's wife had organised a birthday party for him at their club the following evening. But the shrewd girlfriend had her way of celebrating her man's birthday first, just as she intended to, in the guise of the new year's party. The unsuspecting wife was pleased to be part of her husband's circle, and did not suspect anything amiss. The man was pleased at his girlfriend's cleverness in getting her way without any suspicions on his wife's part. Sujata remembered the scene with a shudder of disgust.

It was after the DJ took over from the MC that Sujata got up and joined Radhika. She was now near the bar. Radhika then requested

 Shuvashree Chowdhury

the bartender to make them another of his signature cocktails. He proceeded to hand both the ladies an exotic flame-topped glass each. He had churned out blue concoctions in them, by pouring ingredients out of various bottles into the tall glasses that he then set afire, much to the thrill of the watching crowd. After handing over their glasses with an exaggerated bow, the Italian resumed displaying more dramatic fire tricks. Sujata and Radhika watched on, cheering enthusiastically with many others. In a while, Radhika moved on to socialise with other guests, leaving Sujata much calmer. A lady approached Sujata, whom she recognised as a well-known fashion designer. Sujata tended to meet her often at parties and they were thus socially acquainted. They exchanged pleasantries and chatted for a while.

Anand now approached the bar and stood alongside Sujata, and together they interacted with guests. With the ease with which they did this, who would gauge the gaping void between them? Sujata was acutely conscious of Aparna's presence in the same hall, more so now that Anand was near her. It was only when Sujata and Radhika proceeded to where dinner was served that Sujata almost walked into Aparna. It was as if this meeting was inevitable. After all, they had been in the same hall for hours and, though acutely conscious of the other's presence, had not gone out of their way to avoid each other. As much as Sujata wished not to run into Aparna, there was a part of her that did, to see how she would react to her. And there would also be the pleasure in snubbing her. But when they did come face to face, there was between them a wide-eyed, shocked expression.

"Hello, Mrs. Anand … It's lovely to meet you … How are you?" Aparna said, after a brief moment.

Sujata, without intending it, instinctively averted her gaze. Then much shaken at Aparna's smug and confident attitude, Sujata consciously turned her face away and walked on without replying. Did she have to play up to this social charade, Sujata thought, in fury? Aparna was shaken by this snub in public, and instinctively her eyes welled up. As much as she had dreaded this meeting, there was not much else she could have done but acknowledge her boss's wife in public. But from Sujata's perspective, what was Aparna really expecting in the circumstances, to be friends with her?

Radhika noticed this exchange, but pretended not to have. She was a sagacious woman. It was not her place to comment on this matter involving her boss. She proceeded to the buffet table and picked up a plate. Sujata, following her, was grateful for Radhika's silence. Seething inside, she was in no mood to talk.

Sujata went about distractedly, getting served small portions of the varied exotic items on to her warm plate, from the live buffet counters, starting with Italian, then Korean, and Chinese. She couldn't forget Aparna's self-assured coolness, in greeting her, as if they were mere social or business associates. The sight and flavour of all the delicious food wafting into her senses could not distract Sujata from her enraging thoughts. What was she supposed to do? Was she to greet Aparna coolly in turn? Even hug her perhaps, the way others in her place might have, in projecting how like one big happy family they were? Was she supposed to show how acceptable all this was to her, and thus encourage Aparna further?

One or other of the staff, Sujata mentally cursed as she went about picking almost every item on the dessert counter, must surely have noticed the interaction between Aparna and her. By now, they would be spreading the spiced version of the scene between the boss's wife and girlfriend. This talk would soon be like Chinese whispers, taking on the dramatic hues of the gossiper's imagination. Radhika knew of this situation well, not that any of the parties concerned had confessed to her. But people at work and outside too did gossip, and she was privy to a lot of it. But she was level-headed and reliable never to comment, or lend support either for or against the faction for either woman. Radhika was rather fond of Anand, having worked with him since his father's time. And in respect for the elder man who was no more but whom she would always be grateful to, she remained silent.

Aparna was livid too, not only at this snub by Sujata, but the humiliation in the way Radhika had looked away. It was Radhika's attitude that had coerced the tears out of her. She fought to control them, walking away in full view of people. Aparna sought the sanctuary of the washroom for a while, making a brisk dash for it. She had instinctively wanted to ignore Sujata, on walking into her uninitiated. But what was she to do, how could she possibly ignore Sujata in public? She was the boss's wife after all. Aparna

 Shuvashree Chowdhury

returned to the hall sullenly, and headed to where the crowd was in full swing to the DJ's expert spinning of the latest Hindi music. Two of her colleagues pulled her on to the dance floor. Aparna did not resist, allowing the rhythm to steady her emotionally. She was still raw and hurting from her grave wound induced by the fraudster Stephan. Could she not have been spared this traumatic experience so soon after, Aparna thought, of being branded as the other woman?

Chapter 24

Freedom at Last

Aparna stood sombrely, with her twelve-year-old son Kartik at his father Nikhil's bedside at the Lilavati Hospital in Mumbai. They had taken a taxi here straight from the airport, landing late in the evening. In the hospital's lobby, they were met by Nikhil's brother and his wife, and led to his room. His parents stood by their son's bedside, shrouded in a lifetime's remorse. Nikhil, it was predicted by the doctors, was at the stage of his rather wasted life, whereupon it might give up on him at any moment. As Aparna looked at him, she barely saw signs of life. He was miserably thin, his cheekbones more prominent, his temples hollower, and his eyes in the deep sockets larger than she remembered them.

Aparna might not have recognised the shrivelled frame, with the pinched face, sunken eyes, and the ghastly colour of his face and neck, as being that of the good-looking man who used to be her husband, if she had walked in upon him alone. He had been rather corpulent, but now he had a dried-up, yellow look. The skin of his neck was loose and wrinkled. As she continued to look at Nikhil, the handsome face with a bright complexion and intelligent eyes she had first met in Chennai flashed to her mind. That face was just as vivid in her mind as the face of death she looked upon now, the contrast shaking her to the core. She looked at Kartik abruptly, coercing her thoughts to concentrate on the present, worried how the boy was absorbing this horrific sight. It was like viewing the ghost of his father in a film, dressed in white, amidst the backdrop of the white bed clothes and medical gadgets. There were needles dug into the top of Nikhil's hand, the only visible body part, the rest of him covered high up to the chin.

But to her surprise, Kartik was calm, and though he looked extremely sad, there was a composure far beyond his years. Aparna

 Shuvashree Chowdhury

had not gauged the extent of deterioration Nikhil's health and appearance had undergone over the years. She had been too busy in the desperate bid to leave her past behind to surge on ahead in her new life to even think back upon those times. But Kartik had reported to his grandparents after his last vacation, as vividly as children tend to, that his father's clothes hung about him as though they had been bought for someone else, and his collar now seemed three or four sizes too large. That his hands trembled continually and when he wrote to help Kartik with his homework once, the handwriting scrawled over the page with shapeless, haphazard letters.

"Nikhil was evidently very ill even then," Aparna's mother had stated earlier in the day, when Aparna reached home with Kartik to pack for their trip. "Kartik told us that Daddy eats little these days, usually only some soup or at most a toast to go with it for dinner. And still he is very sick in the mornings."

Aparna sadly recalled now how in the months when she had been desperate and driven to cure Nikhil's alcohol addiction, she would research its causes and effects. This was after she discovered her pregnancy. She had read then that the reasons for addiction to alcohol or cigarettes is the absence of adequate amounts of a chemical called dopamine in the brain. Insufficient levels of dopamine production in nerve cells are also associated with tremors and motor impairment in Parkinson's patients. Altered dopamine activity is also seen in those suffering from schizophrenia. Aparna had learned further from another article that calcium can help maintain levels of dopamine—a key neurotransmitter—as calcium ions play a critical role in producing dopamine in a normal brain. If normal dopamine levels are maintained, the craving for alcohol can be substantially reduced.

In fact, alcohol at first makes the brain release more dopamine than normal, triggering a feeling of well-being. But as more alcohol is consumed, the brain's reward system is desensitised and less dopamine is released. In order to release the necessary amount of dopamine to feel good, a person increases his or her intake of alcohol. Thus, addiction sets in. This is what must have been happening with Nikhil, Aparna had concluded. Armed with all this information, she had started serving Nikhil large portions of milk or curd with every meal, to increase his calcium intake. But egotistic and defiant, Nikhil had refused the milk and curd outright. He didn't even have curd rice as he hated milk products, and, in fact, even detested chocolate. Aparna had however never told him, out of fear, why she had started serving him milk and curd. Now as Aparna thought back to those times, she regretted not having told Nikhil why she was trying to increase his calcium intake.

The last time Aparna had seen Nikhil was seven years back at the time of their divorce. She had not known how much his alcohol addiction had consumed his bearing since then. But Kartik had been spending his vacations with his father and it was barely a month since he had last seen Nikhil. Yet even he was having difficulty recognising the father of a month ago in the one lying in a state of decay in front of him. Aparna, till the call she received this morning from Nikhil's father, followed by the chat with her mother on Kartik's last vacation, had not imagined Nikhil had wasted away to this extent over the years. Nikhil had deteriorated this much only in the last few days, she learned. Aparna had not paid heed to Kartik's reports on his father's life and health, though if she had really listened, she would have deduced his end was near. Children are observant and can recount minutiae, even if they do not have the knowledge or maturity to decipher their inference. But Kartik, in his unusual maturity, didn't tell his mother much about his vacations or his father, so as not to upset her and to allow her to move ahead in life.

Aparna had not allowed herself to think back on her disastrous marital life with an alcoholic waster in the last years, in her bid to stay focussed on her future. After the long-drawn-out divorce, along with the custody battle for her son, she had mentally closed that chapter of her life. But she never influenced Kartik against his father. In fact, she was rather glad from Kartik's little recounts of his vacations that Nikhil had turned out to be a good father, whom Kartik had grown to adore and even respect. After that, Aparna's relationship with Anand that was interspaced with the whirlwind one with Stephan that might easily have destroyed her, had left her little emotional space to think about anything else. On rare occasions, Aparna had chatted with Nikhil's brother's wife, while

     Shuvashree Chowdhury

Kartik was visiting them on his vacations in Mumbai. She did wonder now and then how her co-sister had managed to stay with her husband, who was also an alcoholic.

But then, his elder brother was not as adamant as Nikhil. He had been coaxed in and out of rehabilitation several times by his parents and wife. After each such stint, he would abstain from drinking for a while, even work well at the family business. And then when he would invariably start drinking over again, unable to withstand his craving, he would agree to return to rehabilitation. Nikhil's ego, on the other hand, perhaps would not succumb to the pressure and threats that Aparna imposed on him to go into rehabilitation as a precondition to stay on with him, or later to return after she had left him. Nikhil, even in the last years when he called Aparna in drunken stupor to coerce her to come back, embellishing his threats intermittently with declarations of love, never admitted that he had a drinking problem.

Aparna had never ceased to persuade Nikhil, even till a year back: "You go into rehabilitation and try to improve your life and circumstances. And I am willing to come back with Kartik and give our marriage another chance, at least for his sake."

But Nikhil never conceded, and would vehemently reply, "You don't have to tell me what I need to do, Aparna. I'm fine and you need not return here."

Then he would not call again for a while. Nikhil's pride could not accept Aparna's condescending attitude towards him, and her lack of empathy for his problem, over which he had lost all control. Dealing with an alcoholic or a drug addict is just as trying as a mental patient. It requires much sensitivity and is taxing for parents, spouses, or caregivers. This is from the difficulty in all cases to toe the line between empathy and pressure to conform, for the victim's welfare. Aparna's co-sister was a relatively docile woman who did not pose any threat to a man's ego, unlike Aparna with her dynamic personality and drive to change her husband. Thus, she was still rowing along patiently in the lake of her marriage, however turbulent it got in stretches. She empathised with her husband, accepting that he was at least trying to come out of the clutches of a vehemently possessive lover—alcoholism.

Aparna had been impatient for Nikhil to change and did not

realise that a person would not become alcoholic if he had the mental strength and control. She had hastily given up on rowing the leaking boat of her marriage, when it was in a turbulent river of problems. Then she had deserted it and swam to shore by herself, while it slowly but steadily capsized along with the drunken boatman. It was as if she was now called to the hospital, to identify her co-traveller—the drunken boatman, who from his afflictions, was unable to row or swim to shore and had thus drowned. She kept looking at the dying man with a sense of sympathy, but also a relief that she had sorted out her own life at a new shore, rather than suffocating with him in the last years till she drowned. She had a life to go back to. All those in the room stood silently for what seemed like a long time, lost in their private thoughts about the man who lay in a drug-induced sleep. His liver had collapsed, from its inability to process the varied drugs administered to control an acute viral attack followed by jaundice, and all systems were following suit.

When Nikhil finally opened his eyes slowly, he first looked at his son Kartik. His dying eyes brimmed with love, and then filled with tears. Nikhil then looked at Aparna, barely able to look her in the eye. She took a step forward, so as to give him a burst of emotional support to be able to face her. He met and held her gaze weakly, guiltily.

"I'm so sorry for everything, Aparna," Nikhil said earnestly, in a voice that was barely a whisper, "I hope you can forgive me someday."

Aparna remained silent, looking back at him gravely. She felt sympathy and a deep regret. How could a man who had all the potential and opportunities for the most extraordinary life have wasted it to this extent?

All she could bring herself to say was, "I hope you are not in too much pain?"

Nikhil looked at Aparna quietly, with all the sorrow and regret it was too late to feel now—of what could have indeed been a beautiful life. All those he truly cared for were in this room now. His sight embraced them all together. It distressed Nikhil that he would not be amongst them much longer. But what crushed him to his bones was to realise how he had callously dashed to the

 Shuvashree Chowdhury

ground all their hopes and expectations of him. He had selfishly taken it upon himself to lead his life the way he wanted. He had not cared that his life was as much theirs as it was his. Aparna had always been right, but he had been too stubborn and egotistic to pay heed to her words. Then it had been too late, to pull the reins of the horse of alcoholism he had let go so wild, until it had kicked him in his guts. But even in his most negligent state of mind, Nikhil had not envisaged his end so soon. He had not thought that a mere bout of jaundice would crack him up, and his body would not be able to fight back to get him on his feet again.

Nikhil turned again to his son Kartik, and what he felt was an immense guilt and shame at having been the worst role model a boy could have had. But to his satisfaction, what he saw in the boy's eyes, exceptionally mature for his years, was not hate but far from it—a deep sympathy for his father, and above all adoration. In many ways, to Kartik, his father had been a good role model. The way he cared for him on vacations in Mumbai, taught him his maths, science, and English lessons, also to swim, and they played tennis at the Gymkhana Club—all this made Nikhil a good father. Nikhil would try to drink as less as was in his control when Kartik was visiting, and would also wake up early. They would drive down to Juhu beach, or to Bandstand or Marine Drive for a jog, then to the Gymkhana Club, where after a round of tennis or a swim , they would have a lavish breakfast. Nikhil had provided Kartik the kind of male companionship a boy needs to have, supplementing what his maternal grandfather who did all in his capacity couldn't fully provide.

Kartik came closer to the bed now and put his hand over his father's head. Then looking at his face lovingly, he stroked his hair, in a strange reversal of roles, as a father might his sick son, in consoling him. Nikhil had on several occasions done the same as he had watched Kartik fall asleep. In Kartik's mind, Nikhil's drinking problem was a chronic illness that was neither his fault nor in his control, so the state he was in now was only because the illness had taken charge. This thinking had been instilled into his psyche, with much care and sensitivity, by his mother and his maternal grandparents. His paternal grandparents avoided the topic in distress and guilt. Thus, Kartik had grown up without any disrespect for his father, which might have been otherwise apparent in a situation as his. The disregard would have harmed his sensitive, impressionable mind, and tarnished his values and life going ahead. As for Nikhil, he was in any case past the ability to be restricted from drinking by his son's negative opinion even if it would have upset him. Though he didn't care what other people thought of his drinking.

Nikhil also had tried his best to uphold Kartik's inherent belief that his father was responsible, caring, and worthy of respect. He was immensely grateful to Aparna and her parents for bringing up his son with respect and understanding for him. Kartik might have grown up to be a rebel, or a confused or meek child, more so perhaps if his parents had lived together and quarrelled constantly. It was best then that Aparna had left when she did, Nikhil had conceded, when he saw how mature and compassionate Kartik had turned out to be. Now in his dying moments, the satisfaction he had through all his physical pain and hopelessness was that his son was a smart, mature, and balanced kid. It was an immense relief that he did not hate his father.

It also somewhat relieved Nikhil's guilt that Aparna was by now self-reliant and had moved on in life without him. He also realised, that his parents, after the initial grief, would be well rid of the constant trouble, worry, and shame he was to them. Nikhil concluded that his family could finally settle into a more peaceful existence with him gone for good. With this thought, a peaceful smile lit up his face and his features relaxed. His body could no longer tolerate painkillers, so they had been stopped. Nikhil's sight lingered for a while on his son now, conveying an eternal love Kartik would hopefully remember him by. Then he took one last look, one by one, at all those gathered around him, and who meant everything to him, before Nikhil shut his weary eyes. He slipped into deep sleep, breathing heavily.

The doctor, who came in presently, told the family, "Why don't you all go home now? Get some rest and return in the morning. It is not likely he will wake up at night. One of you could wait here for any medical requirement or decision."

But Nikhil's mother was reluctant to leave, as she had a premonition these were her son's final moments. What if he should

     Shuvashree Chowdhury

open his eyes, even one last time, and not be able to see them here? Worse still, what if he might think they had all left him here to die? Nikhil, in his sleep, was subconsciously wrapped in the soft cosy murmur of his family's familiar voices. They were still around discussing their next course of action, when suddenly they were startled by a chilling, loud, sound. His chest heaved as if to breathe, and he had a brief seizure. While everyone looked on in alarm, the doctor rushed to Nikhil's side, only to perceive that his breathing had stopped. He then felt Nikhil's pulse, and looked at the heart monitor. It was all over. The loud, ghastly sound had been the death rattle. As everyone watched in shock and grief, Nikhil's jaw fell and his eyes were open wide. The doctor looked into his eyes and slowly closed them with one hand.

"He is no more." The doctor softly announced, fulfilling his obligation, looking sombrely at no one in particular. The response was a surprised but resigned silence, to which he added, "But we'll wait a few hours to make the official announcement, and then prepare a death certificate. After that, you may take the body home or to the crematorium directly from here, after calling anyone else in the family not already present."

Nikhil's mother was the first to take control of the situation. Her face was frozen. To Aparna's amazement, rather than break down or even allow a tear to escape her eyes, as usual she was the one to take the decision on any matter pertaining to her family.

She calmly said, "We're all here, so let's take him to the crematorium from here. What is the point of taking the remains home, when Nikhil has left us already? Moreover, why not let everyone else remember him just the way they saw him last, before the last bout of illness? I would not want people to remember him this way."

Nikhils' mother Nandhini was a tall, slender woman, with striking features, and large eyes, still as beautiful and elegant as in her youth. She was also strong-willed, proud, vain, superfluous, and egoistic. Her heart was cruelly crushed almost to death now, after years of its being trampled upon in helplessly watching the deterioration of her favourite son. But she still wished to shield him from the judgemental opinions of the world, even in his death. She would set up in the front hall of their house, Nandhini decided, the most handsome and happy picture of her son, from his healthy days. Before that, she would have shifted the furniture, including the dining table, and got her special set of carpets laid out for people to sit on. She would call the best florist in town right away—the one who worked for all their family functions, she mentally added, to decorate Nikhil's picture along with the hall and the front façade of the house.

They were a well-known family, so a large number of people would obviously come to pay their last respects to the departed. Whether or not they were sincere, people would ensure participation in this high-society function. This was to watch the spectacle, also be seen and photographed and written about, as media coverage would be high. Nandhini would have to ensure everything was perfectly organised. Her mind was working deftly, thus guarding her from the real emotional impact of her loss. She called her younger brother, who was aware of Nikhil's acute condition of the last few days, to announce her son was gone. She asked him to come to the hospital immediately, if he wished to see his nephew a last time. But this was more as she actually needed and sought emotional support for herself as well as for the whole family.

Nikhil's remains were loaded onto a hearse only nearing dawn. It took that long to complete the formalities and get the death certificate issued and handed over. His elder brother and wife, both pretty shaken at the kind of death alcohol could lead to, brought a fresh set of clothes to dress Nikhil's remains in—which was a gruesome task. His brother and father slipped his long legs into the white linen *churidar*, with help from the male nurses, and it was quite a job to get his arms through the sleeves of the *kurta*. They had got wreaths and plenty of flowers and incense, to take him as respectfully as possible on his final journey. This journey in death was Nikhil's family's attempt to throw a blanket of dignity upon him, after they had lost all power to cloak the indignity he had plunged his life into. Kartik was calm and collected, brave through the entire process, just as he had been when he had learned his father was dying.

When Kartik lit the pyre, Aparna was moved to tears that trickled down her face involuntarily. She fought to control the tears that were more for the big little man, her son Kartik, who

     Shuvashree Chowdhury

had gone through so much in life already, and now this. The last few months had been tough on Aparna too. Her emotions were already overwrought and raw, still sweltering from the successive onslaughts recently in her life. The brutal, prolonged abuse by the fraud Stephan after all the turmoil with Anand, till the public humiliation by Sujata and Radhika last month, all had left her emotionally delicate. Thus now, the pain of her son's loss of his father bled her heart. It was not the actual loss of the dead man that clutched her heart savagely and suffocated her, but love for her son. Though Aparna had loved Nikhil too and still did in a way and his passing did aggrieve her. It was an accumulation of all this pent-up grief that melted out of Aparna's heart in a steady stream of tears. She stopped fighting it, allowing it to flow over the pyre of her past life that could have been good and a marriage and family that might have been beautiful.

It was on the flight back to Chennai just two days later that Aparna was able to view the whole experience of Nikhil's death detachedly. Now she saw it in a fresh perspective. She had left Kartik with his paternal grandparents, so they could all be of emotional support to each other in their loss. She was going to be busy with her work anyway. Kartik also had other rituals to take part in. Aparna felt mentally free, as she leaned back on the headrest of her window seat, recalling the flight she had taken with Kartik two days back. She was surprised at the depth of the feelings for Nikhil that had been stirred at his passing. She understood now, even after the divorce, she had been connected to Nikhil in so many ways, through their son.

In fact, she had been unable to take any independent decision on Kartik's behalf, or make plans for him without Nikhil's consent. This had restricted her life in many ways. When Aparna had been planning to go away to settle in the UK with Stephan, she had prepared to put up a stiff fight with Nikhil and his family, for taking Kartik along. She had been determined to make them see it was a positive move for Kartik's education and future. Kartik could spend one of his vacations in India, and at the others, Nikhil would visit him in UK, Aparna would have convinced him. But all that, or similar situations arising thereon, would not be a problem anymore. Also, Kartik would no longer miss his studies that tended to take a back seat on his vacations with his father in Mumbai, as even his paternal grandparents were rather liberal with him. This was more relevant now that he was in senior school and his board exams were coming up in a couple of years.

Aparna could take firmer decisions on her son's behalf henceforth, convincing both set of grandparents easily. She was even earning well now, after her recent promotion and increase in salary. Aparna was the mistress of her destiny as well as Kartik's. With all these racing thoughts, as she looked out at the darkness outside her flight window, Aparna abruptly thought of Anand. He was the reason she had not made up her mind to move out of India yet, as she had long desired. Yet was it not ironic, that it was in shielding herself from the apparent lifelong pain of remaining merely the other woman in Anand's life, that Aparna had been emotionally driven to Stephan and now into contemplating to leave the country? Why would his wife leave Anand with their growing children and forgo the life they all enjoyed, Aparna had judiciously concluded on the night of the launch of *Elite*. She could not bear to subject herself to any further humiliation on his account. Moreover, she personally knew of some men, incidentally entrepreneurs, who enjoyed the conveniences of one woman taking charge of their home and children, while the other as his mistress gave up her life for his success in business. Both women, though, in such cases were well looked after financially. But Aparna was not going to be content with this contrived arrangement.

She had phoned Anand a few times, since receiving news of Nikhil's illness, to update him as he had insisted on it. In fact, the first time she called Anand in an emotional outburst, just after Nikhil's demise, in pacifying Aparna, he had said softly, "But it's all over now, isn't it?"

"Yes, it is. I am a free woman now," she had agreed.

Her restrictions were indeed all over. Aparna had mentally broken out of the shackles that had tied her down. There would be no one to lean on from now on, she determined, or rely on, and above all to blame for lapses, failures, and disappointments. She alone was going to be responsible for her life.

A bird on the ground, when it flaps its wings to fly, does not fret about being alienated by the universe. It looks towards an

     Shuvashree Chowdhury

endless sky, in assurance that at some point it will be joined by some close friends and some new. Then they will fly in patterns of ethereal beauty for all they left behind to see, not be concerned about whose eyes scorch to look at their brilliance, in the glare of the sun. As the aircraft touched down smoothly on the tarmac at Chennai airport, Aparna tightly shut the lid to her past life. She now had a new lease of life.

Chapter 25

At the Cliff's Edge

It was on a Friday morning during breakfast that Anand was to reach the milestone end of their marriage. It was perhaps his weariness at the long tumultuous journey of over two decades, rough and beyond his endurance now, which drove Anand into this drastic recklessness.

Anand had just finished eating his breakfast of a bowl of mixed fruits, followed by toast and masala omelette, ending with a bowl of sweetened yoghurt.

"Did you give Malathi money last month?" Sujata asked him casually, munching on her buttered toast and omelette.

"No, I didn't give her any money," Anand said crisply.

"But the cook told me you did," Sujata insisted, viewing him curiously. "And then Malathi also admitted to taking Rs. 40,000 from you as a loan."

"Ah! Well, I might have. I'm not sure."

"You're not sure … now what's that supposed to mean?" Sujata said in a sharp, raised tone now. "You give someone 40,000 rupees and then you don't even remember?"

"I have a lot of important things to do and remember, rather than recall precisely what I speak with the maids."

"Yes, I'm sure you do, among which prancing around town with Aparna is top priority," Sujata retorted bitingly. "I need to know, as I gave Malathi the full salary this month, without deducting a part as repayment of the loan you gave her."

"Now that you know, you can adjust the money from the next salary onwards, isn't it?" Anand replied, unperturbed.

"But why didn't you tell me yourself?" Sujata snapped. "Instead of my having to find out from the cook … and then ask Malathi?" Then turning briskly towards Malathi who stood at the kitchen door, she asked, "And you, why didn't you tell me right away, that you had taken money from sir? Why did I have to learn about it from the cook? If you need a loan, it is alright, but you should tell me and always be open and honest with regard to money."

"Akka (elder sister), I thought sir would tell you about it," Malathi faltered, looking towards the floor, "I thought you knew of it."

Sujata looked at Anand seated across her. Her face was a mask of outrage, eyes splinters of venom, as she looked at him menacingly in rigid silence, desperately seeking the appropriate words for her immense rage. It was propelled by her distinct recall now of the conversation she had had with the cook on return from her last trip to Mumbai.

"You know, Akka, whenever I returned from the market, Malathi took ages to open the door. This was if she was alone with sir in the house. Please keep an eye on Malathi. She is very crafty."

The cook's words ringing in her ears now, Sujata abruptly stood up, and looking sternly down at Anand, she raged, "So now you'll even lie to me about the maid, is it? It's more important to humour her ... at my cost, insulting me?"

"What do you mean ... what are you talking about?" Anand said calmly, looking at Sujata curiously. But he rose from the table, pushing his chair back noisily in irritation.

"You're carrying on with the maid too, aren't you?" Sujata screamed sharply, venting the pent-up pain, anger, and indignity she had suffered for so long at her circumstances, that erupted from her soul. Then as if flinging a verbal sharp penknife at him, she vehemently stated, "Malathi will have to leave the house right now. She cannot stay in my house ... not a second more, I tell you. I will throw her out this instant."

As if on cue, like this were a well-rehearsed drama, Malathi fell at Sujata's feet, pleading amidst loud sobs, "I'm so sorry, Akka. It is all my fault. I should have informed you. Please don't throw me out. I promise you I will never give you another chance to complain.

"Stop this acting," Sujata hissed, as if she might strike her, "Just leave."

"Malathi will not go anywhere," Anand said firmly, in a biting tone. "What has she done wrong? It is you who will have to leave, if you must."

Sujata lunged at Anand menacingly, arms outstretched, as if she wanted to hit him, scratch him, and hurt him like he was hurting her with his insulting attitude. In a flash, she visualised Malathi with Anand on their bed and the image drove her wild.

"How dare you?" She yelled, brandishing her hand at him, "How dare you?"

Sujata continued her tirade, abusing him profusely. At this point, Anand stepped forward purposefully. And he slapped Sujata. Seeing the craziness in her eyes alarmed him. It was like she was possessed by a ghost and, if he didn't snap her out of her demonic rage, she might destroy herself and him. They looked at each other in shock, both rooted to the ground. Sujata's face stung from the blow, but it was her heart that was on fire. She noticed Malathi and the cook look at Anand and her from the kitchen, horrified. It sent her into a frenzy of acute humiliation, due to her disgrace being witnessed by the same maid who was the cause of the argument that led to this inimical culmination. How dare he outrage her dignity, Sujata thought defiantly. That Anand would stoop so low, not only to strike her, but also not consider the presence of the maids a deterrent to his outburst, was the first nail on the coffin of their lifeless marriage. What was to follow was quite akin to Sujata's finding the precise nails, to tighten and then lower the coffin underground.

Whoever would consider that Anand, who was typically calm and composed, was capable of this reckless crushing of his long-time marital car? Who could believe him capable of hitting a woman, his wife at that, the mother of his grown-up sons? Wasn't she also the woman who saw him through some of the worst times of his life? Was it then, the other woman in his life Aparna, Sujata speculated, that caused such disdain in him for her? Was there emotional pressure from Aparna to end this journey with her, especially after the way Sujata had snubbed her, at the launch party, in public? Was that the probable cause of Anand's defiance now? Or perhaps it was the lure of a compassionate, peaceful life with Aparna, that so eluded him now, which might have fanned the

Shuvashree Chowdhury

fire to Anand's flying off the cliff thus, Sujata thought in stinging vexation. Much worse, was it possible he might be having an affair with this maid also? After all, she was pretty and young. And their cook had warned Sujata of it.

What struck Anand soon after the shock of his appalling act of slapping his wife, from viewing the horrified expression on Sujata's face, her slight eyes seeming larger than her face, was relief their sons did not witness this nasty scene. They had just left for school, when the argument erupted. This was after they had their favourite breakfast of masala cheese omelettes, with toasted bread, that Sujata ensured they rounded up with glasses of Bournvita milk.

Sujata's anger had erupted violently at Anand's defensive tone, and also because of her own drastic thoughts out of fear of the cook's warning about the maid ringing true. She vividly saw in her mind's eyes—Anand with this maid Malathi in the bed they shared—to her utter disgust. This image is what had brewed into a full blown, high-pitched argument between them. Anand had at first mentally tried to evade getting into the verbal wrestling ring with Sujata, and then when overpowered in it, he used his stinging sarcasm to disengage, but unsuccessfully. The quarrel had peaked into his raising his hand abruptly and forcefully to hit Sujata, only after she got up from her seat and brandished her hand at him along with hurling offensive accusations.

As for Anand, now that his repressed temper had erupted like lava from a dormant volcano, he felt subdued and instantly regretted what he had done. He still stood rooted to the ground, while the maids disappeared into the kitchen. Sujata strode away purposefully towards the living area, her heart and mind aflame. Then picking up her phone from the centre table where she had left it in her handbag, she dialled from it. Anand followed her in a daze, confused beyond words as to what he must do now.

"Can you imagine, he hit me?" Anand overheard her say on the phone and then, after a pause, Sujata added in a shrill tone, "Seriously, Anand slapped me, and you won't believe why … for the maid! That too in front of her!"

She must be talking to Varun, Anand thought with alarm. He was now his mother's best friend. The boys had been privy to verbal showdowns between their parents often, though they had never witnessed physical violence. Anand was thankful that they had already left for school. Sujata would fill them in on the drama that had ensued, but luckily it would not have the same impact as seeing their father slapping their mother. As it is, Anand was having a hard time connecting with the boys. It was only lately that Aparna had made him see the need for it. The boys would never forgive him this offence, he thought dismally. What a negative impact it would have on their young impressionable minds!

Aparna's strong bond with her son Kartik and her insistence that Anand needed to bond with his children as well had struck a chord with him. This was after Sujata's failed attempt to convince him similarly over the years. It was Aparna who had made Anand realise that building and erecting a business empire for his children would not keep them bonded to him. So, he had been making efforts to bond with them lately, however late or little. But this drama would undo all that. He looked at Sujata regretfully, wishing he had pleaded with her not to tell their sons of this incident. But it was too late now, as she had already mentioned it to Varun who as it is avoided his father since he was a child. Sujata now glared at Anand with that indignant look in her eyes that he recognised so well, with her head tilted upwards.

"I'm sorry," Anand pleaded, looking imploringly into Sujata's eyes.

But she just glared at him in stony silence, her eyes radiating a hatred and rage that seared Anand's soul. He had never seen Sujata this angry. Then in a huff, she picked up her handbag, still holding the phone to her ear with the other hand. She walked to the entrance of their apartment, pulled on her sandals lying there, and then unlocking the gate, walked out. Her heels clicking noisily on the stairs as she continued to talk on the phone animatedly, Sujata walked down purposefully. She had already been dressed and ready for work. After passing through the main gate, she waited a few minutes. A large black sports car pulled up right in front of her. Anand watched it curiously from the balcony, in a state of deep regret now. What had gotten into him? Sujata must be going to her office now, Anand thought, but knowing her, she

 Shuvashree Chowdhury

was showing off to him as she tended to lately, that she had other men in her life.

Anand had barely caught a glimpse of the black-sleeved arm that rested on the car's window. He wondered who was the driver. Then he reasoned it had to be the man with whom she chatted incessantly on the phone lately. Manas, once her client and now her good friend, was the only one Anand knew of, other than Shekhar. Manas was besotted with her, and often spoke of leaving his wife, wishing to be with her instead, if she would accept him. Sujata had told Anand of this in one of her attempts to show off. She tended to brag about all the male attention she got lately, through her work interactions. It was to boost her self-esteem in front of a husband who showered his attentions on any woman but her. Anand indulged Sujata in this, as he was relieved she was no longer so focussed on his alliances with other women.

Manas was well aware of the intricacies of Sujata's successful career, as it was often what they talked of, on their beach jaunts, sitting looking at the sun setting over the Marina beach. She had in her the allure of a beautiful woman, but Manas also found the promise of a successful business, if he was in a relationship with her, very attractive. So the steady fire of her problems with Anand were to Manas's advantage and contrivance to fan. He would try and contrast his behaviour to Anand's to look like the better person. His marriage to her would give Manas much more security than he had now. Her firm would be the perfect progression for an HR professional like him. Sujata's firm was already successful, with overseas branches now in addition to branches in the prominent cities in India. She had slowly and diligently consolidated her business out of Chennai first and then expanded it.

Sujata's ambition and craving for a personal identity had arisen out of her determination to be at par, if not above Anand socially. It was Anand's attitude towards her, his taking her for granted and the disrespect she always felt, that Sujata had channelized positively, into a prolific ambition for success and self-identity. She would perhaps not have had such drive for success, if not to attest her capability to Anand and the world. This was in addition to the need to provide a good life for herself and her children, away from Anand. Then she must also prove she was better than

Aparna—his latest flavour, whom he gave precedence over Sujata always due to her inherent smartness. His slap, Sujata considered now, must surely be Anand's bid to control her, in satisfying his fragile male ego punctured often lately by a headstrong and successful wife.

In Anand's view, this incident was the ultimate breakdown of his immense patience. Sujata was more aggressive than ever now and insulting, since she was independent financially, and successful in her own right. It made her feel powerful. But what was more marked, Anand had noticed, was the extreme elevation of her vanity, from all the male attention she received and encouraged, to keep herself afloat in a sea of moral and emotional security. Shekhar, unlike Manas, was still the balancing and calming factor in Sujata's life. He tempered her youthful impetuousness and rage with his maturity and his balanced approach to life. Though Shekhar would be happy to have her and to build a life with her, he was aware that her life really must be with Anand and their children. His wife's death had taught Shekhar the value of preserving a marital relationship, which one invests so much of one's life in.

Anand gave Sujata a life he never could, Shekhar knew. He believed their young children had to be with both their parents. Also, as Anand was much younger than him, Shekhar had the assurance that Sujata would not be alone later in life. But Manas had no such misgivings, and so he wooed Sujata gallantly and with perseverance. He was always with her in person, or on the phone with her, giving Sujata all the attention she craved and had never received in marriage. He showered her not only with time and affection, but also flooded her with expensive gifts, ranging from designer clothes to bags and shoes, and meals at expensive restaurants. They had long graduated out of the mere Marina Beach jaunts. In fact, now Manas openly dropped her off and picked her up from her home and office. Over and above this, the fact that her boys loved and adored him really tipped the scales in his favour. He was perfectly poised for provoking Sujata's insecurities with regard to Anand. It was Manas who had fed Sujata's frazzled, insecure, and unhappy mind, with varied notions of Aparna's entrapping Anand to marry her by devious means.

 Shuvashree Chowdhury

"Don't be surprised if Aparna gets pregnant," Manas had said to Sujata once.

"But why would she be stupid enough to do such a thing?" Sujata had retorted, though Manas's words had the effect he desired.

"So he is forced to leave you and marry her, to safeguard his reputation, of course," Manas said casually.

"As if Anand has an honour really left to defend any longer, or that he cares, the way he is conducting himself publicly with that woman," Sujata hissed like a snake who has been stepped on, though Manas had attempted to make it seem accidental. Then after the stinging pain seeped under her skin, choking her, Sujata muttered meekly, "But if Aparna does get pregnant, it will leave me with an acute loss of dignity in public, more than ever, but above that it'll tarnish my children's lives. We will be the talk of the town."

It was not surprising that Sujata had been behaving so tempestuously with Anand lately. Manas was doing his best to fan the flames by provoking her self-esteem and insecurity. Also, it was Manas who had seen Aparna with Anand at the Marina Beach one morning and conveyed it to Sujata promptly. He described Aparna physically and Sujata recognised who it was with Anand. It was her trust in Manas's finding that was the basis of her conviction, when Sujata threatened Anand with suicide over his dalliance with Aparna. Sujata had confided in Manas about Anand's alleged affair with Aparna, shared her humiliation, anger, and bitterness, which he used to his advantage, in boosting her wrath on Anand.

When Manas received Sujata's hysterical call after Anand slapped her, it seemed to him that this was the opportunity he was waiting for, everything he had worked towards. He now made a show of defending Sujata.

"Your cook is aged, isn't she? So she must know. But more than that, she is loyal to you and knows Anand well," Manas had said when Sujata told him what the cook had said about Malathi and Anand. "Don't rule out her hunch."

Manas promptly picked up Sujata from her gate. After Sujata settled into the car beside him, clutching her handbag as if for moral support, she narrated the incidents of the morning and the audacious slap in detail. She tended to share the events of her day with Manas over the last many months, like they were a couple. He was by now not only her best friend, but also lover, accompanying her on work trips out of town. Sujata considered him her ideal man, as she believed he truly loved her. She had given up on the idea of a future with Shekhar by now, and was considering spending the rest of her life with Manas. She was well over and done with Anand, after this morning.

It was to the police station Manas was driving Sujata to, to lodge a complaint against Anand on charges of physical abuse. Manas convinced Sujata that Anand deserved it. He suggested the official complaint would go down as a record, for proof once she filed for divorce. Sujata repeated the happenings of the morning in minutiae to Manas over again on his urging. This was because she would have to go over the incident several times during the police questioning. She had better be sure of the sequence of events in her head, if she wanted to sound convincing. Sujata's face stung, with every recall of Anand's slap followed by the shocked look on the two maid's faces, viewing them through the kitchen window overlooking the dining table. Manas's idea of instantly registering a police complaint had satisfied her need for revenge.

The last thing on Sujata's mind, even as she promptly agreed to Manas's suggestion of a police complaint, was the negative publicity it would bring. She did not consider in haste the wretched loss of dignity it would cause not only to Anand, but to her and the entire family as well. Sujata did not consider the impact of this drastic measure on her business associates, leave alone on Anand's professional reputation. And what of the impact on their growing sons—once their parent's private life was in public scrutiny—wouldn't their teachers and friends all come to know of it? What would they think of them and their family? But what did such issues matter to Manas, if it expedited his plans to be with Sujata? The end would justify the means.

By the time they walked into the police station, Sujata was determined to make the complaint of being physically abused by her husband. Manas made her repeat the incident, till she was worked up. What was uppermost on Sujata's mind was her seething humiliation and seeking revenge for it. Once she made the complaint, as expected, Sujata was quizzed on the details of her

                              Shuvashree Chowdhury

allegation. It was while they were waiting to meet the senior officer in charge that her sister Ramya called on her cell phone. Sujata angrily spit out the details of the morning, including that she was at the police station now to lodge a complaint for the same. Ramya, in a frenzy, announced this incident to the rest of the family who were still seated at the breakfast table, much to everyone's horror.

"Anand deserves this." Ramya sputtered in seething rage. "He thinks no end of himself, doesn't he? Success has gone to his head, added to the constant attention from all the women in his office, especially that woman Aparna. How does he dare to raise his hand on you, after everything you've done for him—through the business ups and downs and the family illnesses and deaths? I still recall all the harassment you underwent when a corporate house had lodged a police complaint against him and the *National Daily* for some misquotes by Aparna."

Sujata's father, in the meantime, after hastily discussing the matter with her mother, took the cell phone brusquely from Ramya.

"What are you doing, Sujata, have you really lost all sanity? And with whose initiation have you taken such a drastic step?" He said urgently. Knowing better than to argue with her when she was this angry, he added pacifyingly, "Look here, Sujata, I am not asking you not to deal with Anand severely. But to go to the police station with this complaint is stupid, to say the least. Haven't you considered the repercussions of your impetuousness, not only to yourself and your business, but to our extended family? What of the harm it will bring upon your children?

But Sujata was much too convinced of Anand's need to be taught a fitting lesson to pay heed to her father's caution, so she forcefully replied, "It's alright, Dad. I have thought things over, and I cannot live with this man anymore. It is better that everyone knows now what really happened to finally compel me to leave him. Or people will say I left him only because I found someone else."

Sujata knew her father was always in support of Anand, as he had much respect for Anand's maturity and business acumen. If Anand was pushed to hit his daughter, she must surely have pushed him over the edge. That was how his mind would work, Sujata knew. Her father indeed discerned how impulsive and arrogant both his daughters could get in the face of any opposition. They were both like their mother that way. The way Sujata behaved with Anand in that supercilious manner so characteristic of her, any man would he thought…lose his patience at some point. Anand was a stable man, who provided financial and social security to his wife and her entire family, her father mentally conceded. He had no option left now but to get to the police station himself, to prevent any further mishaps on the part of his impractical daughter.

In the meantime, the cops at the police station impressed upon Sujata, "For us to lodge an official complaint of physical abuse, there must be some tangible sign of abuse on the victim's body … is there any mark where he hit you?"

As if on cue, Sujata instinctively felt the stinging sensation on her left cheek, and she put her hand over it. Manas shoved her hand away lightly with his own, and looked intently at her cheek. In his mind's eye, he visualised a red slash on her soft fair skin, but to his dismay, there was nothing there. The cop sitting across them, along with the one standing beside him, peered at Sujata's cheek.

The one seated asked again, "Is there any visible sign of abuse?"

"It's been a while, and so the marks don't show now," Manas replied falteringly, and then in a more convincing tone, he lied, "But I saw the marks. They were distinctly there. We applied ice and so the marks have faded by now."

"But then we cannot lodge a complaint. Without any marks, it is not valid."

Sujata and Manas, much disappointed, rose to leave. It was just then that Sujata's father walked in and, looking at him, Sujata froze. She had not expected that he would actually come over, however anxious he had sounded. Now he would see Manas with her and think the worst, and impose upon her to stay with Anand. However, her father was mature enough not to comment on the presence of Manas, or to tell Sujata what he really thought of her actions. He realised that Manas was the one who she trusted the most. After learning the police would not register a case as there was no physical proof of abuse, Sujata's father walked out with them. But unlike them—dejected but determined to get a medical report to validate their claim of abuse—he was really relieved.

   Shuvashree Chowdhury

When Sujata reached home, her father dropping her off, while Manas went on to his work, Anand was getting ready to go to the office.

As she walked into their bedroom, he spontaneously said, "I am sorry, Sujata! I didn't mean to hit you … You must believe that. It was just a reflex action from what you said. Whatever problems we've had, I would never intentionally hit you."

Anand kept looking at Sujata, watching her as she maintained a stoic silence and pretended he didn't exist.

Suddenly, much to his surprise that she was even speaking to him, he heard her say, "I'm leaving for good, Anand. This is it. I've had enough of this marriage."

"I am really sorry," Anand pleaded. "I mean it sincerely, trust me."

"But it's too late. You might like to know that I am coming from the police station now. I filed a complaint against you on grounds of physical abuse. If you are called upon by the police at home or summoned there, don't be surprised."

"You did what?" Anand blurted in alarm, his voice bitter as he reiterated. "You went to the police to lodge a complaint against me, your husband. Is that it?"

"You heard right!" Sujata repeated.

She was immensely pleased at Anand's displeasure and apparent fear. The objective of the complaint had been to shake Anand out of his cushy throne, where he sat perched mentally, to look down upon her. He was even compassionate to the maids—whether or not he was having an affair with Malathi was irrelevant—and brutally humiliated Sujata in front of them. That is why his slap was so excruciatingly painful to her. Also, now that she had found companionship and adulation through Manas after the acute loneliness in her marriage, Anand's stinging attempts to crush her self-esteem seemed intolerable. In the face of her enhanced value in the world, from being respected and trusted by her clients and senior candidates who had an assuredness about themselves and their place in the world Sujata could no longer tolerate Anand's devaluation of her.

"What are you trying to prove by going to the police? Is this drama to publicly malign me?" Anand snapped, his anger resurfacing. Then fighting to rein it in, he added, "You know well that I did not mean to really hit you."

"Your physical slap was only a manifestation of the humiliation you've put me through all along with your womanising. What with the insults I've faced with people laughing at my back, and forced to feel inadequate over those women you shower your attentions on though they do not score over me." Sujata stated this in a flat tone, then feeling the calmest she had in a long time, she continued evenly, "And then now, an affair with Malathi of all people … But let's say, even if I'm wrong in imagining your association with the maid, can you deny your steamy affair with Aparna? Then you're so involved in your life that you forget the children, fulfill no responsibilities in their upbringing whatsoever. It's like I'm a single parent. And if all this is not enough, after all I have done for you, your slap is proof of your treacherous streak, the extent to which you take me and our marriage for granted. Why then would I think of your reputation, when you've never cared for the need to save mine? I'm going to my parents' place as soon as the boys return from school."

Anand remained silent, in shock at the cool vehemence of her words. Sujata had never been so calm during their fights. For once, he had nothing to say to counter her allegations. He knew she would not listen to anything he said at this point. Yet he must attempt to justify his stance.

"But how can you imagine I'd have anything to do with a maid?" Anand said, in a placatory tone, "It's your cheap insinuation that triggered my impulsive rage."

"Well, it's pointless, isn't it … going back and forth over this now? I am leaving for good to live at my parents' place along with the boys," Sujata announced firmly.

Now that her mind was made up on what she must do, Sujata felt a serenity that was shocking even to her. There is nothing as disturbing as indecision. The anxiety over what the future held for her and the boys could not supersede the relief at having made up her mind over her defunct marriage. Anand perceived the detached tone and recognised her calmness. He realised intuitively that this was not the same as the many times Sujata had threatened to leave or gone away to live with her parents. Sometimes, there is more

   Shuvashree Chowdhury

love, attachment, and sentiment hidden in silence or heated words that stem from hurt and disappointment, than the emotional vacuum in the coolest words. In spite of being sorry for having hit her, Anand could not find it in his heart to stop her from leaving. He could not try to undo the tortuous knots in his marriage now. He was just so tired.

Anand and Sujata had withdrawn from each other with a resigned attitude to their circumstances. They realised they were headed to the end of their marital road, even the mere charade it had been reduced to lately. He couldn't handle her erratic moods that swung like a pendulum between high-strung tantrums to steely silences and back. She took his total unresponsiveness to her varied demonstrations of her hurt feelings and lack of emotional display as proof that he didn't care enough.

That Sujata would go to the extent of going to the police station to lodge a complaint against him was the final proof to Anand of their reaching the dead end of their marital road. It was Anand's slap that had brought Sujata to the cliff's edge, grabbing her with fear of what might happen if she took even a small step ahead with him. Her going to the police station and now leaving home for good was like the gunshot going off, in commencing the individual new races of their lives.

Chapter 26

The Hairpin Turn

The morning after her return from Mumbai, after Nikhil's cremation, however washed out she felt emotionally and physically, Aparna went to work as usual. It was her diligence to her work, the Friday magazine *Elite* now having picked up well, which made her return in haste. But she had awoken rather late this morning, as Kartik was not there for her to worry about getting him ready for school. Her mother had prepared the breakfast Aparna preferred of *uttapam* and three *chutneys*. And while she ate it along with her parents, she narrated in detail the sequence of events from landing in Mumbai to returning to Chennai last evening. Though she had kept Anand abreast of all the details from Mumbai over WhatsApp, she had called her parents only a few times and kept them posted about the important details. She had been finding it too difficult to deal with her own emotions to have to worry about their worries.

As she drove to work, Aparna was relieved to finally be alone. The chat with her parents had raked up old bruises, adding to the numbness she had felt. Her car, the maroon Hyundai Ritz she was still paying the EMI for since the last four years, was now her haven. She was trying to sort out her thoughts and overwrought emotions before she got to office. It was on these drives to and from work that Aparna listened to her favourite music. It was in the car that she squarely faced the emotional upheavals life never ceased to embroil her in. This was why she had become so fond of this car. It was her only private space, her sanctuary, where she could hide from the world, without any doubt or misgiving on her absence from life and responsibility. Now with the marital chapter of her life sealed, with Nikhil's death allowing Aparna the opportunity to finally move on, she looked ahead with renewed hope.

    Shuvashree Chowdhury

She thought about a great job opportunity she had been apprehensive of committing to, even though she had been toying with the idea of moving out of town after the humiliation by Sujata and Radhika at the launch party. The appointment letter from a reputed international magazine, for their Middle East supplement to be launched shortly in Dubai, was still in her Gmail inbox. The franchisee of this new supplement owned a popular TV channel in Pakistan. Aparna had read the appointment letter several times, the last being on her phone, while waiting at the security hold of Mumbai airport last evening. She was in a dilemma—should she turn the opportunity down? It was not worry for Kartik that caused her indecision. He could stay here with her parents, to complete his current school session, while Aparna proceeded to join the new job. And she could get their new home and his school settled before hand. The thing holding her back from what might be the greatest progression of her life was her love, loyalty, and gratitude towards Anand. If only she could get a grip of her feelings for him, she would throw them upon a sea of opportunities and set sail in search of new shores.

On walking into office, Aparna proceeded straight to her desk in her own cabin. She worked independently now, reporting to the chief editor directly, not to Radhika as before. The new editor had segregated the charge and responsibility of the supplements—*Urban Plus*, the *Sunday Magazine*, and *Elite*—each reporting to him. Radhika Nair was still in charge of the daily *Urban Plus*, but they had a new man from Delhi now in charge of the *Sunday Magazine*. The Friday magazine *Elite* was doing well under Aparna and had created quite a secure market place by now in spite of the varied magazines vying for reader space.

Aparna left her bag in the desk drawer underneath. She considered having a cup of coffee quietly at her desk first. And then she would meet her team, as she did daily at noon, by which time everyone would have surely come in. But just as she sat at her desk, her cell phone in her bag beeped, announcing the arrival of a WhatsApp message. She quickly retrieved it and checked the message, as it might be important. Aparna had muted the nonstop threads of conversations of her school and college groups. With so much going on in her life, a torrent of thoughts ensuing on her work and family constantly, she had no inclination to casual and daylong chit-chats like many of her batch mates. Yet she spontaneously replied to any message they independently sent her, and also tried to attend the get-togethers these groups organised as and when she could. But this new message was from Anand.

"Please come and see me as soon as you arrive," it read, to her surprise and apprehension at the urgent tone of the message.

Now what, why this early summon today of all days, Aparna wondered in exasperation. She was not yet in the mood to meet anyone, not even Anand. Was he calling her to talk of her days in Mumbai in detail? But even as she got up to leave, Aparna thought it was unlikely that would be the reason he called her. As over and above keeping him posted from Mumbai on WhatsApp, she had had a chat with Anand on the phone on her drive home from the airport last night. As Aparna hurried to the furthest end of the building where Anand's office was located, on the ground floor, just as her own, she had a gnawing sense of foreboding. Was there some major error in the stories or in the editing of the last issue of the Friday magazine, or perhaps in the current one of this morning? She recalled she had scanned everything online last night one final time. Aparna smiled warmly at Anand's secretary, seated at her desk outside his office.

"How was your trip, hope all is well now? The secretary Rose, asked her warmly, and then she added urgently, "Go on quickly, he's waiting to meet you. Doesn't seem to be in a good mood since he arrived this morning, so be careful."

As forewarned, Anand looked sombre and in a thoughtful mood, when Aparna first caught sight of him on entering his cabin. He looked up and watched her walk up to his desk briskly. Noting the harassed look in his eyes, his forehead deeply furrowed, Aparna knew instantly that something had to be terribly wrong to fluster Anand's usually calm countenance this way. As Aparna sat down, without waiting for him to ask her, he looked straight into her eyes. But he wore a sheepish look.

"You just won't believe what happened this morning…." he started without preamble, and after a pause, he added, "I hit her." Then noticing Aparna's narrowed eyes staring uncomprehendingly

    Shuvashree Chowdhury

back at him, her face reflecting her immense confusion and impatience, he added hastily, "I hit Sujata."

"What ... You did what?" Aparna blurted, the turmoil of the last few days making her oversensitive and irritable now as she glared at him in shock. But then, she soon registered from Anand's expression that he was much troubled and this was not another sinister joke of his. She asked, in a concerned tone, "But why ... and how?"

Anand recounted the incident that had led to his sudden physical outburst, rather calmly. In recounting it in detail, as Aparna stared at him in horror, Anand felt a renewed guilt and was miserable that he could do such a heinous thing. But while talking about it, he realised that the act had suddenly eased the anger built up in him over years at Sujata's extreme dispositions towards him. It made him feel liberated in a way, from the deep animosity that had built up in him for her.

Anand, regaining his composure by now, concluded his narrative by saying, "This might perhaps cost me dearly. Losing the children ... you know ... ending our being a family as we were even till this morning. It might be the termination of my marriage surely, but then I'm the one who rang its death knell with the unwarranted slap, aren't I?" Then looking into Aparna's eyes with profound sadness, Anand continued, "It was as if I had felt compelled to ring the bell ending a class, of a trying and difficult lecture or examination. In our school, a student was allotted to ring the bell at the end of periods and I did that for many years. What is left now is for me to await the results of my impulsive act akin to a written exam I've taken, by a divorce decree perhaps. Sujata's family will consider her physical and financial security in supporting me initially, disapproving her idea of a divorce. But with her insistence, they will give in ultimately to support her."

Aparna listened to his story, letting the implications of Sujata's leaving Anand along with her children sink in well. She was close to achieving what she wanted out of life: to be rid of Sujata, thus enabling Anand to consider a life with her. Though she knew marriage may not be possible soon, for the sake of his children.

But to her surprise, Aparna found herself almost involuntarily exclaiming, "But how could you hit her, Anand? Whatever Sujata said about you and the maid was disgusting, no doubt … But it does not justify your slapping her for it. I can't even envision you doing it, let alone believe you could do such a thing."

"I didn't do it with a level head," Anand blurted softly. "I just lost my temper."

"It really is no excuse, to raise your hand and say you lost your temper," Aparna said forcefully, exasperated by Anand's casual and smug attitude to all his faults. Then recalling how he had unnecessarily drilled her at meetings in the early years, that used to insult and enrage her, Aparna added. "Well, if I were in Sujata's place, I might have perhaps done what she did too and filed a police complaint."

Anand was silent, looking down at his hands lying limply on his lap. He really had no defence for what he had done, he knew. He was talking to Aparna about this now only because he felt compelled to talk to someone. And he had no real friend whom he could trust with something like this, other than her.

"Even you know, Aparna, though I've often talked to you openly about my marital circumstances that tend to bring on my uncontrollable temper at times, that I would never hit her intentionally. I was truly pushed beyond my endurance this morning," Anand stated after a prolonged silence, even as Aparna continued to look at him quizzically, studying his expressions for signs of sincerity. "But then, the way Sujata marched out, a man picking her up from the gate promptly, and headed straight to the police station with him, makes me doubt whether she was pushing me so I would go over the edge. She could earn her freedom without taking any blame whatsoever. It all seems like a well-orchestrated plan to me. Sujata did not even need any time to think what she wanted to do. There is a man in her life, as she herself blatantly told me a month back. Very calmly, she had added that she wanted to leave me for him. He is obviously the one who has been giving her the moral support to turn her against me to this extent. I'd been telling you how Sujata has been more difficult than ever. With my hitting her, it's as if she got exactly what she sought. It all seems pre-planned to me now."

"Well, if you ask me, she just acted on impulse, I think." Aparna replied judiciously, her tone firm, not about to make up her mind

     Shuvashree Chowdhury

on this so soon. "But as for your behaviour, what you describe as an impulse … you really have no pardonable excuse." Then, in curiosity, she asked, "By the way Anand, who is this man she wants to leave you for?"

"Ah, that! You just won't believe this … It's Ramya's ex-husband's younger brother, who has always had a crush on Sujata since they were young. It was her friend Manas who picked her up last evening from our gate, but I know for certain that she is not in love with Manas and she understands rather well neither is he in love with her and has been aspiring to climb the social ladder through her. But she has played along, using him as an esteem booster and for easy companionship, and lately not to raise any suspicion on the real man in her life. Sujata's family will never approve of Jai, after what transpired between both their families since Ramya's first marriage to his elder brother Aacharya, which led to the bitterness of their divorce."

"What! What are you talking about, Anand?" Aparna retorted irritatedly. Then she looked at him with disappointment, feeling the loss of respect for him sting her, as she continued, "This complicated new set of allegations you're making against your wife after hitting her is really absurd and stranger than fiction. Don't try to justify your behaviour to me, least of all to yourself!"

"It truly seemed a fabrication to me too, when Sujata told me a month back, rather firmly, that she had found a man and wanted to leave me for him," Anand said sharply. "I thought she made it up to spite me, but now thinking it over, I realise she really meant it. The man can't be anyone else but Jai, in my view. Ramya did tell me a year back that she had got in touch with her ex-husband Aacharya on Facebook, then met him at his office. Sujata had spoken to his younger brother Jaiditya, who had once been a close friend, through Ramya's initiation. Then they too had met up over coffee. Since then, Sujata and Jai have renewed their friendship that, with their long-time familiarity, might easily have blossomed into a deep love."

Aparna looked at Anand quizzically. But Anand was right on his instincts over Jaiditya having become the true love of Sujata's life in a short time. She had met him at the popular Chamiers Cafe in R.A Puram, and over their first meeting after two decades, they had picked up from where they left off since Ramya's divorce and Sujata's subsequent marriage to Anand. Jai was married too, though very disenchanted, to a socialite fashion designer, who ran her own boutique in Nungambakkam. Jaiaditya liked everything about Sujata that Anand had taken for granted for long. Her simplicity, loyalty, and inherent sincerity in every aspect of life including her profession, that Anand had trampled on callously, often brutally, Jai loved. This was more so now, being married to a shallow, frivolous woman Neeta, who only cared for her butterfly image in high society.

Jaiaditya, a year younger than Sujata who was now forty, was a handsome man, with a medium height and stocky built. He had soft, friendly facial features and warm curious eyes, with a moustache that toughened his innocent countenance somewhat. He ran his own furnishings and interior decorations business, and was far from rich as Sujata was now, let alone Anand. This was although his father had been president of a reputed multinational firm that retained him as a consulting partner long after his retirement a decade ago and thus he still earned rather well. Jai was a genuinely sincere, open-hearted, broad-minded, and compassionate man, who had an elegant sense of dressing and refined social graces that awed Sujata, and made him popular wherever he went, especially at the few clubs in Chennai he was a member of through his father.

Jai was always there for her when Sujata needed him. One night, rather late, when she had called him in much pain from a sudden bout of food poisoning on return from Mumbai on an official trip, he had rushed to her house with medicine and stayed with her till she felt better. He often picked her up and dropped her off if she didn't feel up to driving, and he also prepared tea or coffee and had even cooked for her a few times at her place. All this was when Anand was travelling. Sujata and Jai were best friends and compatible in every way, including their physical chemistry, all of which was lacking in her marriage to Anand. The way her two sons adored Jaiaditya and were so free with him, as if he was a dear friend and father figure, endeared him to Sujata most.

Above everything, what made Sujata make up her mind on him was Jaiaditya's protective streak towards her. This contrasted with Anand's deprecating treatment of her ever since their marriage.

			Shuvashree Chowdhury

Jai's transparency with her, on all facets of his life, proved he respected and adored her just the way she was, for the woman she inherently was.

That evening, after work, Aparna drove home exceptionally fatigued. Her chat with Anand in the morning, having stirred up the hornet's nest of her feelings for him, added to the tumult of the last few days in Mumbai. As for work, she was used to the pressure and responsibility by now and could tend to it instinctively, without much exertion. Aparna had spent the day in perceptible calmness, over meetings with her team, planning the next supplement of *Elite*. She had lunch in the canteen with Radhika, where she casually discussed the Mumbai trip, also the latest on *Elite*, in a bid to stay connected with her. But inside, Aparna had been a heap of smouldering coal emotionally, and yet no one sensed her turmoil. It was as if she were an iron furnace, insulated from the fire of agony gnawing inside. She had become used to exuding an aura of calm elegance about her, irrespective of the intensity of her feelings, what with the torrent of fire splinters destiny chucked her way to constantly scorch her heart and soul.

On the one hand, there was Sujata's departure, and what it could mean for Anand and her. Then there was the nagging fear that she was just Anand's mistress, for Aparna was not sure how he truly felt about being with her for the long term. Even if his intentions were all honourable where she was concerned, would Anand ever want to marry her, even if he were to divorce Sujata? Anand's insecurity over the position of his two sons in his company might take precedence over Aparna and her son, and prevent his actually marrying her, Aparna feared. Sujata's sons were after all Anand's own and he would want what was best for them over and above anything else. Moreover, Sujata surely would not let go of her marriage without securing the best for her sons financially, irrespective of how much she earned independently. She had lately been demanding to be made joint managing director, and with a divorce, she would make more demands to secure her children's future. Where did all this leave Aparna, but with a social insecurity lifelong?

Wasn't she much better off then, Aparna concluded, in taking up the opportunity in Dubai, to ensure her freedom—both financial and emotional—from Anand or any man for that matter? Aparna thought of the lonely life she might be subjected to, once Kartik was grown and had left home for higher studies or work. And she had firmly decided that she would not expect anything out of her son materially or emotionally either. She would offer her friendship to his wife someday, just as to him, and be happy with their love and friendship from afar. It is but natural to expect of children to take care of aging parents, but with the pressures of occupational and personal lifestyles ever on the increase, this tends to lead to disillusionment on both sides. She had come to accept that it was no use expecting children to become a prop in one's old age just because you gave your life to raising them.

By the time Aparna stepped into the elevator in her building, she had decided to accept the opportunity in Dubai. But as she met the smiling faces of her parents, after her mother answered the bell, the way both their eyes lit up on seeing her, her heart constricted. Aparna promptly rescinded her decision. How was she going to leave them at this juncture, when they did not expect anything from her, but just to see her gave them so much pleasure? They must have worried about her well-being all day, after the ordeal they knew she had gone through in Mumbai. Aparna had noticed a missed call from home over lunch, she now recalled guiltily. But she had become so busy later that she had not returned the call, and then it had slipped her mind. This is how it becomes difficult to meet the expectations of parents, despite all good intentions, she thought sadly.

But her parents were not perturbed by Aparna's lack of response to their call. They had called her office to ensure she had come into office safely, and were satisfied by the reception desk confirming it. The fact that they were ready to reach out to her without undue expectations, understanding that they were now retired from service and free while their daughter had too much on her plate, ensured there were no hurt egos from unwarranted insensitivity. Aparna went into her room to shower, after giving her mother and father a hug each. The few moments of basking in their warmth gave her an immense sense of security and well-being now. By the time she had come out to the living room, her mother had served on the centre table a portion of *medu vadais* with mint and onion

　　　　Shuvashree Chowdhury

chutneys, Aparna's all-time favourite snack. As she sat down to eat hungrily along with her father, her mother brought cups of filter coffee.

It was in the privacy of her room after dinner that evening that Aparna recalled word for word all Anand narrated to her that morning.

She became acutely troubled, then cursed him aloud, "Damn you, Anand!"

Only he had the capacity to get right under her skin with his tales of woes or joy. When he was going through the trying time of his brother's efforts to oust him from their paper after winning their mother's sympathy, Aparna had been as anxious for his circumstances as she might have for herself. Anand had then been compelled to keep Murali out of the *National Daily* for good, with support from the board of directors who believed Anand was best at the helm. This had severed any ties with his mother and brother, just after his father had passed away. Aparna had been through all these upheavals with him, as Anand's only friend, one he could trust implicitly. All of this had conversely made Aparna more emotionally dependant on him than before. She had become drawn and bound to him, at first with all the problems of her life, then in being part of his.

But those problems paled in comparison with Sujata leaving him now. This could impact Aparna's life, so what was she to say to him? Was she expected to sympathise with Anand's confessions of his violent outburst which had compelled Sujata to leave him? She was a woman too. How could she support his act of violence on another woman, his wife at that? Then there was Aparna's newfound fear that he may become violent with her too at some time, with sufficient provocation. With Sujata having gone to the police, this messy issue might attract dirty publicity, and was surely going to bring Anand disrepute. It would drag Aparna along, sooner or later, if Sujata had her way, and Aparna had her son to protect from all the mudslinging that could surely follow. She couldn't be a disinterested friend to Anand, not when this development had so many implications for her. Aparna had been too rattled by the speed with which her circumstances were changing in the last few days to have offered Anand any empathy. All these signs from God now seemed to Aparna, as if the doors of one life had shut with Nikhil's death to open another with Sujata's leaving Anand right after. Was it all preordained then?

It was Monday, after the most anxious weekend Anand had ever spent over a series of discussions with his in-laws over the state of affairs of his marriage. The intercom line on his desk rang, breaking through his troubled thoughts.

"May I come in and see you now?" Aparna said, on hearing his voice, promptly elevating his mood. "I need to discuss something important with you."

"Yes, come on in. You are just the person I need to talk to now."

In fact, Aparna was the only person Anand could tolerate meeting now, in this mental state. With her, he would not need to put on an air of calmness he far from felt. Little had he envisioned that the end of his marriage, as is usually the case, would be worse than its worst moments in all these years. What had he been expecting—that Sujata would just go away if she must, to allow the children to visit him at his will, then resume all responsibility towards the boys once they returned to her? The thought of the long-drawn explanations and discussions, the effort to hold on to his ground, that it was Sujata who wished to leave, and she could still return at will, was stressful. He just needed solitude and peace, till he could get a grip of the rage that was again erupting from being blamed for everything that was wrong in their marriage. As Anand expected, Sujata's parents wished for her to remain in the marriage—to go back with the children and live with him. So they purposefully counselled Anand, much to his vexation, to mend his ways, so their daughter could consider giving the marriage another chance.

Anand dialled his secretary Rose and asked her to order two cups of filter coffee. Just then, Aparna walked in. He noticed that she looked distraught. What might be bothering her now, he wondered? Was she still sulking over the loss of her marriage irrevocably now, with the death of her ex-husband? Aparna sat down across him quietly, without being asked. She abruptly placed an envelope in front on the table, avoiding his gaze, and then looked down at her hands on her lap. Why was she avoiding

    Shuvashree Chowdhury

his gaze? Had she lost all respect for him, after learning he was capable of hitting a woman, his wife at that, Anand thought, with a sinking feeling? But he had told Aparna because she was the only one he could talk to about it, who he considered would understand him without judging. Had he been wrong then, in deducing she loved him, the real him and all of him, with all his strengths and flaws?

"What is that in the envelope you have there?" Anand asked, sounding casual.

"It's my resignation," Aparna blurted, without any preamble.

"Look, Aparna, I'm not in the mood for such hideous jokes right now, even if you think it might cheer me up. In fact, it's the worst time ever."

"It's not a joke," Aparna said softly, still looking down, avoiding his piercing gaze resolutely. "I am serious. I've taken the decision to move on. And I have accepted the offer I had mentioned to you, from the magazine in Dubai. I've just given a copy of this resignation letter to the chief editor too before coming here."

"How could you do this ... that too right now? Why are you doing this at all? I don't understand it!" Anand said, almost choking with emotion and shock. "You know how much I need you here and now ... more so, with everyone leaving me one after another. My father and mother have already left me. Now Sujata walks away abruptly. I only have you."

"You will be fine, Anand, trust me ... you will. You don't really need anyone in your life," Aparna replied reflectively, in a soft voice. Then firmly, trying to control her trembling voice, hoping desperately she would survive his appeals to her feelings, she continued, "Then this is not about you, it's about me. I must go, really, and be independent emotionally and financially, learn to take charge of my life myself."

"What about your parents, Aparna? How can you just leave them when they need you the most now?" Anand said desperately, seeking a straw to cling to even as his emotional ship was sinking, its anchor ripping out of the shore so abruptly.

"In fact, this decision to move to Dubai is as much theirs as mine. They convinced me I must go and make a better life and career. This was just when I was planning to turn down the offer.

I spoke to my father this morning over breakfast, before taking the final decision to turn down the offer. But instead he urged me to take it up, that both he and Mother would come along with me and live wherever I would go. They knew I could well do with their support now, especially with Kartik."

Anand shoved the ultimate bait at her, as he said: "But what about us, Aparna? Now that Sujata is leaving ... we could be together. I know this is what you've wanted all along and I want it now too. It's just that I was confused on how to deal with the circumstances. But now I've made up my mind about us, our future, firmly."

"Which 'us', Anand?" Aparna said wearily, emphasising the "us", looking him full in the eyes. "There never was an 'us' ... It was just you and me with a candle called hope that I lived with alone for long. The flame had diminished over time, but burned bright again when you told me of Sujata leaving. But I don't want this fire to consume me, so I would rather extinguish the steady flame now. I might have to live with the residual molten wax of pain and regret all my life, of how beautiful it could have been between us, even as our candle of love lit up the world. But I can't be with you and risk destroying myself. Eventually, I'll move on ... that's the hope I'd like to carry with me."

Just then, the waiter from the canteen knocked on the open office door. He stood there with the tray of the coffee ordered. Anand nodded to him, signalling him to come inside. This was after Anand peeled his pained gaze away from Aparna's face, with much effort. The waiter ambled in, with the tray balancing a white and gold bone-china pot, along with two matching cups and a plate of biscuits. Aparna took this as a cue to get away. It was pointless prolonging this official farewell. She had to serve a month's notice period, but Aparna was determined to avoid Anand as much as was possible during the time. There was no way she was going to sit through a cup of coffee with him now, with a heart that was steaming hotter than the brew, out of the love she still felt for him and perhaps always would. Anand might just succeed in changing her mind, which as it is felt like putty in his hands now.

The waiter began pouring the coffee into the two cups on the tray. Aparna looked at Anand as if for the last time, with

                    Shuvashree Chowdhury

all the love her heart was capable of ever feeling. It melted into
the tears stinging her eyes, threatening to roll down. She shoved
the envelope closer to Anand on the desk, then abruptly got up,
turned around quietly, and walked out the door. She had reached
a hairpin bend in her life's path. She must not falter now or ever.

The End